ALSO BY KELLY FINLEY
"THE QUEEN OF SPICE"

-Interconnected Books & Audiobooks

Available in Kindle Unlimited & Audible-

HOLIDAY FOR SIX

HALLOWEEN FOR SIX

with cameos of MCs from characters above and below!

VERY SPICY, LOTS OF FRIENDS TO LOVERS RomComs & AUDIOBOOKS

BELLES & BRATVA BEASTS

NASH

AXEL

SIRE

LOCH

JACE

SHAMELESS PLAY

SHAMELESS GAME

featuring Blair, Beau & Colton

featuring Silas & Eily Van de May with Cade and Redix

A Forbidden Cinderella Retelling Poly Romance

AFTER HIM

WITH HIM

An Angsty Second Chance to an MMF Why Choose Duet

PROTECT HER

PIERCE HER

HUNT HER

CHASE HER

A Spicy, Romantic Suspense, Bodyguard/Celebrity Trilogy

Join my newsletter. I share sneak peeks, giveaways, and more.

HALLOWEEN FOR SIX

KELLY FINLEY

DEAR READER

This is a story celebrating all consensual adult love. It's a sweet and spicy tale about finding your happiness and family.

Along the way, polyamory and consensual non-monogamy are celebrated, and real-world challenges are explored such as infertility and polyphobia. The use of terms varies as do the people and communities who use them.

If the idea of a lot of love for all excites you, this story may be quite the treat for you.

All of these characters have their standalone,
interconnected romances available
for free on KindleUnlimited.

For details and a suggested reading order review
Also by Kelly Finley

For bonus content, sharing more of their sweet and spicy
life together, visit my website at
KellyFinley.com

For every reader who deserves to get their spooky freak on.

HALLOWEEN FOR SIX PLAYLIST

Midnight Island by Harrison Brome
Body by Loud Luxury, Brando
Souls by BONES UK
The Devil is a Gentleman by Merci Raines
Adorn by Miguel
Love Bites by Def Leppard
Bloodletting by Concrete Blonde
Maneater by Nelly Furtado
Principles of Lust by Enigma
Dancing in the Moonlight by Toploader
Us by MOVEMENT
E.T. by Katy Perry
Devil Inside by INXS
Closer by Nine Inch Nails
Rabbit Heart by Florence + The Machine
Listen on Spotify

HALLOWEEN FOR SIX

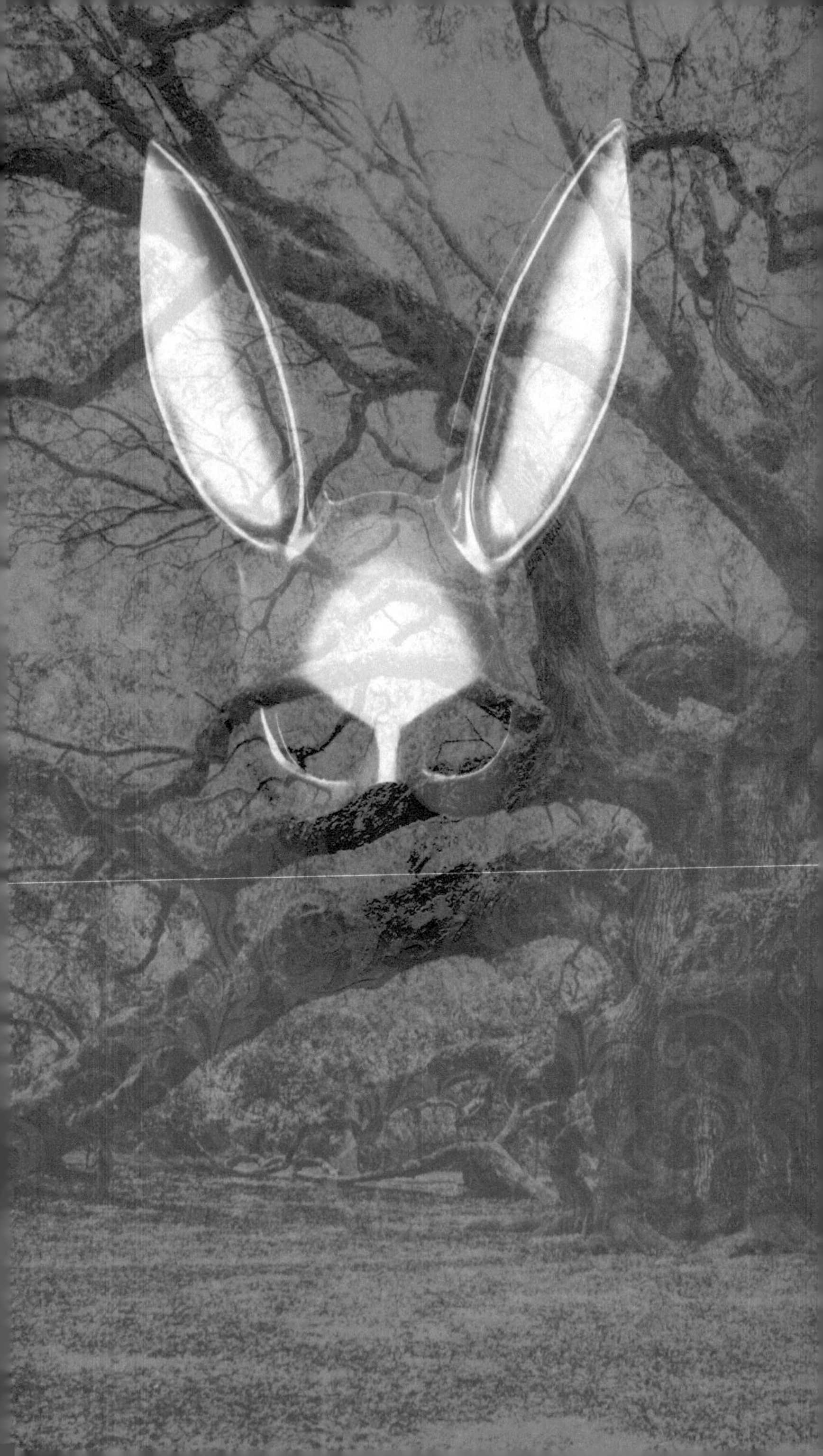

Eily

CHAPTER ONE

EILY

THIS IS HALLOWEEN HO PREP 101.

How do you prepare for hosting a Halloween for sex ... I mean ... for *six*?

Me? I start from the bottom up.

Lying on a table, naked ass in the air, I prop my chin on my forearms, gazing at a painting of a perfect peach.

"Now, you may feel a little tingle," the spa technician warns, like this is my first assperience. "Ready?"

I grin.

"Blast my ass, Doc."

Nope, she's not a doctor, but she *is* about to play cosmetic laser tag with my rump, zapping it into a perfect peach, too.

"Eily, you have some *assplaining* to do," Cade chuckles, naked ass up, too, and lying beside me with her lips smushed against the table. "I can't believe you talked us into this."

"Yeah," Charlie, lying on the other side of Cade, wonders aloud, "like ... how is this a *facial* when they're putting a green, goopy mask on my *ass*?"

"This is the Top Tushy Treatment, ladies," I boast. "Today, our peaches get steamed, zapped, peeled, masked, and creamed."

Cade scoffs, "My peach gets creamed a-plenty at home."

I glance at her and Charlie.

Our three treatment tables are lined up, probably for when innocent bridal parties come in for spa days, but this is equally momentous.

This is Halloween Ho Prep 101.

"Look," I school them on our sexcapades, "we're about to have our asses out for five nights in front of fourteen guests—seventeen if you count us—and I, for one, plan on having a perfect pumpkin for the hallowed feast."

A technician glides a wand over Cade's booty. It zaps her flesh, probably erasing a little pimple.

"Ouch!" But it makes Cade jump.

"Someone's being a butt baby."

"No, I'm not," she huffs. "But I'll have a *roasted* pumpkin if we keep this up." She sniffs the air. "Hair. I smell burning hair."

"Like your pound cake hasn't been roasted and toasted in hotter ways than this before."

Charlie snorts, amused by the truth.

Cade rolls her violet eyes at me.

"Besides," I remind her, "you're both so busy, I have to schedule a derrière date just to see you."

Charlie sighs, propping her chin in her palm.

"I know. Sorry. It's been a crazy year, and I need this break, too. Lately, I've been hiding in the bathroom to get some me-time. But no. My kids think I sit on the porcelain throne to hold court, resolving their latest fuss."

"Think that's bad?" Cade says, "I had an erotic dream about Paw Patrol the other night."

Charlie laughs. "Which one?"

"The girl pup *and* the police pup. Should I be disturbed? Was it a sign?"

"Girl, that's a sign you should be properly fucked."

"Exactly!" I blurt. "We got Brazilians, butt facials, and, oh, let's do spray tans today, too!"

"Nope." Cade puts her verbal foot down. "You can zap my peach but not bronze it. We're not porn stars."

"No. We're even luckier than pro pussies."

The technician zaps away at my fanny.

Do I smell burning hair, too?

Meh. *Maybe.*

But I'm too excited. I've worked too hard. So hard that I'm now a Pornified Party Planner.

I even made the certificate for myself on Canva and framed it.

"We're a polycule of six," I continue, "about to host eleven friends in an epic Halloween week of kinky tricks and treats, and you two are my slutty ghouls, so spread your vertical grins about it."

I don't care that the technicians can hear our every word.

I'm not ashamed of our lives and love.

Are we non-traditional?

Yes, and a-haunting we will go.

You see, celibate, miserable, old White men made most rules about marriage and sex, and I'm not dumb enough to follow them.

What did they know about love, anyway?

Are we controversial? Six people fucking? And loving?

To some, I guess.

I'm a happily married woman. I'm supposed to be devoted to my husband, and I am.

Silas Van de May has my soul.

Every morning, I wake up in his tan, beefy arms while he kisses my neck, his lush lips softly whispering how he loves me while his hard morning wood eagerly pounds on my door.

And usually, I open wide for him with a smile.

Silas is my paramour.

He's my every breath.

But my heart? My body?

I'm exactly like my husband. Our hearts are big enough to love more than one, and our bodies won't be shamed into following rules we didn't make.

And with the way we break those rules? It's too much fun.

Yes, you're welcome to join my vaginal vigilante crew, too. I'll make us some T-shirts.

So, now it's the six of us—at least—when we have the rare time.

There's me and my husband, Silas; Cade and her husband, Redix; and Charlie and her husband, Daniel.

"The Six," as we call ourselves.

And yes, we share more than sex. We're close friends. We're a chosen family. Hell, some of us work together, but not this week.

This Halloween getaway is for adults only. It's for taboo tricks and treats.

"You know I'd be smiling about this," Charlie says, "if our husbands were here, spreading their cheeks, too. I call bullshit on anything women are *supposed* to do that men don't have to do as well."

"I call it ironic," Cade adds. "Because our men are gold-medal athletes in the anal Olympics. Where are they, anyway?"

"Shopping," I inform Cade.

"Shopping for what? You have everything ready. You've been planning this erotic extravaganza for months."

"I have. I've decorated romantic glamping tents for each polycule and—"

"*Glamping?*" Charlie squeaks. "And they're *decorated?* On a Lowcountry *island?*"

Can her voice get any higher?

"Bitch, I'm an artist." I laugh. "Like I won't go glamorous, even in nature and shit. We've built huge canvas tents that I decorated, putting cozy beds in them with white linens and indigo blankets, of course. I found cute furniture for each and hung twinkling lights on all the high wooden rafters. I even found huge white fuzzy carpets, like giant porno rugs. And I scored huge steel drum bathtubs. There's one on each tent platform we built and—"

"You mean platforms *Silas* built," Cade corrects.

"Hell, yes, he did." I swat her arm, all playful. "Give that man a project and some power tools, and he's a pig in shit. Besides, Silas loves spending his money on others. So, after our Halloween, we'll leave the glamping tents up and let charities use them for retreats."

"You mean *after* you buy new beds for the tents," Charlie warns, "because we'll ruin them."

She's not wrong. We've learned the very fun way that some love leaves permanent stains.

Y'all, Tide detergent has nothing on our trysts. To be fair, we test its strength with silicone lube.

And who, other than charities, does my husband, Silas, like spending the fortune he's inherited on?

Me.

For our wedding present, he bought me a private island on the Lowcountry coast of South Carolina. He named it "Indigo Island," after the local art I create. Then he planted an indigo farm for me before he and a crew built my barn-sized art studio and a home we plan to fill with our kids one day.

But while I'm trying to get pregnant, I'm like Silas.

I love spoiling our friends.

I live for hosting our get-togethers.

Nice ones and naughty ones, too.

"So, what do you call the fancy tents we used *last* year?" Cade asks. "Roughing it?"

"Oh, those were tiny yurts. Our group was smaller last year. Hell, you and Scarlett were pregnant and couldn't even play our games."

"We got in the spooky spirit." She reminds me, "We painted pumpkins on our bellies every day."

"That was so cute." Charlie kicks her feet. "Who's coming back?"

Last year, I convinced Silas we should host a Halloween week on our island. But not everyone we invited was able to come ... or play. Bellies and balls got in the way.

A.k.a. pregnancy and the NFL.

But this year?

Things have changed, and I'm brewing up naughty plans.

Drawing a breath for this list, I'm not exhausted by it—no. My kitty is sweeter than candy corn over our guests.

"Well, it's the six of us, of course. Luca and Scarlett are returning, and Stacey will be back with her husbands, too."

"All *three* this year?"

Hmm. *Noted.*

Charlie's kitty sounds excited about Stacey's men.

"Yeah," I reply. "Stacey's husbands, Ford and Mateo, are returning, and finally, her husband, Luke, is joining us. He's on a thirty-day leave. He's coming and—"

"Oh," Cade goes for the pun, "it sounds like we're *all* coming this year."

Devilishly, I nod. Trying not to get distracted by the word "coming." It's like a bright, shiny object to my dirty mind. It has ADD.

Not *that* ADD.

My dirty mind has Active Dick Delirium.

That's what you get when your husband has a talented one.

"Yeah," I focus, "and football won't get in the way this year, either. Zar can come with Nick since Nick's on Injury Reserve again this season."

Charlie tsks, shaking her head. "Poor guy. His fucking ACL. Players tackle his knee, knowing it's his weak spot."

"And since Zar and Nick are coming this year," I keep ticking down the list, "Beau Bronson and Blair Monroe are coming, too. But Colton Hawke, their partner, has a home game in Atlanta, so he'll join us later."

"Why didn't they come last year?" Cade asks. "They were invited."

"Because," I shrug, "that's like asking newbies to pilot the Space Shuttle with only a single-engine plane license. We're kinda intimidating."

"We *are*?"

Cade doesn't get it, but I do.

Silas was my first, and he'll be my last. But, when I literally fell into his world, my big, rebel-hearted, future husband was already in a hot throuple with Cade and Redix.

And those two were already soulmates.

Cade and Redix were childhood sweethearts with a past that needed healing, and Silas did just that—he brought them back together.

At first, once Silas found me, he didn't want to share me with them. He was too protective, and with good reason, given my past.

I admit I was intimidated, too.

Redix Dean was Hollywood's bad-boy Romeo, and Cade Bryant was a former model turned cop. Like, she's his Juliet. Long story, but theirs has a happy ending.

And it was one I immediately felt.

You can't be around us and not feel the intense connections.

And I didn't want to change one long, tawny hair on my husband's sexy head. So, I insisted on joining his throuple with Cade and Redix.

Best. Decision. Ever.

Like winning a Lotta Love Lottery.

I didn't know friendship, intimacy, and sex could be that great.

Then Charlie and her husband, Daniel, joined our foursome on our New Year's cruise.

Talk about sailing on a Sea of Sin.

With the intense history Charlie and Daniel have? With how Charlie grew up with Silas and was his first megacrush? And with how Daniel works with Redix now? They're two of Hollywood's leading men on a scorching hot show, acting like closeted Vice cops in love?

Yep, we were a powder keg, exploding with passion, love, and lots of lube that week.

Oh, and Clone-A-Willies, too.

Thus, The Six were born.

But here's the thing: birds of a poly feather flock together.

So, our friends and their polycules are coming, too.

Coming.

See? How can I avoid the pun?

"So, that's seventeen people total?" Charlie counts on her fingers. "Six women and eleven men? Holy Halloween holes to be haunted."

My imagination sparks, picturing the Halloween slasher series *Scream.* Hoping how, yeah, we'll be screaming friends, alright, but it won't be over Ghostface.

No, we'll be screaming with seventeen *O* faces.

"But not everyone is open." I wag my finger. "Some are closed. They'll be more about parallel polyamory. They'll celebrate *with* us, not *be* with us."

"And yet," Cade lilts, "we've seen how some change, even if for a night or a holiday."

"Yeah," I shrug, "if that's what they want. Like last year with Scarlett and Stacey's husbands."

"Damn," Charlie sighs, "talk about a Halloween bone-yard. Luca and Ford were two alphas who got off dominating each other and lucky Mateo. Their wives sure loved it, too."

"Oh!" I jump.

Glancing over my shoulder, I admire my technician spreading cold aloe gel over my booty and...

How cute!

It looks so shiny I shake it. "Y'all, look at my booty. It's The Great Pumpkin."

Charlie laughs with me, but leave it to her to count

heads, too. Like we're going to war and not a week of cock-n-cunt parties.

"We'll be outnumbered," she says. "That's almost two men for every woman."

My eyes get wide. "And the problem *is*...?"

"No need to padlock your pussy." Cade dismisses Charlie's cock count. "Not every man is open to other women."

"Well then..." Charlie rises on her elbows, letting her white towel fall away, exposing her proud breasts and sending a tingle to my core.

Zing. It reminds me how most of our network, like me, is bisexual.

Charlie's so fucking hot. So is Cade. So are our men.

Our sextuplet is just that: sex-y.

"How will we know," she asks, "in the orgy pit, who can fuck or suck who?"

I love how candid we are. We gotta be. There are too many cocks and cunts involved to beat around the bush.

Beat. Bush.

There I go again.

Break out the pun scoreboard.

I'll be chalking up points all week.

"I mean," Charlie continues, "the six of us agreed to be open this week, but others may not be. And Eily," I stop shaking my Jell-O, focusing my punny mind, "you're trying to get pregnant."

It's sweet how Charlie worries, "Only Silas can have you bare, but what if it's dark and—"

"Don't worry," I sigh heavily.

I'm not mad or sad. Well, maybe a little ... but I am discouraged. Silas and I have been trying for months with no luck. So, honestly? I've focused my frustration into my party.

"Here's the plan..."

Both women look my way.

And while, yes, I've planned a week of Halloween sex to die for, we live for our bond.

When you find souls who match yours, you hang on. You cherish how great love can be—together.

The beautiful thing is, every year, our intimate network only grows.

That's why it took some thought. I felt like a happy, horny little witch concocting this spell...

"I sent out RSVPs with kink quizzes and consent lists," I explain. "Then, I sketched it out—five nights of five kinky tricks. I've assigned different guests to host a night in our Trick Tent, the biggest, most lavish on the island. They'll surprise us with their theme, toys, and costumes for all, etcetera. That way, each night will be different, and that's where the guys are. They're shopping with Silas for the final night."

Cade drops her sultry voice. "Other than me"—she's always investigating like a cop—"*who's* hosting, and *what* are their tricks?"

I chew my lip, unsure if I want to ruin the spooky surprises.

So, I torture her with a smirk. "You already know you're doing the first night, and Silas is hosting the last. The rest? Wait and see. But if you don't host a night, you get to draw names for who's the treat to be tricked—"

"Who's the *treat*?"

Thrill shrieks Charlie's voice. She's an out-of-tune Mariah Carey.

"Three treats," I clarify. "We'll draw for a turn."

"Why can't we *all* be treats *every* night?"

I laugh at Cade. "Is your woo woo whining?"

"Uh, look here ... my woo woo didn't get tricked last year. I was seven months pregnant. So this year?" Playfully, Cade shakes her tush, too. "My *Boo Tee* needs lots of haunting."

See? She's gonna be thankful she had her pumpkin polished.

"Don't worry." I wink. "You'll get your scream night. We all will. And when it's not your turn, you can watch or—"

"*I* want to know if you've invited that masked villain again." Charlie looks deadly serious. That's worse than dead serious. "I never did figure out who it was, except it's a man, and I swear, last year when he scared me in the shower like *Psycho*. Fuck being a screaming bitch. I almost snapped his neck."

"Yeah," Cade huffs. "Whoever he is, tell him not to sneak up on a former Marine, a black belt, or a retired MMA fighter. And that's just her, me, and Scarlett. Our men are nothing to fuck with either."

I press my lips together...

Nope. Don't do it. I'm not blurting this secret.

I mean, the seventeen of us are an intimate network—mess with one, and you'll get fucked by all.

Yes, dammit.

That's another pun, but it's also Poly Rule #1.

So, it's not easy trying to scare the ever-living shit out of people who trust you, who get your back.

But don't worry.

I'm not a trained fighter like the women I love. Nope, I'm the smallest and youngest of us, and I have a quirky limp. It used to make me insecure. I used to be a wallflower until Silas.

Until he made me feel beautifully fucked, free, and fearless. In that order.

And now?

My mouth is my weapon. It has no silencer, no filter.

So, leave it to me to find the perfect man for an evil task and not be too shy to ask.

I spotted the villain in the dark corner of the sex club many of us frequent, the same corner I used to hide in. He was twirling his signet pinky ring, eyeing me. Not creepy, just admiring me with Silas.

Then, Fate found us bumping into each other on Meeting Street in Charleston, of all haunted places.

The villain bowed his head like old-world nobility. "Good afternoon, Mrs. Van de May." He shocked me, knowing my married name, greeting me with Southern manners and a smile so devious it was delicious.

Did I scurry away, all scared?

Hell, no. I'm a preacher's daughter who rebelled from the flock.

I flew straight into hell.

Secretly, I followed the villain's wide, tapered back in his dark gray suit down the shadowed, narrow sidewalks of the French Quarter, from Meeting Street to the ivy-covered, cobblestone alley beside Delta's, Stacey's exclusive adult store.

When he unlocked the back iron gate to her historic row house-turned-salacious destination, I grinned.

If Stacey knows him, I can trust him.

I entered through Delta's front door and confronted the villain on the third floor. He was about to disappear behind a locked, black door I've never seen the other side of.

Still, I wasn't afraid.

I grabbed his concrete biceps, whipping him around to stand toe-to-toe with me, my nose barely reaching his hulking chest.

"Since you're a stranger who knows my name," I demanded, staring into his rakish eyes, "you'll get a strange thrill helping me, too."

So, this year, the villain returns. He'll haunt Indigo Island, but this time, there are more victims to terrify.

And Cade clocks it across my guilty face.

"Aw, shit," she mumbles. "I know that look."

"Who me?" I profess, drawling, "Why, I'm innocent."

I touch my chest like I have the vapors, whatever the hell that means; it's a Southern thing. I just hope it works.

"Eily," Cade smirks, "you're as innocent as triple *X*-rated Tinker Bell. I know you're brewing promiscuous potions for all."

"Then hocus, pocus, my bitches." I blow a kiss. "Are y'all ready to have your heart racing faster than in a haunted house?"

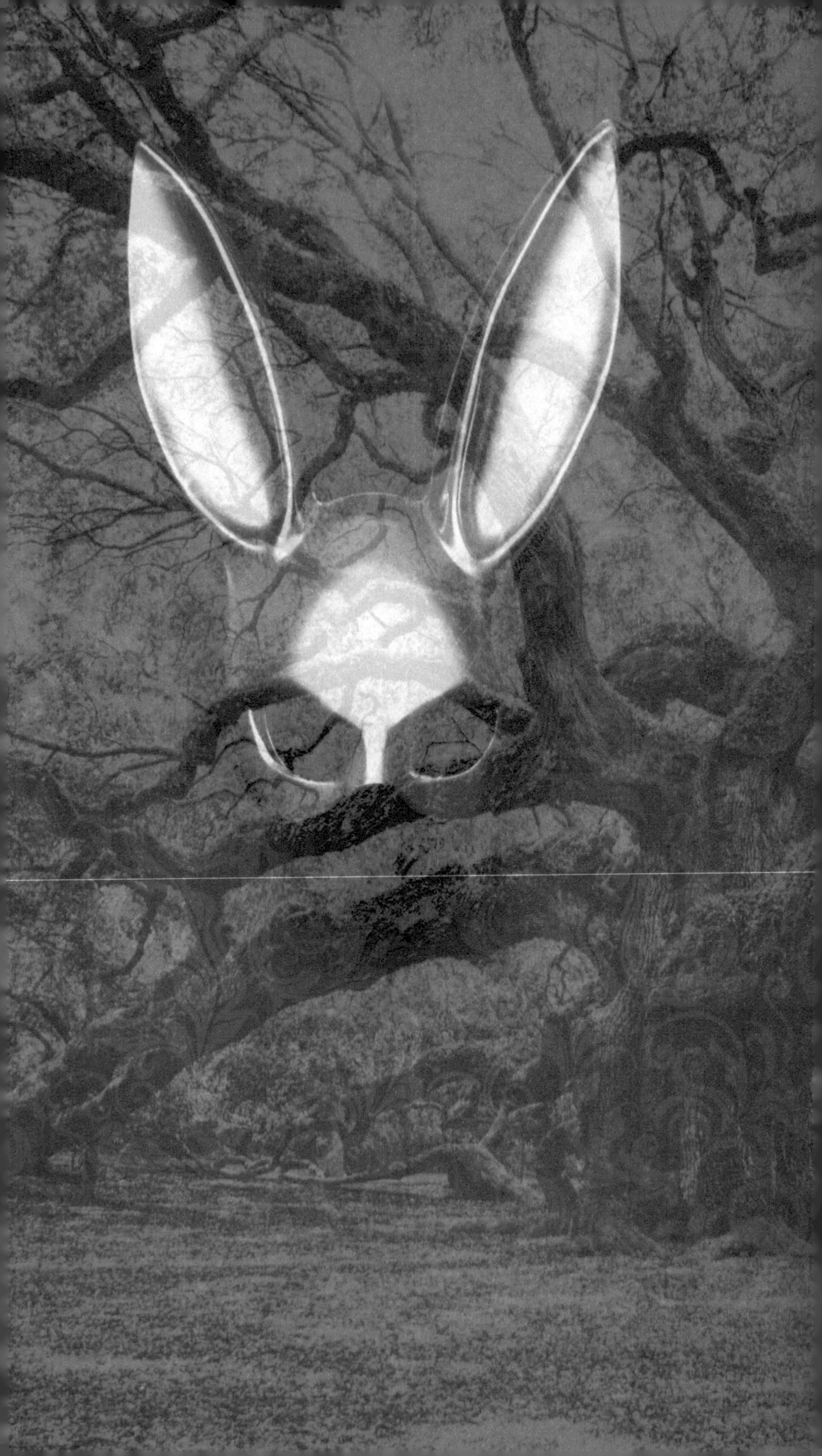

Silas

"Your penis isn't Pottery Barn!"

"Ever use one of these on your junk?"

I wave a penis pump at Redix and Daniel.

"Don't need it," Redix answers, twisting his lips into a cocky grin.

"Looks like it sucks, mate." Daniel flashes his million-dollar smile.

"Ain't that the point?"

I admire the clear acrylic tube with its black tip and blue digital display.

Then, I admire Daniel.

As usual, he dressed up for our shopping excursion. His navy sweater is paper thin. It barely contains his muscles while his gray pants hug his infamous ass.

Yep, I'm admiring that, too.

Grabbing a different model off the glass shelf, Daniel

warns me with a smirk, "If you pump your Big Ben even larger, it won't chime inside anyone's hole."

"Well, yeehaw." Redix elbows between us. "Sign my hole up to try." He grabs another pump off the shelf, tapping my biceps with it. "Here. Use this one. It's the biggest."

I glance across the lavish, second-floor showroom of Delta's.

"You want me to pump my pecker right here?"

Yeah, I'm used to this swanky adult store. And yeah, they had to close it for us to shop because Daniel and Redix are too famous.

"You're welcome to use one of our private rooms," the store manager, Vale, advises, dressed like Wednesday Addams while she leans in the doorway. "Or, if you don't have any questions, I'll excuse myself. The store is yours for the afternoon."

"Thanks." I nod my chin at her.

Vale's been awesome every time we shop here. She's the one who told Eily to start eating yams to increase her fertility and for us to switch to fertility-friendly lube. Hell, we'll try anything to get pregnant, and Vale has a PhD in sexuality, so we appreciate her expertise.

So much so that Redix waves a penis pump at her like we're in class. Like he's eager to pass an erection exam.

"Do you sell lots of these?"

"Actually," Vale answers him, "we do. Some men report longer-lasting erections, and research has proven they can help people with erectile dysfunction achieve satisfying benefits."

"If something pumps my dick even bigger," Redix praises the device in my hand, "it would be *damn* satisfying for us all."

"Satisfying," Daniel lowers his brows, "and sore. I wouldn't be able to sit on my arse for days."

Coyly, Redix leans Daniel's way, nipping his ear, teasing, "Oh, my mate, but how your Big Ben would thank me."

They pause, their accents clashing while they grin, exchanging a heated stare before sharing a hungry kiss.

Dare I say they're dying for each other because...

They are.

Redix and Daniel can't afford to make our relationship public. They have to hide it on the set of their show or in public.

While we have our trusted friends who love us, others won't. You know how it is.

People will judge. They'll be cruel, and Daniel and Redix are too protective of our chosen family. They have kids and I want one, too. We have to watch out for each other.

Their lips part.

They grab a breath before Redix turns to me.

Yes. It's my turn.

But a gruff voice interrupts us.

"Use the pump for about fifteen minutes with some lube." Jace, the bodyguard for Delta's, stands behind Vale. He looks like her shadow, dressed like Gomez Addams for Halloween next week. I turn to him while he shares, "I was curious and tried one. Damn thing did make my dick even thicker ... and longer."

Vale whips around. "Tried it with *who*?" she asks.

"Noneya," he answers her with a smirk. "But maybe you and our accountant should try pumping his number even bigger."

She backhands his biceps. "Shut up."

"Alright." I'm inspired. I ain't shy. "I'll try it."

"Aw shit, I gotta see this." Redix steps back. Plopping

down on an ivory velvet chair, he plucks his phone from the back pocket of his ripped jeans. "I'll FaceTime the wives."

"Where are they, anyway?" Daniel asks.

"Getting their fannies fried." When Daniel arches his dark brow quizzically, I explain, "Getting an ass facial. Like a laser treatment and lotion and shit."

"Huh." Redix wonders, "Should we be prepping our backyards, too?"

"Nah." I wave my hand—the one with a penis pump in it. "We manscape and know how to prep. Besides, I got enough to worry about. I'm not sure what to do for the last night."

"We, uh, have your selections so far, packaged and ready to send," Vale tells me before glancing at Redix and Daniel nervously.

I told her I'm planning a surprise even my partners don't know about.

"If you find anything else today," she says, "I can discreetly send it to your island."

Vale's been full of ideas for our Halloween week. So, part of me feels like an asshole not inviting her, too.

But Stacey, who's part of our network, is Vale's boss and is already coming with her husbands. And this year, Vale's twin sister, Blair, is coming with Beau Bronson and Colton Hawke.

So, yeah.

I'm proud of our world, but some polycules shouldn't cross.

"You've made *selections?*" Daniel asks. "Like what?"

"Please say costumes," Redix drawls. "I wanna play Doctor Dean, giving dirty exams with latex gloves again."

"Bollocks." Daniel laughs. "We did that last year. No repeats."

"Easy for you to say." I scan the showroom for inspiration. "Eily said the same thing, and lemme tell ya: I can be kinky, but it ain't easy being original, too."

"Then let us help you," Daniel offers, his tone cheeky. "You know … when we put our three heads together … lots will come of it."

I grin at his cocky joke.

At his intimate offer.

At how I can't believe sometimes that Daniel is my partner, too.

Was I always attracted to his badass wife, Charlie?

Hells yeah.

Long before Daniel Pierce ever came around with his superhero body and British swagger, Charlie Ravenel was my first crush. Like a mega-crush. I was going to marry her, but she friend-zoned me.

Years later, I met Cade, then Redix.

Yep, that was fate.

Because sharing Cade and Redix's love left me aching for my own, and that's how my heart finally found Eily Dove. *Again.*

So, I had to make her Mrs. Van de May because I'm never letting Eily go.

Hell, I was willing to give up everyone and everything for her, but she wouldn't let me.

Eily is a fearless firecracker of love. She's hot, tiny but mighty, and all mine.

She's the air I need to live.

But when I stop joking around? When I let myself get all sentimental?

Yeah, I love Redix and Cade, too. I love how Charlie and I finally crossed over from the friend zone into something more intimate—something way hotter. I love how Daniel and I have a strong bond, too.

The six of us will always be together.

Heck, they don't know it yet, but I'm building homes for their families on Indigo Island. I dream about us and our kids growing old together.

But this week? I'm skeptical. I ask Daniel, "You sure you wanna help?"

Planning sex games ain't Daniel's thing. Playing them? Yeah. But he's too busy being a Hollywood heavyweight to plan a damn thing.

"Bloody right, I do." Daniel strides across the showroom toward the ivory-lacquered drawers full of high-end lingerie.

Told ya, we shop here all the time.

He slides open a bottom drawer, plucking out a package. "Let's do a night wearing these."

"Dude!" Redix roars. "You and your fishnet fetish."

I approve of the men's black fishnet shirt Daniel's suggesting. But I taunt, "Only if you pierce your nipples like the model on the package, too."

When Daniel smiles like that, panties *and* boxers combust.

He winks at me. "I'll pierce my package for you, but only if you chaps join me." He nods at Redix. "You already go mad when we tongue your nipples."

"I can arrange it for you," Vale says. We have professional piercers here."

"You do?" Though, why should I be surprised? "Is that what's on the third floor?" I ask, "In that room with a black door that's always locked? A piercing room?"

I know my way around Delta's.

Eily and I have enjoyed several demonstrations of their

sex furniture in the parlor on the third floor. Our partners have, too.

You know—for *educational* purposes.

But no one, not even Stacey, the owner, mentions what's behind that black door at the other end of the hall.

And like any horny mind with a heartbeat in an adult showroom, that secret door only makes me curious AF.

As a proud bi, poly man ... that's a lot.

I'm curious to know who is Eily's secret villain.

The fucker followed me one night last Halloween, down the shadowed trail on my island, past the crumbling headstones by the edge of the inky water.

At least ... I hope that eerie cold sliding up my spine was her villain.

The others freaked out about him last year, and I can't tickle or seduce the truth out of Eily, but I know her. I know he's connected to Delta's somehow.

We don't let just anyone onto our island, and we trust the people here.

Especially when Vale blushes, stammering to answer, "That's ... uh. That's ... uh ... just a storage room and—"

"Ahem." Jace clears his guilty throat.

We're all over six feet tall, but he's a giant. And ... he's a huge, horrible liar.

It's obvious.

That ain't a storage room they're hiding on the third floor.

"Secret rooms. Fishnets. Piercings." Impatiently, Redix shifts on his chair. "Whatever. Quit stalling," he tells me, "and test that pecker pump."

Vale points. "There's complimentary lube samples in the basket by the window. So, I'll leave you gentlemen to explore."

She turns, gently shoving Jace down the hallway. He

glances back over his granite shoulder, wanting to watch, and I wouldn't mind. I'm dedicated to my partners, but we agreed to be open this week.

But now, it's just us calling our wives.

I UNBUTTON MY SHORTS, telling Redix, "Call them. Let's see if they approve of my purchase."

Yeah, it's late October, and I'm wearing khaki shorts with a black linen shirt because this is also Charleston. The forecast looks perfect for today and next week, with mild days and brisk nights.

"Hey." I hear Cade answer Redix's video call. "Where are you guys?"

Redix turns his phone screen. It lands on me, standing beside Daniel with a wall of glass shelves brimming with sex toys behind us.

"Good!" My wife blurts, "You're at Delta's. Ask Vale if my glow-in-the-dark pumpkin butt plugs came in. They've been on back order." Eily giggles. "Pun intended."

"Baby girl," I call for her, so Redix aims his screen at me.

My wife appears on it, her long brown hair sprouting from a cute ponytail at the top of her head.

Sipping a pumpkin latte because that's her M.O. and 'tis the season, she nestles beside Charlie, sipping the same, I'm sure.

But Charlie's long blonde hair always looks like she just got off a motorcycle. Like she's a badass, reclining against Cade, whose brown bangs always cloak one of her violet eyes while the rest of Cade's sexy hair is short.

The three cuddle together, wearing Halloween tanks covered in skulls and ghosts.

They remind me of those hot women I see on reruns of *Charmed*. But instead of being a cute trio on a witchy show, they're sprawled across a park bench by the Charleston Harbor. Like they own this spooky town while they enjoy their girls' day out.

I wave the device at Eily. "Should we do a trick night of penis pumps, pumpkins, and pussies?"

Cade starts laughing, but Charlie narrows her gaze. "Don't even *think* about pumping your dicks before y'all fuck pumpkins and our pussies."

Eily giggles. "Maybe that's why they're called jack-o-lanterns. You know? For jacking off."

Redix turns the phone so it captures all three of us. "You know—pumpkin fucking is a thing."

"Says the man with a food fetish." Daniel teases Redix before schooling us, "But Jack-of-the-Lantern is an old British term for night watchmen carrying lanterns. Of course, you Yanks stole that term, too."

"Besides," Cade debates Redix, "pumpkin fucking is *not* a thing."

"Candy Cade," he drawls, "you need to stop watching Paw Patrol and get back to watching porn with me."

"Not if they're fucking innocent orange gourds."

Redix smirks. "What do you think inspired your creamy pumpkin-spiced lattes?"

"Redix! Eww! That's gross!"

But he makes Cade laugh. The sexy asshole always does.

They can banter all day, but my wife's pixie face is worried.

"Silas," Eily pleads, "what if you use that pump and

break your dick again? Then, I'll never get pregnant. Besides, you're supposed to save your baby gravy for me, not blast it into a tube."

"Baby girl, don't worry." My shorts fall to my ankles before I tug my gray boxer briefs down. I'm hanging, half-excited for this. "I can make people paste all day."

Daniel tosses his cleft chin up. "Bloody hell, you two and your semen synonyms."

Charlie matches her husband. She's laughing, too, but I focus on my wife and surge even harder.

I love teasing Eily, pleasing her, and giving her all I have.

"Mrs. Van de May," I coax, "imagine how much *love* I can pump inside you after I pump my pecker, too."

Eily leaps up from Charlie's embrace, pleading to me and all of Charleston's Battery Park.

"But, Silas!" she exclaims. "Your penis isn't Pottery Barn! If you break it, I already bought it, and I don't *want* to return it! You don't need to pump your penis even bigger! I love you just the way you are. And what if you hurt Mister Twirly?"

Redix smirks up at me. "Mister *Twirly*?"

"Yeah." I start stroking it. "That's what I call my hose when he slings soap bubbles in the shower. But now, he's too hard."

"Oh my god!" Charlie's howling. "Daniel calls his Mister Slappy. He jumps on the bed, popping his hips, making it slap his belly."

Now Cade's rolling, too. They're falling over each other on a park bench.

"Redix slaps his from side to side," Cade says, "calling his Daddy Ding Dong."

Redix corrects her, "Not Daddy *Ding* Dong. He's Daddy

Dangle Dong because some days he dangles left, some days he hangs right."

But I'm not dangling.

I'm exposed, erect, and loving this.

There's something about the six of us, even when three are on a phone screen.

I feel free. Loved. And *horny as hell.*

I've missed us. We're always so busy we rarely get moments like this.

I tug my hair out of its knot, letting it tumble free before unbuttoning my linen shirt. Letting it fall to the floor, I kick free of my shorts and boxers, relishing how Eily sighs, "Silas, that's NOT fair. You know you're caramel man candy, and we can't resist a bite."

Standing naked, I tempt, "Then let's see how many pumps it takes to get to the center of my Tootsie Pop."

"Thought it was *licks*?" Redix mimics, licking his lips.

"That, too."

I rip open a packet of lube with my teeth. Glossing it over my fat tip, I make our laughter fade away.

Daniel stands beside me, staring at my aroused cock. When he starts sucking my neck, his hand caressing my bare ass, moans crawl up my throat, making Redix rise from his chair.

As he approaches the glass shelves behind us, I turn, watching Redix prop his phone on a shelf so our wives can see us.

On cue, Daniel kneels before me, his back to the phone.

Then Redix joins him.

Though our wives can't see the lustful smirks on their handsome faces, I can.

"Show me." I fist my base, teasing my tip over their parting lips. "Show me how you get off looking at my cock."

They stare up at me, tugging their pants down along with their boxers, their erections springing free.

Our wives know what we're doing.

We always take turns like this. We always share. We always love. We give everything to each other, men and women.

"You guys can play," softly Eily commands from the phone, "but Silas, save it for *me*."

I groan, fisting my rigid shaft.

It's heaven and hell how Eily's been making me wait. She figures out when she's going to ovulate, then teases me days before, making the tension build. She seduces me, then won't let me come.

So, when she finally frees me, it's like she's in heat, and I'm a rabid dog.

I'm on her for two days straight.

Every position. Every part of the house. Hell, even on my boat, the side of a road, or a Starbucks' bathroom. Anyway I'll take Eily, and she wants me. Nothing and no one is better than fucking my wife.

Mostly, it's fun.

But lately, it's frustrating. Not for me. For her. I want a family with Eily any way we can. But she wants me to get her pregnant, and I want to fulfill every dream she has.

That's why this week will be good. It'll be a break from the pressure she puts on herself. It'll be fun.

And with everyone who's coming? It'll be damn hot, too.

"Let's see how big your cock can get for us," Redix teases, flicking his tongue over my tip, letting me watch him lazily stroke his curving length.

"Let me help," Daniel offers, his voice gruff with desire.

I hand Daniel the pump. Then I sigh, watching him carefully wedge my hungry tip inside the tube.

While Daniel focuses on the erotic task, Redix reaches for Daniel's exposed erection. It makes Daniel grunt at Redix's expert tug while Daniel slowly eases the tube down my lubed shaft, securing it around my thick base.

I hold it there, creating a tight seal.

It's a crazy sight. My hard dick fills a clear tube, and it turns us on.

"*Fuucckk*," Daniel growls. "This is hot."

"Click the button and pump my cock," I agree, loving the sight of Daniel serving me.

Not one muscle on his perfect form, even under his sweater, isn't bulging with power while his coal waves glisten, his famous tendril falling over his forehead. And his lips? They part, doing this to me, pressing the button on the pump over my firm cock.

"Uhh," I grunt at the new sensation, at the pressure. "Oh fuck."

It's odd. It's weird. But this is arousing, watching Redix and Daniel fixate on my swelling shaft.

"Don't hurt him," Eily gently chides from the phone, and I glance up at the screen and swell more.

She's lying back in Charlie's arms. It looks like Charlie's lingering her fingertips over Eily's erect nipple, thinly covered by her soft, ghostly tank top.

I'm a damn lucky man.

My wife doesn't wear bras. Her small breasts drive me crazy with lust, and they arouse Charlie, too.

Her braless nipples are erect under her white tank because I can see how Cade is doing the same to Charlie. How Cade's teasing Charlie's nipple.

They're aroused. Our wives are getting off in public to us, their husbands together, and that turns me on more.

"Baby girl," I growl for my wife. "This pump feels good. You and us and this thing are fucking turning me on. I won't be able to hold it."

Suddenly, Daniel clicks the pump twice.

The rush of blood to my cock is so intense, making my thick shaft inflate even more. It's filling, expanding my erection, my swollen tip almost reaching the end of the tube.

"Fuck," I grunt.

"Damn," Daniel mutters. "You can't take much more. You already fill the tube."

With one hand stroking Daniel's bobbing cock, Redix reaches his other hand between my thighs, wedging his fingers behind my balls.

When Redix finds this spot on me, the one he discovered first, massaging my tender perineum, along with the intense pressure Daniel clicks over my cock, "Oh fuck, yes," I growl even louder, glaring at my wife on the screen.

She'll be ovulating soon, so I've been waiting for her, and she can see it. How I can't hold back.

"Fuck, Eily," I beg. "Please. I need to come. Just once with them, then I'll save it all for you."

"Let him," Cade urges. "He looks like he's in pain."

"Fuck, I am."

This sensation is too weird and new. I'm so used to my dick, how it's big; I know. But this erection feels different. It's a massive, bursting demand I can't control.

"Okay," Eily sighs, writhing on the bench as Charlie pinches her nipple, pebbling under Eily's thin tank.

I'm gonna lose my fucking mind to the sight of Charlie getting my wife off while they get off watching me, too.

"Okay," Eily says again. "Let them taste you, but look at me when you come."

I nod, guiding Daniel's hand with mine, gently tugging the pump off my shaft. Inch by inch, we free my swollen cock until I'm free, until it bobs full, almost dropping heavily in pain for release.

"Damn," Redix licks his lips at it, "your cock is fucking huge."

Lowering his mouth, he keeps massaging the sensitive spot by my tender ass while the tip of his warm tongue drags along the throbbing vein on the underside of my exposed dick.

It makes me shudder as Daniel leans forward.

He's fisting Redix's length. I can watch Daniel do it while his blue eyes taunt my hazel ones. Laving his warm tongue over my leaking tip, Daniel slurps my drops with relish.

"*Fuucckk.*" I beg, "Suck me now. Fucking swallow me. Make me come."

Usually, my control is epic. Usually, I focus on my partners, not me. Usually, I get off making others come, but I need this so badly now.

Maybe it's the months we've been preparing for this week. Maybe it's the taboo tricks and treats we're planning. Maybe it's the familiar bodies I crave and the new ones, too.

I know we'll share the most debauched, devoted nights to fucking and more.

And maybe I can finally give Eily every dream she wants.

When Daniel, then Redix, then Daniel again, sink their hungry mouths, scruffy with whiskers, down my throbbing dick, my thighs tremor. I palm their skulls, fisting Redix's long hair like mine and Daniel's short, thick waves.

They suck me off.

They jerk each other off.

Redix teases near my ass while Daniel's big hand chokes my aching base, and my breath thins, my gaze burning through the phone screen.

It's like Eily's standing right before me, and I know our beautiful women.

I know they'll tease the line of public indecency on that park bench before they finger each other, sucking nipples and getting off in the back of Eily's car.

I've watched them do it many times.

"Oh fuck, yes, baby girl."

I'm about to come to the thought of it. Of our three sexy women. Of my two hard men. Of all the hot women and men joining us this week.

Eleven hard cocks and six glistening pussies.

"Oh fuck, I'm coming in your throat," I warn. I celebrate.

Brutally, I yank Daniel's hair, and he moans, loving it, gagging on as much of me as he can.

Then, Redix flicks his tongue over the exact spot on my shaft, over my thick vein, knowing that's my trigger, and I explode. I grunt. Locked on Eily's green eyes, I fill Daniel's eager, moaning mouth, tremors quaking with sweet release down my body.

I'm still coming, spurting as Daniel pulls off. I shoot across his cheek while he shares my load with Redix's waiting mouth. The lewd way he drizzles my cream over Redix's waiting tongue makes Redix come in Daniel's jerking fist.

But Daniel doesn't come. He's hard, and my mouth is watering to taste him, too.

I love him. I love Redix. I love us. There's nothing I

won't do for them, and I want to please him, too. Daniel's been so tense lately. And beyond our sex, he has my heart—they all do. I burn to make everything right for him, to take care of him, too.

I'm about to lower to my knees to do it, to tug Daniel to stand, but he wedges his swollen cock back under his black briefs.

"Let's buy eleven pumps," he jests, changing our vibe, "one for each man this week."

"Dude," Redix sighs, reaching for Daniel, kissing his neck, sharing the same urge I feel to take care of him. "It's your turn."

"No." He cups Redix's cheek. "I'm saving it for your jack-o-lanterns."

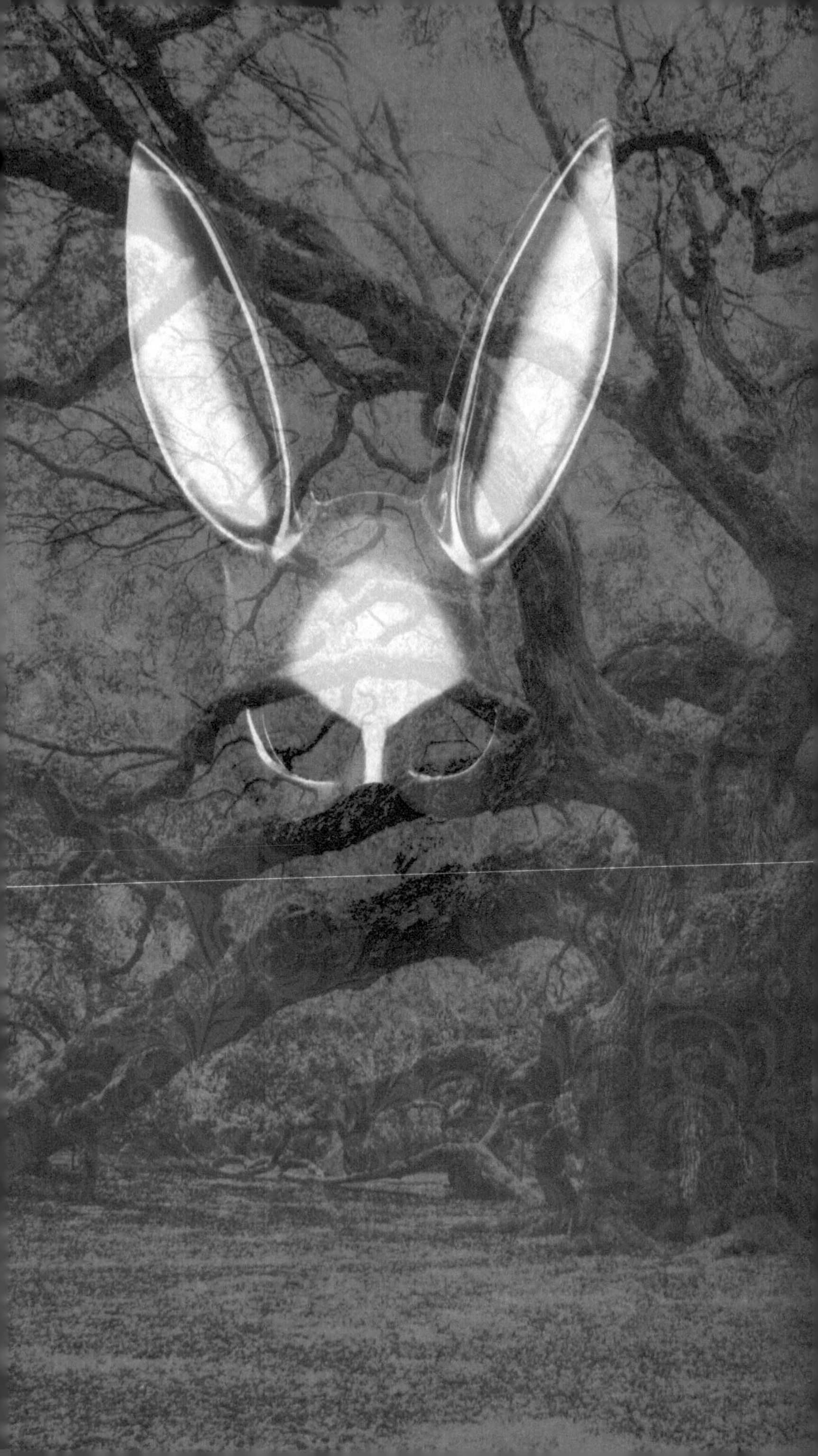

Charlie

CHAPTER THREE

CHARLIE

CHARLIE

T HAT'S WHY I LOVE THIS; FEELING HAUNTED AND HORNY AT THE SAME TIME.

"Oh, my god. This is nicer than our house!" I marvel, gazing around our glamping tent. "That's it. We need to redecorate."

"*Charlie*," Daniel almost scolds, "no more throw pillows. We have enough to build the Himalayas."

"But our furniture is covered in sticky applesauce. We need real adult stuff like this." I sweep my hand like a real estate agent, like I'm selling this. "A bamboo wardrobe for our costumes and lingerie. An indigo-washed dresser. Gorgeous paintings. And look at the rugs. No fruit juice stains! This is perfection. Eily's creativity never ends."

"Neither does Silas's generosity." Daniel plops our luggage down on the massive bed. "He had this custom-made for us. More than six can comfortably sleep here."

"More than six can populate the world here."

I'm amazed by the bed, too.

Draped in sumptuous white linens, cozy indigo blankets, and ivory cashmere pillows, once our six bodies are wrapped under those sheets, why leave?

Summon our kids.

Let them run wild around the island while we make more.

Or at least while we pretend to.

Daniel's been snipped, and Redix is thinking about it. But Silas is fully loaded.

I'm sure it'll happen for him and Eily soon. But just in case, Cade and I have implants. We really want this for Eily. It's finally her year to get pregnant.

"Speaking of populating and penises." Gently, I approach Daniel, touching his chest. "Will you be okay this week? I noticed what you did at Delta's yesterday. How you didn't let Silas and Redix even try."

He nuzzles his forehead to mine. "Babe, I've just been so knackered and stressed. Five times lately, I couldn't spunk, and now it's blocking my head, too."

"Was it me?" I worry. "Do you need someone else to do it? To make you come?"

We've been married for too long. We love each other too much. Daniel and I talk about everything.

"Never." He laces his hand through my hair. "Charlie, you're so fit, that's the problem. I come home, and you give me stiffies. But work, lately, gives me stress—all the pressure and demands. I feel like a bloody cork, needing to pop, but I can't."

"Daniel, just tell Redix," I urge. "Tell him you want to wrap the show and let him help. You're writing, producing, directing, and acting, and it's a lot. You wrote the show for three seasons only, so fuck the studio if they want you to sign on for three more. That's *not* what you envisioned."

"It's not just Redix," he answers. "It's all the cast and crew and their families. They depend on my show. They've made Atlanta their home. I'll gut their lives if I don't sign on for more."

My husband. He's won Emmys and Oscar nominations. They even voted him the sexiest man alive twice, but he's also the sweetest.

I kiss him because I don't know what else to say. This is Daniel's decision. He just needs my support.

Tugging at my waist, drawing me closer, he needs me, too. His deep kiss declares it, so I sigh over our heating lips, our bodies melding.

"Wanna try popping your cork now?"

"Later." He grins. "Let's unpack. Let's relax. I'm sure once I do, I'll empty my wank tank."

Since he has a sense of humor about it.

"Oh, I'm sure you'll be very inspired once Luca gets here, and Stacey, oh, and Beau Bronson, too."

Daniel smirks.

Like I can't clock who twitches his cock, whether we know them well, like Luca and Stacey, or have only met them once, like Beau.

"And you?" He taunts, "I know your type, too—anyone in a uniform."

"My twat doesn't have a type," I huff. "I'm frustrated, too. Even when we get a chance to fuck, and *come*, we have to be so damn quiet."

His nose keeps nuzzling mine. "That's because when I make you scream, our daughter thinks I'm hurting you."

"What does that say about our sons? They don't knock

on our door? They don't care if their mommy's getting hurt?"

"No. They're my little mates. I told them Daddy needs to get his leg over Mummy."

I swat his chest. "They're too young to know about sex."

"Not about sweets. I tell them I'm stealing your candy and bribe them to keep quiet about it."

"Daniel!" It's not fair. He's too sexy when he jokes. "When are we going to tell them for real? About the six of us? How we're a chosen family. I feel like we're the kids, afraid of getting busted when we're doing nothing wrong."

He pauses.

It's not my career or fame that gets in the way.

It's his.

"Soon," he answers. "We'll talk to the others about what to do. I don't want us hiding forever, either. I just don't want us going it alone."

"Well, look at what Beau, Colton, and Nick did," I say, full of hope. "The first players to come out in the NFL? And how they did it as a group? It was smart. We could do the same."

"Maybe." His shoulders sag. "But let's just bloody relax for now. I need a week with my wife, our partners, and some naughty games. Reality can wait."

We kiss. We agree. I unzip our bags and start unpacking, only using two of the six dresser drawers.

What have I learned on our holidays for six?

One—clothes are a waste of fucking time. Literally. Only pack a little.

Two—but yummy robes are priceless. I recommend silk, cotton, and cashmere ones. The sex is always hot, but the temperature isn't.

Three—pack your personal care items. Lots of them.

And I mean.

Lots.

On our first group holiday, I loved our gushing sex. But afterward, I felt like a glazed donut, all squishy and dripping for hours.

I gave new meaning to sticky sweet.

So, I discovered Dripsticks—intimacy clean-up sponges. They're like little mops for your pussy. And Cade found vanilla cupcake personal wipes.

Who knew genitals could taste like a French bakery?

You see, you can't get this intimate with this many without getting over the awkward stuff.

I hand Daniel my toiletry case and his, asking with a kiss on his cheek, "Can you take these to the honeywagon?"

Redix told Silas and Eily about them.

Honeywagons are RV trailers used on film sets. They're luxury bathrooms on wheels and perfect for our glamping needs, too, so Silas bought a fancy, eight-room one.

This week, two of us will share the individual dressing rooms with private showers and such.

But this time...

I'm locking the door when I use it.

Last year, we left the doors unlocked as invitations, and it was fun. We learned how a max of three could fit in the shower. More than that, and someone's drowning.

But one night, I went alone.

After our night of Dirty Doctors and Nasty Nurses, I was a blissful mess.

Lathering in pomegranate body wash, I sighed, relaxing. But when I opened my eyes, the lights oddly flickered, a sudden chill skittering across my wet flesh, though I stood under hot water.

Then ... a thud shook the RV.

"Hello?" I called out, assuming Daniel and Silas were joining me like the night before.

But no one answered.

And the lights flickered lower.

I could barely see.

I needed to grab a towel and investigate, so I ripped the shower curtain open.

To find an evil silhouette eclipsing the flickering light.

Disguised by a black and gold horned mask with a lecherous smile, the demon shocked me, but I didn't scream.

And the devil didn't speak.

It just tilted its perverted face as if it recognized me. Then it dragged an eerie, onyx glare down my naked body, relishing my heaving breath, my dripping breasts, my nipples erect with fright.

Clad in a sinister black, dusty suede topcoat, it was obviously a male. No woman looms that large.

But this woman is skilled.

I'm too trained.

Instinct had me pulling back a punch aimed at his throat, but something killed the power. The flickering lights and pelting water stopped, darkness with an eerie chill flooding the space. I couldn't see as I heard no footfalls, no slamming door while I just stood naked, heart pounding, pussy oddly aroused.

Then the lights jolted back on.

And he was gone.

It left me half terrified and half thrilled.

And this year?

My pulse races. No telling what will terrify us.

"Babe," Daniel asks, "where are our handcuffs?"

He's ignored my request about our toiletry stuff.

Instead, Daniel's unzipped our garment bags, inspecting our costumes for tonight.

"Here." I hand him two pairs from our luggage. "It's kinda weird this year, not hosting a trick night."

"It's kind of fun," he rumbles. "I like the idea of others playing with *us* this time."

Yep, there goes another zap under my zipper.

Never did I think I'd be fucking my friends and more.

And never did I think my hot-ass husband would eagerly join me.

But *never* doesn't really exist.

Not when you invite change. Not when you invite lust and love into your life.

"Are you going to let him do it this week?" I tease Daniel. "Luca wanted you last year, but Ford and Mateo beat you to it. So, this year? Are you up for Luca's whip?"

"It depends," he answers.

"On?"

"On what my wife is willing to do. I'll try new things and partners if you do, too. We have to be equal. That only feels right to me."

Warmth floods my heart. I close the distance, kissing his granite jaw, then tenderly, his lips. "*You* always feel right to *me.*"

He knows it's my answer; it's my permission.

Brushing his thumb over my lips, he asks, "Do the others still feel the same?"

The others are our polycule: The Six.

We always talk. We always make sure. And anyone can always change their mind, and we'll stop. We honor our partners first and our paramours, our spouses, above all.

"So far," I answer. "I assume once everyone's here, we'll chat."

"Where are they, anyway?" He taps his watch for the time.

"Silas and Redix are ferrying the guests from the mainland. And Cade's setting up for tonight in the Trick Tent, while Eily's disappeared inside her house. She's forbidden us to enter."

That's where Silas and Eily house the small catering and event staff who usually help.

I know they've had them sign NDAs. They've secured their phones. They're paying them a generous sum, inviting the staff to enjoy their sprawling home by the water, too.

As long as the staff thinks this is just a Halloween party inside the tents.

As long as they don't leave the house at night.

As long as they don't get curious and wander down the sandy path under rows of swaying palmetto palms to the clearing where our glamping village stands erect.

Because this setting is spook meets spunk.

Bless my heart. I'm turning British. But you get the idea.

Seven tents rise in a circle. Five standing side-by-side. They're white and rectangular, like this one. They're where the polycules will sleep ... *and more.*

But two black tents soar together. They're giant round event tents.

One is where we'll eat and hang out during the day. One is where we'll be tricked every night.

And all hover on wooden platforms two feet off the ground.

This is a coastal island, after all.

Silas cleared this side of it, facing the wide river, swirled with swaying marsh grass. He didn't remove all the trees, just the low brush and scraggly baby pines choking the view.

What's left are the sprawling ancient live oaks, their wide, low branches dripping with Spanish moss, forming ghostly canopies.

By day, this place looks like a sultry island getaway.

Like where you want to honeymoon in a romantic Lowcountry tent village with the blue Atlantic shimmering in the distance.

But by night?

Holy shit, it's on.

I live on a Lowcountry island, too. Daufuskie Island, and I know.

Once the sun melts into the ocean's horizon and all lights dim as the lapping water lulls the eyes of the living asleep...

The darkness awakes, creeping through the shadows as the full moon slides behind the night clouds, conjuring...

The Haints.

Silence your naive mind long enough, and your soul can sense them haunting here.

Because haints are unique.

They haunt this watery land of ancient decay, decadence, and evil deeds. They're said to be malicious spirits, jealous of your life.

That's why, in the Lowcountry, we paint our porch ceilings watery blue. It's lore. It's a spell, scaring the haints away.

Don't believe in ghosts?

Fine.

But Home Depot does. They even sell Haint Blue paint.

So, when you finally feel one shiver up your spine, its cold breath raising the hairs on the back of your neck? You can buy pretty blue paint to ward off that evil looming spirit ... and hope like hell it works.

Daniel catches me musing. "What are you grinning about?"

"Nothing." I tuck our empty luggage under the bed.

"Bollocks," he laughs, toiletry bags in hand, standing at the threshold of our tent.

Its canvas walls are secured open, pulled back like a curtain to a stage.

And why do I know that's how we'll sleep?

The polycules will leave our tents open. We'll be too excited to let others watch and maybe join us. We'll want them more than we'll worry about what else may creep in, too.

Gators. Bobcats. Snakes. *Haints.*

That's why I love this; feeling haunted and horny at the same time.

"Come on." I smack my man's ass. "Let's get our spook on."

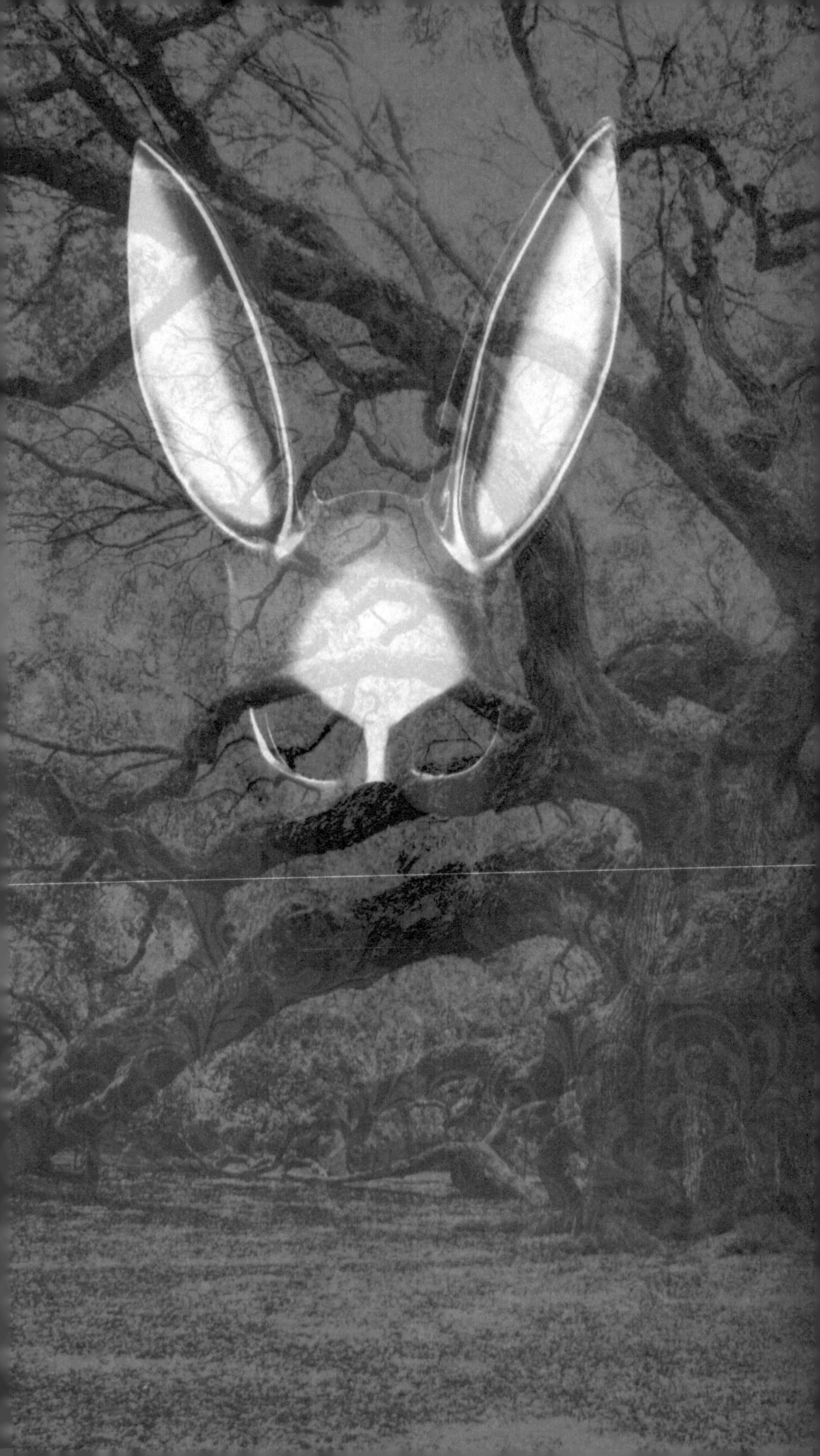

Cade

CHAPTER FOUR

CADE

You gotta tease and ease, not plop and pop.

"Need anything?" Charlie's voice calls out.

"Cade," that's Daniel, "we got bugger-all to do. Let us help."

They wrap on the flap of the Trick Tent. I rush their way, grabbing the canvas panels, poking my head through the flap.

"Boo!" I answer. "And fuck off. Literally. Go fuck and quality test the beds."

"We're not snogging while others work."

Huh … Daniel's too hot to look so tense.

"Alright." I shrug. "Redix just texted. They're five minutes out. Take some carts and help them on the dock. Help everyone get settled into their tents."

"Race ya!"

Charlie turns, charging toward the row of parked golf carts we use on the island. She makes Daniel lighten up.

She makes him race after her, scooping her up and tossing her over his shoulder with a squeal.

Good. They'll help Silas and Redix welcome our guests to Indigo Island, while I finish in here, putting the finishing touches on our first trick night.

An ice-breaker night.

Wait.

It's gonna get so hot in here; ice won't have a chance in hell.

Of course, I'm talking about our erotic games, not the autumn temperature. These event tents can be cooled or heated, but it's perfect outside.

And it's perfect in here, too.

This Trick Tent is glam meets gruesome.

Eily's had the inside of it draped in black velvet. From the center pole, billowing down the rails, velvet pools over the wooden platform covered in a mismatch of plush, dark rugs.

Spider webs and Spanish moss sway from heights, too, while dozens of tall candelabras flicker with faux candles.

Once the sun goes down, orange and green uplights will add to the spooky feel. That and the dry ice machine, misting an eerie, sandalwood-scented fog through the tent while a speaker system pumps wicked, wanton beats.

Silas has been working on the playlist for months.

Hundreds of starry lights twinkle above. It looks like a spooktacular night sky above five sofas made of garnet velvet square cushions.

More like blood-red velvet.

With their low height and generous size, the sofas are perfect for ... *everything.*

Eily arranged them in a cozy pentagon, framing the tent's center. Their black, acrylic side tables gleam ... *empty?*

Huh. Where's our stuff?

Lubes, condoms, wipes, and toys.

No one in their raucous mind has an orgy without them.

Since she won't let me near her house, I text Eily.

> Where are our fuck bins?  

Quickly, she replies:

FAIRY O' FUCKS 

Behind the curtain opposite the door flap.
We made a little room to stage our stuff for
each night

See if you can find my pumpkin butt plugs

> Some guests are too new

> Zar & Nick. Beau & Blair & Colt

> We can't go from handshakes to
> hotdogging in one night. That'll scare them
> away

They trust us. They're 🐃

> WTF? A rhino?

🐃 No more Paw Patrol

🐃 = horny

> What happened to the 🐗?

Satanists canceled it

Besides, imagine 😏

Pumpkin butt plugs glowing in the dark

17 glowing butt plugs?

Like Ass-O-Lanterns in the night?

That's a hard pass

Wisely, Eily assigned the first night to me.

This ain't my first raunchy rodeo. I'm the OG. I started our first throuple: Redix, Silas, and me.

Or did Redix start it?

Or did Silas plan it?

Tough to say.

But with each person, we've added more love, more lives to share, and … more bodies.

So, you can't rush this.

You can't ask seventeen people to bend over for a luminescent butt plug like a witchy spell of, "Poof! Now glow and fuck!"

That's a yeast infection and a yelling match waiting to happen.

No. Communication. Consent. And tonight? Costumes and carnal games are required.

You gotta tease and ease, not plop and pop.

I refocus her.

How's dinner going?

FAIRY O' FUCKS 

Good

We're serving Morgue-a-ritas, virgin and slutty

And finger foods. Literally. Severed-finger
cheese sticks with bloody marinara sauce.
Witch hat dippers. Halloween bat wings

Bat wings?

Chicken wings. As if

The Treat Tent is almost set

That's what we're calling the tent beside this one.

The Treat Tent is for friends and food.

The Trick Tent is for fucks and fun.

Dusk falls as golf carts whir, guests chatter outside, and I prepare adult games. I hear them enter and exit the Treat Tent next door, grabbing dinner bites and drinks.

Then slamming doors to the honeywagon let me know the hour is near. Everyone's taking showers, getting dressed in costumes, as I finish by covering the rugs in the center of the tent with the black Fuck Sheets that Silas bought in bulk.

Yep, they're a thing.

And yep, we'll be washing dozens this week.

I check my watch.

Thirty minutes til Boo Time.

Cloaked by the night, I dart from the Trick Tent to the honeywagon, to the dressing room I share with Redix.

I open the door.

"Well, hey there, little lady," Redix tips his cowboy hat, greeting me shirtless.

"Oh, my god!" I beam. "You're really going for it! Leather vest, chaps, boots, and turn around..."

He does it proudly, with his arms like "praise me," and I chew my lip, so in love, so in awe.

You can slurp champagne from the deep side divots in Redix's ass. His hard glute muscles have no tan lines.

I swear, you can take the boy off the surfboard, but not the man. He still lays out naked with his long hair, kissed by the rays, too.

But it's the scar on his backside that he doesn't hide anymore. It fills me with love, my eyes biting back tears. He got that scar because of me, and for too many anguishing years, I never knew until it was almost too late.

But now Redix shows it off in black assless chaps over a mouthwatering black leather jockstrap.

"Alright, alright." He turns back around. "Your cowboy is ready to ride." Hooking his finger over my jeans, he yanks me to his lips. "And I sure want my partner."

Slowly, he kisses me, cupping my cheek, his tongue laving over mine. My core melts, softening with heat, my soul dancing with her match, her mate. We were teenage sweethearts. He was my first so many years ago and still, Redix knows how to claim me.

We'll never part, but…

"Holster your pistol, cowboy," I huff over our lips. "I gotta put my costume on and get back to the tent before everyone else."

"Just a quickie," he begs.

"Just a hell no." Gently, I wedge him away. "I'm hosting tonight. So hurry and help me get ready."

Even while I slip on my matching assless chaps, boots, vest, and hat, Redix plays.

He sits on the vanity countertop, tugging at the strings of the tiny red and white gingham bikini I'm wearing underneath.

"Quit it," I laugh.

It's like I'm a picnic, and he wants a bite.

"Dayum," he sighs, coasting his fingertips over my belly. It's obvious we've had two daughters together, and we're proud of it.

"My wife looks too damn beautiful to share," he says. "I may keep you to myself this week."

I snap my glance up. "Are you serious?"

I'm not mad.

Sometimes, he or I get possessive. We only want the other. Sometimes, one of our partners feels that way, and we understand. When we go to Luca's hotel or Stacey's showroom, sometimes we stay closed as couples, or as a group.

No matter what, though, Redix insists, I'm the only woman he'll kiss—ever and until his dying day.

But I want Redix to kiss Silas and Daniel, and when he does, it's beautiful.

Those three used to be closed, but they're opening to other men in different ways. It's up to them. We wives let them decide.

Because Charlie, Eily, and I do the same. We've always been open to other women, though Charlie can be more reserved, and we love her for it.

When it comes to the women with the men? Usually, we're with our paramours. For us, that's our spouses. But sometimes we share, and sometimes we swap. It depends on the mood or the need. We never judge, and we always talk about it.

Because we all have our thing.

Like Silas will only hold Eily when he sleeps. He has to wake up with her every day. And Charlie only wants Daniel when she's upset. Only he makes her feel like it'll be okay. And Redix has scars and memories only I share, only I can hold.

That's your paramour.

The one you need above all.

"Nah, I'm kidding." Redix keeps tickling my belly. "You were pregnant and didn't want to play last year, so you should get your groove back."

"So I *lost* my groove?"

"Whoops!" He laughs, tossing his granite chin up. "I just stepped in a cowpaddy."

Silently, my glare replies.

He licks his bottom lip. It shines as his blue eyes tease. "Damn, woman. Your fury gets my fish stick hard."

"Redix!"

"Candy Cade!"

"Have you got a death wish?" I narrow my gaze. "Never, *ever*, reference fish and pussy in the same breath. And don't tell a woman who gave birth ten months ago that she lost her groove, or you'll lose your balls, too."

He wraps his legs around my thighs, making me fall into his waiting arms. Arms wrapped in shredded muscles, so it's damn hard getting mad at him.

"I'm saying..." He lifts my chin, my lips to his. "Beautiful women like you, ones who give birth or take care of kids or just put up with dumbass men like me, deserve to let us give back some of the joy you've given us."

His kiss is tender, familiar, and teasing.

"Smart answer." I love it, nipping his lip.

"Honest answer," he says. "I love watching you have fun."

"So you're okay if we're inclusive? If the six of us have more lovers this week?"

"*Only* this week," he clarifies. "I like the Garden Party poly stuff. When it's only a few times a year, but the rest of the time, it's just us. That's what we agreed to unless someone changes their mind."

"Silas may change his mind—at least about Eily. He really wants to get her pregnant."

Redix brushes my bangs back, sweetly studying my face like it's the first time he's seen it. Not like he hasn't been the love of my life since we were ten.

"Silas loves Eily like I love you. Always and no matter what," he answers. "So, we'll be careful with her this week. I think he just wants her to have some fun. He's got a big surprise for her."

"What?"

"I ain't telling on my man. Not even for my wife," he lies.

Redix will tell me if I insist. We don't keep secrets. But we love surprises more.

"Fine then." I tug his hand. "Come see my surprises for tonight."

Silas admires our group of sixteen, sprawled across the pentagon of sofas.

He boasts, "We look like a council of Jedi knights."

"No," Redix grumbles beside me. "We look like a pile of sixteen burlap sacks."

Everyone laughs, and that's part of my plan—fun before fucks.

"This lets us do our big reveals," I explain, standing with my husband, cloaked in a brown cape tied around my neck, too. "We worked hard on our ensemble costumes, so let's appreciate each reveal."

"What does the winner get?" Charlie jokes, "A gold trophy or a gold dildo?"

Eily claps. "I want a gold dildo! That's year-round fun."

"We'll see," I answer.

"Well, since you're standing there," Daniel suggests, "you and Redix should go first."

With a shared glance, we grin and untie our capes. They flutter to the floor, revealing our raunchy cowboy and cowgirl costumes.

Luca whistles, then shouts, "Turn around and show us what we can ride," and we do.

Redix and Luca are close. So, we shake our asses for him, too.

More admiring whistles fill the air.

"Look at those peaches!" Eily cheers.

I twerk mine. *Sure glad I had a tushy treatment.* It looks great, I know, as I make our guests laugh even harder.

"Alright now," I turn, telling her, "you and Silas go next."

They stand, their robes falling to reveal their elaborate, sexy wench and pirate costumes.

Wow. Silas is wearing a shirt! That's rare. But, of course, it's a white pirate's shirt hanging open, revealing his dozen-pack.

And Eily's allergic to bras. She's wearing a thin, off-the-shoulder shirt, her hard nipples raiding our minds as Silas ties on a velvet, indigo head sash before Eily unveils her swashbuckling hat with blue feather plumes.

Damn, they're hot.

Damn, they're perfect.

Stacey calls out, "You look like the rogue rulers of Indigo Island!"

"Argh!" Add Luke and then Mateo, who agree with their wife.

"You four should go next."

I point at Stacey so she and her three husbands stand.

Even in dull robes, they're a breathtaking quad. I can't stop staring.

Stacey is a former blonde beauty queen turned Southern sexpreneur. With her exclusive Delta's adult stores, she and her alpha men, her husbands, break all the rules.

Ford is the rugged, older Dom. Mateo is the middle man with mesmerizing ink. And Luke is the young hero, the Army Ranger.

But when they drop their capes, they reveal their bond and sense of humor, too.

"Yes!" I love it as we all clap. "You nailed it!"

Stacey is a sexy Dorothy from the Wizard of Oz, wearing ruby slippers and white thigh-highs under her tiny gingham dress. Luke is the golden scarecrow, with scraps of clothing tattered in all the hot places. Mateo is the tin man in silver shorts and paint, barely covering his ink and muscles. And Ford is the lion, the most ironic costume because he's not afraid to wear furry orange shorts with a tail and nothing else.

I can't help it.

After what happened last year, I glance at Luca.

Yep, he's scoping Ford again.

It's like he's looking in the Dom mirror. And Stacey's eyefucking Luca's wife, Scarlett, too.

There's always been an attraction between them, so I gesture.

"Mr. and Mrs. Mercier, care to go next?"

Scarlett smiles, quipping, "Cade, you read me like a Ouija Board."

Last year, Scarlett was pregnant like me, so we got close. We binge-watched Halloween movies while the others played, and I can tell she's like me this year, too.

Scarlett's feral and in the mood.

So, as Luca takes her hand, rising beside his wife, their capes remain on the sofa, and, *holy, freeballing gods.*

Luca's imposing bronze frame and godly member are barely covered by his costume. His short, white Greek warrior's toga, black hair, and crystal eyes add to his mythical look.

With her flaming waves, Scarlett looks like the sex demi goddess Luca stole from the mortals. A gold leather corset and a flowy white skirt barely cover her.

The applause doesn't stop, and I want all to feel welcome. So, I turn to my left, asking our newest guests, "Would you like to go next?"

"Sure," Beau answers, tugging at his fiancée's hand.

Well, actually, Beau is engaged to two. Blair Monroe, the stunning raven-haired beauty rising beside him, and Colton Hawke, the wide receiver for Atlanta's Super Bowl champs.

Beau, Blair, and Colton are very close to Nick and Zar, who sit on their other side.

Zar and Nick invited them.

What Beau, Colton, and Nick—proud pro football players—did changed professional sports forever for people like us. It makes that sudden instinct flood my heart. That warm feeling I trust.

They belong.

They need this, too—love that understands, love that's bigger than two hearts.

"Now," Beau announces, "I think we should score extra points tonight."

He's getting into the spirit.

"Our fiancé, Colt, has a game tomorrow," Beau says. "He'll be here the next day, but he's ready to play with us, too. He's in costume at home and waiting for our call."

"Hell, yeah!" Silas admires. "That's gotta be an automatic win."

"Could be," I tease.

"Well, let me explain," Blair chimes in while Beau calls Colt.

I love it.

Blair's not shy.

Besides, she knows us. She used to work at Delta's, Stacey's sex shop, before Blair moved to Atlanta to be with Beau and Colton.

"My guys," Blair continues, "are big geeks like me. We love anything alien or superhero."

Chuckles rumble.

We know where this is going.

"So this week," Blair continues, "Beau and Colt are totally fanboying, and I'm fangirling, too, not to make it weird or anything."

All eyes land on Daniel.

Redix howls, "Aw shit," loving when this happens. "Please tell me one of y'all is Superman."

Daniel blushes. He can't hide it because he gets this all the time.

But still, when Beau Bronson, the NFL's legendary quarterback, drops his brown cape, revealing his red Superman cape and sculpted, steely blue costume. And then his fiancée, Blair, reveals her cosplay, her detailed Wonder Woman look with the perfect long, black hair, too...

KABOW!

The group goes wild.

"Wait! Wait!" Beau presses his phone, holding the screen up so we can see.

It takes a moment before Colton Hawke appears in costume, growling, "I'm Batman," and we start roaring again.

Colton looks impressive, too. He's big and brawny, with his square jaw clenched under that iconic black leather mask.

They get a standing ovation. And yeah, they'll probably win.

"Hope you don't mind." Beau casts his smile at Daniel. "We're huge fans."

"Not at all." Daniel's a gentleman. He makes humble look hot. "You look better than I did in that outfit."

It's sorta true. How perfect Beau looks. How Daniel obviously admires him.

But I'm shocked … and kinda clit-thrilled … to see my girl Charlie admiring Beau and Blair, too.

"Okay, okay," I calm our little crowd. "Let's welcome our other new guests."

"New?" Zar drawls, grinning at me, his gaze taking his time, admiring my form. "Darlin', we've seen your hot bacon sizzle. We ain't new."

If I close my eyes, Zar sounds like Matthew McConaughey but looks nothing like him.

Zar is brunette and bronze. He looks Greek, like Luca. Hell, he's Luca's CFO and sub. They have a dark history. And somehow, Scarlett, Luca's wife, is involved. She subs with Zar, too.

But Zar's man, Nick? He's lighter with strong features, his dark blond hair cropped and styled.

They're a striking couple of opposites.

And yes, we do know Zar and Nick. We all got quite intimate at Luca & Scarlett's engagement party at Luca's hotel.

"Well, then," I tease Zar back. *Damn, I'm curious about him.* "Show us your sizzling costumes."

The way they smirk with swagger. The way Zar and Nick turn, rustling with something they were hiding on their sofa, their robes fluttering to the floor as they turn around, facing each other...

It makes Daniel boom, "Bloody hell!" Even his laughter sounds British. "It's cocks in a box!"

And it's hilarious.

Zar is dressed like a sexy UPS driver in tight brown shorts and a shirt. Nick is a hot FedEx driver in tight blue shorts and a shirt. But between them, they hold a white cardboard box over their cocks.

"What are you delivering?" Redix asks what we're all wondering.

So, Nick and Zar kiss before they laugh, lifting the box, revealing their cutaway shorts over matching, white mesh jockstraps.

"Penis packages!" Eily blurts.

"Talk about packing heat," Scarlett admires what bulges in a double dose before us.

"The newbies win!" Charlie proclaims, laughing. "We got the Hot Justice League and the Dick Delivery Duo. Who can compete with that?"

"Not so fast." Beau sounds quite curious. "You can still win. Just show us what you're hiding."

And again, I sense it.

The attraction.

Beau and Blair may be fans of Daniel's. Hell, millions are. But everyone admires Charlie, too.

With that scar on her gorgeous face, she's stunning. In particular, Blair keeps staring at her.

Daniel and Charlie are the last to reveal their costumes. So, Daniel nods for Charlie to go first.

Jaws drop along with her cape.

My stare. Everyone's stare lands on Charlie's mouth-watering cleavage. It's exposed by the open zipper of her black satin micro dress. It's tight and adorned with a silver police badge, a holster slung low, and handcuffs dangling to her naked thighs clad in laced-up combat boots.

Then, Daniel reveals his costume.

It's equally kinky. I expect bachelorettes with dollar bills to appear.

His black silk cop pants and tight sleeveless black button-up bulge over his muscles. He can't be contained.

To match Charlie, he's wearing a silver badge and handcuffs. But when Daniel dons the British Bobby police hat he was hiding under his cape, it doesn't match, and it sure looks arresting on him.

"Hey, officers." Silas offers his wrists for their handcuffs. "I just ripped a tag off a mattress."

We laugh, admiring our group, standing in a wide circle —sixteen here and one on the phone.

It's an arousing sight.

Our Halloween is off to a spine-tingling start with *that* other tingle—that luscious one we love—quickly traveling south for all.

"So, who won?" Eily's always curious.

"We all will," I answer. "Because we got more games to play."

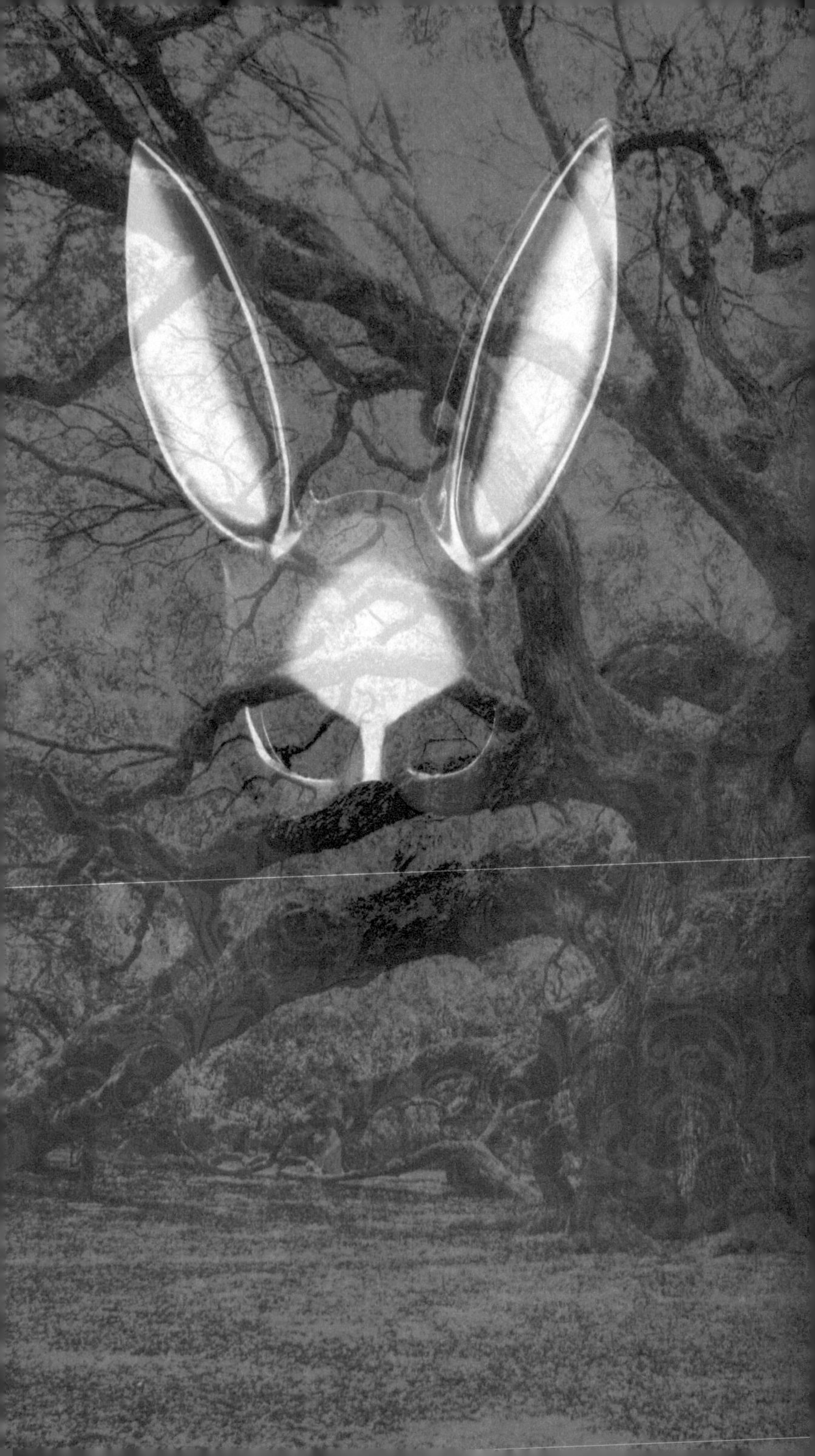

Cade

**IT'S LIKE GAME OF HORNY THRONES.
SWORDS RISE EVERYWHERE.**

All refresh their drinks, chatting and admiring the costumes.

"Help me set up the next game," I whisper to Redix, who assists as we lift a light metal frame covered in a black silk sheet into the middle of the room.

Once all are seated, I pass around a small, black glass cauldron.

"We have a black-and-gold tradition," I announce. "So, in the spirit, pull out one chocolate candy kiss. Most are gold, but if you draw a black foiled kiss, you play the game."

The cauldron only has fifteen kisses. For this round, three are black. I'm not playing this game, and Colton's not here, but he's watching on the phone Beau holds up.

Once all select, Stacey, Eily, and Zar are up to play.

I uncover the first game, and Stacey laughs. "Is that a sex swing frame?"

"You'd know." I wink. "And yes. But tonight, you're bobbing for donuts hanging from a string on it while blindfolded with your hands tied behind your back. The first to eat all four donuts in their row wins."

It's raucous, watching them lick and snap the air. With each vigorous bite, their glazed donut sways away, making them stagger to find it.

"Jeez!" Eily proclaims, her lips glossed with sugar, her tongue swiping the air, blindly trying to find her second donut. "Licking beaver is easier than licking these Krispy Kremes."

"It's like licking a virgin." Zar finishes his first donut. "She won't keep still."

Nick asks his man, "How do you know?"

"Ahem." Luca loves cajoling them, "I made Zar let me watch him tongue a few in college."

Yeah, you'd tongue a bath drain for Luca Mercier.

And yeah, the idea of letting Zar serve me for Luca?

Hmm, my kitty purrs.

But Stacey's quiet, devoted to her tonguing task and winning, besting Eily by one donut.

Pecking Stacey's glazed lips when we free them, Eily praises her, "Congratulations, you've become quite the cunnilingus Queen."

Stacey gets high-fives while Redix helps me push the frame away, replacing it with a covered silver basin.

"What's that?" Colton wonders from the phone, so Beau holds it closer. "Oh!" Colton suspects, "You're bobbing for apples!"

Apples?

Now, where's the kink in that?

The cauldron passes again, and three get black kisses. Since the men outnumber the women, it's Daniel, Luke, and Beau, who passes his phone to Blair to hold while they play.

"Kneel, gentlemen," I demand.

"Yes, ma'am," Luke, dressed like a sexy scarecrow, answers with a suggestive smirk. He looks aroused to serve.

"What are we doing?" Beau wants to know, looking thrilled to kneel next to Daniel, too.

I wish I had a lasso for this, like a whip or something.

Should've asked Luca. Oh well.

"Together and with your hands tied," I answer, dramatically snapping the black sheet off the basin, "you're bobbing for *dildos*."

The group erupts.

I knew this would be a hit.

"Fuck yes! Someone record this!" Colton begs from the phone in Blair's hand. "I'll give Beau shit for this forever."

From his knees, Beau winks at Colton on the screen.

"I'll use my phone." Eily plucks hers from a side table. "I found the perfect porn filter. We use it for our videos all the time. It makes Silas's balls look great."

Silas laughs. "Baby girl, please tell them *all* our secrets. Why keep anything, like my balls, private?"

It's cute.

Silas kisses Eily because she can't. She can't close her big heart and cute mouth.

Once I tie the men's hands behind their backs, it's a sloshing, sexy sight, watching three sizable hunks—one a cop, one a scarecrow, and one Superman—dunk their handsome faces in cold water.

They're laughing, their mouths searching, pushing, and

nudging a full basin of floating dildos in a rainbow of colors, but with no luck.

"Bloody," Daniel huffs, "I can't get a cock in my mouth."

"That's *not* what he said." Redix laughs. "*Yesterday.*"

Mateo taunts, "You gotta open bigger, man."

"Yeah, let's work together," Luke suggests. "Push a cock in my mouth."

"Yeah," Beau adds, water dripping from his dark-trimmed beard. "Then he can use his cock to shove a cock in your mouth, too."

Half of us snort while Eily records them, cooing, "*Ahh. Look.* They're becoming fellatio friends."

Daniel almost drowns, laughing with us, but he follows Luke's orders. Of course, leave it to the Army guy to organize group maneuvers, even bobbing for dildos.

"Good! Good!" Beau's such an athlete. He coaches Daniel, too. "Way to execute! Now, with your mouth, almost kiss him while you shove that purple cock into Luke's mouth. Then, with his cock, he'll shove that fat pink one or that long, lime green cock in yours, but you gotta open big for it. Don't like drown, but keep open for it so he can shove a cock in."

Do you hear this?

I'm gonna piss my chaps, I'm laughing so hard.

"Then together," Beau's too focused on winning, "your cocks can shove that blue swirly one in my mouth." And we're too busy laughing. "That's it, Luke. Take the purple cock. You got it. Good! Now, Daniel, take it. Open your mouth. Take the pink cock. Good! Luke, shove it! Shove it in his mouth! Harder. He's almost got it." He tells them, "Good! Good! Now, shove a cock in my mouth while you bite your cocks hard so you don't drop 'em."

"Again," Redix is rolling, "that's *not* what he said."

Ford adds with his deep gruff, "Actually, I like a little teeth."

"Duly noted," Luca teases, and I almost can't keep track of everyone.

Of who lusts for who. Of who loves who. Of who belongs to who. Of who's allowed to play with who and how much.

I'm sure, over the week, I will.

It already feels like there was never any ice to break, only donuts and dildos to eat.

Finally, all three men lift their heads, hair dripping, faces streaming wet with dildos proudly clenched in their grinning teeth.

"Say 'dildos'!" Eily snaps the pic.

While the laughter won't stop, we refresh again. Some go to the honeywagon; some go for drinks. Charlie helps me clear the basin away. Then, Silas helps me cover the floor with dry fuck sheets.

"What's next?" he wonders.

But all I share is, "Everyone, grab a drink and relax. All play this round."

Once settled in the pentagon again, I randomly pass out black envelopes, each embossed with a gold number, one through seventeen.

"Colton," I wave an envelope at the phone Beau's holding again, "I'm saving this one for you."

"Deal," he says. "I'll be there in forty-eight hours."

I sit beside Redix and explain, "This is a game of Intimate Treats. You've each been given one and a person, a number, to share it with.

"But," I pause for clarity, "this is *optional*, and that's our rule all week. We always talk. We always ask for consent, and we can always change our minds. So no obligation. Only fun. Okay?"

All nod.

"I'm number one." Mateo waves his envelope. "I guess I'll go first." He rips it open, reading aloud, "Moon number fifteen."

"That's me," I answer. "And please do."

Mateo smirks, approaching, eyeing me beside Redix, and no one can miss how hot Mateo is.

Black hair to his shoulders. Deep brown eyes. Light brown skin smeared in silver paint over his sculpted pecs and arms covered in striking black ink.

"Dayum," Redix, with his arm draped over my shoulder, admires Mateo as he turns around.

Aiming his impressive backside our way, with a zip and a tug, Mateo pulls his silver shorts down, arching a bit, letting us appreciate the sight.

"Damn," I mutter, lusting as Redix does for him.

Then Mateo thrills us.

Dropping his shorts to his ankles, he kicks them away. Covered in silver, his ass is nude, and when he turns around, *oh, my towering Tin Man.*

The Tin Man wanted a heart in the story, but ours needs a defibrillator. They're pounding because Mateo's got the longest cock I've ever seen. And if you saw Redix's, you'd be like, *damn*, too.

Redix licks his lips at it. "Goddamn." It's the word of the night. He won't stop praising Mateo, who's half-hard as he returns, sitting with Stacey, Ford, and Luke.

That's the perfect start to our game.

"I'm next." Nick announces before reading his card, "Take off three pieces of clothing for number seven."

Hell, three pieces are all Nick is wearing.

"That's me," Ford rumbles. "Ready to receive packages."

But Nick looks at Zar first, and Zar nods, smiling like he's fine with them being a little open tonight.

So, Nick stands before Ford, stripping for him, unveiling his trained physique before snapping off his jockstrap. Then proudly, Nick strokes himself for a minute. "Special delivery," he taunts Ford, Ford's husbands, and his wife.

All enjoy Nick's delivery, and I chew my lip.

That's two men nude so far.

Then Eily draws Luca.

"Mimic your favorite sex position for three minutes," she shares her treat, and Luca nods, consenting.

"Get ready for the ride of your life," Silas chuckles, admiring how his tiny wife, Eily, fearlessly hikes up her wench's skirt.

Eagerly, she climbs on Luca, confidently straddling him on the sofa.

With Luca's toga so short, he's got to feel Eily's slick enthusiasm grinding over him. I know she's not wearing panties. She thinks they should be banned, but Luca doesn't touch her.

It's like he's holding back, so Scarlett climbs behind Eily.

Together, they mimic riding Luca. They give him a dual lap dance as Scarlett tugs Eily's top down, exposing her pert breasts, and teasing Eily's nipples for Luca's smoldering gaze.

"She's a dirty little girl." Scarlett taunts her husband. "She's so aroused for you, isn't she?" She tugs Eily's nipples. "Maybe we should share her?"

"Yes, share me," Eily begs, making Luca lick his lips.

It's hot watching Luca, the powerful Dom, submit to two women. When they climb off, giggling, Luca's toga is lifted, his meaty cock exposed, soaring hard, his eyes aflame with lust.

The sight of Luca's arousal makes Daniel clear his throat.

Then Charlie takes her turn. "Let number eleven play with your nipples."

"Who's number eleven?" Luke asks, exchanging a hungry look with Charlie.

Oh, Luke is interested in her. I guess it's a military thing.

But is Luke free to play?

I glance at Stacey, Luke's wife. She grins like she wants him to enjoy his time with us.

"Me," Blair answers. "I'm eleven."

"Hell, yes." We hear Colton on the phone.

But Blair turns, asking Beau, "Are you okay with it, too?"

This is new for them, you can tell. Beau's smile is thrilled, but the way he narrows his gaze is unsure.

"Dude, let her," Colton urges from their video call. "We're all bi, and you and I have each other, so our woman should have this, too."

They negotiate like we do. They talk it out. *That's real love.* You can tell they share it.

Slowly, Beau pushes his thumb over Blair's plump lips, demanding her suck while he asks, "Is that what *our* dirty girl wants? You want us to watch you with women this week?"

Eagerly, Blair nods, sucking his thumb before she lifts away, suggesting, "I think you and Colt should play a little, too. Not all the way. I know you don't want that. But these are our people. Finally, we're safe here. We belong here. We can explore with them."

"I agree," Colton says. "We know the lines we won't cross, so have fun tonight. I certainly will when I get there."

For sure, every heart in the room, like mine, understands the feeling of finding kindred spirits. Of finding people you're more than safe with; you're free.

And the beauty is ... that's when your life *really* begins.

"Okay," Beau agrees, holding the phone and letting Colton watch. "Show us, kitten," he tells Blair. "Show us how you love playing with pussies, too."

Charlie rises in her sexy cop dress, dragging her zipper down to her belly button while she stalks Blair's way. Tugging her dress aside, she exposes herself, so Blair stands, greeting her, tugging her Wonder Woman bustier down, too.

"Dear god," Zar drags his hand down his face, sighing, praying, "I know it ain't Thanksgiving yet, but thank you for this breast fest."

I chuckle, letting my gaze admire Zar a little longer than the others. I like him. He refuses to be imprisoned by expectations, and it's attractive. Intriguing.

Blair and Charlie stand in front of Beau with Colton on the phone, letting all watch as Blair teases Charlie's nipples, slowly circling them before palming their lush weight, making Charlie moan.

"My sexy wife is very naughty," Daniel taunts them. "Charlie likes her nipples sucked hard. And bite them, too. It gets her wet."

"*So* fucking wet," Eily sighs. "Charlie's the goddess of the gush."

Licking her lips, Blair goes for it. She heeds Daniel's tease, craning her neck, lowering her mouth to suck, then bite Charlie's nipple.

Charlie gasps, cupping her there, hard and fisting

Blair's raven strands. Both women moan, writhing together, before Blair lavishes Charlie's other breast with the same attention.

"Fuck," Beau growls. "Fuck this is hot."

"Told you," Colton says. "Am I the only one jerking off to this?"

"No," Daniel answers, and I glance right.

Daniel's unzipped his cop pants. He's stroking his thick shaft, and when I glance back, I catch how Beau is more than a fan of Daniel's.

He's aroused by him, too.

Under his costume, Beau surges hard. He's sharing his hero's arousal for how his fiancée, Blair, and Daniel's wife, Charlie, clearly want each other.

"Who's turn is it?" Impatiently, Eily sighs, "Or can we all just start fucking now?"

Silas laughs. "Time. That was three minutes."

"Bullshit," Redix replies. "That was a good five minutes. But yeah, it's my turn now."

Gently, Charlie kisses Blair before returning, tits out, to her seat beside Daniel.

I grin.

My game is working.

Charlie's flushed and smiling like Blair while Redix reads aloud, "Time for Penis Play. Act like pirates swinging big swords with number ten."

Silas whips his sexy grin at me. "Cade! You set this up! *I'm* number ten."

"No, I didn't," I scoff. "How could I? It was random. I didn't know you'd be a pirate tonight."

"Really?" Eily's skeptical and right.

"Okay, fine," I admit. "Of course, Silas is the ultimate pirate. But I didn't know Redix would draw his card."

"Well, then," Redix stands, "prepare for plundering."

Silas rises with him.

And when they do...

They're almost too beautiful together.

Tall, tan, shredded with muscles, and long, tawny hair, some mistake them for brothers, but clearly, they're not.

Silas saved Redix in ways I couldn't. He gave him back his innocence. And Redix taught Silas how to love, how to sacrifice everything like Redix did for me.

That's how Silas found Eily, too.

That's the past and love we share. The happiness, too.

"I'll swing my big sword," Redix unsnaps his leather jockstrap, coaxing Silas, "if you swing yours."

Silas, in his pirate pants, tugs them down his thighs, his incredible cock, indeed, stabbing like a steely sword, wanting a public duel with Redix.

"Ahoy, my matey," Silas taunts Redix back, but then it's passionate, how they reach for each other, how their breath changes.

Fisting their hard cocks, they rub them together, tip against tip, then shaft to shaft. It makes Redix grab Silas's hair, kissing him like he'll never stop.

I glance around.

It's like Game of Horny Thrones.

Swords rise everywhere. Unsheathed in fists.

Zar and Nick wield theirs. Beau, Daniel, Luca, and Stacey's husbands are stabbing, too.

Everyone's aroused. It fogs the room like the sandal-wood-scented mist, music coaxingly pumping in the background.

If I give them more time, Redix and Silas will come. It's obvious by their hungry thrusts and grunts.

"Can we please fuck *now*?" Eily begs me.

"No," gently, I chide. "All get to play, but no one fucks."

"What?" Stacey's on Eily's side. "We're at an erotic Halloween week hosted by The Six, and no one's *fucking*?"

That makes Redix and Silas stop, lips to lips, tip to tip.

They turn to me, surprised, too. But I give them a look, a tender one they can read, and they sit down, cocks hard, but understanding.

"Not tonight," I clarify. I feel responsible. I care for these people. "Let's keep getting comfortable together and make sure we know our limits, too. Just tonight. No fucking. Not even spouses or partners. It'll be hotter that way."

"Cade's right," Luca declares. "Waiting makes it better."

"Says our Pleasure Dom," Scarlett adds, rubbing Luca's thigh. "You get off on it, but some of us have waited a year for this party."

I blow a kiss at Scarlett. "I've waited a year, too, so one more night won't hurt. I promise."

"Speak for yourself." Ford fists his hefty cock. His hooded stare lingers from me to Daniel, who's still fisting his cock, too.

Damn, Daniel has stamina. He's been hard forever.

"Some of us need relief," Ford demands.

"Okay," I reply. "We'll finish our game, then get off solo."

"Like a circle jerk?" Luke reveals, "I've done a few in the Army. It's fucking hot. All of us getting off and coming together and—"

"No," but Charlie interrupts. Nervously, she glances at Daniel, then at me. "Not *all* of us," she insists. "Some are still new. Some may have boundaries. Just *one* of us comes for all."

"Just Cade!" Eily jumps on Charlie's bandwagon. "Just

Cade, our horny hostess. She's earned it tonight. Right, y'all?"

Eily gets all to agree, especially me.

So Scarlett goes next. She takes her turn for three minutes, massaging the ass of number thirteen, Stacey. It's obvious when Scarlett plays under Stacey's gingham dress that she massages her clit, too. She almost makes Stacey come, but they don't break the rule.

But then Beau takes his turn. And though it seems like it, I didn't set this up.

"For three minutes," Beau reads his card aloud, "massage the crotch, over the clothes, of number nine."

"That's me," Daniel practically groans, still stroking and hard. He consents.

But Beau turns his phone, asking Colton, "Is this what you mean by us playing?"

"Yeah." Colton sounds gruff. He sounds aroused. "Do it if you want, and let me watch you."

Charlie moves over on their sofa, letting Beau recline beside Daniel.

But Daniel's cock is already exposed. It's not under his clothes. And though Daniel looks like he's burning with lust, his muscles glistening with sweat and tense with need, he won't force a situation.

He'll honor Beau and Colton's boundary.

Daniel huffs, asking Beau, "Should I zip up?"

"No," but Colton answers. He must feel so aroused, yet needing control, watching us from his phone. "Can you massage Beau instead?" Colton asks Daniel. "Over his Superman costume? Fuck, it's kinda funny, yet kinky."

All smile, agreeing, but it's up to Beau.

There's something about Colton, Beau's obvious and

only male love, watching him, permitting him. So, Beau nods.

He's already hard, his cock swollen under his blue costume.

But once Daniel reaches over, cupping Beau's girth, slowly massaging his rigid shaft, covered by blue spandex, Beau groans. His back bows, thrusting his hard cock into Daniel's grasp while he stares at Colton on the phone, then at Blair, across from him on a sofa.

Blair's aroused.

She's breaking the rules, covertly fingering herself under her blue skirt, but it's obvious Colton's getting off to this. For those who can't see him on Beau's phone screen, we can hear him.

"Fuck yes," Colton growls. "Stroke him off," he tells Daniel. "Feel how hard he is. He's always been hot for you. We both have."

Daniel's hard, too. Not at the praise of fans, but for Beau.

Who wouldn't be?

We all know what Beau did. He's an incredible man. He's beyond hot, with his thighs shaking. He's going to come in Daniel's grasp if Silas, the timer, doesn't stop them, and Silas won't.

We want this for Beau.

We want this for Colton, too.

They're the newest men, with their woman, in our group, and it's what they want. Just a bit of kink and play without breaking any promises.

They need it like we do—the safety, the freedom we rarely get off this island.

"Fuck yes," Beau groans at Daniel's efforts. At Daniel's

mammoth hand, his palm, expertly pressing, rubbing down, and lavishing Beau's tip, too.

"Oh fuck, yes," Beau grunts.

"Come, baby," Colton urges Beau. "Come in Daniel's hand. Look at how hard he is, how fucking big he is stroking your thick cock."

It's true.

Daniel is swollen.

You can see his veins pulsing to come like his cock is aching to do it, but he won't. He's focused on Beau. He's watching his hand give Beau the release he needs.

"Come on," Daniel urges Beau. "You know you love this. You love a man fisting your thick cock." His accent alone does it. "Come on. Cream in my hand. Show us how you love it."

Beau can't speak.

Instead, a growl crawls up his straining throat, his chin tossing up, his lips parting. He grunts, his body jolting while Daniel squeezes his shaft, making Beau's milky cum spill inside his suit.

Daniel's an actor. He knows the power of his glare. He keeps milking Beau's cock, "Give me more," he demands while staring at Colton on the phone screen.

When Daniel makes Beau grunt, spurting again in his fist, it ends Colton.

"Oh fuck, babe," Colt huffs. "Oh fuck, yes, babe, I'm coming, too."

We all want to. We all need to.

Bodies are squirming.

Eyes are searching.

Breath is huffing.

Since I'm the hostess, and they told me to come, though Beau already has, I crawl down, kneeling in the middle of the floor on top of the black sheets.

Tugging my bikini bottom aside, it won't take me long.

All the ache. All the desire. All the love in this room, I feel it thrumming through my veins.

I watch Redix. I watch my husband.

Then, letting my stare roam, meeting the eyes of people I trust, a group I desire, I touch myself for all to see. My gaze lingers on Zar, and I moan.

My fingers slide slick through my tingling folds, the ridge of my middle digit strumming over my sensitive clit. I rip my vest, then my bikini top aside, pinching my erect nipple with one hand while I fuck myself with the other.

"Yes, Cade," Redix coaxes, returning my gaze to him. "Finger that sweet pussy. Show them what a beautiful wife I have." *Oh god, they're looking at me.* "Show them how you're a hot little slut for me." *Fuck yes, I am.*

My fingers dip inside.

"Come for us," Redix demands, and *yes, I will.* "Show them how you want them all week."

Yes, I do.

I'm right here on my exquisite edge, about to fall. Feeling their heated gaze, I'm swollen and proud, pounding my fingers inside.

They can hear my arousal.

I can listen to their panting breath.

I can see lust in so many eyes.

Redix reclines, grinning. His cock surges hard, watching me, almost making me do this, making me finger myself for everyone, and I love it.

"Do it, Cade," he coaxes. "Make me a proud husband and come like a beautiful slut for us."

"Oh god!" I cry out.

Because I am, I'm clenching. I'm coming so hard my muscles seize, and I can't move.

Only my stare can.

And I groan, coming with another spasm, but this time with a lewd, depraved shudder, too, because...

Behind Redix.

Lurking in the dark shadows of the tent.

Where no one else sees but me.

Is the devil.

He watches as I make myself come for sixteen people. He watches as I make myself come for him.

Redix

> "We're so right and raunchy; the devil wants to join us."

Bacon. I smell bacon.

Umm, and yummy breasts.

I cup Cade's succulent one in my grasp, burying my nose in her soft neck, my chest pressed against her warm, silky back.

This is heaven.

Forget cracking my eyes open, even though my stomach growls at the aroma of a legit Southern breakfast being served in the Treat Tent, and my dick stirs to my wife in my grasp and Silas's backside, his ass rubbing against mine.

I don't want to wake up.

This is a dream.

"Dude," I growl at him. "It's too early. Keep still."

"What time is it?" Charlie mumbles on the other side of Cade.

We're piled in our new bed, our six bodies cozy under blankets, while the crisp morning autumn air makes me want to stay here forever.

"Fuck," Daniel huffs. I hear him fumbling for something on the nightstand. "It's ten bloody o'clock."

"Shit," Charlie gasps, "it's late."

"Shit, let's cuddle here all day." I squeeze Cade tighter. "We never get to sleep in. Glory and Lola wake us by six."

"The other morning," Daniel rumbles, "Duke jumped on our bed at five a.m. He leaped across Charlie and landed on my morning knob, smashing it with his little foot, and I almost honked everywhere."

"Barfed," Charlie translates. "He means barfed, not the other thing."

I grin with a shudder against Cade. "Thank god our girls aren't rowdy."

"Not yet," Cade murmurs, rubbing her ass against my dick. "Coffee." She knows how to bargain. "I need coffee."

Reluctantly, I sit, stretching. "Yes, ma'am."

Rubbing the sleep off my eyes, I look to my right, to Daniel by the edge of the bed. He's holding Charlie, whose legs intertwine with Cade's.

"Tomorrow morning," I tell him, "it's your turn to play pussy-whipped husband."

With sleepy lids, Daniel smirks at me. Like he ain't doing shit. But like, I don't know.

Sexy British bastard. He's proudly whipped for his wife, too.

Then, I look to my left for some backup. But that's all I see ... a back.

Silas's ripped back.

He's got it facing me on the other end of the bed. His body engulfs Eily in his embrace.

"Shit," I huff. "Guess I'm the bareass barista this morning."

Wedging the sheet and blankets down, I crawl out of the middle. It ain't easy.

"Nice moon," Daniel admires my awkward effort.

I joke, my bare feet greeting the cool wooden floor, "Wanna land on it?"

Daniel tempts me, "I got my rocket right here." He's always horny in the morning.

So am I. So is Silas.

What man isn't?

I don't have to peek under the covers to know Silas is sporting morning wood, too.

Cade reminds us, groaning into our pillow, "No fucking until tonight."

"Fine by me." I scratch my morning shadow, pressing the button on the coffee maker. "Because our solo shows last night were mighty fine."

Eily put a table with a coffee station in every tent, and it's official. I'm nominating Eily for President of all Poke Parties. No one runs them better.

Poor thing. She must be exhausted. She hasn't blurted a peep this morning.

"Hey," so I ask Daniel while we wait for java to brew, "where did y'all go last night? You missed the show. Luca was hot as hell, making Scarlett, Zar, and Nick kneel for it."

"I wanted him all to myself," Charlie answers for Daniel, wedging her face deeper into the canyon of his massive pecs while he kisses her hair. Like they share a secret.

"Oh, so y'all broke Cade's rule?"

"Never," Daniel answers me. "We know better than to piss her off."

"Amen to that," Cade mumbles before clocking my steps toward our open tent flaps. "Where are you going? I'm comatose without caffeine."

"To squirt the dirt," I answer, squinting.

Naked, I step into the bright, brisk morning, but it ain't cold enough to shrivel my piss hard-on. I try to be discreet, aiming it over the side of our tent's wooden platform.

Then I laugh, catching the backside of Luca doing the same from his tent next door.

Damn, that man has a cut ass.

I call out to his broad, naked back, "You look like one of them Roman statues of boys pissing in a fountain."

"Greek! Not Roman." He laughs but doesn't turn around. "And I'm no boy. I'm a very hungry man."

He shakes the dew off while I do the same. Then he turns around, giving me a mischievous smirk before disappearing inside his tent with Scarlett, Zar, and Nick.

Like a stiff branch, I crack my back, arching as I turn to see Mateo, our other neighbor, reading on their deck.

Resting between his legs, under a cozy blanket on their lounge chair, is Stacey, reading a book, too. Ford and Luke must still be in bed.

I wave. They wave back.

Then I grin, catching Beau and Blair naked and in an odd position.

They're in the tent on the other side of The Quad, which is what we call Stacey and her three husbands.

Guess Beau and Blair's fiancé, Colton, will join them after his game tomorrow. So, for now, I call out, "Whatch y'all two doing?"

Blair answers, "Morning yoga."

"Airplane planks," Beau explains, lying on his back, his powerful legs rigid and in the air. His feet flex flat, easily holding the weight of Blair on her belly, flying above him with their hands clasped.

Aw, they're cute.

They're smiling at each other. They're buck naked and obviously in love.

I joke, "Looks to be more than yoga real soon."

"We won't break the fuck rule," Beau answers. "We promise."

"We trust ya," I reply, and that's rare for me. To trust. But I do. That's all I feel with this group.

I get why Cade wanted us to go slow last night.

Well, slow for us.

This is supposed to make us stronger as couples, as groups. We build bonds here, not break them. Having a constellation of souls like ours means too much to us. Some of us can't be out in public. The cost, the risk is too high.

But here?

I take in our peaceful glamping village, the sunlight burning off the morning fog through the sprawling oaks with Spanish moss swaying from branches.

This is connection. This is freedom. This is Halloween fun and fucking for some ... and coffee.

The rich aroma hits me, making my mouth water, so I retreat inside our tent.

"Your new man's outside," I tease Daniel. "Beau's naked and waiting to play ball with ya. And Charlie, your titty sister, Blair, is out there, too."

Cade giggles into our pillow, keeping it warm for me, while Daniel and Charlie just laugh.

Because it's half a joke and half true.

Everyone can sense, if not outright know, who is whose primary. Some of us have one. Like, Cade is mine. She brought me back to life. Or how Scarlett is Luca's or Zar is Nick's.

But some have true multiples. They can't love one above another. Like Beau, Blair, and Colton. Or Mateo with Stacey, Ford, and Luke.

But then again.

I'll never stop loving my partners, either. They're forever in my heart.

Like Silas.

Who hasn't said a fucking word which is weird. Usually, he's raising hell with the dawn.

Pouring a cup, I stir in some coffee with Cade's sugar and milk. She likes everything candy-sweet.

"Hey, dude." I talk to Silas's back, "Are y'all alive over there? You need some mouth-to-mouth? Or dick-to-mouth?"

"Uhh," he grunts.

"They're knackered," Daniel says. "We broke our hosts."

"How?" Charlie asks. "Silas can go all night, and Eily makes the Energizer Bunny look sedate."

I pour a cup for Charlie, too. She likes it black. I'd pour a cup for Eily, as well, but damn, she's quiet.

That ain't like her.

"Hey, fun size," I try rousing her. "You asleep, too? I thought for sure you'd be up early for your fuckathon."

Barely, Eily moans, her long brown hair spilling over Silas's biceps. He's got her practically under him while he stirs.

While his hips move, slowly rolling ... and *hang on...*

I know his thrusts. I know her moans. I know Silas's favorite position. He likes taking us from behind.

"You fuckers!" I laugh. "You're fucking!"

Eily moans louder. She loves getting caught.

"What?" Cade flips the white sheet off them.

Like a cop, she investigates before demanding, "Stop!" Like they're committing a felony in traffic, not fucking on our bed.

It only drives Silas. He starts humping Eily harder. He loves breaking rules, and he loves us watching his naked ass do it.

"Ah, let him get a leg over," Daniel endorses what Silas is literally doing.

He's got his leg over Eily, wedging her open, her tiny body helpless, lying on her tummy with her back arched. She's taking Silas as his massive cock drives inside her. We can hear his effort. We can hear her moaning, melting into the mattress.

I whine, "How come they get to fuck, but we can't?"

"Shhh. They're trying to get pregnant," Charlie whispers like they can't hear us.

Like they aren't right there, humping like animals at a zoo. Like they're behind glass, inside their natural habitat, while we're on a school field trip, witnessing biology at its best.

Hell, I would've passed that class if it had been entertaining like this. But I did like sex ed. In high school, I applied my education, chapter by chapter, with Cade.

So, I wait with two steaming cups in hand. No way I'm delivering hot coffee to our bed while they're fucking on it. Talk about scalding hot sex.

Instead, I love this. I live for this shit.

Watch.

"Need some help fucking that sweet, little pussy?"

I grin, cuckolding Silas, who growls back at me like a feral beast, every muscle on his sculpted back tense with effort. Hunched over Eily, it's like he'd rip the throat out of anyone who touches her right now.

She's his. He's mating her. He's breeding her. She gets his seed.

"No," Eily huffs at me. "I mean, yes, Silas. Yes. Harder. Harder. Don't stop. I'm gonna come."

Silas growls again, and yes, he'd even kill *me* if I came near his wife.

I set the cups down and lean against the table.

Charlie pulls Cade into her and Daniel's embrace. They hold each other, giving our partners more space.

It's fucking beautiful, actually, how Silas loves Eily. How he'd die without her. How he fought for her, even back in high school. He'd give his life for her, and now ... they want to make one together. They're trying so hard.

Damn. Can men get hormonal? Like all monthly and emotional? Is that why I'm craving chocolate?

Because this is hot, but if I let it, I'd kinda cry.

I want this for them. I know it'll happen for them. Our kids will grow up together.

I glance at Daniel, and he winks at me. He remembers doing this with Charlie, just like I did with Cade.

That primal instinct. That deep urge. That over-whelming honor. That tiny hope. You have no control, only a dream.

"Silas!" Eily always calls his name when she comes. It doesn't matter who makes her do it; *Silas* is written across Eily's soul.

He holds her hand, squeezing it as his body locks, groaning deeper than he does with anyone else. *He's coming. Real hard.* My rousing dick knows it. Then we hear it with his soft murmur, "Eily. Eily, baby girl. Fuck, I love you so much."

He wraps around her so tight I can't see her. He loves her that much, and she's that small against his tall, protective frame. All we can do is hear their muffled kisses, her sighs of love … and my stomach growl.

"*Now*, can we drink our coffee?" I ask, making them chuckle.

"Yep," Eily's voice peeps from under Silas's weight. "I just got all the cream I need," she jokes, "but I'll take five sugars like Cade."

"No way," Cade answers her. "No coffee for you, our Haunting Ho. Not until you tell me who the hell that devil was last night."

"What?" Eily bolts up, her hair mussed like it got caught in a blender.

Silas rolls on his back. He turns to Cade, too, while Eily declares, "There was no one here last night."

"Don't play spine-chilling, mind fuckery with me," Cade replies. "I saw him. I saw your villain. He was lurking behind Redix, and then he disappeared."

"Damn," I huff. "All y'all got spooked last year, and I still haven't seen him. And he was right behind me last night?"

"No, he wasn't," Eily replies. She sounds legit. "He wasn't here last night."

"Yes, he was," Cade volleys. "I was coming in front of all of y'all, then I saw him and—"

"Wait." Charlie sounds serious. "Who is this man, and can we even trust him? If he was in the tent with us and—"

"But he *wasn't*." Eily's honest tone won't waver. "He can't be here until later this week, and yes, we can trust him. Well, sorta. But I'd never invite someone who'd out or hurt us. He's just for shock value. He wears his black pin-striped suit and Black Mask and scares the shit out of y'all."

She huffs, falling back on her pillow. "But now, my spooky surprise is ruined."

"What do you mean a 'Black Mask'?" Daniel asks. "Like from DC comics and Batman? Like the mafia crime king who wears a skeleton's mask that's all black?"

"Yeah." Eily stares at the tent ceiling. "It's kinda perfect for this guy. A businessman. A criminal mastermind. An impersonator. A little sadistic, but really fucking hot. Trust me." She sighs, "I worked so hard to get him, but now my fright night is fucked."

"Ah, baby girl. No, it's not." Silas turns, cupping her flushed cheek. "He can still terrify us. Don't worry. We'll be frightened."

I snort. *Silas misses the point.*

He sounds caring, not creeped out by Eily's villain.

"No, he can't," Eily debates. "Y'all are no fun. I can't scare you. You guys are too smart, and our women are too badass. I'm surprised Scarlett didn't punch his throat last year before Charlie sniped him out, and Cade dumped him in the ocean."

"But..." Charlie stammers, like she's adding it up. "But, he doesn't wear pinstripes and a black skeleton mask. He wears a dusty topcoat and an antique demon mask with horns and—"

"Yeah," Cade adds, "it's a black and gold mask ... like our colors. It's like he knows us. He knows about our games."

And don't judge, but I swear a shiver crawls up my naked spine.

"But," Eily croaks, popping up again, "he *doesn't* know about us. I swear. I never told him about our black and gold sex games."

We're silent, eyes darting before searching Eily's face, which looks innocent.

Which *looks scared.*

All of us but Daniel are Lowcountry-born and bred. And around here? We know our ghosts are real.

"Aw, shit," I crow. "Hell, yeah. Our satanic sex conjured a haint."

Eily blurts, her petal lips insisting, "We're not satanic! We're beautiful—all of us. I love our sex. There's nothing wrong with it."

"Yeah," Silas laughs, "we're so right and raunchy; the devil wants to join us."

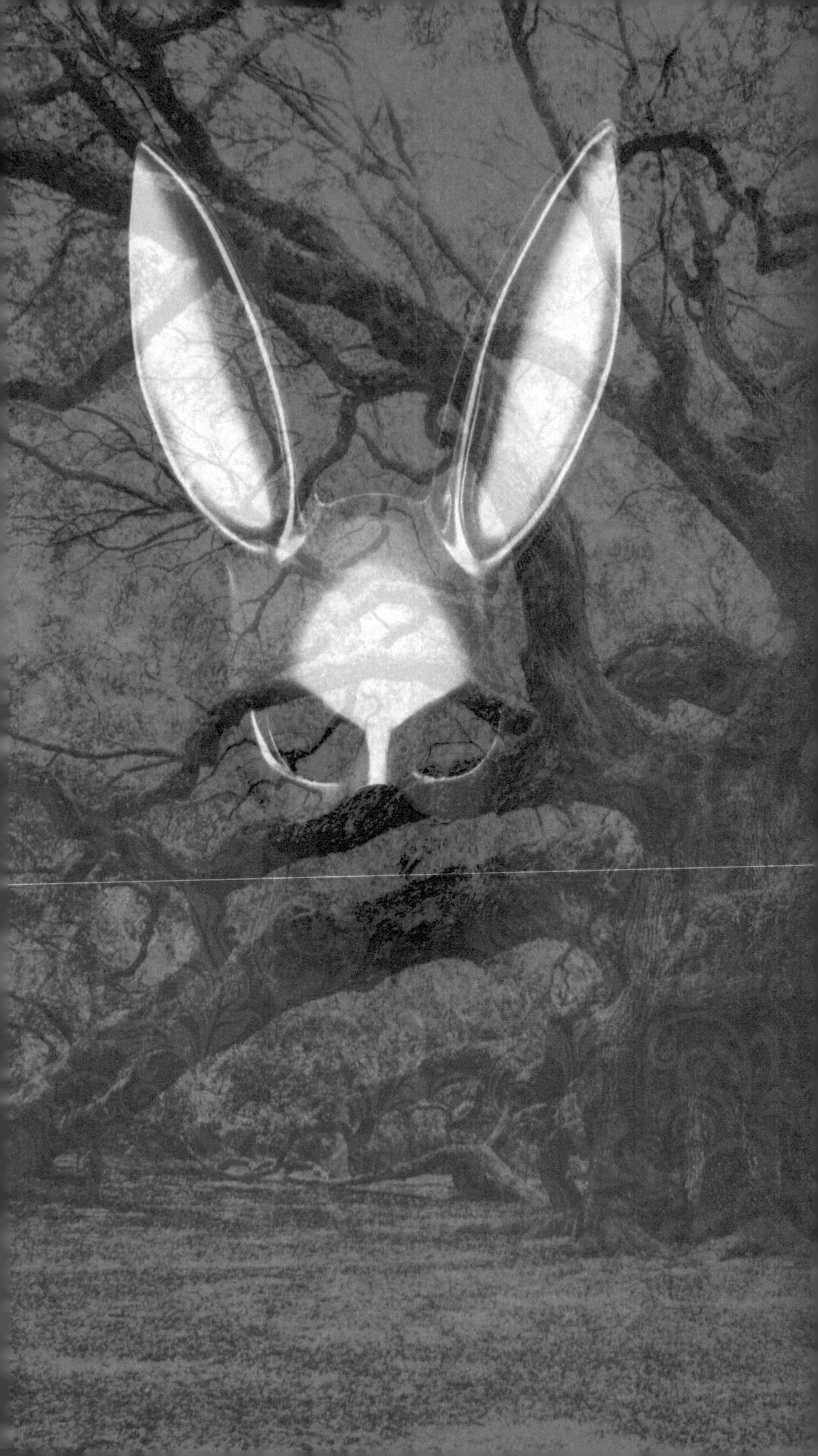

Daniel

CHAPTER SEVEN

DANIEL

> "WE'RE BOUND TO GET DICK DELUSIONS AND VAGINAL VISIONS ALL WEEK."

"So, you're not a fan of shrimp and grits?"

A lush accent interrupts my untouched brunch. I glance up. Luca's taking a seat across from me.

"I prefer scones. But I've learned to love biscuits. *Southern* biscuits."

"Likewise." Luca sips an espresso. "Though ... I still crave the taste of home."

"Greece, right?"

He nods. "And you? Do you miss London?"

"Actually, Cornwall is home and..."

I glance across the Treat Tent. Its side flaps are open, the autumn sun spilling in.

I have more in common with the fifteen people sitting at hand-hewn farm tables or nestled together on piles of ivory floor cushions than I do with the average Englishman.

Not all accept our life ... or our love.

And I care bugger-all if they don't.

"Though, I like it here." I turn back to Luca. "This is home. With my wife. Our kids. With you lot, our friends. I'm relaxed here."

"And yet," knowingly, he traps my gaze, "something haunts you."

Crikey Moses. The fork in my hand stalls. I've barely eaten. I can't. For weeks, my hollow stomach's been in knots.

And this makes it worse.

"How did you know?"

Luca leans back in his chair, his white linen shirt falling open, his jeans faded and relaxed.

"I watched you eat breakfast with Redix," he says. "Well ... he ate, then left, yet you remained like you needed to tell him something, but you didn't. You can't."

"Bloody hell." I'm not upset. I'm impressed. "You got all that from watching us?"

He smirks. "I gain a lot from watching."

Luca is a Pleasure Dom.

For a moment, I forgot what I've witnessed of his expertise so far.

He likes to restrain, to control, to watch until you let go, until you come for him, breaking into someone new.

I know his fetish saved him from grief. I know that's why Zar means so much to him. And I know how he lost his first wife. I know how he'd kill for his second wife now. Luca worships Scarlett.

"You saw all that?" I raise a brow. "That I need to tell Redix something?"

"I know Redix well." He sets his cup down. "He's been a close friend for years, and I know you can tell him whatever has you, uh…" He licks his bottom lip. "Whatever has you *bottled* up."

When someone can read you like a book? Like an erotic one of your darkest secrets, should you be scared? Or aroused?

And when that someone looks like Luca Mercier? Like a merciless Greek sex god? I mean … a *Dom*.

Should I submit to him, too?

Sweat hits my pits, beads forming over my top lip, too.

"How do you know I'm," I grab a breath, "*bottled* up?"

I don't know why I can confess to Luca what only Charlie knows. That for weeks I haven't been able to spunk. Translation: ejaculate.

Yes, I'm in pain, but this finally feels good. It feels good talking to a man about it, too.

"Has it ever happened to you?" I whisper. "You know? Your bottle gets hard, but your cork can't pop?"

Luca's chuckle is deep, not judging. "A few times. Once, it was stress from inheriting my hotels. In the past, it was grief or guilt. And, father to father, you'll understand; I can't always … *pop my cork* … if I fear my daughter may interrupt."

I toss my chin up, laughing. Relieved and validated. "It's a wonder parents ever fuck again."

His tone drops. "Eventually, the urge in us is too strong."

We pause. The room, full of our friends and partners, falls away.

It's just Luca and his crystal eyes mesmerizing me, asking me, "What do you need to tell him?"

"Redix?" I lower my voice because Luca looks worried that I'll hurt his dear friend.

"It's not about our love," I answer. "The six of us are well—quite well. It's about our work, our show."

"What about it? It's a hit. You won an Emmy."

"I want to end it," I confess. "I never saw the story lasting this long, but now hundreds of good people depend on it for their jobs, and Redix loves his role. He deserves to win for it."

Slowly, Luca nods. "And you feel guilty because you're co-stars, but you won last year, not him."

I look down, pushing grits across my plate.

"It gutted me. To win when he didn't."

"Because you love him." Luca understands. "And now, it's tough when you need to do what's best for you but not for others."

"I feel guilty, and it's bloody killing me. The studio wants to know next week if I'll sign on for more seasons, so I must decide. That's why I can't—"

I can't even say it.

Every time I think about it, it gets worse. The pressure. The frustration. The embarrassment. Eventually, everyone will know. Charlie's trying to help me hide it. But why should I? I trust these people.

They'll understand.

Bloody hell, I more than trust them. I want them.

We're open this week. Rarely, does our polycule do this. Usually, it's only The Six. Mostly, it's me and my wife.

But on our holidays, the exploration, the erotic play, and sometimes the new lovers make us stronger. I only return, more devoted to my partners, more in love with my wife. My wife, Charlie, who supports me. She sees who raises my eyebrow.

Yes, I fancy Stacey. Of course, I do. She looks like Charlie.

Yes, I think Beau is fit. He's an all-American man, a perfect athlete hiding a bad boy underneath. I can tell, and it's intoxicating.

"But you will," Luca commands, interrupting my silent panic. "Your cork will pop tonight."

Of the new partners I crave this week, it's Luca.

I wanted him last year.

His whip intrigues me. All my muscles and might can take it. I'd relish it. Fuck being the boss this week; I need a break. And with the way Luca lowers his dark brows, his lush lips curling up, it's like he knows exactly what I need, and...

"Heads up!" A deep voice booms.

I glimpse a blur, a football expertly aimed, landing in my shocked grasp.

"Come on!" Beau shouts for me and Luca. "It's flag football time. Shirts versus skins."

"Women are skins!" Eily cheers, jumping up from the cushions and flinging her T-shirt off.

She's so cheeky. Bras are a joke to her.

"If you play tits out and topless," Silas protests, rising beside her, "it ain't fair. The men will be too distracted."

"Speak for yourself," Nick boasts, leaning against a table. "No offense to our beautiful ladies, but I'm immune. I'm the only gay man here."

They all begin gathering in the middle of the tent, dressed *or not,* shirts and bras flying off for the daytime game.

Only Luca and I are seated, witnessing their standoff. It's entertainment at its best.

Eily throws her arm over Charlie, who throws her arm over Blair. Then, Stacey, Cade, and Scarlett join their topless line.

Like a firing squad of a dozen mouthwatering naked breasts aimed at the men, our women aren't playing fair.

They planned those little black dolphin shorts they're wearing, too.

They make Hooters look like Amateur Hour while they stand like the Champs of Chichis.

"Beau plays with us," Blair announces, "and you guys get Nick because he's a pro. He'll help you since the rest of you fellas say you can't control your blue-veined junket pumpers while our tits are—"

"Our *what?*" Redix howls. "What the fuck is a blue-veined junk—"

"She knows a million names for it," Beau interjects. "Donut holder. Frankendick. Hole puncher. Jawbreaker. Meat flute. And my favorite … a salty yogurt slinger."

"I'm marrying two of them." Blair shrugs. "Gotta be creative."

Silas smirks. "Hell, that names Redix before breakfast. Donuts, yogurt, and all."

Cade quips, "Don't forget his Frankencurve."

"You mean his giant hoochie hook!" Eily jumps in.

"Fine then," Redix says, untying his shorts. "I'll play with my hook out and catch you all."

"Yeah," Mateo unzips his jeans, "our jawbreakers will distract the ladies."

"Aww, hell nah." But Luke cups his crotch. "I gotta protect Big Jim and the twins."

Ford wraps around him, biting Luke's neck. "Take one for the team, and if Jim gets hurt, I'll kiss him and make him better."

A shirtless Beau asks, "So … we doing this?"

Gawd blimey, that man is fit. Something about his beard turns me on.

Luca stands. So do I.

"We'll play," I announce, tossing the ball back to Beau. "Knobs versus knockers."

Beau catches it. "Play on my team," he says, "to even it out."

Quit tempting me.

"Whose team is the ghost playing on?" Silas jokes.

Zar drags his shirt off. He's ripped and bronze underneath. "Some of y'all are pale, but you ain't ghosts."

"He means our *haint*," Redix explains.

Her tone worried, Stacey probes, "Our *haint*?"

"Yeah," Silas answers, "Cade saw him. Charlie saw him. And last year, I felt him following me. We conjured him with our wicked sex."

"Silas," Eily huffs, rolling her eyes, "no one conjured a haint. We're not wicked. Cade was just having a horny hallucination. There's going to be seventeen of us. We're bound to get dick delusions and vaginal visions all week."

Luca smirks. "My kind of nightmare."

"But y'all," Stacey warns, "haints are real. I sense one at Delta's all the time. Like it suddenly gets icy cold in the middle of a warm room. That house is almost two hundred years old and haunted."

Don't be fooled by her beauty queen looks. Stacey's a smart woman. She's sussed this out, raising my pulse because I believe her.

She gestures to the clearing outside. "And what about this island?"

Silas stifles a yawn. His default mode is relaxed. With a stretch, he fills us in.

"Books and records say there was an abandoned French mansion here. Old letters say they heard screams from it.

But it's long gone. It belonged to some pagan Marquis, hiding his depraved rituals from the English Puritans. Marquis Lois Ravenel and—"

"And he's *not* my ancestor, you little shit." Charlie's fists land on her waist.

But it *is* her last name, and her people *are* from here.

Still, I can't tell if Silas is taking the piss because they always go on like this.

"Charlie girl," he flips her ponytail, "don't be scared. It's just your kinky ancestor who turned his mansion into a wicked brothel during the Revolutionary War."

She swats his arm. "You're lying."

"No, he's not." Stacey aims her stare, searching the dark shadows of the thick marshy forest on the edge of the clearing. "That's the history of these islands. People used them for all kinds of dark deeds and rituals."

"Y'all," Cade fears, "we're haunted."

"No," Beau twirls the football in his fingers, "we're playing."

For hours, we play.

For hours, the lads tease the ladies with every ghoulish genital joke you can imagine.

It's a wonder no one gets their jibbly bits smashed.

Half of us are starkers except for our trainers. All of us are sweating with black or gold flags dangling from the belts around our waists.

Still, the ladies, Beau, and I lead by one point until Nick summons his lads into a huddle for the final two minutes.

"Shit," Beau huffs, glistening with sweat beside me.

Bloody hell, I can't stop glancing down at his abs. His trail. *His bulge.*

We kept our gym shorts on. No sense in distracting our team with balls and bats, too.

Wrong sport. Right image.

I wipe my brow. "What?"

"Nick may play defense for Carolina," Beau warns, "and he may be injured and not running the ball today, but he's got a cannon for an arm. Watch out. Here comes the final trick play."

"Whada we do?" Scarlett asks.

Beau studies our beefy opponents. "Cover your man," he coaches. "Literally."

But that does fuck all.

Redix snaps the ball to Nick, who expertly holds, waiting. Because instead of running away and avoiding flags getting ripped off, the lads charge us. They trick us.

While Luke stays open, running down the field for Nick's throw, each man sweeps a woman off her feet, like a regency romance on steroids.

Silas spins a giggling Eily around. Redix has Cade wrapped around him. Stacey takes on Mateo, who scoops her up like a damsel. Our ladies laugh as Ford rushes Beau, defended by Blair and Charlie, and Luca aims for me.

Because Zar tricked Scarlett, tossing her over his shoulder. She's slapping Zar's naked back while I tower, smirking at Luca's approaching blitz.

I match him in size, and that's an impressive amount. We stop, nose to nose, bodies dripping, grins muzzled.

"Tonight," Luca dares. "You're mine."

Or is it a promise?

Bleeding hell, I hope so.

We leave the game a draw and take our showers.

After a leisurely dinner of calzones shaped like skulls, I notice Luca summoning Redix. Nervously, I watch them leave the Treat Tent.

I trust Luca. He'll keep my secret. He'll let me tell Redix what's troubling me, but their exit is odd until Eily catches me watching.

"It's Luca's turn tonight," she shares.

Sitting on Silas's lap beside me, she swirls her fingertip through orange icing on a chocolate cupcake, teasing, "Not me betting a million on BDSM treats and tricks for all."

Please be right. Please be right.

Fuck, I've wanted this for so long.

The rush heightens when Redix returns with garment bags draped over his arm.

"Alright, y'all," he announces. "Put on a cape, but the red lingerie and men's shorts are optional."

Scarlett unzips the bags as if she knows what her husband has planned. "Here you go." She hands cupless bras and crotchless panties to the women who coo, admiring their quality.

"Nice." Stacey fingers the chrome buckles. "Mariemur's red leather line."

I assume the women know the designer reference, while all men know BDSM kink when we see it.

Holy fuck, my stirring cock sure recognizes it.

Luke studies the black leather shorts in his hand. "Don't think I've ever worn men's fetish wear before."

"No fatigues this week." Stacey drapes her arms around Luke's neck. "It's Halloween and time to play with our husbands."

"What are we playing?" Ford asks.

"Put on your vampire capes." Redix whips his over his broad shoulders. "Tonight, Luca is playing Love Bites."

Daniel Pierce, this is going to suck ... and you'll bloody love it.

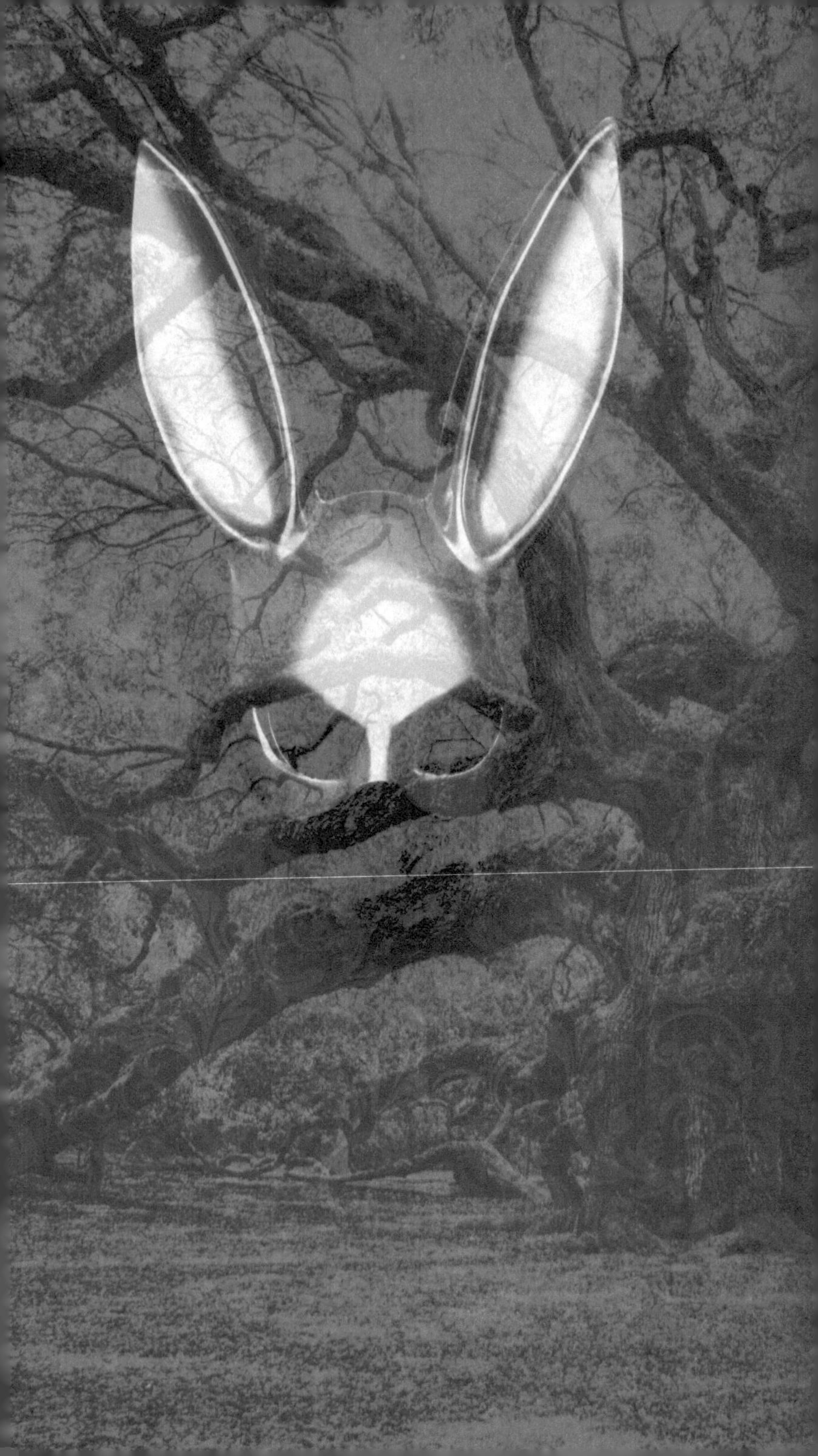

Daniel

CHAPTER EIGHT

DANIEL

"MY ISLAND. MY ORGY."

Love bites?

Yes, even the song plays in the Trick Tent.

And most would feel like a bleeding idiot dressed like this, but I'm used to elaborate wardrobes.

Besides, sixteen of us are standing in a circle, draped in vampire capes. It's not embarrassing if it's on trend. Right?

Luca wears the most elaborate cape. Instead of fetish shorts, he's laced into black leather pants. Instead of being bare-chested, his white ruffled shirt hangs open.

Cast him as Dracula. With his onyx hair and crystal eyes, Luca IS the deathly Dom ... except for his bronze skin.

He must've fed recently.

But not on Redix. They don't cross that line. Don't think they ever will.

"Damn," Silas admires Luca. "Who are the lucky ones getting impaled tonight?"

On the other hand? Silas would clearly pole-vault over the line with Luca.

As would I.

Luca presents the black cauldron to us. "We will suck three victims tonight."

"But no blood play!" Eily yelps. "I mean, no judgment, but I'll barf."

Stacey chuckles. "That sounds judgy to me."

"Really?" Eily's eyes get wide. She didn't mean to offend. "You do *blood* play?"

"No," Ford firmly barks. "We're not into blood kink, but Delta's has some rare, respected clients who are."

"Who?" Of course, Cade investigates.

"I bet I know," Silas speculates. "And I'll donate a hundred thousand to any charity if you tell me what he hides behind that black door on the third floor."

"Ahem."

Stacey coughs. Her body, strapped in red leather lingerie, suddenly fidgets, and Ford cuts his wife a look. Stacey cuts him one back. Like *What? It just slipped out.*

"See!" Redix gloats. "It's obvious. Delta's third floor hides our demon haint with his black horned mask and gold monster cock."

"Silas! I mean, Redix!" Eily stomps her bare foot on the rug. "Both y'all. Quit it. There's no demon."

"Ah, baby girl." Silas wraps around her from behind, kissing her cheek. "Who cares who's haunting Delta's when we got our very own horny haint right here on Indigo Island?"

"We are NOT haunted!"

Eily keeps insisting, and I don't know what to believe.

Is there a strange man Eily has enlisted to scare us? Apparently. Is he a friend? Or is he a foe, as Charlie always fears? Maybe. Is this villain mindfucking us as planned? Obviously.

Or is this island, like many places along these dark, swirling waters, haunted?

Definitely.

"I sure hope we're haunted," Blair chimes in. "I need inspiration for my next smutty book. Like lonely demons who crave romance."

She's an author. She's thrilled by the paranormal: fact or fiction.

"Enough." Gently, Luca commands the room, "Let's draw."

Passing the black cauldron around, Eily grins, selecting a black foiled kiss. Then Beau gets one. Then I do, eyeing Luca like he planned this, though I can't figure out how.

"Can I be Bella?" Eily chomps her chocolate. "Can Beau and Daniel be my Edward and Jacob, but this time, Bella fucks both? At the same time?"

"Aw, shit," Silas grumbles, rolling his hazel eyes. "Not with these damn *Twilight* movies again."

Eily snaps, "They're *books.*"

It only makes Silas chuckle, "They're bullshit."

"Yeah," Redix cups Silas's ass, "because the real saga is Edward secretly wants to suck Jacob, *remember*?"

I laugh at the memory. At how this was an ongoing debate on our New Year's cruise.

But Beau clears his throat. "I'm ... um. I'm not really open like that."

Blair grabs his hand. "But you can play a little. Colt wants you to, and so do I."

Play a little? Yes. No harm in that.

Kissing her cheek, Beau insists, "I'll never fuck anyone but you and Colt. Ever."

"Of course," calmly, Luca interjects. "We understand. This is for fun, and we all have hard limits. For example, touch my wife, and you die."

"He means you can't fuck her pussy," Eily clarifies. "But you can lick it." She asks Scarlett, then the others. "Right? All can lick kitties this week?"

Eagerly, the women nod. The men do, too.

Scarlett chuckles, "Right. Games of lick-a-clit are open to everyone, and so am I for other play."

"But I'll kill anyone who fucks Eily's pussy."

Whoa! Silas sounds aggro. Like mad possessive, which is rare for him.

"She's about to ovulate, and she's mine." He squeezes her tighter.

"But I'm like Scarlett." Eily claps. Silas's embrace can't tamper her enthusiasm. "I'm open for other play. I insist. My island. My orgy."

Cade laughs, holding her hand up like we're in primary school. Like we're learning the orgy rules, lest we be punished and sent to stand in the corner.

In leather fetish wear.

Did I just grin at that image?

Cade suggests, "Can we please establish whose holes are open to who?"

"To whom," Mateo hints.

"Who?"

"Whom."

"Who?" She's confused.

"It's open to *whom*," Mateo explains.

Fingers start pointing to people, parts, holes, and humans.

This is a bit of silly chaos until Luca booms again, "Enough! No one is fucking!"

"Not again." Stacey rolls her eyes, looking annoyed.

"I mean," Luca explains, "we're open to our spouses or partners tonight, but first, we play my way."

Annoyed, he snaps off black sheets and all gasp. Except me.

I groan.

Jesus, Mary, and Joseph. Thank you all.

Luca's way involves three bondage tables. They're similar to massage tables but with two holes in the padded, black cushions.

"This is for your face," Luca gestures to the top hole before his stare demands mine, "and this other hole is for milking."

Fuck, that's kinky.

Fuck, my cock swells.

I ache for Luca to do it. He has the skills, and the pressure in my groin knows it. I'm straining against the laces of these leather shorts.

"Do you consent to strip?" Luca asks me, Beau, and Eily.

"Yes!" Eily claps, answering for us.

"Do you consent to be bound while we feed on you?"

"Hell, yes!" Eily fist pumps the air, almost clocking Silas's nose, while Beau grins, nodding, and I chuckle, "Please do."

Luca probes, "Do you wish to be punished for being our dirty treats tonight?"

"No," Silas answers for Eily.

His new aggro ways may start a tiff. After escaping her father's rule, Eily does what she wants. Usually, it's what Silas wants, too.

But Eily shrugs with a grin. I think she likes this version of him. "Pain's not my kink anyway."

Luca looks at Beau.

"Not until Colt's here," he answers. "Then he'd love a Dom and Dominatrix night."

Blair caresses Beau's biceps before Luca turns to me. "And you?"

Charlie squeezes my hand. My wife knows what I desire.

"Yes," I answer. "Punish me."

Though the tent mists with a scented fog, lights glow low, and candles flicker around, I witness the darkness fall over Luca's eyes.

"Not too much," Zar warns Luca like he can sense his Dom's blood rising. "He's not used to it like me and Scarlett."

"How about five?" Touching my arm, Scarlett suggests, "Start with five whips. You have all week if you need more."

I nod. "Five."

"Six." Luca picks up his leather flogger from a side table. "You'll take two lashes for yourself and two for our other blood dolls."

Charlie gulps, "Blood dolls?"

"Those are mortals who let vampires drink from them once a day to keep them alive," Scarlett explains. "The mortals get off on being eaten by them."

"Okay," Eily twirls her ponytail, "so maybe I'm *not* so against pretend blood play."

But I search Luca's eyes, and this isn't pretend. He wants this. I *need* this.

"Six," I confirm. "Six lashes."

"Turn around," Luca demands, so I do. I face the long bondage table while I hear him command, "Secure his hands."

Charlie steps aside as Zar appears on my left and Redix on my right.

Suddenly, heat steams against my cape. The press of a firm man is behind me.

"If you want me to stop," it's Luca, lifting my cape and leaving it to drape over my shoulder, exposing my backside, "you say, 'Red,' and I will stop."

His hand reaches around, drawing open the laces of my shorts. I glance down, watching his long fingers brush over my firm cock.

"If you need a break or less pain but still want my whip," he nips my earlobe, "you beg, 'Yellow.'"

With both hands, Luca wedges my shorts down, my cock springing free. It soars, eager for his touch.

He leaves my leather shorts straining around my thighs. It's part kinky and part to protect my tender flesh there, I know. I trust him.

"But if you want more." Luca grabs my buttocks, teasing, tugging them apart. "If you need my pleasure and pain, you say, 'Yes, Master.'"

Inches from Zar, I see a smile ghost his lips.

I know their ritual. We've watched it.

Zar is Luca's sub. He calls Luca his "Owner." And Scarlett, Luca's wife, calls him by his name. "Luca" is her green word.

So, Luca respects his subs. He gives me a different Dom name to use for him.

"Yes, Master," I answer.

The mere words off my tongue send a pulse down my jutting cock.

"Hold him," Luca commands Redix and Zar. "Feed on him. Mark him while he takes my punishment."

"And the others," Luca calls out. "Gather around. Watch Daniel take my whip."

There's something about the others watching, eyeing

my hard cock as they circle the table. There's something about two powerful men like me, restraining my wrists with my palms braced against the table while Zar kisses, sucks, and bites my neck, while Redix does the same. There's something about my fit wife watching my surrender, my moans, while Silas and Eily suck her nipples for my gaze.

Luca's stinging lash whips my arse so fast, the first slice so intense, so biting, a grunt strangles my throat before I bellow, "Yes, Master."

I like it.

I need more.

I need to let go.

I'm held down by men mauling me. I'm watching my wife get fondled. I'm taking Luca's razor whip. I let my cock ache while my arse suffers.

Two. Three. "Yes, Master." Four. Five. Six cracking slashes across my burning flesh … and I heave for more.

The pain breaks my chains. I'm out of my troubled mind, and I want more.

But Luca stops.

Warmly, he's behind me again, biting my neck, his hand reaching around, gliding down my abs, dewy with sweat. With a tease, he swipes his bare fingertip over the angry tip of my cock.

My swollen, dry tip.

Passion swirls with pity in his voice. Like Luca suffers as I do. "Do you need more?"

"Yes, Master," I grumble, this frustration familiar. It threatens to ruin my night … again.

"Come caress his marks," Luca commands. "Take care of him. Praise Daniel's sacrifice, then strip our other dolls, too. Bind them for the feeding."

Redix and Zar keep their grasp on my wrists, their palms sweating, their mouths still hungrily marking my neck, shoulders, and pecs.

Love bites, indeed.

Then other hands, soft, small ones, and firm, big ones, gently linger over the burning welts on my arse, kisses brushing my backside, caresses lingering between my thighs.

It's erotic. It's loving. It soothes the ire boiling in my blood.

Once all touch me, I strip and crawl onto the table, turning to lie face up, trusting Zar as he secures my wrists in padded cuffs to the sides of the table. With padded straps, he binds my ankles, too.

I turn my head left and see Scarlett carefully securing Eily, and on my right, Ford secures Beau.

Luca looms at the center where our tables meet. I lift my head, glancing over my toes, watching Scarlett hand him a jar containing a dark red gel.

"There is no blood play tonight," Luca assures. "Instead, we use this to feed. It's a sensitivity lube designed to stimulate the nerves. It's edible and cherry-flavored. It appears blood red on the flesh, but it's harmless."

"It's delicious." Zar tugs my thighs apart, making me lie with them open wider. "It thrills whatever it touches." He eyes my heavy cock. "Your clit or dick will thank you."

Nick joins Zar. He holds him with his back to his chest as the couple admires my naked body, bound to the table. I'm hard and open for their stare.

Like he understands. Like he respects him, Luca slowly paints the first dollop of red gel over Eily's pussy. She gasps at his touch as he invites Silas to begin.

"Feed on your wife," Luca urges him, "until she's ready for us."

With her legs parted, Eily's ribs heave for this. She lifts her head, watching as Silas lowers his mouth, his handsome face aimed between her parted legs. With his first lick up her pussy, she moans, her tiny body restrained but arching for more.

Silas devours her, and she keeps moaning his name, trying to lift her lips to his mouth as he holds her thighs open. He is clearly the one who introduced her to this pleasure, the one who owns her body like no other.

"Everyone," Silas lifts from his meal, his lips red and glistening, "join me. Eat her, too."

"Yes," Luca praises, swiping gel over Eily's pebbled nipples. "Feed on her. Make our dirty doll come."

"Oh god!" Eily cries out when Silas, Redix, and Cade take turns licking her pussy. Then others do it, too, heads lowering to feast on her sex. All while Stacey sucks Eily's nipples, ravaging her breasts while her husbands join her.

They're taking turns on her.

In the darkened room, it does look like a feeding frenzy of bloodsuckers over her body. Black capes hunch. Sounds of wet flesh, hungry mouths, and satisfied moans bewitch with the music.

I can't see Eily.

I can only hear her wails.

She's coming.

She's in ecstasy.

I glance at Beau. He's watching, too. He's waiting for his turn, his muscles tense and ready. His cock angles, heavy and hard for it.

Then he turns his head, catching my eyes admiring his swollen length. I can't help it. I meet his stare. I can't move, but my cock does. It jumps for him, and Beau catches it, making his eyelids droop heavy with lust.

I know Beau loves his fiancés. I know he'll be their devoted husband, as I am to my wife.

Like fire burns, I live for Charlie. There is no air, no life without her.

But attraction is welcome in this room. It's safe. It has boundaries and beauty. Beau wants me as I want him. *Just a little. Not a lot.* It's in his blazing blue eyes.

When it's Beau's turn, Luca honors Blair. He prepares Beau's bound body for the feast, circling the red gel over Beau's nipples, then glossing his thick shaft and coating his tip with it.

Beau moans with each touch from Luca. Like he can't help but be aroused by it.

I'm only watching, and I'm so fucking turned on.

"He's *your* man." Luca nods to Blair. "So, show us how thirsty you are to suck him."

Strapped in mouthwatering red leather, Blair Monroe has luscious curves and a stunning smile. A smile that first takes Beau's lips in a deep kiss, making him groan. She offers him her ample breasts, and eagerly, he sucks them, too.

Blair loves playing with him, teasing Beau while he's tied down. It's obvious.

But then, Blair turns to Charlie. Shamelessly, she asks her, "Will you hold my hair back? Will you finger me while I suck my fiancé's cock and make me come with him in my mouth?"

Oh, it's on.

Cocks and minds will be blown.

"Bad kitten." Beau jerks at his restraints, but he smirks.

Clearly, he loves this. It's exactly what he wants, and it's what they do.

Rarely is my wife aroused by women other than Cade and Eily. But Charlie desires something about Blair. It arouses her, and that arouses me, watching her do it.

Charlie fists Blair's raven strands while Blair voraciously sucks Beau's cock, her plump lips plunging, her throat proudly gagging on Beau while Charlie's other hand must be playing between Blair's legs. I can't see, but by the lull of their moans, Charlie's fingering Blair's pussy. It's feeding Blair's slurping appetite for Beau.

"Others," Luca commands. "Others feed on him, too."

While Blair is the only one who takes Beau's cock, others claim his neck, his nipples, even his toes and thighs.

I glance back at Eily. She's still bound. She's still writhing with Silas solely devoted to her, licking her pussy, relishing what's all his now. He looks about one minute from mounting her.

Turning back, I hear Blair's moans deepen into growls. They turn into her feast on Beau, spit webbed from her lips to his tip, while others take small bites of him.

"Such a dirty girl," Charlie taunts Blair. She's using Beau's words on her. "You love sucking his cock for us, don't you? It's got your pussy so wet. Your clit is so hard, my fingers are sliding inside you. That's it. Feed on him while I finger fuck you."

Fuck, I love my wife.

Fuck, this is naughty.

Come on. Where are my drips for this?

"Fuck yes, kitten," Beau agrees, lifting his head, watching her.

He thrusts his hips, taunting Blair, "You're such a. Dirty. Fucking. Girl. For me."

Even though he's bound, Beau's controlling her. "That's it. Let her finger your sweet pussy while you taste my cum. Then you'll open your dirty mouth and let them see my cream on your tongue."

With a groan muffled by Beau's cock, Blair trembles. Her shoulders quake. She gets off on his dirty talk.

"That's it," Charlie coaxes, tugging Blair's hair. "To his base. Come on. Keep him in your mouth while you grind on my hand. *Yesss.* You're clenching. You're such a dirty girl. Come on. Come for us. Come on my fingers."

Silently, Blair bucks. She shakes. She must be coming. Charlie kisses Blair's shoulder while the orgasm quakes through her body.

Then Charlie takes her fingers, glossed with Blair's milky arousal, and slides them over Beau's parted lips, taunting him, "Taste how much she loves you. How your woman sucked your cock and came on my fingers for you."

Beau obeys and doesn't last. He roars, "Fuck, Blair. Fuck!"

Bodies recede, and only Blair remains.

She relishes every drop of Beau, her hands caressing his flexing abs, her mouth receiving him until he's done grunting. Then, she obeys his command, proudly showing the room her reward before Beau growls for her kiss and takes it.

The whole time, Luca didn't feed on Eily or Beau. He watched everyone.

But he studied me.

I've been lying here for so long, watching this erotic game.

I've been hard like this, my cock swollen with no relief. I can't touch it; my wrists are bound.

I expect Luca to douse my shaft in that special lube. To tell Charlie to suck my cock.

For fuck's sake, please. I need my beautiful wife. I need her to relieve me.

But Luca surprises me. He turns to the side table, lifting a black silk handkerchief monogrammed with a golden *M*. Under it is a box. From that box, he lifts a clear tube.

"Oh fuck." I tug at my restraints.

I know what it is. It's been years since I've used a Fleshlight, designed for maximum exterior grip with a tight, ribbed, choking interior.

But that male masturbator is compact. It's enough for a hand to grip while leaving the rest of my shaft and tip exposed from the open end, bare and desperate for release.

This will be torture.

Sweet, savage fucking torture.

Because I've already tried, several times, to stroke my cock. To give myself relief. I didn't want to frustrate Charlie anymore, so lately, I only frustrate myself.

Without a word, Luca slowly lathers my cock with the sensitivity gel. Warm and cool sensations collide, electrifying my flesh. Blood instantly rushes to my already swollen length.

Instead of inviting my wife to do it, Luca lifts my base. His controlling grip around my cock races my pulse. I'm sweating.

Teasing the entrance of the clear tube over my swollen tip, Luca asks, "Do you want this? Do you want release, no matter what I must do to give it to you?"

"Yes, Master."

The words growl from every tense muscle and frayed nerve in my body.

Make it stop. Make me feel like a man, a satisfied *man again.*

Luca starts stroking my glossed cock with the tight sleeve, and, "Oh fuck!" the pleasure is there. It triggers an intense sensation, making me shout.

This feels so fucking good.

"Feed on him," he commands the others.

Mouths and lips take my flesh, biting, kissing, and sucking.

After Redix and Zar and now the others, I'll be marked. When I return to set next week, I'll have to be covered in body make-up and...

I don't give a fuck.

Let them devour me. Let them mar my flesh. Let them deliver exquisite pleasure. I close my eyes to it. And there it is. The pressure. The stress. It finds me, too. It never fucking ends.

Luca must read the tension across my quads, my abs flexing.

I can't let go.

"Taste him," Luca commands. "Lick him until he feeds us. Until he drips for us."

He keeps pumping my shaft at the base, freeing my length and bulging crown.

My wife goes first, sucking my tip, flicking her tongue over my sensitive seam. She's perfection. She's the best at this.

"Oh fuck, yes, babe," I groan. "Don't stop." I want to sink my hands in her silky hair, but my wrists are bound.

Charlie signals for Redix, and he goes next. He devotes his warm mouth to my cock, making me pant, all while Luca won't stop his tight, pumping control.

"Lift his head," Luca commands. "Let him watch us take care of him."

Nick appears by my shoulder. Carefully, he wedges a small pillow under my neck so I don't strain. I can relax. I can watch this.

The sight is beyond kinky. The ambiance makes this erotic game look like a pagan ritual, all devoted to my pleasure, to my release.

Mouth after mouth, women and men, suck my cock, different tongues laving over my sensitive crown. All while Luca pumps my base. It's like he's driving all the pressure into my opening slit, tongue after tongue trying to make it drip.

"Oh fuck. Oh fuck." It tremors my thighs. It sheens sweat across my naked flesh. It races my heart, my biceps straining against my wrist restraints.

But still.

No release.

This is where I'm stuck, trapped in this hell.

"Do you want more?" Luca sees it. He knows my secret.

This frustration is all in my head. I've let it become too powerful, too much.

But sometimes, we get so focused on caring for others that we lose ourselves. Finding our joy feels selfish, if not futile. We want to give up on our pleasure when it's what we really need.

Maybe I'll never stop being the most powerful man on set, the one studios and crews depend on.

But not here. Not now. Not with the ones I love.

"Yes, Master," I beg. "I want more. I need to be fucked."

The request escapes. Fucked by whom or how I'm not sure.

But Luca shakes his head, denying me. *Or helping me?*

It's like he knows better. He won't give up on me. He's committed to my pleasure, to finishing me like this.

Gesturing to Charlie and Redix, Luca commands, "Stroke him, and don't stop."

Then Luca turns to Mateo and Ford. "Untie Beau," he demands, "and bring him here."

While they obey, Luca returns to his side table. With a snap, he secures a black latex glove over his right hand, dousing his digits in lube. Then Scarlett helps him tug on a left-handed glove, a leather one with silver claws.

Claws?

Latex?

And lube?

I start writhing. *Ehhh, yes. I want it.*

The others gather around. Partners touching partners. Hands pleasing themselves and others.

"Free his ankles," Luca commands Zar, who obeys.

It makes Zar hard, serving his owner, yanking my body to the edge of the table, exposing my arse for Luca's claim.

Beau appears unbound and on my right. He admires my body, his dick surging hard again. It's like my naked need; my torture excites him.

"Daniel wants you to watch." Again, Luca reads my mind. He tells Beau, "Watch his cock while we make him come. And come on him if you want to."

The rush is immediate. A new white heat flames through my flesh, burning away barriers and turning my stress to ash.

Fuck, Luca won't stop with his kink.

He will *make me come.*

Even if it takes all night, I have no control.

This is true submission. Pure trust. Raging lust.

With his thick fingers covered in latex and lube, Luca

teases into my ass while my wife and partner stroke my cock.

Instantly, I writhe, tugging against my wrist restraints and groaning for more.

"Hold his ankles," he commands. "Hold him still. He's too strong."

Ford and Mateo appear, each man grabbing my leg. I *am* strong, so I let them. I let them hold my thighs open for Luca's expert probe, his fingers seeking, searching inside.

"Milk him. Milk him hard," he commands Charlie. "Take turns," he directs Redix.

"God," Charlie marvels, watching Luca's claim. So is Redix. They're watching Luca finger my ass, with three, maybe four digits, I can't be sure.

It's just burning perfection.

I turn, and Beau pumps his dripping cock to it, his lips parted, his eyes enraptured by this carnal and caring act.

Then Luca finds the spot, his fingers curling and pressing up. With brutal pressure, he massages my prostate, that maddening place that sends stars shooting across my vision, my nerves igniting with new desire.

"Oh fuck!" I roar. "Don't stop!"

"*Yessss*," Luca coaxes, his accent thick, his tone heavy. "Yes, we have him now."

With his left hand, his clawed glove, Luca scrapes his sharp, chrome nails down my side, over my tender flesh, raking my ribs, scratching my obliques, making me try to twist away, which only increases the pressure, the intense pleasure in my arse.

"Oh fuck, yes," I groan. "Fuck, punish me and take my ass harder."

"Shit, this is hot."

I hear his deep praise. Focusing my gaze, I turn again to

Beau by my side. He's stroking faster to this, *to me*. I search for Blair, his fiancée, and notice she's sought my wife.

She's returning the favor.

Blair stands behind Charlie, fingering her while Charlie arches her back for it, letting Blair get her off while Redix takes control of pumping my cock for Charlie's gaze.

It makes me crack. The sight. The sensation. The exposure. The taboo. "*Yeesss.*"

Finally, I start to drip.

"Lick him." Luca sees it. He commands Charlie, "Suck your husband's cock."

Charlie leans over, moaning, full of desire to please and be pleased. Blair doesn't stop fingering her while Charlie obeys Luca's command, taking my need into her wet, sucking mouth.

"Aww, yes, babe," I sigh.

Redix, with his choking grip, strokes my base. He's tugging my balls, too. "Fuck yeah," he coaxes. "Suck his cock. Finger his ass. Let's help him come so fucking hard."

Does Redix know? Can he tell? How I've been so stressed, so frustrated?

"Yeah, do it," Beau grunts. "Aw, fuck, do it. Make Daniel come." Because Beau is about to, he's straining for it.

So, I tell him, "Do it for me. Do it on me. I want you to."

With no shame, Beau lets go. He shoots across my chest, warm, creamy splatters of his arousal painting my flesh. He surrenders to his desire, and it frees me.

Finally, I let go.

Watched by the ones I care about. Touched by the ones I love. I let it take me. "I'm coming," I grunt.

"Yes," Redix urges, tightly squeezing my base.

"Now," Luca demands, brutally pounding his fingers into my ass.

"Ummm." Charlie's sucking mouth tenderly moans, tasting my relief, of me about to come. I think she's coming, too.

"Oh fuck, babe. Oh fuck." It starts in my legs, shaking in the controlling grasp of other men, my breath ragged and thin. The white heat, coiled tight at the base of my spine for an eternity, it seems, snaps. "Oh fuck. Oh fuck, I'm coming."

I can't stop it. Plopping her lips, webbed with spit, off my tip, Charlie marvels. All do.

This explosion has been waiting for so long; it's powerful. I can't breathe through it. I don't need to. The pressure releases, and I'm powerless. It happens *to* me. Ropes of my cum spurt so hard from my tip, the salty drops reach my chin, splattering my lips.

"Fuck," I huff, spurting more. My toes curl. My thighs shake. My cock pulses as Redix squeezes and Luca curls his fingers inside me even harder.

They're truly milking me. I groan, spasming again. And again. It coats my abs, mixing with Beau's cum on my chest, pearly streams of all I've been holding back. I'm covered in it. And they won't stop, the sudden convulsions that release more.

In a relieved haze, letting it happen, I turn my head to find breath. To find focus. Gazing into the dark shadows, into the black velvet folds of the tent, I see...

The devil.

Lurking there in his mask.

He's smiling, and I spurt again.

I must be hallucinating.

It's a dick delusion, as Eily said, and I'm too bloody happy to care, to move.

"You look so fucking beautiful," Charlie sighs. She brings my focus back to her.

Breath finds my lungs again. Finally, my voice returns. Finally, my muscles relax. I feel whole.

"Bloody, fucking hell," I rumble. "Fuck me, I needed that."

Redix frees my cock as Luca retreats from my body. With my dazed stare, I thank them.

All around me, love seeks love. Spouses and partners join. I can't focus. I just want my own.

"Babe," I call for Charlie.

While Redix frees my wrists, she kisses me. Tenderly. Deeply. "I love you," I sigh.

"I love you, too." She whispers, "Now, tell him."

Then it's Redix. It's his lips on mine. It's like he knows. We're all too close to hide our hearts.

"I need to tell you something," I confess into our kiss.

Pulling back, Redix brushes the sweaty tendril off my forehead. "Tell me anything," he promises, "and I'll still love you."

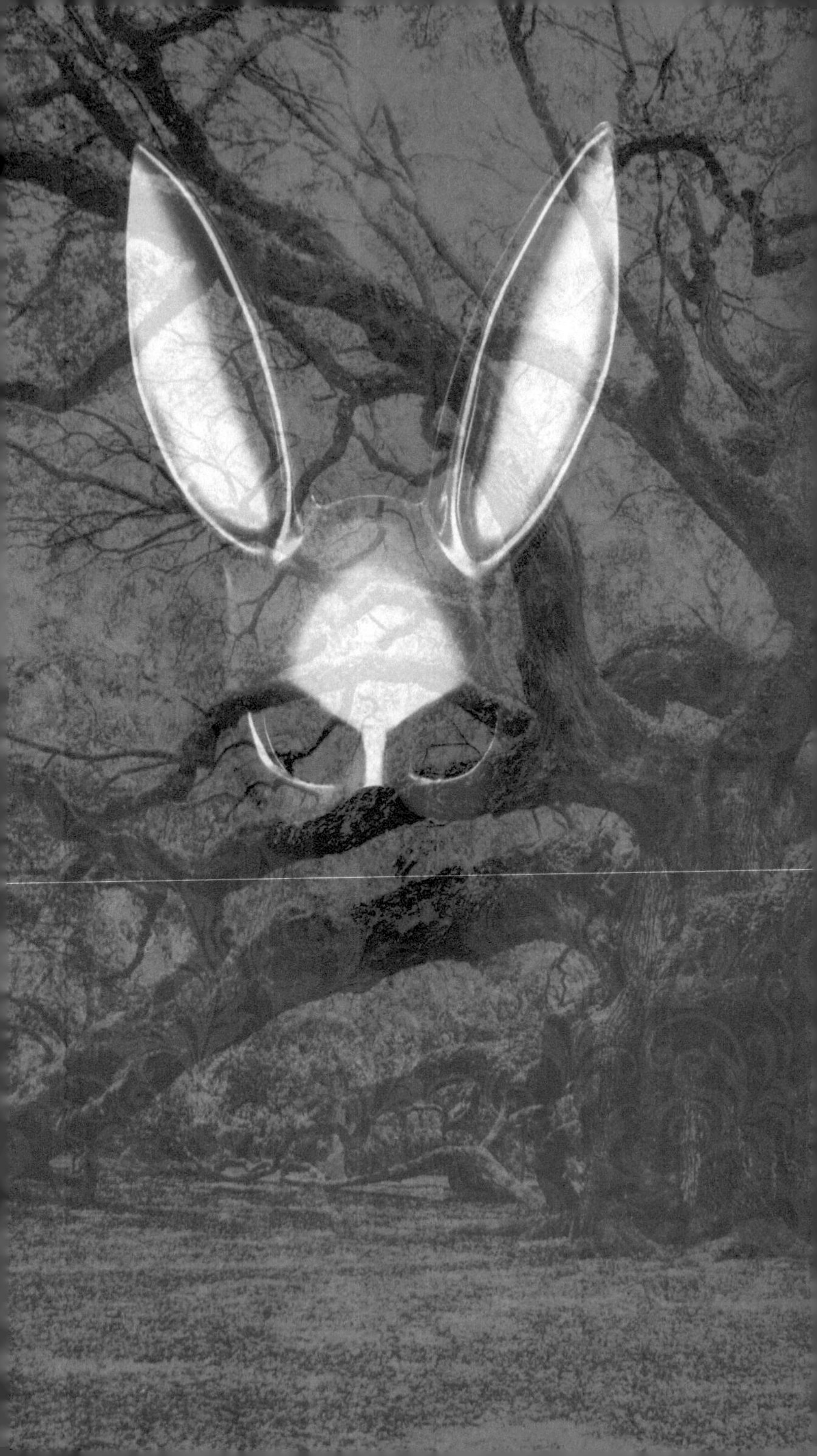

Eily

CHAPTER NINE

EILY

"I'm so sorry I'm a happy slut."

"So, tell me the craziest thing you've seen working in a sex shop."

I should have better manners. I'm talking with a mouth full of candy. But Redix and Cade got me hooked on Lemonheads, and now I'm obsessed with their sweet, tart crunch.

I also read that citrus fruits help with fertility, which means citrus candy, too.

One can hope.

And it is Halloween week.

"The craziest thing?" Blair tugs at her Atlanta baseball cap. "From working at Delta's? That's tough to say."

Beau calls over his shoulder, "Tell her about the guy and the vibrator."

"A *guy*?" Silas casts his fishing line, standing next to Beau, who's doing the same.

It's a gorgeous, sunny, cool day on the water. We're moored at the marina, patiently waiting for Colton.

So, Silas whipped out his long rod—no, the fishing one—and gave one to Beau, too.

And all I know is … they better NOT catch our dinner.

Do you want to see a grown woman look like a complete dumbass?

That'll be me, losing my shit, squirming and squealing whenever one of those slimy creatures flops around.

Silas has tried to cure me of my fear of live fish, but not today, Satan. I swear, their unblinking eyes are the gateway to hell.

But at least, while we wait for Colton, I have more time to score the tea on Delta's.

Do I want to know crazy stories about that fancy sex store?

Ehhh, is water wet?

Do I want to know about my villain, too?

Ehhh—confession time.

I sorta, *kinda* don't know the villain's name. His contact on my phone is SEXY SATAN.

All I know is he's filthy gorgeous, stinking rich, and maybe a criminal.

Just a smidge.

That intel? I got it from his chiseled face, his ruby and platinum signet ring, his Patek Philippe watch, and the cross tattoo … or was it a dagger … on his ring finger? I clocked a lot of ominous ink he's hiding under his starched white shirt.

But if I met him at Delta's. If the criminal has a key to the place. If he's really hot with good taste in expensive clothes … he can't be that bad. Right?

Again, one can hope.

And, yeah, again, it's Halloween. If you're gonna play with devilish dudes, it's the holiday to do it.

Just in case, maybe Blair knows him. Maybe she'll let something slip.

"Yeah," Blair answers Silas, "a *guy*. He came into the store, all preppy, like he left a golf course, and said he wanted to buy the best vibrator in the store."

I scoot closer to her. She has my full, short attention span.

"Which is?"

I'm the consumer reports on sex toys. I'm taking mental notes, always on the search for the best pussy products.

"Depends on the clit." Blair chuckles. "Some like a hummingbird, some like a woodpecker."

Passionately, I nod.

"I like a lap dog."

Silas snorts, winding his reel. "Eily Van de May, you're my water bowl for life."

"Thank you, baby," I call out to my husband before nudging Blair's flip-flop. "Now, back to the guy and the best vibrator."

Blair continues her story.

"So, I showed him the popular models. Clitoral massagers. Little bullets. The ol' reliable wands."

I pine, "I love wands."

"And I told him when it comes to sex toys, orgasms are priceless. And he agreed. He said cost wasn't the issue."

"Smart man."

"Wait for it..." Beau warns with laughter edging his voice.

"What?" I shove my sunglasses up my nose. "He wanted the vibrator for himself, didn't he? Like for his ass, but he was too shy. Aww, poor guy. There should be no taint on teasing taints."

"No," Blair hums, "that wasn't it. He said he'd pay any price, up to ten *K*, for a one-of-a-kind vibrator, and I was like, 'Uh, I can order one in gold for you.' And he was like, 'No.'"

Blair touches my knee. We're side by side on the padded bench over the stern. Wearing sweatshirts, we're in shorts and flip-flops, too. What can I say? It's Southern autumn attire.

"Get this." She pauses for effect. "He said, 'I'll pay any price for a *used* vibrator.'"

"Used!" I start rolling. "By *you*?"

"Yep." She pops her lips. "I got all kinds of propositions working in that store. Lots of couples in particular. I was their unicorn."

"A unicorn?" I lean in. "No judgment. But so ... horse and horn kink is a thing, too?"

KABOOM!

Did you hear that?

That's my mind getting blown once again by new sex intel.

I can't keep up. I can barely remember a password.

Blair laughs. "Yeah, for a few. But a unicorn is a bisexual woman that casually joins another couple."

"What's a bisexual man who seriously joins a couple? Like Silas first did with Redix and Cade?"

"A stallion," Silas boasts.

Blair shrugs. "I've never heard that term, but sure, why not? It's not like there are rules for people like us."

I lower my voice, my eyes darting to Beau's broad back before I side mutter, not wanting to get Blair in trouble, but I'm dying to know.

"Did you ever ... you know ... sprinkle your unicorn glitter with a couple?"

"Uh, yeah, she did," Beau proudly answers for Blair. He doesn't even turn around. "She's a pro. She's still teaching me and Colt things."

"I'm not a *pro*." Blair shakes her head. "I'm a romance author. It's called *research*."

Beau glances our way. The man has a pussy-licking smirk.

"Well, then, lucky me and Colt," he says. "We'll be your Wikipedia of Whoopee for life."

Blair bats her lashes at him. "Promise?"

"We gave you two rings to prove it, kitten."

I glance down, temporarily blinded by the ice stacked on Blair's ring finger. A clear, twelve-carat diamond. A band of emeralds, rubies, and sapphires in rare colors. Like a million-dollar rainbow band.

Her rings are stunning. They're sentimental, I can tell. Just like the indigo sapphire and diamond ring Silas had made for me.

"I did research," I share. "Well, using romance novels and porn. And I'm glad I did. I was literally gonna *blow* giving a blow job."

Blair laughs. "I sure did, giving my first one! I didn't know better."

"See? So, I wanted to learn because I knew Silas was a pro. Not like *paid* to fuck. He's just an expert at it, and I didn't want to blow my chance. Pun intended. But he was so patient with me. He taught me everything I know. I was a virgin before him."

Silas sets his rod in a holder, chuckling, "My beautiful virgin? Yes. A gifted prodigy, horny to learn and quickly surpassing her master in sex skills? That's my hot wife."

His lips lean down for mine.

I blush at his kiss and praise.

Lately, Silas has been the poster brute for cavemen. He's all grunty and fucky and possessive with me, and ... okay ... I kinda love it.

I know he'll mellow. I know once—*if*—we have a baby, his possessive streak will become protective. Silas will be the perfect father.

Besides, he fucks me like an animal lately, and I'm not submitting a one-star review on that.

No, those are five-star fucks.

And sorry, Starbucks, for ripping down your paper towel holder. I just *really* like your pumpkin spice lattes and fucking my husband in your bathroom.

Grabbing a beer from the icy cooler, Silas acts like he's serving me first, but ... he presses the cold can against my neck.

I crook it, squealing, "You're getting me wet!"

He pops the can open, pecking my lips as he hands it to me. "Wasn't that my wedding vow? To love, honor, and get you wet?"

"Take notes, Beau." Blair accepts a beer from Silas, too. "We're putting that in our vows."

"Gotcha, kitten," he replies.

"When's the big day?"

"Valentine's at The Mercier. Your invitations are in the mail." Blair flutters her feet. "I'm so excited. That's where it all started. Well, between me and Beau. He and Colt have been in love since high school."

"Bullshit," Beau laughs. He secures his rod before accepting a beer from Silas, too. "You and me started in college the day you sent a fantasy football stroker to my dorm."

"Like a masturbator?" Silas pops his can last. Even drinking beer on a boat, he has manners. "Like the one Luca used on Daniel last night?"

"Yeah." Beau takes a gulp. I'm chugging my beer, too. "But this was a football on the outside and a fake pussy on the inside. I got so much shit from my roommates and team, and then—"

"*Then* I sent football strokers to his teammates, too," Blair adds. "All with Alabama thank you notes from Beau."

Beau laughs, "The joke was on you. I've never seen a locker room so full of happy men. It became *my* stroke of genius."

They tell us more stories about their college pranks, making us laugh, which makes me pop off impressive beer burps.

Yeah, Beau's eyes widen that a little thing like me can belch like a trucker.

If only it were an Olympic sport. I'd finally be an athlete. In that, or sex.

After our one and only round, the guys return to their rods.

Me? I'd rather them play with the rods in their pants than the ones with tack and bait because it makes me anxious.

Silas keeps casting and reeling, casting and reeling. His rhythm, with its *zzzzzz* and *click-click-click*, makes me fear the inevitable.

Soon, he'll catch a shiny little monster. It'll be on the boat, flopping and staring straight into my soul like *Murderer* and *Fuck you and your tartar sauce.* And its eyes won't blink, its scales all slimy, getting closer to me and—

Eily Van de May, stop freaking out! You're a grown woman, bigger than any fish.

Wait.

No, I'm not.

Have you seen a swordfish? A tarpon? Have you ever stared down a giant catfish? With their creepy, thick whiskers?

Yeah! See? They're demon creatures!

Distract yourself. Distract yourself. Don't pee your shorts.

"So, uh, who were your favorites at Delta's? Like your loyal customers? Other than us?"

I hope the anxiety in my voice doesn't make Blair uneasy. I hope I don't sound like a nervous ninny, though I am. Fearfully, my eyes dart to the tip of Silas's fishing pole.

Is it bending? Does anyone else hear the JAWS theme music?

"Oh," Blair says, "you want to know about the third floor? About the black door?"

Stop the panic attack.

Blair's onto me.

"Uh, I mean..." I pick at my indigo nail polish. "Any floor. Any door. I just like the stories and—"

Blair nudges my foot. "It's okay. I honestly don't know. That room used to be where customers could privately shop our online store for larger purchases. Stacey made demonstration videos they could watch, too. She and her husbands loved making them. But right before I left and moved to Atlanta, she—"

"She *what?*"

Great.

Silas is eavesdropping.

My sweet, sexy husband can't mind his business from five feet away.

"She moved all the furniture out and locked the door," Blair tells him. "And it's a big, beautiful space, the former owner's bedroom with a private view to the back courtyard.

It's a waste to be empty, so yeah, she definitely put something in there."

"You mean *someone* in there." Silas winds his reel up … and me. "That's where Eily met her villain."

"Okay," I huff. "We vowed to love, honor, and, yes, you always make me wet, but that doesn't mean you can read my mind. Silas, that's just freaky."

He laughs, getting ready to cast again. "Baby girl, never work for the CIA. That was too easy."

"Is he right?" Blair wonders. "Did you meet some strange guy at Delta's? In *that* room?"

"Sorta, but I didn't see inside it. I just figured if Stacey can trust him, I can." Blair nods. She agrees with me. To her, I'm a kindred, kinky spirit. "I mean, this guy looks evil but in a hot way. So, I asked him to sneak over and scare us. You know … to spook us. But he said he was busy until tomorrow. So, I don't know who is—"

Like a giant sea squid lurking in the dark water behind me, its long tentacles suddenly emerging from the depths, something wet *flops*, landing in my ponytail.

It's dripping. It's salty. It's…

Squirming!

"SIIILLLAAASSS!!!"

I jump up. Suddenly, my body knows every cultural dance. Suddenly, Mariah Carey is in my throat. "Eeeek! Eeeek!" I'm whistling screams in double *E*. Suddenly, my hands can snatch out every long hair attached to my skull.

"The devil's in my hair! The devil's in my hair!" I tug at my rainbow scrunchie. I speak in tongues. "Cast ye out, demon! Cast ye out!"

Finally, being a preacher's daughter comes in handy.

"Whoa, whoa, whoa." Silas rushes my way. "It's my worm. A fishing worm. Settle down."

A worm?

In my hair?

Settle down?

No, fuck this! I can scream louder. The entire marina can hear my distress call. I'm cracking glass everywhere.

Sorry about your windshield.

"Oh, Lord! Oh, Lord!" I wiggle and jiggle like I got a feeling in *Flashdance*. I'm a retro fan, but I fucking hate this!

"Silas, kill it! Kill it! Die, fucker, die!"

He laughs, trying to hold me. "Be still, and I'll get it."

"I can't be still! It's gonna crawl in my ear and infect my brain! I'll start craving manure, laying eggs, and having dirt dreams!"

"You already have dirty dreams." He laughs, hooking his arm around my waist, lifting my kicking feet off the fiberglass. "Hold still, and I'll find it. Ouch! Quit kicking my shins."

I slam my eyes shut.

"What do you mean, FIND it?"

I can't watch. This is death by invertebrates. And death by embarrassment. I told you this would happen.

"You got thick brown hair to your waist." He lifts my strands. "It blends in. Just a second."

"Oh, Lord," I pray. "I'm so sorry I'm a happy slut. I promise I'll go back to being a miserable prude. I'll never fuck again if you help my husband find this heathen worm."

Silas's chest shakes, laughing against mine, his fingers searching my hair.

"How did this happen?"

I hear Blair ask what I'll be putting in the police report, too.

"Aw, I didn't hook my worm on right." Silas holds me

tight, and I can almost endure this. "When I cast, it flew into her hair."

I cry against his chest. "Silas, I'm gonna pee then die if you don't find it."

"You ain't dying on me," he says. "But you can pee on me."

I mutter, "That's not my kink."

"No," he says, kissing my forehead. "But that's our love. I got you, baby girl. Hang on."

I soften a bit, lowering my freak level to DEFCON 3. I'm always safe with Silas as he lifts the back panel of my hair, combing his fingers through. "There's the little rascal."

"Get it out! Get it out!"

With a flutter through my strands, Silas frees his hand and the worm.

Of course, it starts squirming by our feet, and I scream a lot … and maybe pee a little.

"What do we got here?"

A baritone voice drawls, deep and Southern like ours. It turns my terrified stare to find Colton Hawke standing on the dock in his black joggers, a fitted white tank, his hair in a knot, and lots of sexy ink, with his overnight bag slung over his hulking shoulder.

"Just a little excitement." Beau reaches out, taking his other fiancé's bag. Plopping it down in the boat, he reaches for Colton's massive hand next. It's just to steady his jump down into our boat.

"What's the ruckus?" Colton lands. "I heard someone cursing bloody murder and worms from the parking lot."

"Sorry," I mutter. "That was me."

He greets me, then Silas, and then he kisses Beau and Blair while Silas scoops me up.

Cradled in his arms, he brushes his lips over my ear. "I didn't mean to scare you. You okay?"

"No," I pout because I can.

"Are you gonna pee on me now?"

"No."

"I was kinda hoping you would. Not like to be kinky. But like trusting me with your body because I'm gonna be there with you, Eily, catching our baby. I won't be one of those men who freak out about birth and pass out. I can't wait to share everything with you."

I rest my head against his bare chest, closing my eyes, feeling his heartbeat and wishing for it, too.

I sigh. "I'll always trust you, but you better slay that vile little creature, or I'll kill you, too."

"I will." He kisses my strands. "I'll eat the worm for you."

"Eww! No, you won't!"

"Yeah, I will."

He sets me down on the padded bench before plucking the wriggling beast from the boot deck, lifting it to his full lips.

"Silas, don't!"

He lets it dangle over his mouth before grinning and tossing it overboard.

And that right there, folks, is why I love Silas Van de May. He loves me, saves me, teases me in all the right ways, and the cute gross ones, too.

"Phew." I slump. "If you had eaten that nasty worm, I'd never kiss you again."

He falls over me, bracing his arms by my side, laughing, "You saying you don't love me and my little worms?"

"Your worm is *not* little, and they're *tadpoles*."

"No, they're *yours*. Now, give us a kiss."

He's got me there. Hell, he's got me everywhere.

I pucker tight, providing minimal lip-to-lip contact, still mad about my mortification, but he goes for it, taking my full kiss.

Will I forgive him? Maybe. Does he love me like a scandalous prince? Thank you, Jesus.

We turn to our new guest and tell him what happened, and Colton quickly fits right in.

I give up my seat on the bench and stand with Silas at the helm so Colton can nestle between Beau and Blair on the ride back to Indigo Island.

They catch up, congratulating him on winning the game last night.

But after a few minutes, Colton draws back, suspicious, eyeing Beau's neck. Then, he lifts Beau's gray T-shirt, inspecting his torso.

"What the fuck?" Colton laughs. "Did y'all have an orgy with leeches last night?"

"No." Blair wraps her legs around his. "We played Love Bites."

Whoops!

I almost forgot.

Glancing down at my thighs, I can't see my neck, and I don't need to lift my shirt like Beau to admire how I'm covered in hickeys, too.

"Love bites, huh?" Colton nods. "Just how did that work?"

We can hear his voice booming over the boat's engine. Besides, Silas is going slow. It's a no-wake zone.

"Luca was Dracula, and Beau, Eily, and Daniel were our blood dolls," Blair tells the story. "The rest of us were vampires. We tied them down and fed on them with this red oral gel. It was so hot. I took the biggest bite of Beau while others just nibbled on him."

"Nibbled?"

"Nibbled," Beau assures Colton. "We said we're not crossing some boundaries."

"Yeah, but did you get to bite Daniel Pierce?"

"Oh!" *I love it.* "Are you hot for Daniel?"

Colton proudly admits, "Who the hell isn't? He gave me my first wet dream. And my second, third, and fourth."

"Same." Beau slings his arm around Colton, joking, "Wet dreams and balls were one of the many things we bonded over."

I sigh, "I wish women could orgasm in their sleep."

"We can." Blair piques my interest.

"How?"

"Baby girl," Silas calls out, "I make you come all day, and now you want to do it in your sleep? You're gonna wear that kitty out."

"Speaking of wearing things out." Colton salutes me. "I gotta thank you for that video you made of my finacés on their first night. I don't know what cleaned my pipe more: my woman licking another woman's nipples or my man getting a handjob from a superhero. I enjoyed it several times."

"You're welcome," I chirp. "I love making deposits in my friends' spank banks."

Colton laughs while Beau grins from ear to ear. "Damn, Silas," he boasts. "I swear we'll be married to the same woman."

Blair blows me a kiss. I catch it and smack it against my kitty. "Backatcha, bitch."

We make the guys shake their heads, chuckling before Colton wonders, "So, what's tonight's game?"

"I don't know what the trick is, but it's Stacey's turn." I bounce my brows. "Expect to get your freaky spook and spooky freak on."

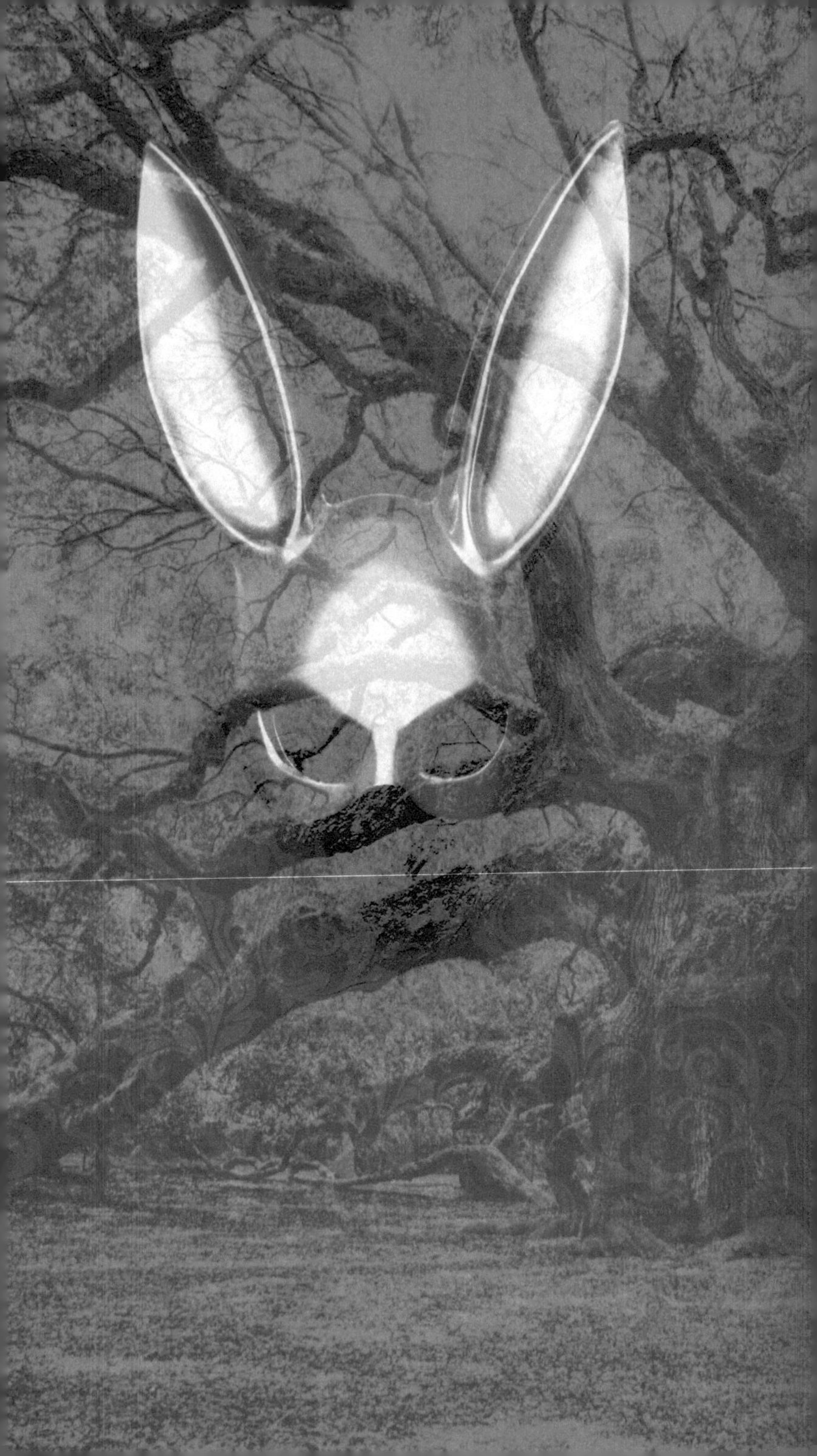

Charlie

CHAPTER TEN

CHARLIE

HOLY, SEE THROUGH TO THE PROMISED PENIS LAND.

Who needs a private dressing room when you've slept with everyone in the tent?

I'm not shy. Not with the six of us.

Eily zips Cade's white lace bustier in the back, so Cade returns the favor.

Daniel, Redix, and Silas tug on sheer white men's briefs. I never knew they made them, and...

Holy, see through to the promised penis land.

Those sheer white briefs lift and contour masculine asses while showcasing their generous packages, front and center, barely veiled by silky fabric held up by a thick, boxer-like waistband.

Forecast for tonight: A storm of Ds is coming.

"Damn," Silas admires himself in the gold-framed floor mirror, shaking his marble ass. I grin. *Like his rear can jiggle.* But I sure feel the earth move to the big show in the front.

"I'm buying a dozen of these from Stacey," he says. "I can get into this."

"You can get into them,"—Redix approaches, cupping Silas's ass—"so we can rip you out of them."

"Hell, nah," Silas scoffs. "These are a hundred dollars a pair. Stacey went all out on our angel attire. You ain't ripping it."

"It's Fleur du Mal." Eily admires Cade's thong, lingering her fingertip over it. "These gold chain *V* strings are like a hundred, too, and all it is is a white silk triangle, a string, and a tiny chain in our butt crack."

Redix shakes his head. "I don't know why you women do it. Walking around with a string in your ass."

"They prevent panty lines," Cade explains. "And they're sexy."

"How sexy can they be when they've been in your butt all day?"

"You never complain when you're in my butt. And you sure like it when we're in yours."

His eyes flash. "Game point for my wife."

"Don't they itch?" Silas asks. "And smell? Hell, I'd burn my boxers if they were melting like cheese between my cheeks all day."

Eily shrugs. "Honestly, I do prefer panties or boy shorts."

Silas plops down on the bed, yanking her onto his lap. "Who are you fooling? You never wear drawers."

Eily pokes his nose. "What's the point? You're always taking them off."

Daniel stares down at his pair, admiring his cock covered in transparent silky threads.

His muscular, ripped thighs. His dark trimmed patch.

His meaty cock, draped semi-hard and snug over his balls. I admire it, too, feeling my kitty lick her wet lips.

"Jesus, Mary, and Joseph," he declares. "These sure make my Christ and his two apostles look good. It's perfect for tonight—for angels and demons."

"Stacey's the queen of this." Cade lifts the girls higher in her bustier. "Leave it to her to plan a Sexorcism trick night."

Eily sighs, "I think it's sweet how Luca gave his turn to be a treat to Colton."

"He can only stay for two nights," Silas explains. "Colton has to go back to practice. It's good he gets to enjoy this. Sure hope we don't scare him, though."

Redix wraps around Cade, hugging her waist. We're all in the handsy spirit. "Ain't that the point this week? Terror and temptation?"

"Speaking of…" Daniel aims my way.

I've tried to fade into the background, knowing they're curious.

"What's under your robe?" Daniel wonders, tugging at its silky rope.

I swat his hand. "It's a surprise."

A surprise that has my clit tingling to this kinky outfit. I'm slick with anticipation.

"You, Colton, and Mateo," Cade says. "The dirty devils we angels have to save tonight. I'm jealous."

My brows shoot up. "You had your trick night. The first night, remember?"

"Masturbation doesn't count."

"Eh, yeah, it does," Eily disagrees with Cade. "I do it all the time, but you got to do it with sixteen people watching you. Looking all cowgirl sexy and hot, fucking your hand. Then we all got off, too."

"Shit," Redix mutters. "I'm ready to get off *now*."

Me, too.

Tonight is going to be delightfully depraved. I can't believe what I've requested.

Hang on.

I lied.

I *can* believe it.

I trust everyone here. I desire them, too, and I'm in a wicked mood.

Something has gotten into me. Like a spicy spell. An erotic potion. A salacious spirit swimming through my veins.

I need to get my Halloween freak on.

Stacey had us draw from the cauldron early, so she'd know who the treats would be in advance. I drew a black kiss. Then Mateo. Then Luca, who paused before handing his to Colton.

"Enjoy," Luca said, the ultimate Pleasure Dom.

Then Stacey asked to meet with us privately, the treats, to explain the role play and explore our consent.

Mateo is one of her husbands. She already knew his boundaries.

"I'm like Mateo," I said. "This week only, I'm open to all. Our group wants this."

Stacey smiled, arching her eyebrow at me.

"Fine, *I* want this. A lot. It'll be fun."

At that last part, did I clap?

Maybe.

But this was new for Colton and his love with Beau and Blair. An open group marriage, even with our network for holidays like this, may never be for them.

We understood.

Honestly, I enjoy my months with just Daniel, too. I love

our intimacy. Our laughs. Our devotion. The way Daniel loves taking candlelit baths with me.

"We want to watch and be watched." Colton was clear on that and a little nervous. "But we don't fuck others."

"I get it." Mateo wrapped his arm around Colton, squeezing a little. "With us? I top others. But I'll only bottom for my husbands. And our wife?" Mateo winked at Stacey. "We love it when she tops us."

Colton laughed, his shoulders dropping relaxed as he continued.

"I want to touch and be touched," he said. "Oral is okay for Blair and me. We've talked about it, but not Beau. There's only one other he wants this week."

"Are we allowed to know?"

Stacey asked gently, and Colton answered by looking at me. It was sweet. Colton was a little shy, asking, "Will you share your husband with us? Just for some fun stuff?"

"I'm sure he'd love it."

Yeah, it was surreal and sexy, too. Like I was accepting their invitation for a playdate in the park, not a sexorcism of demon desires for my famously hot husband.

Millions may crave Daniel Pierce, but I'm the only one with his heart. He's proven it to me. I don't worry. I'm flattered.

That's the moment my hungry kitty started to purr.

And she hasn't stopped.

"Come on, Charlie. Show us your devil costume."

Eily's trying to tempt me into opening my robe. Daniel is, too, pulling me in for a kiss, but I giggle, shooing him away.

"I can't, y'all. It's a surprise."

"Speaking of devils and surprises." Daniel glues his

stare to my cleavage while he informs the others, "I saw him last night."

Eily giggles. "No, you didn't. You're taking a shit."

"It's taking *the piss.*" Daniel laughs. "There's a big difference."

"A big brown difference."

Silas falls back on the bed, laughing, too.

"Y'all, hush." Eily jumps to her feet. "Taking the piss or taking a shit. Either way, you're full of it. You're just trying to scare us. There was no devil last night. Or the night before. Or the night before that."

"Well, then you have a rogue villain." Cade doesn't sound amused. "Because someone is here when he's not supposed to be, and he's fucking with us."

"Hell, maybe that's what he wants," Redix beams. "To fuck us. Next time y'all see him, invite him to join."

"We're sure dressed for it tonight," Silas says. "Fourteen of us are dressed like angels. We can have that demon praising hallelujah to our cocks *and* cunts by the end of the night."

"Eily," but I get serious. I'm deadly protective of the ones I love. "Who is this villain guy? And why is he here, early like you said, and mind fucking us? Four of us have seen him now. He's legit."

"And what's his name?"

Cade interrogates, too, and Eily twists her lips.

She kinda does that thing. Like if she were wearing a demure schoolgirl's skirt and not a sexy thong, she'd play with her hem. Tilting her head. Acting all innocent. "Umm," chewing her lip when she whispers, "I don't know."

Silence.

That's the sound.

That and the fuck beats playing from the Trick Tent and the laughing voices of others in their tents.

"You don't *know*?" Cade looks like an alien landed. And then stole her favorite dildo. "What the hell?"

"I know he's secretly *nice*." Eily strains a smile, trying to convince us not to freak out. "I know he's hot and rich."

Redix laughs. "Oh, well, then. Rich and hot is fine."

"You said he was a criminal!"

Cade's not that mad. She's just shocked.

"Don't be hating on criminals. You're one." Eily gestures up and down to her. "Sorta."

"Aw fuck," Silas sighs. "To a degree, we all are. We're fine, y'all. A villain? A demon? Charlie's horny haint—"

"He's *not* my hainty ancestor!"

Why do I care, though? Honestly?

The Ravenel name goes way back. I have nothing to do with the fucked-up history of my ancestors here. I just inherited the damn name.

And lactose intolerance.

They can take that last one back.

"It's perfect. It's All Hallow's Eve," Daniel assures, leaning against our dresser. "Person or phantom, we have a real bloody demon haunting us."

"Okay," I huff. "I know it's a Brit thing, but *bloody* is not the word to use right now. I'm not mad, but this ain't a game. We need to know who this man is because he knows *us*, and that's a risk I'll eliminate if I need to."

"*Awww, shiittt.*" Silas practically kicks his feet. "Here comes Charlie Girl. Here comes the Marine. If she grabs her rifle, y'all best run. Run like you're on fire."

"Aren't you supposed to drop and roll?" Redix makes it worse. He jokes, too.

I scope our group. We're standing in role-play lingerie, pussies and pricks poised for a fun night.

"Fine," I sigh. "We'll wait. Let's have a good night and not worry about it. We can talk to Stacey tomorrow about the mystery villain and get to the bottom of this. Okay?"

They nod.

And secretly, I want to be at the bottom of a pile of man meat tonight, so let's be logical tomorrow.

Redix adds, "Yeah. And if the demon appears, just ask him if he wants top or bottom."

"*Redix.*" Cade rolls her eyes, but she's smiling.

"Yeah," Silas piles on. "Ask if he wants a devil's kiss."

Daniel snorts. Redix chokes. And Eily asks, "What's a devil's kiss?"

Cade rolls her eyes again. "You fart while receiving oral."

The guys explode. They're laughing so hard they grab their abs.

"I did it one time," Redix confesses through tickled tears. "I didn't mean to. Chili, dude. It'll get you every time."

"You got *me!*" Silas bellows. "It singed my nose hair. That's how I fucking know what a devil's kiss is."

Daniel wipes his eyes. "Poor, Charlie. I got you, too, once. I didn't mean to. Remember?"

I mutter, "Don't remind me or my nose."

The wives shake our heads but can't fight our smiles.

The cute, farting, fuckers.

"Well, nothing starts the night like flatulence and phantoms." Cade lifts her hands, proclaiming. "Let's fuck."

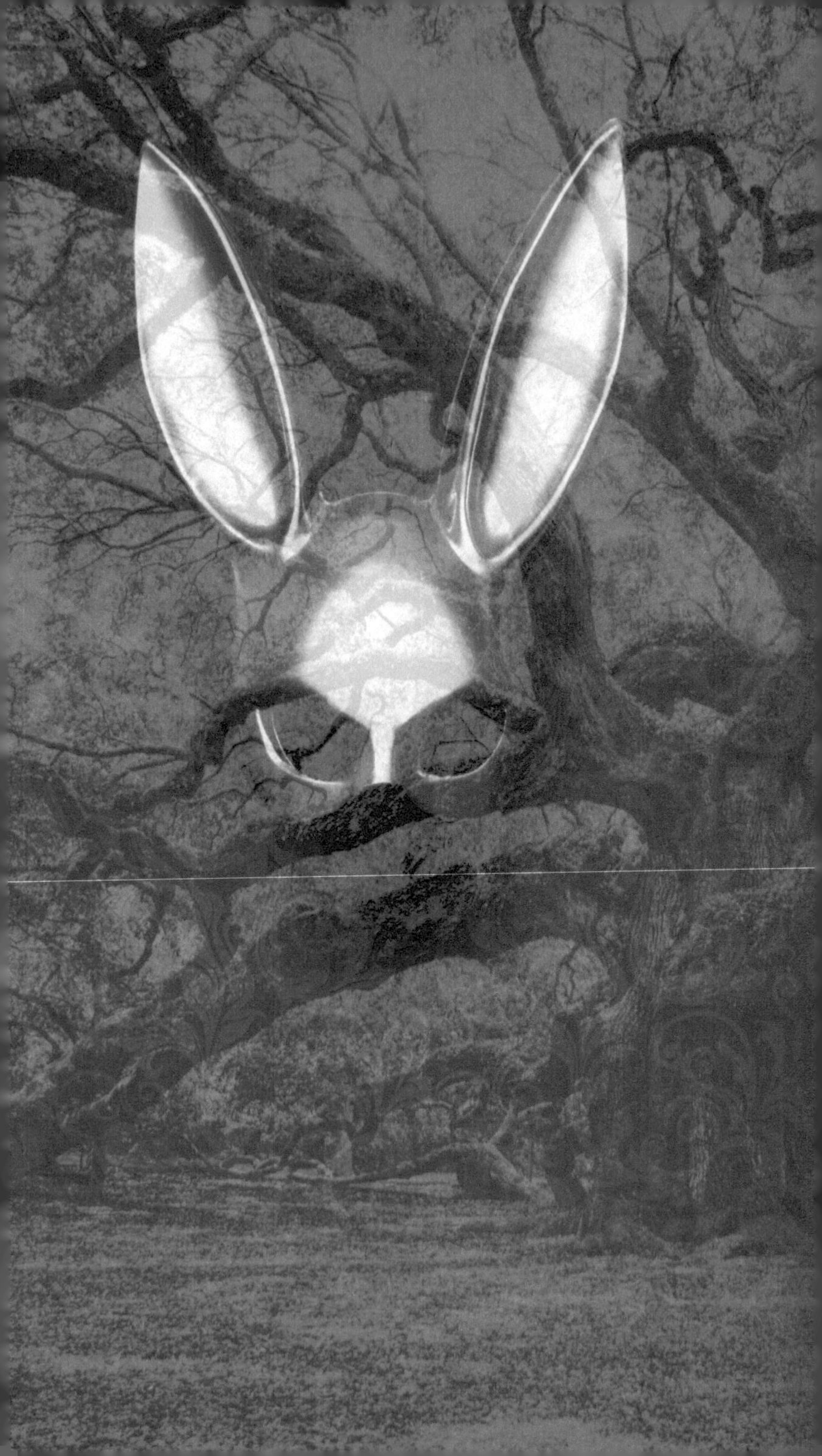

Charlie

I want to be devoured, defiled, lavished, and loved in lewd ways.

Hundreds of faux candles flicker.

Tonight, the mist in the Trick Tent has an amber aroma. The music is electronica, religious chants mixed with erotic beats. I recognize the songs from the nineties.

Three twin beds with ornate, antique iron frames beckon in the tent's center. Red uplights glow underneath each. Draped in white lace and black sheets, they're aligned like a three-point star, and I stand at the center.

Sex toys, lubes, restraints, candles, and red roses are carefully arranged on a long table like an altar.

Stacey went all out.

It's like an orgy meets the occult.

I know she had stuff shipped here, but these beds look like they were found hidden in the marshy forest. Like they're from the French mansion that used to rule this island.

Silas said the mansion belonged to my ancestor, Lois Ravenel, a French marquis who ran a brothel, a pagan who hid from Puritans, and a man who conjured moans and screams in the night.

Is that why, in this tent, I can suddenly imagine his face?

Sapphire eyes. Tousled brown hair. Scruff on his square jaw. A perfect, angular nose. A distinct bow in his pillow top lip. Deep, high dimples when he smirks.

When he pulls his horned mask over his face.

Damn, it's like he's here in front of me. It's like I'm on sacred ground, and our sex so far has been a seance, conjuring his wanton spirit.

It pulses through me: lust in my blood, ravaged wishes in my mind, an obscene urge so strong, it's a specter raising the blonde hairs on my arms.

"I understand you have been *very* bad," Colton teases, standing before me. I focus on him. "The sisters say you're haunted by a depraved demon, that he has tempted you into sin."

It's part of our role-play, and it's working. Colton barely circles my aroused nipple, and I gasp.

"Yes, father."

He's dressed like a priest in a full black robe with a gold-trimmed wide belt and a white collar. He matches Mateo beside him. They look like real clergy except for their longish hair. Mateo's black and Colton's blond strands are pulled back into knots.

I stand before them, my hands obediently clasped.

Stacey thrilled me by giving me a sexy nun costume. It's a barely-there, see-through black and white mini dress with a matching white habit, hiding my blonde hair.

This was so taboo I almost couldn't do it.

Then again.

This is so taboo; *hell, yes, I'm doing it.*

It's just costumes, naughty role-play, and one night I'll never forget.

One night my body is screaming for.

Our angels silently gather around. They stand in a circle, dressed in white, with Stacey, the archangel, in her white BDSM leather lingerie and wide, feathered wings.

Y'all, Victoria's Secret has nothing on her.

Or us.

Why strut down a catwalk for dumbass cameras when your cat can lie down for the group fuck of her life?

"Confess to us, sister." Mateo cups my breast, his palm so warm over my sheer fabric. "Have you been having impure thoughts?"

Colton makes me suck his thumb. "Have you been touching yourself, sister? In that sinful place?"

Dear god, I didn't know this was my kink.

But hallelujah, it is.

I nod.

"Does your demon make you touch others? Like this?"

Colton takes my hand, guiding me to feel his erection under his priest's robe. Mateo takes my other, cupping it over his rigid length.

Over starched cotton, I'm caressing two impressive hard cocks, and the maddening urge to stroke them takes over.

"Yes, fathers."

I do it, moaning as Mateo rumbles, "Do you lust for what's under our robes? Does your demon want to know what we look like? Taste like? Feel like inside that wet place where you touch yourself? Where your demon resides?"

"Yes, fathers," I sigh.

"Amen, this is hot."

An angel drawls. It sounds like Zar.

"Confess to us right now," Colton demands, his baritone voice sexy. "Have you defiled another sister, too?"

I squeeze his cock, grinning. "Yes, father. Sister Blair begged me to ravage her with my fingers, and I wanted to. I did it while we knelt and prayed. I did until her lust dripped down my hand."

"Fuck," Colton mutters, breaking character, his eyelids dropping heavy with lust.

That wasn't in the sketch Stacey gave us. But you know, this is XXX improv. My tease about his fiancée swells Colton's covered cock in my grasp.

He desires the idea of me with Blair. He wants Daniel, too.

Damn, this is getting hotter.

Mateo controls my other hand, guiding it along his impossible length. "Have you sinned, touching another man's hard organ like this?"

Mateo makes me rub my thighs together. I've never stroked a cock so long.

"Yes, father. I confess I let three other priests defile me. Fathers Daniel, Redix, and Silas. Together, they took my flower. I begged them to do it over and over again. And they did. They prayed while they defiled me.

"I swear, a demon possesses me. It gives me impure thoughts. It makes me want to do bad things all the time." I stammer, "It makes me need whoring so much. The heat of lust burns inside me. It wets my sex like a harlot. I need to sin so bad. Help me. *Please*. Please help me. It won't stop."

"She deserves an erotic Emmy."

That's Redix. He makes a chuckle rumble through our group.

"What does your demon tell you to do tonight?"

Mateo stays on script. But I'm not making this part up.

This *is* burning inside me, an overwhelming possession to take, to receive, to be ravaged as my reward.

"It tells me to fuck. Over and over. It makes me crave men's..." I'm supposed to stay on script and say *organs* because that's Biblical, but no. That's not filthy enough for what I feel. "I crave cocks, fathers. Lots of them, all at once."

"Fuck me."

That's Daniel sighing. I'd know his accent anywhere. I know he loves watching me be bad because usually, I'm so good.

I do everything for everyone else. I love taking care of people. It gives me joy, pride, and peace.

But right now?

Curse that.

I want to be devoured, defiled, lavished, and loved in lewd ways.

"There's only one way to get the demon out of you," Colton continues the storyline. It's so cute, corny ... and hot AF. "We have to do a Sexorcism. We have to restrain you while we pray, while we call upon the angels to fuck the demon out of you."

"Yes, fathers," I rasp. "Please, I pray. Call on the angels. All of them. Fuck this demon out of my body."

And if I were on a mountain top, I'd sing it, too, spinning in a circle, Julie Andrews style.

But instead of singing, "*The hills are alive with the sound of music.*"

I'd sing, "*This whore needs a Sex-or-cism.*"

It doesn't match, but that's how happy I am.

And horny.

And loving whorey Halloween.

Colton steps to the altar. As Stacey demonstrated earlier today, he takes the black leather thigh harnesses and returns, buckling them around my bare legs.

The brush of his big, warm hands there excites me.

Then Mateo gets the matching, padded wrist cuffs. Gently, he puts them on me, attaching their gold snap hooks to my thigh restraints.

It's comfortable. It's obscene. It's beautiful, binding my wrists to the outside of my thighs.

I won't be able to fight this.

What naughty nun in her holy mind would?

They guide me to a bed, making me kneel in the center. The bedframe may be antique, but this new, firm mattress is perfect for the ritual.

Mateo starts to untie his robe. "We need to summon the angels for you."

Colton does the same, standing on the other side of the bed.

Their robes fall to the floor. They're nude underneath. They leave their white priests' collars on. They're covered in ripped muscles and dark ink. *Dear Jesus and Jack-O-Lanterns.* They're hard and leaking.

I stare, feeling the devil vamp clawing inside me, thirsty, hungry, crazed. My pussy prays for this.

"Dear god."

Another male voice praises them. It sounds like Nick and all mutter, agreeing.

"Now." Mateo lifts his length to my lips. "Reveal your demon. Let him out. Show us what he desires. What does he make you crave?"

Gingerly, I lick Mateo's tip, tasting his salt while staying in character, acting like I'm shy about this, while Colton glides his velvety crown across my cheek.

"She craves cocks," he teases.

"Yes, fathers," I admit through swipes of my tongue over Mateo's sensitive frenulum, making his breath huff. "I crave cocks," I confess. "Lots of them."

"Confess where you crave them." Colton keeps rubbing my cheek with his. It's so damn erotic. "Where does your demon want our cocks inside you?"

"In my mouth." I suck Mateo's tip. A stifled grunt escapes his throat. "In my pussy." I wish I could touch it, but my wrists are bound. "In my ass." But I can arch my back, presenting it to those behind me. "All at one time."

I'm not performing.

I'm demanding.

It's a craze, a fire in my nerves. An appetite I have to satisfy, or I'll die. It's a luscious curse with no cure. I want the raunchiest sex I can possibly have.

All of it.

All at once.

All night.

Amen.

Colton lifts my chin. I pant, gazing into his brown eyes. Glossing his salty tip over my lips, slick with spit from sucking Mateo's tip, Colton continues our scripted performance.

"Kneel right here and pray, sister," he says. "Watch as we summon the angels for you."

Someone pop popcorn. Then feed it to me because my wrists are bound.

This is about to be a heaven and a helluva show.

Colton kneels, nude, on another bed, hooking his finger, summoning Beau and Blair.

Mateo kneels on his bed, nude, and with a chin jerk, he summons Ford and Luke. Their wife, Stacey, stays with the angels—the others who'll enjoy the show, too.

We watch while lovers kiss and fondle, mouths, tongues, and hands exploring. With every minute, I grow hotter with desire.

Colton gets his wish, letting us watch him fuck Blair, his angel. He has her on all fours, his hands yanking her waist down his shaft. He leaves her thong around her thighs, her breasts bouncing hard in her white bustier. He's fucking her like a beast.

Then he turns his head to Beau standing by the edge of their bed.

"Come here, my other angel," Colton teases Beau, "and let me suck your heavenly cock."

Beau smirks, lifting his erection out of his see-through briefs. Stepping up onto the bed, he straddles Blair and gives Colton his wish.

Mateo gets his wish, too.

He kneels with Ford behind him, with Ford's arm, his biceps popping, trapping Mateo's back against his chest. Slowly, Ford enters Mateo, and his eyes roll. "Oh god," Mateo grunts, receiving his husband.

Then, his other husband, Luke, mimics Beau. He steps onto the bed, letting Mateo's mouth worship his cock, too.

For minutes, Stacey demands we wait and watch their sex. Their love. Their shameless and tempting display.

My core aches.

My sex is so wet.

I'm kneeling with my thighs apart, the cool air thrilling my pussy, barely exposed by my nun's dress. The long veil of my habit tickles my bare shoulders. It adds to the kink while erotic music loops, heightening our indecent game.

With quickening thrusts, it sounds like Colton makes Blair climax. She bucks, gasping, and that sets Colton off, his pecs shaking. He comes with primal grunts, with Beau's cock filling his mouth.

He arouses Mateo to do the same.

Mateo tugs Luke away, and Luke knows his husband. He knows Mateo wants us to watch him come while Ford claims him. While Ford brutally pounds into Mateo's backside. He's making Mateo's length bounce hard, swollen, and begging for release.

"Don't touch it," Ford growls. "You'll fucking come for us. Let them watch you come with my cock in your ass."

Mateo throws his head back, resting on Ford's shoulder. He takes his ravenous kiss while jets of Mateo's cum paint the black sheets in front of him.

"Please, fathers," I beg. "Please, I have so much impure lust. I feel possessed. Please. Let your angels help me."

I'm not lying.

I'm in pain.

I'm obsessed.

Colton's still huffing for breath, but he smirks, answering, "Angels, help our sister."

Stacey clicks my way.

Wearing acrylic heels, the feathers on her white wings flutter as she sits on the edge of my bed. Slowly dragging her fingertip through my slick folds, I gasp when she asks, "Do you want my angels' help? Are you ready for our sexorcism?"

"Yes," I pray.

"Cade," Stacey calls, "come help me prepare her to receive."

Oh fuck, will I ever receive. A lot.

While Cade stalks my way, I glance around the room.

Luca holds Scarlett. He grabs her neck, her back to his chest, while his other hand dominates her pussy hidden under her angel-white thong.

He's controlling her pleasure.

He's making her come.

Nick stands beside Luca, their biceps brushing, their briefs tugged down, while Zar kneels before Nick. He's sucking Nick's cock and stroking Luca's, pressed against Scarlett at the same time.

Beside them stand Redix, Eily, and Daniel. They're waiting for me while Silas won't. He kneels before Eily, cupping her ass. He has her leg slung over his shoulder. She's fisting his long hair, proudly rocking her pussy over Silas's face.

She's about to come.

And I can any second.

Stacey rips off my dress and habit. I'm naked while she teases my pussy, rubbing a generous sheen of lube over my clit, making me shudder. Then she circles my entrance with it, and I moan with need.

I can come right now, but with all my experience with The Six, I can wait. I can edge to an exquisite degree. It makes it so much better.

"Such a demon slut we need to fuck," Stacey teases. "How many cocks does this naughty pussy crave in her tonight?"

Throw away the calculator. Put down your fingers. I've already counted, and Stacey has, too. We already know who is open, who I want, and where.

This may be taboo, but we're also mature. We talk. We plan. We make sure.

"Three," I confess from a fiery place, stirring deep inside. "Three to take turns with my pussy."

Like sorcery, suddenly, visions of nude writhing bodies, sights I've never seen, invade my mind. Like they did this, too. Like they were here. On this island. They were real. I can feel their depraved deeds and desires.

Stacey withdraws, and Cade nudges me forward, pressing my cheek to the mattress. We know how to prep and please; the lewd exposure thrilling me.

Gently, she inserts a narrow lube shooter into my tightest hole while she teases me, "And this sweet ass? How many cocks does your demon crave?"

"Two cocks to take turns with my ass," I sigh, "and the rest I want to taste. I want them in my mouth. I want them all over me."

I'm under a lurid spell.

I'm possessed.

Don't you dare save me.

"Damn." I hear Scarlett moan. "This is gonna be hot."

She and Luca aren't open like Daniel and me, but they enjoy watching my pleasure. So do the others.

Stacey grants my wish. First, she points to Silas, then Redix.

As they approach, their hard cocks straining under their sheer briefs, Stacey directs, "Take her first, my angels. Start fucking this demon out of her."

Silas smirks, shucking his briefs off, his cock springing to hungry life. He climbs behind me, grabbing my waist. His heat triples my pulse.

Lying back on pillows, Silas arranges my body to lie on top of his, my back to his bare, muscular chest. He bends his knees, plants his feet on the mattress, and spreads his thighs.

It makes my body match his. My wrists are bound to my thighs as they fall open, my sex splayed open to the room while Silas tempts, "Say it, Charlie. Say how you want me now."

Never did I think I'd do this with Silas, my best friend for so long. I knew he wanted me, but I didn't feel the same until years later when Eily's love rescued him. She made him into a man you can't resist.

He's also one of the few I trust to do this. I *want* to do this. It only turns Daniel on watching it, hearing my demands while I stare at my husband and answer.

"I want you to fuck my ass, Silas."

Both men moan at my command.

Silas reaches around, spreading my lips open, exposing my tender clit, as he demands, "Lick her. Make her want this while you put me inside her."

Silas knows how to love. He knows how to do this. He'll never hurt me as Stacey and Redix assist.

Stacey bends over, gently circling my clit with her tongue while Redix carefully wedges Silas's crown inside me. Slowly, Silas thrusts, breaching my entrance.

"Oh, god," I gasp at the pleasure, the penetration.

With all the lube Cade put inside me, it only burns for a moment before it feels demonically good, making a voice inside me demand, "More. I want more cocks. Now."

Redix fulfills my wish. He strips, then crawls on top. Braced over me, he gently urges inside my aching pussy. We've done this before, and it always feels so fucking good, my mind melting and body singing because he, Daniel, and Silas know my body.

They know how to please their women.

Like luscious pistons, they alternate their thrusts inside me, and I moan, my eyelids fluttering.

Under me, I feel Silas's warmth. I hear his luring moans while he fucks my ass. Above me is the sultry silhouette of

Redix, his abs flexing, driving his hips, the rhythmic effort of his cock.

But when I close my eyes, visions of bodies intertwined over red velvet settees invade my mind. Memories that aren't mine, furniture, and people that aren't here. They're starving spirits, controlling my senses and driving my demands.

"Fuck me harder," I growl. "Deeper. Faster. Do it. Now."

"Damn, you want this," Redix grunts, his cock obeying. He hammers faster. "You're so wet. So creamy and swollen for this."

"Such a naughty sister," Silas taunts my ear. He takes us there in this dirty role-play, and I start to tremble. "You're not supposed to want this, but you do, don't you, Charlie? You want our cocks fucking your sweet pussy and tight ass all night? Such a slutty sister."

Reaching around, Silas pinches my raw nipple while Redix leans down, sucking and biting my other one.

"Oh god!" I scream. "Oh god, oh god. I'm gonna come."

"See." I hear Eily giggle. "It *is* a sexorcism. Count how many times she screams, 'God.'"

It's cute. It's fun. It takes away the shame because there is none.

This is pure, savage pleasure.

It storms through my core, my orgasm rising, building into a blinding crest. My muscles, my nerves, my pussy, everything tenses, clenching for the wave's arrival, for its sweet destruction.

Silas thrusts his cock in my ass, stretching me, filling me, heightening the sensation in my pussy filled with Redix's pounding length. With his curve that rubs that spot, that *G* spot, Redix was born to please.

I start seeing stars. I fight to make this last forever.

But then Stacey leans down, rattling her tongue over my electric clit, and I explode.

"Oh god!" I gush. I release. My pussy pulses as my core bursts.

"Oh, fuck yeah. Look at her come." Redix pulls out. In a gasping haze, I watch him marvel as I soak him, his hard dick, his lap, the bed.

"Fuck, Charlie," Silas grunts, squeezing me hard. He thrusts harder into my ass, and I moan with more spasms, with my arousal leaking from my sex. "Fuck, I can feel you dripping on me. Fuck, you make me come when you squirt."

With a sudden groan, he does. I love Silas. I know him. I know his sounds, his carnal strain when he comes.

"My turn." I hear the voice that owns my soul. "Give me my wife. *Now*."

It's Daniel. I can't focus, but I can sense him. He's not mad. He's hungry. He's aroused for more.

Just like me.

Carefully, Redix lifts away while Silas rolls us on our sides. Gently, he pulls out. "You're so horny tonight, Charlie," Silas murmurs. "I've never seen you like this." He kisses my shoulder. "Good for you. It's fucking hot."

"Thank you," I sigh as Stacey calls, "Luke." Then, I moan. I can't believe I'm about to do this, too.

Wait.

I lied again.

I *can* believe it.

Stacey and I discussed it this afternoon when she asked if I'd do this.

"I know Luke loves me," she said. "But he's only been with me and his first girlfriend, and I want him to have this. He risks his life daily, and I want him to feel like he's *lived* it.

And you were a Marine. You understand what can happen to him and—"

I reached for her hand. "I understand. Like Luke with you, Daniel was my second. It was just us for years until we were with the others."

"And," Stacey grinned, "Luke thinks you're hot. I mean, we look alike. I can't blame him."

Stacey loves Luke so much. She kisses him by the side of the bed while my love, my husband, takes Silas's place.

But unlike Silas, Daniel gently turns my chin. He kisses me, praising me, "Bloody hell, babe, you got me so hard. I love you like this, taking what you want."

"I want *you*, Daniel Pierce," I sigh.

"Oh, you fucking have me. For the rest of my life."

He makes it sweet, kissing me again. Then, he spreads my legs, making it dirty.

It's like an erotic ritual. My body resumes the same position. I'm on top of Daniel, my back to his concrete chest. My sex is weeping and open, demanding two more men.

I don't hurt.

I hunger.

"My naughty girl," Daniel rumbles. "I can feel another man's cum dripping from your arse." He reaches under, wedging his cock in. Carefully. Slowly. Obscenely. "I'm going to have to fuck this slutty, tight little ass until it's mine again. Won't I, Charlie?"

"Yes, sir."

Anal is Daniel's favorite. The way he does it, he makes it mine, too. He's a master at it, savoring my slow stretch, relishing my aching gape. He makes it last. He makes me come so many times I go blind.

But not tonight.

I'm full and claimed by Daniel as I watch Luke kneel between my thighs with Stacey kneeling behind him.

She tugs his briefs down. Luke's swollen cock bobs free, and I gasp. At the sight. At Daniel's urging inside me. At Stacey's tease.

"See her glistening pussy? See how she drips?" Her fingertip tickles my clit, her lips taunting Luke's ear. "She wants you to fuck her, too."

"Is that what you want, Charlie?" It's sexy how Luke asks, his hand gliding over my thigh where leather binds it. "Do you want me inside your pretty pussy, while your husband fucks your ass?"

Stacey's trained Luke well. He makes consent hot as fuck.

"Yes." I'm pulsing for it.

But Luke surprises me. He unclips my wrists, freeing them while he demands, "Then put me inside you. Show me where you need my cock."

"Fuck yes," Daniel rumbles.

He's going to love this. It only makes me tighter for him, increasing his pleasure, too.

Bracing over me, just as Redix did, Luke takes position while I reach for his thick shaft, my new touch making him grunt.

"Stacey," he moans. "Stacey, are you sure?"

She urges, "Do *you* want this?"

"Yes," Luke confesses. "If you let me. If you love me. Then yes, I want this."

Stacey wraps her hand over mine. Together, we guide Luke inside. "Fuck her," Stacey sighs over his ear. "Fuck her and enjoy it. Feel how she wants you, how she needs you. Just like me."

That drops Luke's eyelids. He moans at my penetration,

at his slow entrance. It's like he can't believe he's fucking another woman. That his wife wants him to while my husband wants him to as well.

"Fuck," Luke sighs as Stacey watches him fully take me. "Fuck, this is so hot."

"Oh god." I can't stop moaning it. Screaming it. What other words can I conjure at this bodily bliss? At this fleshy fuck of my body and senses?

They go slower, their thrusts more languid and lush than Silas and Redix's force, both sensations pleasing me. I like it hard. I like it tender.

I like it all.

I start calling from somewhere ancient, some desire suppressed, some lust unleashed. "I want more. More. Please. Please, give it to me."

I'm so in my body. My body being taken, used, filled, and pleasured. My mind drops into a carnal trance as velvety, salty tips press to my gasping mouth, demanding I suck them, and I blink.

I think I'm sucking Zar's cock. Then Mateo's. Then Colton's. And I want to. I'm obsessed. I'm in dark heaven. I'm in the past. I'm in the present. I'm getting fucked senseless by so many men.

I know it's my husband driving inside me, stirring, grinding, sending luscious shocks from my ass to my clit, while Luke fills me, too. His hips circle hard, driving his cock deep into my clenching pussy, matching Daniel's maddening pressure.

And...

Without sound or warning, I come. I burst. I have a cock in my groaning mouth while the drenching spasms control me. Over and over, pleasure pours from me.

"Shit," Luke grunts. "Shit, she squirts so hard."

"It's so hot." I hear Stacey. I feel her mouth sucking my clit, and I do it again. I groan, exploding.

I have no control.

This isn't me.

This is lust.

"Give her more," Daniel demands. "Don't stop. Everyone. She wants more. Luke and Redix, keep fucking her. She'll keep coming."

Hands, real ones, warm ones, caress my flesh. Fingers, strong ones, Luca's, *I can barely see him*, pinch my nipple, tugging at it. While a cock, the hard tip of Beau's, teases my other one.

With every part of me ravaged, I fall into a depraved dream—a wicked fantasy fulfilled. I relish the men devoted to my pleasure.

They're everywhere, and I'm right here. Blinded. Panting. Shaking. Pulsing. Squirting and screaming and taking them. I come so hard; it hurts so good.

So good as I stare into a man's sapphire eyes...

Eyes that aren't here.

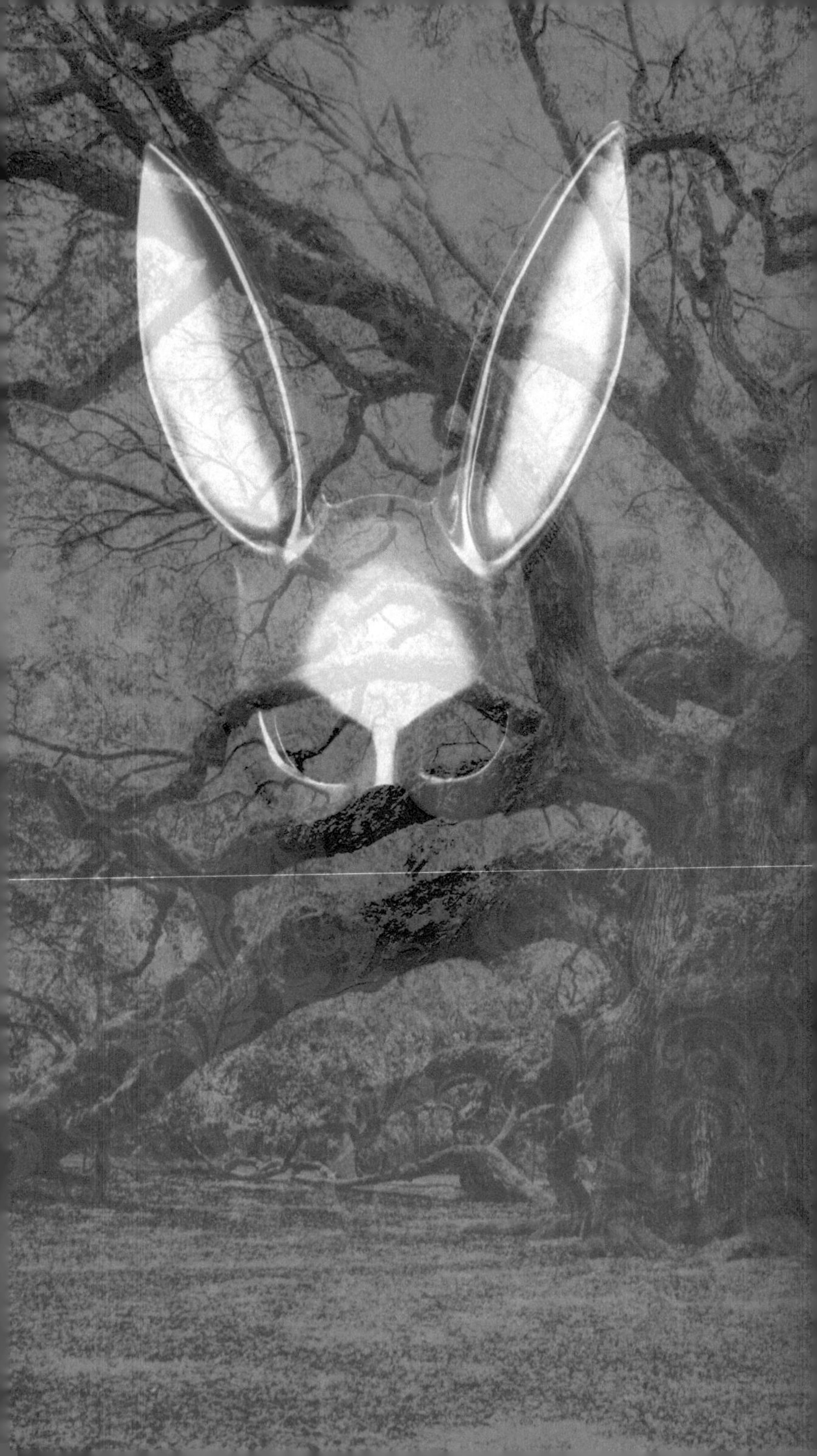

Cade

CHAPTER TWELVE

CADE

Tapping.

"Pssst."

Who's tapping me?

"Pssst."

They have a death wish.

"Pssst."

I'll murder whoever this is.

Cracking my eyelids, I see Eily. Like one of those cute prairie dogs, she's popping up, eyes big, neck craning, looking over Redix. "Pssst." She's trying to wake me up.

"What?" I mouth back.

She nods toward our tent's open flap.

I lift my head. I can barely focus on the silhouettes standing there—all women, all nude, all with bath towels slung over their shoulders.

Charlie. Stacey. Blair. Scarlett.

What the fuck?

The Amazons are summoning me at dawn.

"It's Charlie," Eily whispers. "It's Lip Love Time."

That's all I need to hear.

Sliding out from under Redix, I scoot from the middle where we like to sleep and leave him naked in the bed with Silas and Daniel.

Once my feet touch the plush, "porno rug," as Eily calls it, she hands me a bath towel equally plush.

"Come on," she mutters, urging me to join them.

Are we about to freeze bras?

Are we about to draw dicks on the sleeping foreheads of our men?

Not that they'd complain. But the sight of Luca Mercier with a black Sharpie dick on his forehead would be damn amusing.

Without a word, like a clatter of clandestine cunts, we quietly prowl from our tent's platform, across the sandy path, my bare feet not minding the crushed pine straw, too.

Whatever we need to talk about, I'm here for it.

Lip Love Time is my favorite.

It's what me, Eily, Charlie, and whoever has two sets of lips do after a fun night. I mean ... a fuck night.

We debrief. We dissect. We die laughing. And we usually pop ibuprofen and put ice packs between our legs, planning the next round.

Eily leads our group to the fifth guest tent, the one not being used. The large tub on its platform steams, full and bubbling in the brisk morning. Silas turned these huge silver basins into outdoor hot tubs with teak wood benches and stools inside.

Climbing over the ledge, one by one, we use the three-step ladder to ease into the tub, settling into a circle.

Charlie's the last to climb in as I ask, "What's going on? Are you okay?"

From the ledge where rolled towels and spa products are arranged, Eily, our pornified party planner, pours three cups of sandalwood-scented bath salts into our water.

She turns our tub into a soup of perfumed pussies, while Charlie answers, "I'm fine. I just … I just…"

She trails off.

"Was last night too much?" Scarlett worries for her. They're close. Charlie used to be her boss. "I mean … you took on a lot of dick last night."

"And she won!" Eily, with her long hair piled into a messy top knot, blurts with pride. "I mean, Charlie, we know you can squirt. Lots of us can, especially with our men's skills, but last night, you were like the Hoover Dam, cracking to come, bursting with the water of life. Like it was Vegas, and you were a fountain show of fucks. A woman's wet dream. Or a volcano erupting. You were Mount St. Pussy Goddess hotly spewing forth new life onto this planet and—"

Charlie's rolling. We all are because Eily has an imagination and no filters, but those are facts, too.

"Y'all," Charlie sighs. "I don't know what got into me last night."

"Six dicks."

Stacey smirks, her arms slung over the back of the tub, her glorious breasts bobbing in the water. "That's what got into you last night. Six beautiful dicks."

"*Six?*" Charlie's eyes get wide.

"Shit." Stacey's face drops. "Don't tell me you don't remember? Don't tell me that's not what you wanted?"

I guess Stacey feels responsible. The Sexorcism was her trick, and like her, I thought we all enjoyed the treats.

But apparently...

"You were moaning, like screaming for more," Blair adds. "It sure looked and sounded like you wanted it. You were fisting dicks and getting fucked and literally moaning, 'Cocks. Give me more cocks.'"

Eily giggles. "Is this a bad time for a that's-what-he-said joke?"

"No." Charlie chuckles. "I mean, yes. I did. I did want it. I remember. It's just that..."

She trails off again, her stare landing on the sprawling live oak at the edge of the camp as if entranced, and we fall silent, letting the tub bubble.

In the distance, we can hear the birds. Closer by, we can hear men, their grunts of lust distinct.

Someone's fucking.

"That's Beau and Colt," Blair says. "They wanted me, too, this morning. This place is really turning them on. I swear," she turns to Eily, "did you put something in the water? Because I feel it, too. This must be what bitches in heat feel like."

"Same," Scarlett adds. "It's like I can't get enough. I even wore Luca out last night. I told him to lie there and let me do the work. He wasn't complaining, but after two more times, he had nothing left in him. And still, I was horny."

Around the tub, our heads nod.

We all feel it.

And even though I have spent a lot of time on this island, sharing some of the most erotic moments of my life, something *is* different this week.

It's in Charlie's sapphire eyes that must reflect mine. I

glance around our circle; every woman has that intense gleam and sparkling demand.

They say men are the horny ones. Yeah.

But women are the hungry ones.

And this week, we're ravenous.

"Okay." But I can't help it. I may be getting my freak on, too, but I'm still a detective. "Tell us what you remember."

"I remember Silas and Redix," Charlie answers. "Then I remember Daniel and Luke."

Stacey sighs, "That was so hot. Luke got so into it. He liked me touching him while he was fucking you. He was getting off on me telling him how to do it, telling him to watch how you were creaming on his cock, and I was rubbing your clit, showing him, and—"

"Quiet." Eily giggles. "You're getting me horny when I need a cup of coffee first."

"Ditto," Blair sighs.

"Oh, I remember that. And then"—Charlie closes her eyes—"I remember Redix again, sharing me with Luke, giving me a DP with Daniel. I remember Mateo, Zar, and Colton were in my mouth. And then..."

She keeps doing it.

She trails off, her stare mesmerized by the old tree.

It's like it's interrupting us.

It's like it's calling her name.

I don't want to lead the witness, but she's acting odd. Charlie's mind is a steel trap. She's the CEO of a security company, for fuck's sake. She doesn't forget people and details. Much less dicks and who was giving them to her.

"And then, what?" Gently, I ask Charlie, "What do you remember? And it's okay if you don't. We're not judging."

"Yeah, I get dick delirium all the time." Eily tugs out her bun, assuring Charlie, "Sometimes I want it so bad; I know it's Silas inside me, but when Redix and Daniel are there sharing me, too, it becomes a blur. No, not a blur. It's like I zoom in on a porno and only focus on dicks fucking me everywhere."

She makes us laugh, especially Blair. Her raven hair is wet and falling slick down her back.

"That's an image," she says. "And it's going in my next book."

"Oh, please write a book about us!" Eily claps. "Just change our names. You can do that porno name thing. You know, your first pet and the street you lived on. Mine is 'Princess Spanker Lane.' It's perfect!"

Scarlett chuckles, adding, "Mine is 'Rocket Butts Avenue.'"

Blair laughs while I stay focused on Charlie. "Can you remember what happened next?"

"Yeah," Charlie answers. "But I don't know if it was real."

"If *what* was real?"

"If it was Mateo next. That's who I wanted. That's who I called for, right? And Ford?"

"Right." Stacey smiles. "You wanted all of my husbands, and I was happy to oblige. We don't usually do that. We're not usually open. But once they saw Luke getting into it. I mean," she chuckles, "getting into *you*, I think it turned Ford and Mateo on. They wanted to share you with him and for me to touch them while they did it, too. And you wanted them. You called for them."

"Yeah," Charlie mutters, "I remember the calling."
Yeah, I heard it.
What she just said.
And does Charlie look high? Like stoned on DP memories?

"*The* calling?"

"That's what it felt like." Charlie focuses on me, confessing, "Something was screaming from inside me."

Eily tilts her head. "Like shouting from your pussy?"

"I sure feel my kitty calling sometimes," Blair adds. "She's got a dirty mind of her own. Usually, it calls when I should be doing laundry or emptying the dishwasher. But who wants to do chores when you can do cocks?"

Eily throws her arm over Blair's shoulder. "I know you already have a twin, but I think we're triplets."

Yeah, they don't look alike, but they sure have matching minds and mouths. Blair doesn't use filters, either.

They keep cutely interrupting my interrogation, but I want to get to the bottom of this.

It's not that anything wrong happened last night. Clearly, it's what Charlie wanted. She said so, and she's not the kind of woman—none of us are—to do a damn thing she doesn't want.

But something odd happened.

I can't describe it either.

Like Charlie, my mind stammers for words.

Last night, while she was getting the gorgeous gang-bang of her life, her body erupting with lust so many times —we are definitely turning that mattress into a shrine— the rest of us were under a spell, too.

I was with Blair and Scarlett while their men watched. Luca and Beau, in particular, seemed possessed. It turned me on, seeing their cocks get so raging hard while they watched me fuck their women with my generous strap-on, making them come, then their men took their turn with them.

The night was an erotic dream.

But it wasn't. It was real. I have the strap marks on my thighs to prove it.

"So, Charlie, what are you saying?" I ask. "That you were—"

"Possessed."

The word escapes her lips and doesn't fall into the water.

No, it rises with the steam into the morning mist. It trails, wisps weaving into the branches above, lacing through the silver moss, swaying like ghosts.

A cool breeze suddenly caresses our shoulders, making goosebumps shiver over our skin, not emerged in soothing, warm water. I can see its path travel across our flesh.

Stacey drops her chin. "Possessed?" Her tone believes it. It just doesn't want to.

"I guess that's what it was," Charlie answers. "Not like I have experience with the demonic. But... No. That's not what it was like. It wasn't evil or painful. It was the opposite. I wanted it. I would close my eyes and see people—"

"I see dead people!" Eily blurts. "It was like that movie? You saw dead people like that boy who's talking to the nice cop who doesn't know he's dead the whole time and—"

Blair laughs. "Spoiler alert if you haven't seen *The Sixth Sense*."

Charlie laughs, too. "Yeah, I saw nice, dead people."

Blair leans forward. "Details. I need details."

Yeah, this is definitely going into her books.

"They didn't look dead," Charlie answers. "They looked alive. Like they were here, but centuries ago. I saw furniture and candles and figurines everywhere. It felt like we were with them. Like we were fucking in their ritual."

Blair grins. "Like an ancient orgy ritual?"

"Yeah," Charlie says. "I don't know how I know it, but I

felt it. That's what they did here centuries ago. Rituals. Ceremonies. Orgies. It's like our sex is conjuring them. It's like when my eyes were open, I saw our men fucking me, and I wanted them. And when I closed my eyes, I saw those people and wanted them even more.

"Maybe I made it up. Maybe it was a fantasy, but I saw that man. The one Silas said was my ancestor here. I swear I saw him. I *felt* him. He made me want to do things."

"Oh my god," Eily sighs. "I'm so jealous. You were possessed by a gangbang ghost. And when I die, I'm doing the same thing. Whenever people are fucking, I'll haunt them in a sweet way. You know, like work a woman's clit to make sure she comes."

"Why wait until you die?" Blair teases Eily. "You didn't last night. Thank you, by the way."

Eily pecks Blair's cheek.

Last night, she took her turn with Blair, too, licking her pussy while Silas fucked Eily, spanking her ass, making her get off on being his "bad girl."

I almost forgot that part.

See?

It was a slutty seance.

"But I have to admit," Charlie says. "Whatever was in me last night, my body sure feels it now. I may need a break tonight."

Stacey chuckles. "It really was a sexorcism but in reverse. We were fucking the spirit *into* you, not out."

"I don't know." Blair jokes, "Charlie, you sure were loving it so much. You were pouring out the praise—like squirting a sexy sermon."

Hiding behind her hand, Charlie blushes. She giggles. She shakes her head.

What the supernatural shit? Since when is Charlie shy?

"Girl," I amaze, "you're serious, aren't you? You were *possessed?*"

She's still blushing. "Yes, I swear I was."

"Big dicks and sweet demons." Eily claps her hands. "This week keeps getting better."

"And hotter."

"And wetter."

"And dirtier."

"It's a horny haunting for sure."

The women agree. Like witches, each adding her erotic ingredient into our potion.

"So, y'all don't think I'm crazy?" Charlie asks. "I woke up this morning worried I had lost my mind or that it was all a dream. But I'm so sore, I know it wasn't."

"You're not crazy." Scarlett caresses her shoulder. "Whenever I scene with Luca, I go into a trance. Some call it sub-space, but it's real. Your body is so overwhelmed with sensations that you lose control of your mind. It is sorta like a dream."

"Dicks, demons, *and* dreams." Eily sighs. "It just keeps getting better. And look at us. All gathered, brewing in our own potion. We're like a coven." Her eyes grow wide. Get ready for the blurt. "A *cunty* coven! That's it. That's our name."

We laugh. We nod. We high-five.

And I know this is Eily's dream.

All she wanted was for us to have a good time, and she needed it, too.

I know she's stressing about getting pregnant, but she tries to hide it. Always smiling and joking, that's Eily's true spirit, but she's human, too. She and Silas have this sweet dream, and so do we. We hope they add to our family, too.

That's why she went all out on planning this week. She needs the fun. And the distraction.

No.

A *dickstraction.*

Hang on.

She needed it so bad, forget a hot haint haunting us with orgiastic urges.

What about the real criminal Eily invited, too?

"So," I persist, "now that we know Charlie was officially possessed by her amorous ancestor, let's get to the bottom of this other man. The real one you invited to fuck with us, too."

Eily twists her lips.

Guilt darts her happy glance away.

"Yeah." Charlie sits up, her clarity returning. The fuck fog lifts from her eyes as she asks Stacey, "Who's the man who hides at your place? You know, the one Eily met at Delta's?"

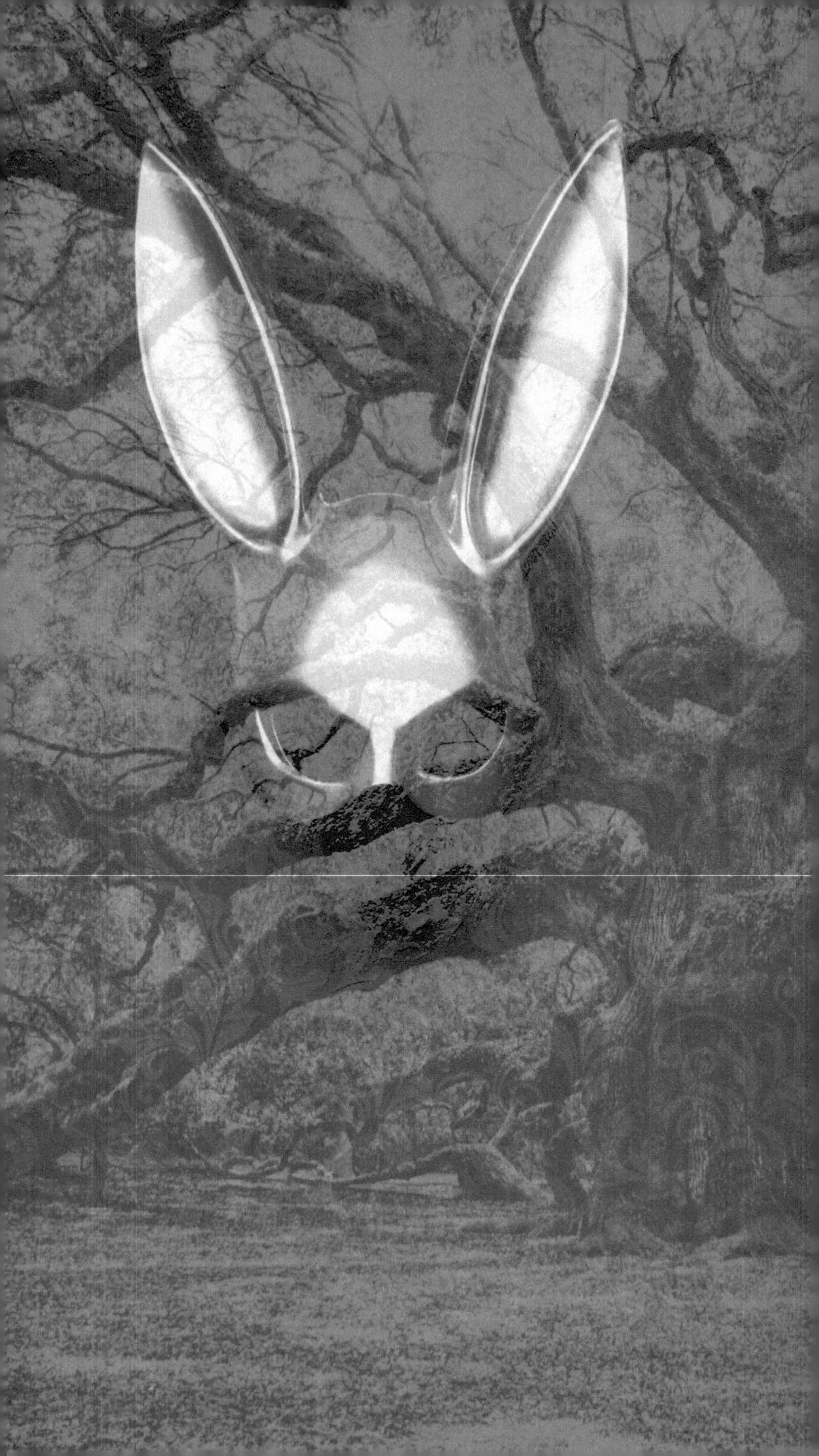

Silas

"You're fucking aggro, and it's adorable."

"You know what they say about life giving you lemons?"

Redix bounces his brows. "Make them into candies and eat them off your wife's fine ass?"

He ain't joking. That's precisely what he does with Cade and Lemonheads.

"Damn, you and your candy fetish." I adjust the nozzle on the hose to full blast. "All that sugar is gonna rot your teeth out."

"All the better to suck you with."

He's on a roll. He's excited this morning.

Last night, while we were having an orgy that would make porn stars applaud, it poured. The rain and Charlie.

Damn, she was like a woman possessed last night, and not a soul complained. It's like we all caught the spirit. I was on Eily twice. I swear, if she isn't pregnant by the end of this week, I'll…

Well … I'll always love her, and we'll figure it out.

But if my plan today doesn't make her happy, about a hundred other things will.

Eily makes cheerleaders look lethargic. Nothing gets her down.

I squeeze the nozzle in my hand, filling the muddy hole the rain made last night with even more water. It's a brown, murky pool, promising fun. I just drove my truck over, loaded with tools and a water tank to make it an even muddier mess.

"No," I preach, finishing my sermon, "when life gives you lemons and mud, you make lemonade and mud wrestle."

"Here, here!" Daniel boasts, digging the hole deeper in spots.

It's like Mother Nature wants this. This spot on the edge of the trail out of camp does this every time it rains. I was going to backfill it, but I got too busy fishing.

This will be a Halloween tradition: rain or shine.

Mud wrestling.

"Watch out for gators."

Redix tries scaring Daniel, who only slings mud back at him, splattering his laughing face.

"But seriously, dude," I tell him. "Chase all the snakes out."

Daniel pauses, lowers his brows, and gives me *that* look … the one you see on screens all the time, the one that tests the fabric of undergarments everywhere.

"Oh," I shiver, giving him shit. "When you give me your wolf gaze, I get all gooey inside."

"Keep it up," he arches a brow, "and I'll give you something else inside, too."

"What-ever-the-fuck. All of us emptied our wank tanks last night. Oh, and this morning. Even *I* need until lunch before my banana can make more cream."

"I'm just glad I can finally empty my tank." Daniel shovels, slinging mud over the brim. "Now that Luca finally cured me."

"Now that you finally told me about our show." Redix shakes his head. "Dude, you should've told me about the studio pressuring you. But at least now I can help you. We'll tell them we'll wrap after this season."

Daniel wipes his brow. "You deserve to *win* for this season."

Redix softens his face. "Is that what you were stressed about? Me winning an Emmy, too?"

"Yeah. You deserved it more than me."

"No, you did. You wrote us a helluva story: VICE cops realizing they're in love; it's kind of been our story, too. So, we'll end it like you imagined. It'll make the story tighter. Stronger. Hell, let's end it *Sopranos* style."

"What about the crew? I worry about them."

"Man, we love you." I mirror Redix, shaking my head. "You worry about everyone, but we're fine. Quit being the oldest."

"Look," Redix squats, his hands dangling between his legs, his focus on Daniel, "we'll pitch another show to shoot in Atlanta and hire the same crew. They'll be fine. I just can't believe you kept all that stress inside."

"Literally," I agree. "But damn, when you finally blew..."

It ain't like us to keep secrets. It ain't like us to share our bodies but not our hearts. But that's just Daniel. The oldest.

The most responsible. Sometimes, he worries the most about us. Sometimes, that makes him the hottest, too.

He finally grins. "Oh, I blew, alright. For Luca. For you lot next."

Yeah, he did.

That vampire night, it was like once Luca helped Daniel let go, Daniel couldn't stop. While I took his ass, taunting his ear, "Come on. Give us more. Show us how you love us," Charlie, Cade, and Eily knelt before him. Then Redix took him while Daniel took Charlie.

Not a drop of stress was left in him once we were done.

And if I thought the Love Bites night was hot?

Our sexorcism last night?

We cast out every demon until two a.m. Then we showered in pairs and groups, all scurrying under umbrellas, back to our tents, tugging our partners into cuddles under covers before the smell of a late brunch awoke us.

That and Redix's mouth.

Our women were gone, so we men shared our special way of waking each other up.

Nothing like blow jobs before breakfast.

"Damn, I'm sore." Redix rubs his junk. "I may need y'all to kiss it again and make it better."

"Charlie sure kissed it last night. She made lots of men better."

It doesn't offend Daniel, me talking about his wife. He knows I love her. He knows Charlie went from being my babysitter to my best friend to our group's "Queen of the Cumshot" as my beautiful wife has anointed her.

He knows, all hot sex aside, I can't live without *my* wife, and I sure love living with my partners, too.

Daniel smiles, stirring his shovel through the mud. I

wasn't joking about the snakes, but none slither out. We're clear.

"Gawd blimey," he says. "I've never seen Charlie like that. It's like she couldn't get enough. She kept moaning for more. Fuck, she was beautiful. So beautiful, finally taking what she wants."

"All our women need a gangbang from time to time." Redix rakes the grass around the hole. "I guess it's Cade's turn tonight, then Eily's."

"Touch Eily's pussy, and I'll cream your corn."

Redix hits me with a smirk. "Promise?"

My nostrils flare. "I'm fucking serious."

"You're fucking aggro, and it's adorable." Daniel sloshes out of the mud pit. Sludge drips from his navy shorts, clinging to his ripped thighs. "You'll make a great dad one day."

I let go of the nozzle, watching muddy bubbles pop over the murky pool, thoughts of fun escaping me. I've been needing to talk to them about this.

"But *when* will I be a dad?" I ask. "We've been trying for a while, and what if it's me? What if I'm shooting blanks and can't get Eily pregnant?"

Daniel shrugs. "Did you get your swimmers tested?"

"I'd be willing to. But then, what if it's *not* me? That'll only break Eily's heart, and I'll die before I do that."

"Look." Redix cups my cheek. Fuck, it melts me every time. "Give it a couple more months, and if nothing happens, go to the doctor together, and if there's a problem, we'll help. Hell, we got extra eggs and swimmers if you need 'em."

"We ain't there yet."

"Well, y'all ain't alone, either ... no matter where you are." Sincerity drops his voice; his scruffy lips kiss mine.

"You know I love you. *We* love you. We're always here for you."

I cast my stare over his shoulder to the tidal marsh behind him. To the spot where I usually see a pod of dolphins. And there they are, their fins cresting, working together like a family, corralling baitfish.

"Huh," I share. "Last month, Eily told me about a dream she had. She said we were here, and she was in a birthing tub on our porch. Cade and Charlie were coaching her, wiping her brow, and I was in the tub with her, holding her legs back, encouraging her, like telling her to push. And y'all were taking care of your kids. She said you answered their questions while they watched our baby being born. She said it was so real."

I sigh, "She said we had a boy, and we named him Indi for indigo."

Sniff.

Sniff.

Ahem.

"Dude?" Redix glances away while I ask, "Are you crying?"

"Yeah, man." He turns back, grinning with tears in his eyes. "That's sweet as shit. That's my fucking dream, too."

"Mine, as well." Daniel stabs the shovel into the ground before matching Redix, reaching for my other shoulder. "I dream of living here with our families. I want to raise our children together. This feels like home. The six of us feel like home."

"Yeah." Redix jerks his chin. "You got a few acres you can spare?"

"Acres? I got two houses I'm gonna build for you."

They blink. They stare. They look at each other before Daniel grips me harder.

"Bloody hell, are you serious? We can do it? We can make our homes here, too?"

"I was gonna surprise you." I grin. "Then I figured your wives would get ill as hornets if they don't get to design your homes, but yeah, I already got the land staked out."

"Speaking of wives." Redix trumpets, "Here they come!"

Come?

No.

They're racing. They're Formula 1 drivers in golf carts, cursing and squealing as they try to run each other off the sandy road.

"You bitch!" Eily laughs, swerving when Charlie tries muscling her off the path.

So, Eily, with Cade in her passenger seat, muscles back, aiming for Charlie's cart.

I swear, my wife has no fear. She's why I have a First Aid Kit that would impress an EMT.

But Charlie has training. Racing with Stacey in her passenger seat, she hits her brakes, slowing, and about to nudge the back left corner of Eily's cart when Cade shouts, "It's a pit maneuver! Break!"

Eily trusts Cade's training, too. They screech to a halt, avoiding Charlie's tactic, laughing as they flip her and Stacey off.

Damn, the laws of physics mean nothing to them.

Why be careful when you can scare the shit out of your husbands?

"If y'all fuck up my golf carts!" I shout, "I'll—"

Eily tilts her head, putting my way. "You'll what?"

Like I can ever be mad at her. "I'll buy you more carts with matching helmets."

She bounces closer. "I want a rainbow cart with a matching mohawk helmet."

I'm sure they exist. I'm sure I'll buy her one. And I'm sure if they don't ... *my cute wife will make one.*

She stomps the brake pedal, flips the key, and turns off the cart. So does Charlie. They jump out and march our way.

"Aw, shit," Redix mutters. "Who kissed the hot hornets' nest?"

Our women look so fiery with Stacey in tow, they don't even notice our mud pit, waiting for some wrestling fun. Visions of muddy bikinis and briefs fill my head, and yep, my banana stirs.

"So, we just got some intel on our villain." *Shit.* But it sounds like Cade's in Sergeant mode. "Stacey," she nudges her arm, "tell them what you told us."

"I already told you I don't know his name."

"But tell the guys what you told us about him. Like, the other part."

So, this is why the women disappeared this morning? They're getting to the bottom of our villainous threat.

Stacey shrugs. "I signed an NDA with him. My entire staff did. I'm not supposed to say anything."

"But this is about our safety." Charlie lifts her sunglasses. Damn, her cheeks glow after getting royally fucked last night. I lost count after five cocks. *I'm so proud of her.* "Just tell the guys so we're all up to speed because this is some freaky shit."

"Freaky shit?" I ask. "Good freaky or bad freaky?"

"Is there a difference?" Redix lifts his arm off me, quickly pulling Cade into a hug. It looks like she's in killer mode, so he jokes around, "Because any freaky is fun to me."

"Uh, yeah, there's a difference." Charlie's fists land on

her hips. "Good freaky is fucking us. Bad freaky is fucking *with* us."

"And?" Daniel cocks a brow. "What does this bloke want? He's been watching us fuck for days."

"That's just it," Charlie answers. "He hasn't been watching us. It wasn't him."

"What?"

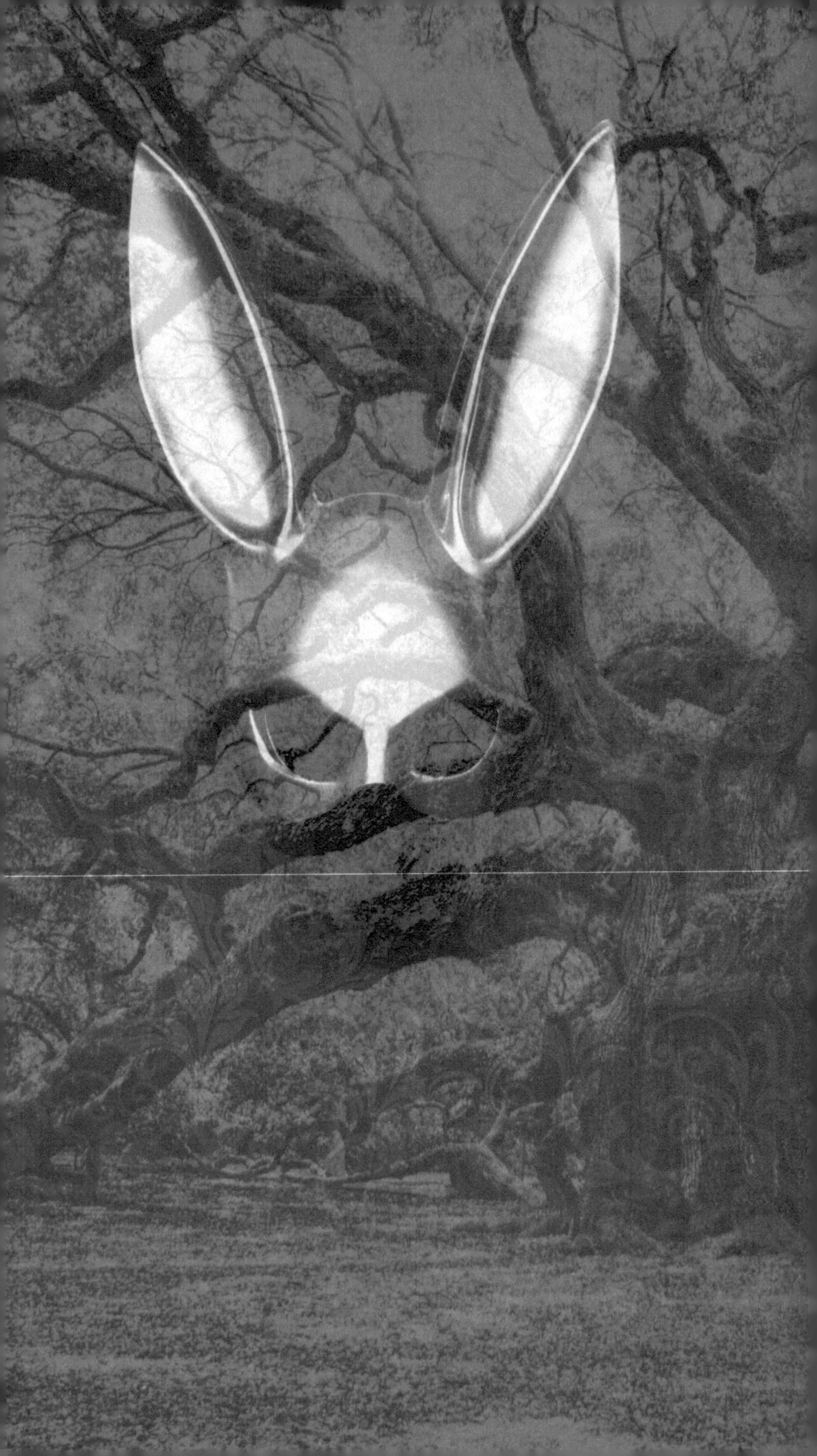

Silas

"He's a sweet savage."

Now, I'm getting pissed.

Who the fuck did Eily invite to our island? And I swear to god, if he betrays my wife's trust, I'll chain a cinder block to his ankle and send him swimming. It won't be the first time I've done it.

Ask Charlie.

"Okay." Stacey lifts her palms. "Don't freak out, but I don't think this man has been here. At least, not yet. He flies to New York the first half of every week. He's not back in Charleston until Thursdays."

"How do you know?"

I'm interrogating now. I'm not fucking around when it comes to my island, my partners, *my wife.*

Stacey rolls her eyes like it's painful to reveal this, but she's loyal to our group. "He's a lawyer, okay? Like, by day. He has a practice in Charleston and one in New York."

"So, if he's a lawyer, why don't you know his name? It doesn't make sense."

Redix is with me now. He's sounding pissed, too.

"Oh, I can tell you his pseudo name," Stacey answers. "It's Michael Cummings."

"Cummings?" I'm shocked. "Like from the law firm on Meeting Street? We've closed real estate deals with his firm. Hell, he handled the closing on this island. But, I never met him, only his partners."

Cade jumps in. "No one's met him. Or at least, only a few have. He's an enigma. Few know his face, but all know not to fuck with Michael Cummings."

"Can y'all just give me some points?" Eily laughs. "My villain is *Cummings*. I swear that pun just keeps on giving."

I brush past it.

Usually, Eily makes me laugh. She is punny.

But this?

I don't like it.

This is our island. This is our home. This is everyone I love, and I have a loaded Remington with an itchy muzzle and a pile of concrete blocks and chains if someone doesn't tell me what the fuck is going on.

"So, who is he then? And if he hasn't been here," I press, "then who the hell has?"

Stacey sighs, "I can't share his real identity. That's where the NDAs come in. He rents the room on the third floor of Delta's from me. He uses it for meetings."

"Meetings with who?"

I knew it. I knew something, more like *someone*, was behind that black door.

"I'm not allowed to say," Stacey answers. "But..." She shakes her head as if she's torn between helping us and betraying him. "I can tell you no one's getting hurt. Well, not *good* people. He's meeting with them. He's hiding another life. His lawyer gig is a cover."

"He's using a sex store as a cover?" Daniel grumbles. "A cover for *what*?"

Yep, even our gentlemanly Brit is fuming.

Sure, we love our women. We trust them. We support them. Hell, they're usually in charge because they look so goddamn sexy being right all the time.

While me?

I feel too damn protective over Eily, over the future we dream about, to risk it for some Halloween fun that may backfire.

"He's mafia." Cade pops off.

Like it's no big deal.

Like it's what's on the dinner menu.

Organized crime with Uzis.

Please pass the salt.

"Bullshit," Redix scoffs. "There's no mafia in Charleston. It's too fucking hot and humid for gangsters."

"Bless your heart." Charlie's amused. To the point of murder. "Call them mafia. Call them savages in seersucker suits. Whatever. But Michael Cummings is a front for organized crime."

Eily muses. "Then what's *disorganized* crime? Like messy criminals? They leave cookie crumbs at the crime scene?"

Okay. I gotta laugh at that. "Baby girl, get serious. You've invited a gangster to haunt us, and now, it ain't even him sneaking up on our sex."

"But don't you see?" Eily's eyes get big. "It *is* him. I found someone so organized that he's fooled us. And his fake last name is Cummings, so I insist on points for that."

Cade twists her lips. "It could be him." She's sold on the

possibility. "Cummings could've made an exception and not flown to New York. Maybe he gets off on scaring us."

"Hang on." My head is spinning. I went from organized mud wrestling to organized crime on my island. And it ain't even noon. "So you're saying that we know him? Well, his fake name and his law firm?" The women nod. "Then call him. Ask him if he's been here this week."

Flirty glances dart. Top teeth bite sexy lips. Four hot women scope each other, but no one will break their pact.

I swear. They're the sisterhood of the traveling wet panties.

They won't rat each other out.

So, I gotta play it.

Rarely, I do.

I save it for times like this. Times when being a man is necessary. Patriarchy has its privileges—lots of them.

"*Eiiilllyyy.*"

I level my stare at my wife, playing my HUSBAND card. My king card.

"Yes, Silas."

She bats her lashes, holding the WIFE card. It's the ace. It's my heart in her hand.

"Have you called Cummings?" She snorts. *That pun is her favorite.* "I'm serious. Tell me. Did you call him, and what did he say?"

After four skipping steps, she wraps her arms around my neck. Craning her petal lips for my kiss. Giving me that bewitching look that convinces me to buy dildos for her in every color. Or to eat spinach because it's good for my sperm.

I'd drink lava for her.

She knows.

But she'd never hurt me.

Now, drive me crazy? In the cutest damn way? Welcome to Eilyville. Yes, you'd want to live here, too.

"My sweet, sexy husband." She pecks my lips. More like I can't resist leaning down to kiss her even though I'm being played like a royal flush. "Have I told you today how much I love you?"

"*Eiillllyyy.*"

"How you have the biggest cock ever?"

"*Eillllyyy.*"

"How horses are jealous?"

"Do you want a spanking?"

She beams. "Yes, daddy."

I raise a brow.

"Fine," she sighs, "I have called Cummings," then giggles again.

Dammit, she loves that word.

"And?"

"And..." She kisses my neck, gently biting it, too. It makes me squeeze her tighter, feeling the raging storm of passion and protection she has stirred inside me ever since I met her. "And you're too sexy to get mad at me." She grinds on me, raising my dick like an Eilyville flag.

"I won't get mad if you tell me." Caressing her hair, I say sweetly, "Now, goddammit."

"And he didn't answer." She winces. "Not my text or call, and not Stacey's."

"He's gone radio silent," Cade adds.

But I don't break my stare, lost in my wife's jade eyes. I find my dreams here every time.

I really can't get mad at her.

Under all the spritely fun and naughty antics, Eily has an old soul. She's been through enough, and that's what I love most about her. Despite what she's survived, Eily chooses joy.

And she loves sharing it.

Lots of it.

All the goddamn time.

"So, it *could* be Cummings who's been here?" I nuzzle my forehead to hers. I know she did this for our friends, for our Halloween party. She just got carried away. "He can just be a good mobster, scaring us for fun?"

"Yep!" Eily blurts. "So, don't worry. I promise. He's a sweet savage."

"Or," Redix taunts, "it's not Cummings, and we really are haunted."

"Like Charlie was last night. A haint possessed her." Charlie whips her stare at Cade, who shrugs. "What? Was that a secret?"

Daniel's tone drops. "Charlie, what does she mean you were *possessed*?"

Whoops.

That took a hard right turn.

Is Daniel aroused or pissed? Tough call. His accent is so rich and seductive when he leaves voicemails ... people save them for solo pleasure.

"I'm sorry," Cade stresses, solely focused on Charlie. "I didn't know it was a secret."

"Charlie? Are you keeping a bloody secret? From *me*?"

Yep. Daniel's pissed.

Nothing's lost in translation now.

"It's not a secret," Charlie sighs. "We were just having girl talk."

"Yeah, we had Lip Love in the hot tub," Eily adds. "We do it all the time. We talk about your dicks and how much we love them." We're silent. "I mean, we don't *use* you for your dicks. We really love you too. All you guys." She squirms. "Didn't you know?"

I did.

I overhear Eily on the phone all the time. And I gotta admit ... hearing how I have a "donkey dick" makes my day.

But Daniel gives that wolf look again, and it's legit. He's mad. It masks his pain, fearing Charlie is keeping secrets from him. Which she never would. I know her. She'd kill for him. Again.

"It was just us gossiping." Cade jumps to Charlie's rescue. "We always debrief after a good dicking down."

"Yeah," Eily rescues Charlie, too. "It's like a five-star review of our fucks. Oh, we should start doing that! We should start journals. Oh, and scrapbooks, too. I can do some character drawings of us and..."

She trails off because Daniel locks his glare on Charlie.

"Which was it?" he fumes. "Was it girl talk, or were you possessed? Because I've never seen you like that. Is that not what you wanted from the men last night?"

Ah, that's where this is coming from.

Daniel loves Charlie so damn much. It takes the greatest trust for a man to share his wife like that. To fulfill her fantasy. To give her what she wants, *if* it's what she wants.

Because Daniel will kill a man who touches Charlie otherwise. Painfully. Like ripping limbs off, one at a time, before slowly spooning out his heart.

That's why he's mad. He feels responsible for her. He protects her.

But wait.

Does that mean he believes in haints, too?

Charlie wraps her arms around his waist, not caring

he's covered in mud. "I wanted everything last night," she gently assures him, "and thank you for giving it to me."

He accepts her tender kiss and then another, cupping her cheek, the one with a scar.

"And maybe it was so incredible, I felt possessed." She caresses his muddy pecs. "That's what I told them. That I felt spirits. That I had visions. That I saw and felt you all, but when I closed my eyes, I saw and felt people that weren't here, too. Or more like … people who were here long ago. And one man in particular. Every time I came, I saw his face so clearly before he pulled his horned gold mask on."

Eerily, cold slices up my spine, making my ears suddenly ring. My hair, tugged into a knot, tingles over my scalp.

My pulse skyrocketing…

All the nights I've spent on my boat, searching over the dark water here. All the evenings I've wandered through the marshy forest. All the moments I felt someone lurking. Calling. Making my head turn. Looking over my shoulder into the shadows, the palms rustling, the moss swaying.

But no one stood there.

I was sure.

Something lurked there.

That's a haint.

It's not a person. It's not a ghost. It's a spirit, a soul craving to live again. But it can't, so it lives through you.

If you let it in.

I joke with Charlie, "So, it *is* your horny ancestor, Lois Ravenel, haunting us?"

It's either that, or I let this scare the shit out of us.

Out of me.

On this island, I've felt it, too—a possession, a power,

an urge to do something, and it's not my will making me do it.

Months ago, when I was clearing the land for our tents, I found something hidden at the base of the live oak. It's the largest tree on my island and must be at least four hundred years old.

And when I say *found*.

I mean ... it found me.

It made me dig, brushing away dirt until it gleamed back at me.

A gold rabbit.

An antique ceramic figurine as big as my palm was smudged with dirt, but its flaking gold leaf paint still caught the light peeking through the oak branches above.

It wasn't a cute bunny for Easter. It wasn't an old child's toy or a treasured family heirloom.

No, it looked...

I don't know how to describe it except ... occultist. Ritualistic. It was half sinister rabbit, half erect man.

The timing unnerved me.

It found me the day, just hours after Eily and I started to try to get pregnant. That morning was our first time without birth control when she was ovulating.

I didn't know if it was a good sign or a bad omen, so I looked it up online.

Long before Easter bunnies and stuffed animals, pagans used rabbits as fertility signs. Rabbits and eggs—go figure. It's like modern religion turned them into harmless, candy-sweet symbols, masking their hidden sexual meaning.

So I never told Eily.

She was too excited that day. She hoped we'd get pregnant right away, and I didn't want to jinx it.

The next day, I buried the rabbit where I found it, returning it to its hallowed grave. Choosing joy, as Eily taught me, I hoped it would be a good omen.

It's still there, hidden, beckoning at the base of the ancient oak on the edge of camp. I swear I can sense it. I swear it has a voice.

"Maybe you're right," Charlie answers me. "Maybe I was possessed by my pagan ancestor. I can't explain it, but I sure felt something. *Someone.*"

Eily chuckles. "Yeah, you felt dicks galore, and it was heavenly."

"So you don't believe in haints?"

Redix grins at Eily. He loves teasing her.

"Oh, I do." Eily lifts her chin. "But compared to living hot and hung humans, ghosts aren't sexy. Haints aren't hot."

"Wanna bet?" Charlie cocks a grin. "Because that haint I saw last night when I closed my eyes was hot."

Eily wrinkles her nose. "If that's true, isn't that like fucking your family?"

"More like your hot uncle, twenty times removed." Stacey chimes in, gently slapping Charlie's ass. "The French do like to keep it in the family."

Charlie just smirks.

She won't deny it. She won't admit it.

But I've had enough.

Is some morally righteous mobster scaring us? Maybe. Is some salacious spirit spooking our sex? I don't hate the idea as long as it doesn't ruin the week. As long as Eily has fun.

I found that gold rabbit ten months ago, and I'll believe in anything to get Eily pregnant.

For now?

I just want her to smile.

"Alright, y'all. Shut up about good mafia and ghostly monsters." All look at me. I squeeze the nozzle, wetting T-shirts and screaming faces. "Time to mud wrestle."

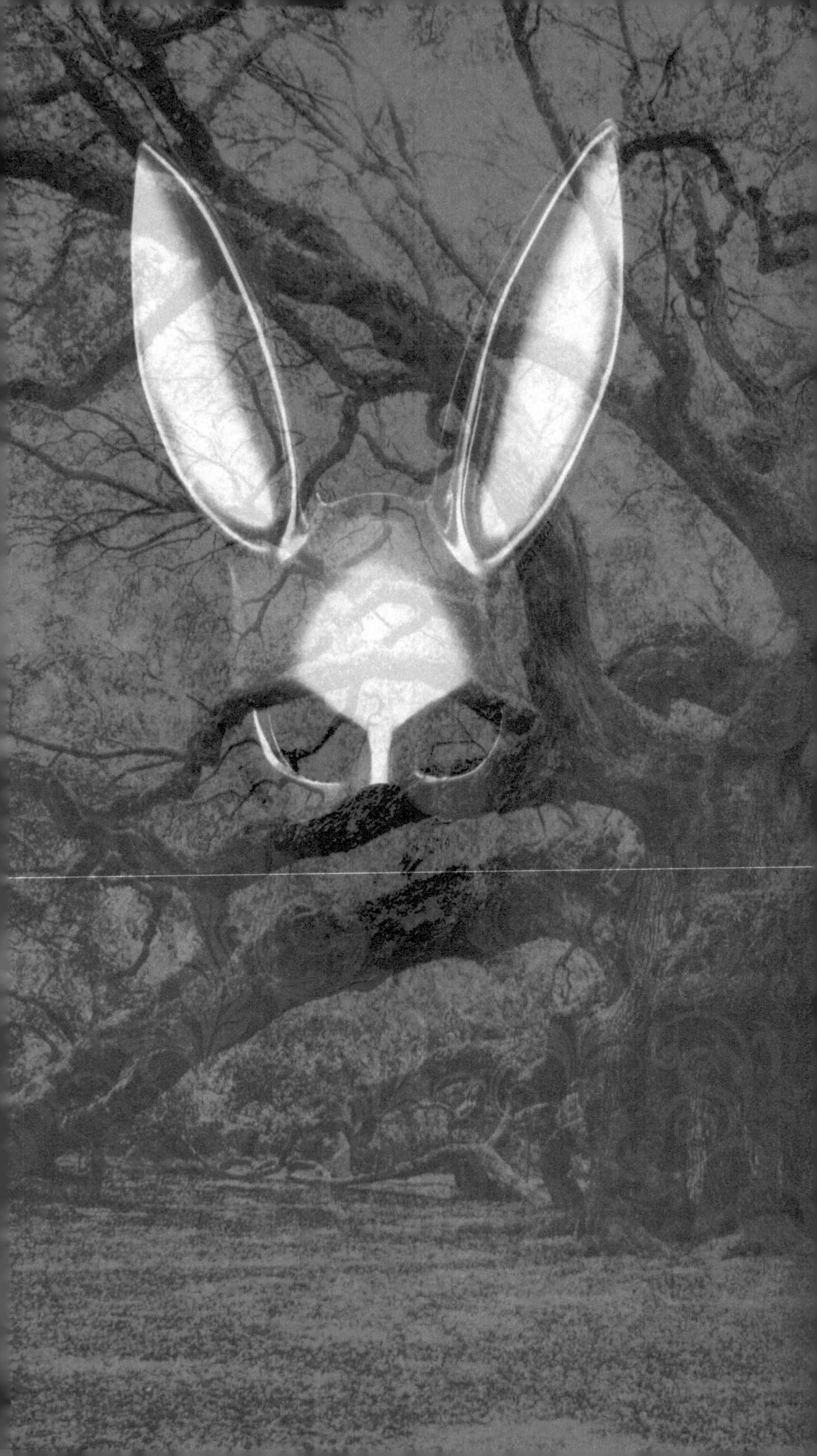

Cade

CHAPTER FIFTEEN

CADE

"Your tent or mine?"

"Punch his balls!"

"Give her a titty twister!"

"Are assholes off limits?"

"Do. Not. Put. Mud in assholes!"

"And don't punch balls! We need them tonight."

"We need titties, too!"

The crowd's shouts around the mud pit, coaching me on how to beat Zar Rollins in a wrestling match, are comical.

I'm choking on sludge and laughter.

I have a black belt and a great set of muddy tits. Zar's muscular, six-foot-three frame and enchanting brown eyes don't stand a chance.

Especially when we wrestle, and I feel how it makes him hard, how he's loving my dirty ass whooping.

We square off, swaying in a fighting stance from scalp to toe, covered in caramel slime.

I smirk, swiping mud off my lips. "You give?"

"Me? *Give?*" Zar's bright teeth contrast with the mud dripping from his dark, trimmed beard. "Darlin," he drawls. "I'm gonna make you and those gorgeous tits give an ass whoopin' all day."

Scarlett laughs from the edge of the pit. "Watch out. He gets off on sparring with women."

"Good," Redix boasts. "Because my wife gets off on kicking men's asses."

"Does that include yours?"

Someone asks Redix.

I don't know who.

My focus is trained on Zar. I'm waiting for one of his hulking shoulders to drop, revealing how he'll lunge for me again.

Redix taunts back with his whiskey voice, "Nah. I love my wife doing other things to my ass."

With a muddy smirk, Zar huffs with his eyes on me, "Lucky man."

Sexual chemistry charges the molecules around us. Seventeen people are gathered, half-clothed, half-topless, some covered in mud, and all having fun.

It's women versus men in mud wrestling, and Scarlett went first. She took on Ford, then Luke. They have military training but she's a titled MMA fighter. And when she took her bikini off?

Yeah, the women are playing dirty.

She won, and I won the next round for us. Luca took my first beating. I think he loved being choked between my legs. The victory was too easy.

"It isn't fair." I hear Blair sigh. "Half of the women are

trained killers, and the other half are like pro-seducers. If we don't win with chokeholds, we'll win with cleavage."

Zar's left shoulder drops.

I catch it.

When he leads with his right, stepping to grab me, I kick, sweeping his right foot. He laughs, splashing down into the gloopy mess as I fall over him. He doesn't even fight me. He lets me straddle him, grabbing his wrists and pinning them over his head, his biceps popping. And if he didn't let me, I could bend his fingers back, making sure of it.

"Sergeant Bryant," he smiles up at me, "you sure are arresting. You got me feeling criminal enough to take you on," he winks, "or *in*."

Nick calls out. "Leave room for me."

"Always, baby," he answers.

Under my soaked bikini bottom, I feel Zar's length stir. Lust sparks in his eyes. It reflects mine.

This week, Zar is open to women. He'll always sub for Luca. He'll always sub with Scarlett. Usually, she's the only woman he serves for Luca, while Nick is the only man he's with.

But Luca wants this. It's like he's giving himself and his subs a reward. His watchful eye caught our attraction days back, and their foursome—Luca, Scarlett, Zar, and Nick— wants something new this week.

I understand.

Our sixsome wants it, too.

And there's something about Zar: the sexy, taunting scoundrel. He's new to me and a worthy opponent. Smart. Strong. Sexy. And hard...

I tease, squeezing his wrists, "Have you been a bad boy, Mr. Rollins?"

"Does a rooster crow?"

"Can you handle me?"

"I'm ripping my britches for ya. Rumor is you pack a helluva strap-on."

"Damn, y'all." Silas protests, "Can we not get through four rounds of mud wrestling without fucking?"

"Ain't that the point of mud wrestling?" Zar argues, rocking his hips under me. It makes me grin—*dirty, hot bastard*. "I mean ... look at her," he says. "All sexy, covered in muck, and beating my ass. Darlin," his grin is pure sin, "we can be like pigs, fucking in the mud."

"No one is fucking in mud," Blair, our resident sexpert, proclaims. "That's an infection waiting to pounce. Shower first."

"Ah, that's as exciting as a mashed potato sandwich," Zar jokes with his stare glued to my ample cleavage swaying above him.

Clearly, he wants it dirty. Why I even wore a bikini, I don't know. It's ruined, and it's coming off any minute.

"That's hygiene," Blair answers. "And I have a big trick night planned, so please don't ruin tonight with yeast infections."

Ah, ha. So, it's Blair's turn tonight. I've been dying for that intel.

"Yeah," Eily chimes in. "We already roll the dice every time we let Redix play with whipped cream."

"Fun size," Redix answers her. "With the sweet fun we have with desserts, a little infection is worth it."

"Speak for yourself," Charlie laughs. "It ain't your vag burning."

"Dicks burn, too," Daniel adds.

"Jeez, y'all," I pant, squeezing Zar between my thighs.

Damn, I'm feeling frisky. "Can we skip past the Dos and Don'ts of orgies and get to the orgy part?"

"Agreed."

A rich accent breaks the group.

It's Luca.

I'd know his dominance anywhere.

"Shower," Luca insists, "and then we fuck."

Trapped between my legs, Zar cocks a smirk, relishing Luca's permission. It's like he's been told he can play, and I'm his new toy.

"We're pacing ourselves." I glance up. Beau answers, "We're helping Blair set up for tonight."

Colton nods, agreeing with him.

"Same," Daniel adds. "We'll wait and help them set up."

Oh, I catch it. The looks, all hot and itchy, between Daniel, Beau, and Colton. The way Blair chews her lip at them. The way Charlie does, too.

Yeah, that's on.

"We'll wait, too."

That's Ford, with one arm draped over Stacey, the other over Luke. Mateo stands, wrapped around Luke, too. They've missed him. They're family. They need their time together.

I get it.

Every day, I need Redix. And sometimes, I need my partners, too. Just the six of us. Our laughs in bed, our bodies cuddled on a sofa, our dance parties in the kitchen while we cook.

Damn, when six people hug at the end of a shitty day, it feels like you can survive anything.

Like, I love our birthday tradition. The six of us throw a party with no sex allowed. Instead, we sit by a fire pit, on a dock, or by a pool; it depends on whose birthday and the season. But the tradition is we tell that person for their birthday ten reasons we love them. It's the only gift we exchange because no one has been promised the next birthday.

Okay, honestly.

Do we break the no-sex rule?

I mean … who wouldn't? Sometimes we get so loaded with emotions we have to. But at least we wait. We wait until love fills our hearts, too.

But this week? Since I didn't play last year?

I want this.

I want my husband. I want this man. I want his woman and her men, too. If anyone else wants to join us?

Please, pile on.

Staring up at me, a smile ghosts Zar's full lips, his muscles tensing, eyes gleaming. *Oh shit, he's going for it*, and I let him.

Like a gator, he rolls lightning-fast in the mud. He takes control, quickly flipping me on my back, his hands pinning *my* wrists now. The sudden movement makes my bikini top surrender. My breasts pop out. They're free.

Zar stares at them, his gaze rimming my nipples, his eyelids dropping with lust. Rivulets of mud stream over his pecs, clinging to his dusting of chest hair, finding the path down his deep happy trail, wandering over his flexing abs.

He's cut and strong, taunting me, "Seems I've been commanded to shower and then serve you, ma'am."

He's raging hard.

Barely, he thrusts into me and...

There it is again. The lust. The desire. The primal urge this island shoots through my veins. With Zar on top, I want him to serve me right here, in the mud, like animals, and everyone can watch.

But...

Nothing ruins a week like vaginitis.

"Your tent or mine?" I proposition.

"Mine," Luca commands.

Zar rises, holding my hands. Even covered in mud, he's a gentleman, helping me stand. Then he smacks my muddy ass, his smirk negating all manners.

I love it.

We leave Silas and Eily behind. They want to slosh in the mud pit with Stacey and her husbands.

Daniel and Charlie disappear into the Trick Tent, happy to help Blair, Beau, and Colton set up for tonight.

And see how else they can "help" them.

Redix and I shower without a word, only hungry kisses. We know what we want. Redix is hard for it. I'm wet for it.

There's always been a connection between Redix and Luca. They're best friends. They don't cross some lines.

But others?

They're attracted to one another and curious, relishing the other's pleasure. Redix devours the sight of Luca and most crave the sight of my husband.

Holding my hand, he leads me across the clearing, over the sandy path, kicking through fallen oak leaves. We're wrapped in plush robes with flip-flopped feet, hearing our partners and friends, their laughter echoing across the early afternoon.

Part of me wants to wait for tonight.

Part of me can't wait for this.

Rarely do I want new partners. I'm so in love with my husband and the ones we have now.

But sometimes, something new for a day only adds to the beauty of what you'll cherish for a lifetime. When I spot how Luca has kept their tent open so the others can watch us, how we won't hide what we're about to share, desire pools in my core.

This feels right.

This is why we're here.

This is nothing but lust and love.

We trod up the stairs to Luca's tent and step inside. Yes, it's Scarlett's, Zar's, and Nick's tent, too. But it's their arrangement. It's their consent. They give Luca the power to be their Dom, and he uses it with great care.

And a glorious whip.

"Good afternoon," Luca greets us, wearing only black silk pajama pants.

The man is a bronze mountain of muscles, rivaling my husband, and my gaze drops to his silk-draped bulge … then it falls on Zar and Scarlett kneeling before him.

Naked and freshly showered, their wet heads are bowed.

Nick reclines nude on their bed, propped on pillows. His athletic form is a sight to admire. He likes watching, too. It's obvious with how his length lies, half hard, craving a show.

Redix unties his robe, his gaze intense, telling Luca, "Dude, you know we trust you, but I won't ever be into pain. I've had enough of it and can't watch Cade take it, either. I'll kill anyone who hurts her."

Luca nods.

He loves Redix.

Like me, he knows how Redix got his scars. It makes me reach for my husband's hand, squeezing it, thankful we've come so far together.

And we didn't do it alone.

The ones responsible for our second chance at love? They're here.

"Then tell us, please," Luca answers, caressing Scarlett's

flaming strands and Zar's dark waves, "how we may serve you. That's what we can share today."

Aw, he's so sweet. This must be daytime Dom Luca. Like he's almost tender while the sun is shining, but by night, he'll whip your ass into coming for him.

Gently, Redix tugs me to him, my back pressed against his chest. Opening my robe for them, he exposes me, demanding, "Serve my beautiful wife today. She deserves it."

Hell, yes, I do.

Possessively, he brushes his hands over my shoulders, sliding my robe off and letting it pool by my feet. Then he cups my breasts, palming them, twirling his fingers over my nipples.

I moan at his touch, falling back against his tall, granite chest. My life belongs to Redix, so I let him share my body like this. I let his hand glide down between my legs, his fingers splaying my slick lips apart, my clit exposed for Luca's stare. For Luca to lick his lips.

"My wife wants your man." Redix knows how to taunt Luca and how to thrill me, too. "And so do I. If your man wants me to let him fuck my wife, he needs to serve me first."

Oh, fuck.

My bared clit sparks, lust flooding my sex.

Redix isn't usually like this. Not with Luca, I mean. With me, Redix is so dirty; he's sweet. He's rough, and I love it. But he's behaved himself around our friends.

Until now.

I think the island is talking to him, too.

He's acting even more alpha than usual.

Luca reaches, lifting Zar's chin. "Does my stud want this? Do you want to earn his wife?"

Like Luca, Zar licks his lips. "Yes, my owner."

Luca looks at Nick. He'll never disrespect him as Zar's future husband. "Can your man serve us?"

"Please," Nick smirks, his cock rock hard. Lazily, his hand strokes it. "I've always wanted Redix Dean, too."

Yep. That's the cost of fame, and I don't mind. Who doesn't want my husband? He earned his reputation as Hollywood's bad boy. But now?

He's *my* bad boy.

I love him offering me like this.

"Take him," Luca offers Zar to Redix. "Let him earn your beautiful wife while I fuck mine."

A soft gasp escapes Scarlett's lips.

She's into this, too.

By the foot of their massive bed, over the plush rugs so wisely placed in each tent, I stand nude. Not moving. Only watching as Redix tosses his robe aside. His shredded body, impressive. His curving cock, mouth-watering.

Luca steps aside, commanding the space in front of Scarlett. He lets Redix take his place beside him, standing before Zar.

"Whatever my stud does for you," Luca gazes at Redix's erection, his eyes burning with lust, "my dirty wife will do for me."

Scarlett licks her lips. Luca's degradation is her drug.

Redix stares at Zar, kneeling before him. Hooking his finger under Zar's bearded chin, even with Luca's permission, even with Zar's consent, Redix will never take. He fists his shaft, teasing it across Zar's parting lips. "Do you want me? Do you want to earn my wife?"

"Yes, sir," Zar answers. "Make me serve you. Make me earn her."

His words are compliant, his eyes willful and aroused. So is his cock. It surges hard.

"Do you think she's beautiful?"

"Yes, sir."

"I agree." Redix fists Zar's waves. "Do you want to fuck her?"

"Yes, sir."

"If I let you have her sweet pussy, how will you earn her?"

"However you desire, sir."

Redix flares his nostrils, pausing, relishing this. "Then suck my cock if you want to fuck my wife."

Eagerly, Zar does. With no hesitation, he grabs Redix's base, his whiskered lips plunging down his curving length. The sight makes me so wet, my sex starts pulsing. It's obvious Zar's good at this, and Redix throws his chin up, groaning in appreciation.

Luca admires their display before fisting Scarlett's auburn strands. "My beautiful whore," he taunts her. Her eyelids drop; *she loves it.* She fingers herself while Luca tugs his pants down, his shaft heavy and hard. "Do you want his wife, too?"

"Yes, sir." She flicks her clit for him.

"Then show them. Show them what a sweet whore you are for me."

Scarlett moans. She matches Zar. Fisting Luca's shaft, her tongue shamelessly swirls over his swollen crown.

Standing side by side, Redix's biceps brush Luca's. Their thighs touch, too. It's erotic. Their towering dual display. Their cocks surging hard together. Zar serving Redix. Scarlett serving Luca. Me, standing here. Waiting to be used. To be shared.

And Nick's entranced. His eyes are glued to Redix's

curving shaft. To his man taking what he can of Redix in his mouth, in his gagging throat.

"Oh, fuck yes." Redix gazes down at Zar, then over at Luca's cock, at Scarlett, taking what she can of it, tears leaking from her eyes, spit drooling from her lips.

"Give it to him hard," Luca growls, telling Redix. "He's a skull pussy. He likes gagging on cock. Give it to him."

Zar groans. Drips leak from his swollen tip, his cock rigid and ready. My thighs get weak watching it.

With Luca's permission, Redix smirks. Cupping Zar's head, he thrusts into his mouth, unrelenting, unleashing.

"Oh, fuck yes, he loves it," Redix growls. "Show me. Suck me. Swallow every fucking drop of my cum if you want to fuck my hot wife."

Nick grunts, pumping faster as moans escape my lips. And Zar's. And Scarlett's.

Luca commands Scarlett, taunting her, too, "You're going to suck her clit like a good little whore while my stud fucks her pussy, aren't you? Aren't you my sweet whore, wanting my cock in your ass while you do it?"

Holy fuck, they're so dirty, they're hot.

Scarlett rolls her eyes, moaning.

Damn, she's the perfect match for Luca. With her titles and training, she could inflict damage if she wanted to. She wouldn't hesitate with any other man. But not with Luca. She loves him. She belongs with him. She craves serving him.

And Luca worships her. He'll destroy for her. He'll torture, maim, and relish pain for Scarlett.

"Cade," Redix growls for me.

In two steps, I'm by his side. I'm kissing him, his tongue lashing mine while he caresses my breast, pinching my nipple and moaning into our mouths. Another man greedily sucks his cock, and Redix grunts, his teeth gently biting my lip as he comes in Zar's throat. I know my husband's sound; his desire is woven into mine.

He finishes over Zar's tongue, then tugs his hair, staring down at him.

"Show me," he demands. "Show me how you loved earning my wife."

Zar smirks before parting his lips. He swallowed. He's hard. He loved it.

Gently, Redix guides me down on the rug. "Get on all fours for him. The man's earned it. He's earned that sweet pussy to fuck."

Luca tugs Scarlett's hair. "Serve her, too."

It's a dance of bodies. Of Scarlett lying on the rug, facing up before I straddle her face. I stare at Luca while he kneels between Scarlett's legs, and I feel Zar kneeling behind me while Luca calls, "Nick."

Rising from the bed, Nick joins us. Carrying a bottle of lube—it's so sexy—Nick's done this before. You can tell. He hands the lube to Luca like it's their ritual.

But I'm already soaked. I don't need lube.

Not when I feel Zar nudging his fat tip into my entrance, teasing it there, rubbing that tingling, tender opening spot. Not when I relish Scarlett's tongue hungrily circling my swollen clit.

She's licking, panting into my sex while Luca preps her ass, rubbing her clit with his thumb.

I'm about to get lusciously fucked, watching Luca hug Scarlett's legs to his chest. His slow plunge into her ass makes her moan ravenously into my pussy, taking Zar.

Zar's relishing it, making me groan at his first long, slow plunge inside my aching walls. His rhythm is perfect, matching Scarlett's tempo, her tongue slowly laving over my excited clit, then down to where we're joined, teasing Zar's shaft before she's back, worshiping my screaming nub.

It's care. It's carnal. It's crude and cosmic, as if our bodies were divined to do this.

It's like once you're brave enough to break earthly rules, you'll find the heaven you've been searching for.

I moan. I rise on my knees, straddling Scarlett, taking Zar, and palming my breasts for Luca to relish while he fucks his wife's ass.

I can hear Luca's stud, Zar, sucking Nick off, and I can watch my husband, my beautiful husband, kneel beside us.

Redix grabs my neck, gently squeezing, gazing down at my body being lavished.

"Fuck," he sighs. "Cade, you're so beautiful. So beautiful when you're a slut like this. Take it, baby. Take what you deserve."

Our tangle of bodies is beautiful. Our sex is loud and primal. The tent is open, and I glance at others watching. Admiring. And when I feel my husband lower his mouth, latching his lips around my nipple, his suck so brutal and breathtaking...

I cry out.

I close my eyes.

I let it claim me.

This carnal urge. This wanton desire. This wild island. This vision of nude, moaning, intertwined bodies doing the same as us. This man in a black and gold mask, sitting on a chair, watching, lording over our sex.

He lures us even deeper, seducing us to fuck for him, possessing us to come for him. For his pleasure. For his ritual. *For his island.*

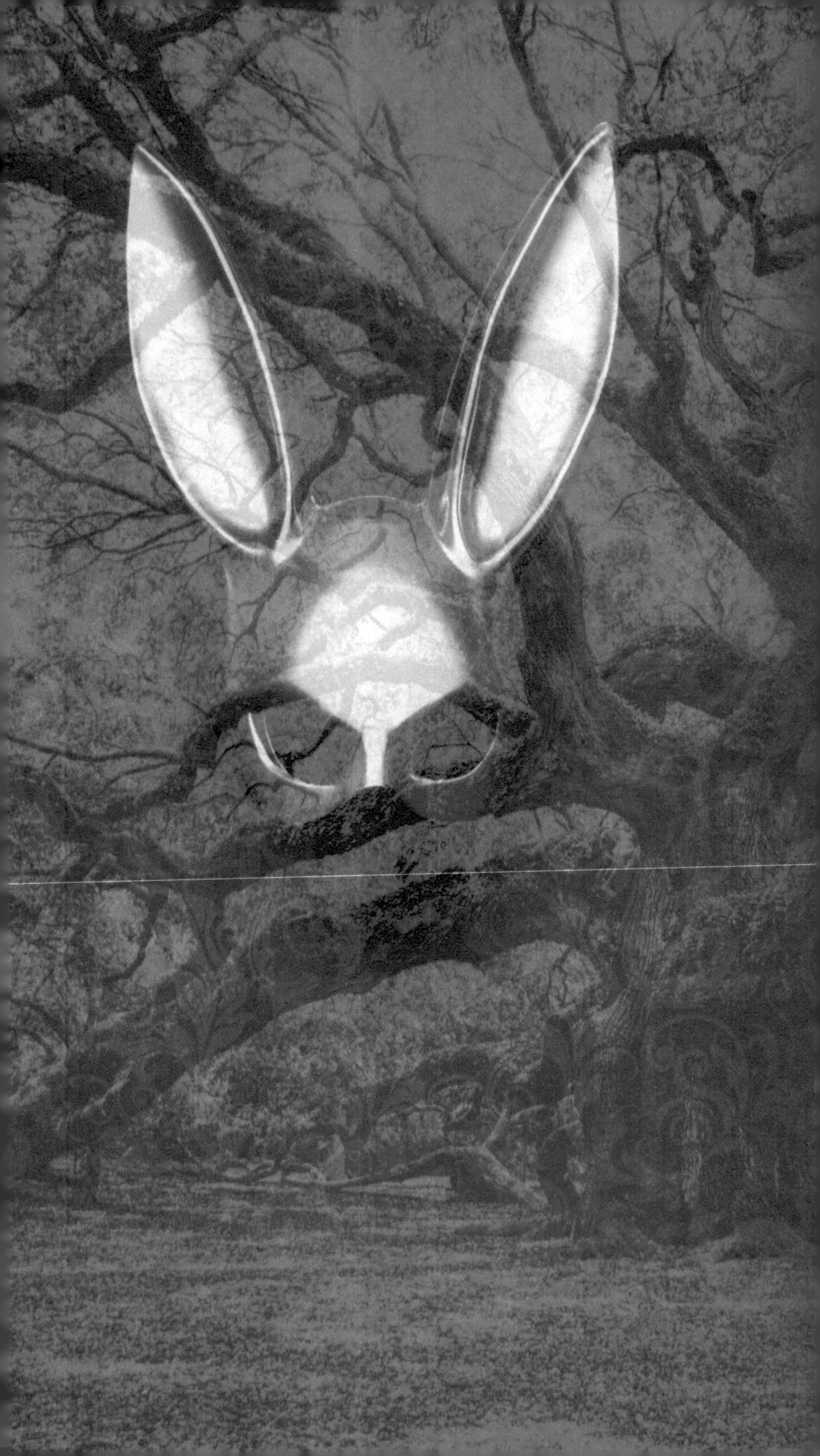

CHAPTER SIXTEEN

DANIEL

> "Get your weenus off me."

An elbow nudges mine, jolting me awake.

"Get your weenus off me."

"My *what*?" My eyes snap open. Dusk takes the afternoon light outside as I turn my head on the pillow.

"Your weenus." Redix lies beside me. He's on his back, grinning, his knee nudging mine, too, but the cheeky fucker won't open his eyes.

The six of us reunited for an afternoon nap before the big night. We've had five minutes of silence, of attempted sleep, and now this.

"What in the bloody hell is my weenus?"

He doesn't answer.

Now I'm intrigued.

"Do you mean *penis*?"

"No. You can rub that on me all day. But not your weenus."

I glance down.

I'm naked. So is he. We all are. And yes, I'm half-hard, but he's guilty, too. That's the constant state of our cocks when we're in bed together and when my nude wife is by my side, the white bed sheet twisting over our feet. It's the perfect temperature with the cool air and our warm bodies. No covers needed.

It's quite a sensual sight, actually—our six nude bodies in a cozy, tangled row.

"My weenus?" So, I'm confused. "Is that some Yank slang for my cock since I'm not circumcised?"

Redix chuckles. "Hell, no. It's hot, you're uncut. It's natural. And it makes your tip so damn sensitive."

"I'm jealous," Silas mumbles from his edge of the bed. "I wish my dick was that sensitive."

"Your dick is perfect," Eily, wrapped in Silas's arms, assures him. "So is yours, Daniel. All dicks are perfect. Whether they look like resting weiners wearing flesh helmets or tube socks hiding a big snake."

"Well, then..." I stare down at it. Under my scrutiny, it salutes like a good soldier. "What's wrong with my weenus?"

"Oh my god." Cade, on the other side of Redix, sighs, "Nothing is wrong with your penis, Daniel. It's natural and super thick, and thank god, you know how to use it. We all love it. He's just giving you shit. A *weenus* is the skin over your elbow. You know, that saggy, loose part when you stiffen your arm."

"Ah, then." I elbow Redix, who lazily laughs. "Take my stiff weenus in your ribs again, you bloody bastard."

Silas mutters, "Speaking of cheeks and stiff arms."

"You had your chance." Redix yawns. "You should've played with us in Luca's tent."

"By the sound and sight of it," I say, "no one was play-ing. That was serious fucking."

Cade chuckles. "Seriously."

Eily giggles, whispering to Cade, "How was Zar?"

"Oh my god," Cade starts to answer her. "It was so good; I felt possessed. He does this thing with his tip and—"

"Y'all, hush." Redix sounds cheesed off. "Come on. We need a nap before tonight."

We agree. We fall silent. Charlie twitches, falling asleep next to my chest. I wrap my arm tighter around her and close my eyes, but Silas mumbles, "I got a boner."

I chuckle. I can't help it.

Redix mumbles, "You'll have to wait till tonight."

"Yeah, save your love liquor for me."

"Climb on, baby girl," Silas answers Eily, "and I'll give you a big shot right now."

"No fucking, y'all." Redix barks, "Sleep."

He can be the kindest man. He'll give his life for anyone. But not his sleep. I get it. He has two little ones at home. Lots of sleep or sex? Either feels like a vacation to a new parent. And if you get both?

Well, that's fucking nirvana.

With a sigh, I close my eyes again.

Sleep is about to claim me, then...

"Speaking of love liquor." Redix elbows me. "Did you give Beau a shot of yours today?"

"I thought you needed a kip."

"A what?"

"A nap."

"I'm trying," he says. "But Cyclops over there with his love butter has me thinking about yours and wondering if you finally gave Beau a taste."

Eily sighs, "God, y'all. Could you imagine if cum tasted like butter? I'd be toast every day."

Silas laughs. Cade and Charlie do, too, but I'm curious.

No ... I'm worried.

Something in his tone.

I turn to Redix, giving him my weenus in the ribs again. "Mate, are you jealous?"

Redix opens his eyes, turning to me.

I know him. I love him. I'd never hurt him. Charlie's my world. My partners are my priority.

I search his ocean eyes for the truth like I've learned to do so well, in character or real life.

I never knew I could love this many, this much. But when you do. When you choose to devote yourself to your wife and kids. To dedicate your life to your partners, too. To do everything in your power for your shared happiness. You fight for it. You sacrifice for it.

Softly, he answers, "Nah, I'm not jealous."

"Are you sure?" I ask. "We haven't done anything yet. And if you're not okay with me being with Beau and Colton tonight, then—"

"Oh, he's more than okay with it," Silas chimes in. "We both are. But he's lying. He is jealous—jealous that Beau and Colton want you and not us, too."

"Is that it?" I ask Redix. "Are you sure? I mean ... I want them, but I don't *need* them. Not like I need you."

"I'm fine."

I stare at Redix. At his dark hair, licked by sunshine, spilling over his pillow. At his granite, scruffy jaw. Every angle on his perfect face is chiseled; it's hard, but not his tender eyes.

"I mean it. Cyclops is right. I'm not jealous of you being with them. I'm jealous we're not joining you."

"Then I won't do it."

"Do it," he says. "I want you to. I mean, I was with Zar today, and so was Cade. It's only fair."

"That's not how we work." I search for his hand, resting on the bed beside mine. "Love isn't about what's fair. It's about what we feel. Some partners make us jealous, and some don't. We have to honour that and be honest about it."

"I'd be jealous of Charlie with Scarlett." Cade pops her head up, resting it on Redix's chest so she can tell me, "Don't ask me why. It's not rational. I just know I would be. I think it's hot when she's with Blair or Stacey. But not Scarlett."

"I don't want Scarlett," Charlie mutters beside me. "No offense. She's fucking gorgeous, but we're not attracted to each other like that. I love her like a friend, not a partner."

"But what if you change? What if you want her one day?" Cade asks.

Charlie shifts to mirror Cade. She rests her head on my chest, answering her, "I'd never hurt you. I'd never make you jealous. I love us. No orgasm is worth messing us up."

"I'd get jealous of Luca fucking any of us." Eily sits up, adding to our chat, her hand lingering over Silas's abs. "So please, don't."

Redix answers, "Fun size, you don't have to worry. Luca only fucks his wife and Zar. Everyone else, he dominates with pleasure, not his prick."

"Yeah," she moves, rising to straddle Silas so she can cast her stare over the five of us. "But that's what I mean. We all have our primaries, then our partners. But sometimes we open up. Like what Stacey and her husbands did with Charlie, and that was so hot. Or like what y'all did with Zar today.

"But can't you just sense which lines we shouldn't cross? Like Luca?" She tells Redix, "You guys are so close. You have this sensual bond, but it's not sexual. It would mess things up if you cross it."

"I agree." Redix gets serious. "I can't lose Luca as a friend. I know he has complicated feelings about who he's with, and I know why. And I love him. I'd never risk regrets between us."

"So," I ask him, "would you regret me being with Beau and Colton? Be honest. I'll never risk us either. Remember, we're raising our families together. We're going to live here together."

"What?" Eily blurts. She looks at Silas. Then back at us. Then back at him. "Is this a trick or treat?"

"Y'all," Silas drawls, flopping his arm over his eyes. "That was supposed to be a surprise."

"Bloody hell," I wince, "tell a mate then. Sorry."

"Wait." Charlie perks up like Eily.

Matching her on Silas, she crawls on top of me, her palms grabbing my pecs, her stare not believing me, either.

"You want to move here with the kids?" she asks. "You're finally willing to do it? For the whole world to find out about us? Because they will. You and Redix have millions of obsessed fans. They'll find out."

"Y'all, it's kinda perfect," Cade adds, climbing on top of Redix.

It's like we're stallions, and our women are ready to ride us, Paul Revere style, telling the world the news about our polycule.

The six are coming! The six are coming!

"The timing is smart." Cade tells Redix, "You and Daniel can wrap your show this season. Then, you won't have to worry about pissing off the studio or risking the press hounding the cast and crew about us. Production will wrap, then we'll release a statement and weather the storm. Before that, we can secure the island. We can be ready for them."

Charlie nods. She's already imagining how she'd lock down Indigo Island like a fort.

Our children, our families would be safe here.

"Please don't be teasing me." Eily reaches for Cade's hand, her other resting on Silas's heart. "I know I joke around, but not about this. Not about *us*. Are we serious? Will we really do this? All six of us and your kids on this island? Like we'll grow old together? Because I'm already buying more rocking chairs in my mind."

Silas reaches up, caressing her cheek. "Their kids and *ours, too*. You gotta believe, baby girl. Don't give up on us."

"But," she stalls, blinking back sudden tears, "it hasn't happened yet, and we've been trying for months. Something must be wrong with me. Maybe I'm too small or something."

"You're not too anything but too beautiful." Silas cups her face. "It's probably me. I got so damn lucky finding you; I gotta earn the rest of our dream together. I gotta work for our future because you fell into my yesterday like an angel."

"Dayum," Redix sighs. "Y'all are too damn cute."

"It'll work out." Gently, Charlie assures them. "Eily, your mom is smaller than you and had you and your sisters. And Silas is too damn in love with you to ever give up. One way or another, you'll have a family. And apparently, we'll be joining you. We'll make a *big* family together."

Charlie leans down, kissing me. I've surprised her, I know. But it's what she wants, and now I can't imagine our lives any other way.

"What will we call ourselves?" Cade wonders. "I mean, like, how do we explain our love to our kids?"

"That's what I wonder," I confess, shifting my hips under Charlie. "What do we name our love?"

There aren't rules for our family because we break so many. Which is a load of bollocks because why are there rules against this?

It's love.

It's just love between more than two.

We're more than one family.

We're three families who found this family together.

"Well, we aren't their aunts and uncles because we fuck." I adore her. Filters escape Eily, but she's right. "I mean," she says, "we'll share a bed like this sometimes. Right? Please tell me we will. If Silas and I have kids, too, I don't want to hide us from them. I don't want to act ashamed because I'm not. I want our children to be raised surrounded by love."

"Sometimes we can sleep like this." Redix jokes, "But Silas snores too much, and Daniel's weenus pokes me all night. We'll need our own houses and beds to get some damn sleep. Evidence: today."

"Shut up," Silas huffs. "You're the one who kicks like David Beckham in your sleep."

"Uh, yeah, and like him, I bend it when I score with y'all every morning, too."

Redix makes us laugh, but I can see it.

I can see our three homes here. We'll have our bedrooms with our wives and our busy, daily lives with kids, school, and work and all.

But I can see us sharing weekends.

I can see us and our pile of kids watching Friday night movies together, popcorn everywhere.

I can see us putting them to sleep in a room of bunk beds and stuffed animals before we crawl into our big bed together, quietly sharing a night.

I can see one of our kids sneaking into our shared bedroom Saturday morning, poking an eyelid, wanting pancakes.

I can see afternoons spent on the water, teaching them to fish and ski, and I can see us gathered around a huge table for Charlie's famous Lowcountry boil every Saturday night.

I can see the headlines, the posts, the viral torture we'll get, too.

The Sinful Six.

The Salacious Six.

I can imagine the horrible shit some will say.

But I can see every Sunday morning, drinking coffee in our row of rocking chairs on the covered porch, watching the sunrise. The six of us, with some hands held, will share laughs while our kids run around. We'll hang tire swings from the live oak.

The world will judge. They'll give us hell, but we won't care.

Because it will be our little slice of heaven.

"I can't sleep now!" Eily bounces on Silas. "I'm too excited. Are we thinking coastal chic or modern beach for your homes?"

"Don't know," Charlie answers. "But I think we should connect our homes with raised porches."

"Yeah," Cade adds, "we can grow jasmine vines from them and—"

"Come on, y'all." Redix groans, almost begging, "This ain't the Magnolia home show. Just ten minutes. Let's nap for just ten damn minutes."

Cade falls on his chest, letting him wrap around her.

Silas pulls Eily into a hug, and I look up, cupping Charlie's cheek.

Silently, she kisses my palm. Tenderly, she twists to lie beside me. Taking my hand, she wedges her body against mine, her warm back to my chest. Slowly, she guides my fingers down between her thighs.

We're too in love. We're too good together. We're too aligned, our souls matching. I know how to do this as I quietly slip inside her. I know how to share the same dreams with her, too.

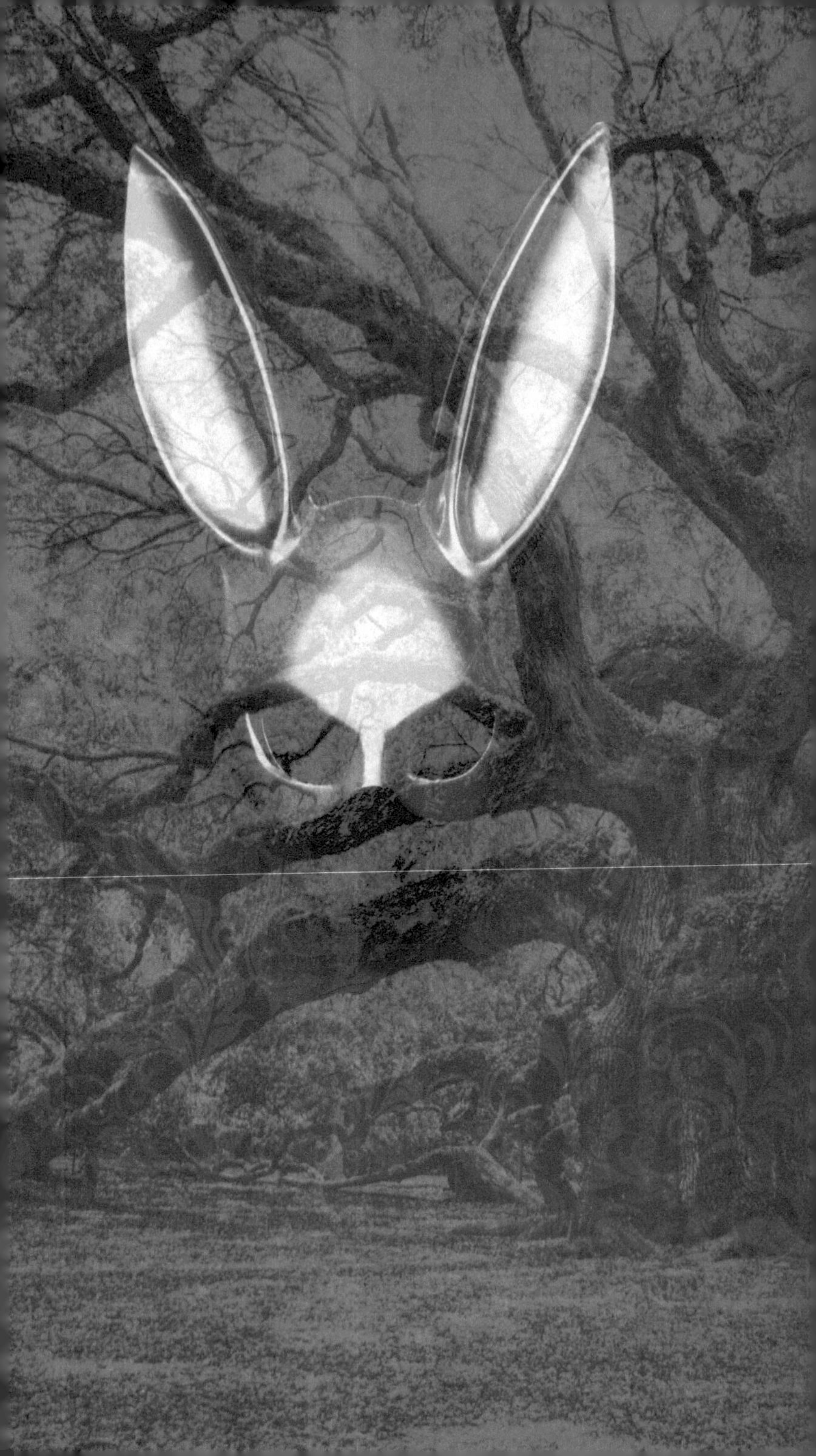

"**May the force be in me!**"

"I better win a fucking Emmy for *this*," I snort. "Literally."

"They should award those, you know. I heard sex scenes are tough to shoot. Is it true?"

Blair swirls day-glo body paint across my back, and I don't hate her hands on me.

She's hot. She's fun. She's damn creative with her trick night: an alien love story.

"Hell, yeah," I answer. "Fucking modesty patches stick to my pubes or body hair. Depends on where wardrobe puts them. And pasties rarely stay on tits, especially when we get sweaty under the lights, so I try to avert my eyes, respecting my colleague's nipples, even when they're right in my face. All while I make sure I don't move my ass wrong for the DP."

"DP?" Blair squirts goop on my glutes. "You've shot a DP scene before?"

"Director of Photography. And no. A DP sex scene is crossing over into porn." I laugh. "I'll only shoot that for free with y'all."

She chuckles. "Does that mean I can put this night in a book?"

"Sure. Just gimme a cool name. Like Redix the Railer."

"Redix the *Raider*."

"Even better."

She squats behind me, getting my hamstrings. With all the prep involved tonight, it does feel like I'm about to shoot a sex scene.

"So, we just go in there and start snatching bodies?" I ask.

Blair paints my calves. "You can change your mind." I'm almost covered, chin to toes, in blue body paint, with purple and yellow paint contouring my muscles. "You can switch and be a human sacrifice."

"Luca is going to lose his mind watching this."

Scarlett stands beside me. We're the lucky treats tonight, so we got to pick first: alien breeder or human sacrifice.

She chose human sacrifice.

I chose breeder.

Big shock.

I know.

Securing her hair in a bun, Scarlett is dressed like a businesswoman. Her white silk blouse, black pencil skirt, and Louboutin black heels are elegant. I like the sexy geek glasses she's wearing, too.

Nice touch.

She really does look like a woman, innocently walking

to her car in a parking lot before amorous aliens suddenly abduct her.

Now, the person who I can't believe is such a good alien sport is Ford Alexander.

I like the guy—a lot.

Yeah, he's a hot-as-hell, grumpy motherfucker, but he's a good one.

He loves his wife, his husbands, and their kids. He fought for his country and has the scars to prove it—especially the big one down the center of his chest.

But he's into this, too, because, deep down ... what man doesn't dream of it?

Who doesn't want to dress like an alien warlord about to breed humans so both species can survive?

It's the plotline for Blair's best-selling paranormal romance books, and now...

"Damn, Blair." I spin around, pondering aloud, "Your books would make a great movie. No. A great *series*."

She stares over the rim of her glasses. "Don't tease me."

"I ain't teasing. I'm serious. Aliens falling in love with humans instead of fighting them? That's fucking gold. We could co-write it. Daniel could produce it. He and I could star in it, and you could be our consultant on set, making sure you like it."

Her jaw hangs open, speechless.

"We can pitch it to the studio." So, I keep convincing her. "We can shoot in Atlanta so you could be near your husbands and—"

"Stop," she begs, tears welling in her eyes. "Just stop. Redix, you're talking about making my dreams come true." She throws her arms around my neck, getting blue paint on her costume.

"Ah, darlin'." I peck her cheek, hugging her back.

"That's what we're here for—making fantasies come true. Whatdayasay?"

"Sold, and excuse me while I pass out."

"Don't pass out." I squeeze her tighter. "We gotta pitch it first."

"And we gotta rehearse it tonight," Scarlett adds. "Because, my god, it's a hot plot."

"So, if they're dressed like humans, we can fuck them?" Ford asks, standing at attention like he's afraid he'll get body paint all over our dressing room in the honeywagon.

"Yeah." Blair lets me go. She shakes her head, still processing my proposal. "I gave everyone a choice: aliens or humans. If they're humans, they want to breed tonight."

"If they're aliens like us," I ask, "can we fuck them, too? Like alien to alien sex?"

"And are we supposed to fuck them, humans or other aliens, with those?"

Ford points to the open silver suitcase on the vanity containing alien cocks.

They look like a pile of fluorescent candy. All giant, brightly colored monster dicks in a variety of shapes and sizes. Some are cock sheaths. Some are dildos. And all look out of this world.

Pinch me.

I can't believe my life.

I can't believe this fantasy.

Screw, turkey. Halloween just became my favorite holiday.

I mean ... candy galore, giant colored cocks, and gorgeous cunts to breed. What other holiday can compete? Maybe Valentine's, but come on, Halloween has kinky costumes, too.

I pick up a long purple and blue cock sheath. It'll add inches to my dick—the potential making it twitch.

"Do your aliens breed the men, too?"

"Yep," Blair proudly answers me. "My aliens have no preferences. Only love."

"Aw, that's sweet," Scarlett replies. "Do they do anal, too? I mean … asking for a friend with a hot, Dom husband who's claimed her pussy forever."

Blair winks. "Yes, they can breed vaginally or anally. As long as the humans are dripping with alien milk by the end of the night."

Ford laughs, tossing his bearded chin up. "I hope you brought a mop because that fake cum lube is a bitch to clean up. I swear we've been through a dozen rugs at Delta's."

"Oh, I know," Blair says. "Beau and Colton learned the hard way. We've already had to replace the carpet and repaint. Now, we play on hardwoods only."

I snort. "*Hardwoods.*"

Scarlett laughs with me. "That's why we have a private hotel suite for our scenes."

Blair sighs, "I love The Mercier Hotel."

"We all do," Ford agrees.

Hell, I'm a fan, too.

I love how our world is growing, our partnerships, too.

From Ms. Faye's Sex Club, where we're members. To Delta's, Stacey's adult store, where we all shop. To Luca's secret suite at The Mercier Hotel. I've heard stories about Zar's beach house. And then there's Silas's yacht, the *Indigo Dream*. And now here, where our homes will be.

Indigo Island.

Yeah, maybe the island is haunted.

I don't mind. The haints can fuck with us, too. It only adds to our fun.

"Okay." Like a director, Blair focuses us. "They're ready in the tent. The scene is set. Your alien soldiers have gathered and handcuffed the humans to breed in the sacrificial field, and now you two, the warlords, have captured Scarlett to breed first. You must breed her and a male and so on. There are three each to be sacrificed."

Scarlett chews her lip. She's nervous. Which is cute and fucking sexy because she could put a hurtin' on us if she had to.

"Don't worry." Gently, Ford caresses her shoulder. "I got ya. I won't do anything to disrespect your husband."

Her husband, Luca, is smeared in blue and gold body paint when we step into the tent. He went for the alien role tonight, as did Silas, Mateo, Nick, Beau, and Colton.

The rest of the men are humans.

Of the women, I glance around, only curious about my wife.

I smirk; *that's my woman.*

Cade's a human, dressed like Scarlett for the sacrifice.

But when Cade sees me covered in contoured body paint, a tattered brown suede loincloth knotted right above my aroused blue vein ... her eyes get wide ... and hungry.

"Beam me up, Scottie," Silas mutters, standing beside her. He has Cade cuffed with Charlie beside them. She's an alien, and so is Eily.

Scarlett, Cade, and Stacey are the women to breed.

But I clock it. Daniel is dressed like a businessman—a male we can breed, too.

I suspect our sixsome had a strategy tonight.

Charlie's still recovering from her sexorcism. Eily is being careful since she's ovulating, so Silas is devoted to her. That leaves Cade and Daniel as the ones from our group we'll sacrifice.

Yeah, my alien soldiers, Beau and Colton, don't look mad about it.

From the other groups, the sacrifices are Zar with Scarlett and Stacey with Luke.

And Blair?

I'm not quite sure what she'll do dressed like a Galactic Babe. In her story, she's the first human bred by an alien. Cue the romance because *surprise* she fell in love with one, then two, alien warlords, aka Beau and Colton.

But in reality, I know her threesome has boundaries. Still, we can't neglect our fearless leader. I'll encourage someone to take care of her tonight.

The scene is set, and I don't need Blair to call, "Action!"

I'm feeling it.

So is Ford.

We drag Scarlett into the tent's center. She's resisting enough to make this real, to make this hot.

"You fucking, beasts," she snarls. "When I get free, I'm gonna fucking kill you!"

"Silence, human!" I bark, scanning the circle of six empty breeding benches, instantly rousing my dick.

Wow, this IS *an epic story.*

Blair went all out, using Stacey's help, I'm sure.

Under Blair's black lights, our alien bodies glow in an evil neon rainbow. Erotic music pumps unearthly beats. Uplights beam bright green and blue in a circle along the dark edge, like we're under our ship, hovering above. A fog with clean water, sugar, and sin aromas mists the tent.

It does feel like an alien breeding. Like we're in the desert of Area 51 with humans we stole for our pleasure, for our survival.

It's kinky as fuck.

The black leather breeding benches will present each human on their back, their legs raised and open, their ankles secured to two poles, presenting them helplessly if we bind their wrists to the bench, too.

I see it clench Luca's jaw as we handle Scarlett, roughly restraining her first. Ford secures her ankle while I rip her skirt enough to open her legs so I can bind her other one.

"Fuck you!" She growls with her legs splayed open, her ass at the edge of the bench.

"Oh, human," I mock, lingering my blue finger over her exposed, pink lace panties. "That's what you secretly want, isn't it? An alien fuck?"

A devilish sparkle hits Scarlett's blue eyes.

Atta girl. She's loving this.

Then ... we're all loving it.

The aliens grab and grunt, binding the humans. The humans resist and play fight, cursing us. Body paint gets on clothes as I catch smiles ghosting snatched bodies.

Once all six are bound and ready to be bred, I smirk at Ford. I swear, he can read my mind.

I approach Daniel while Ford returns to Scarlett on the bench beside us. They could fight us, but they don't.

Ford glances at Blair, standing between our benches. He's waiting for her next move.

On cue, Blair rests her hand on Scarlett's arm, then Daniel's. "This is our only way to survive," she pleads in her role, "but it doesn't hurt that bad, I promise. And if you let it," she practically purrs, "their big alien cocks can feel so good."

"Help me, Obi-Wan Kenobi. You're the only one who can fuck me."

Zar jokes, bound and ready for his turn and we burst out laughing.

Except Eily, who cocks her head. "I don't get it."

Silas wraps around his alien wife. "Oh, we're bingeing *Star Wars* next week."

"Quiet!" Ford shouts to our soldiers, his lips twitching, suppressing his laugh. "We don't have much time. We inseminate, then leave."

Eily snorts. "*Inseminate*. So sexy."

Ford twists his mouth, trying not to break. "We use our huge *cocks* and fill the humans with our alien *seed*."

Eily winks. "Better."

"You creepy, perverted alien fucks!" *Hell yeah, Scarlett gets an alien Emmy.* She rattles the chains cuffing her ankles. "Don't you dare touch me with those big, freaky dicks!"

"Do it!" Daniel tries to snarl, but I hear his laughter. "If you're going to fuck us, then get on with it." *And his arousal.*

I step between his legs. "Oh, you'll get it, human. You're all about to get more cock than you've ever had."

Daniel smirks, so I smirk back, commanding the other aliens, "Strip them!" I start improvising. "And prepare their holes to breed!"

Damn, I'm getting into this.

Pointing, I direct Eily and Silas to play with Stacey. Mateo and Charlie can tease Luke. Nick, of course, belongs with Zar while Ford hooks his finger, ordering Luca to join him with Scarlett. There's no fighting that.

But for Cade?

Oh, she'll love this.

"Human!" I glower at Blair, stabbing my blue finger at Cade's bench. "You say they'll love our big alien cocks? Then prepare her to take mine!"

"Hell yes," Cade whoops. "May the force be in me!"

Zar laughs, and I swear those two are Star Wars peas in a pod.

Blair smirks in her thigh-high white boots, clicking Cade's way.

That leaves Beau and Colton searching my eyes for permission.

Daniel was reluctant, but I'll prove this to him.

I'm not jealous—not in the way that threatens our love. Nothing will ever break the six of us apart.

So, yeah, it's my ego. I wouldn't mind if the hottest pro football players wanted me, too.

But I get it.

Beau and Colton are usually closed, and they may always be. I can't imagine what they've been through together as closeted football players. How they had to deny and hide their love until they found Blair. It seems she saved them.

Maybe this is a one-night-only for them. One night to fulfill their man crush on Daniel. Like millions, they lusted for him for years, and now, they get to have him.

I'll make sure of it.

"Prepare him to take me," I command them, which is odd. They're as big as me.

But hey, I'm rehearsing to be Redix the Raider.

And this is their fetish.

Beau and Colton use one of the fabric knives Blair gave the aliens. Clothes are cut open and ripped apart, our offerings exposed.

"Fuck!" Daniel mutters as his fine gentleman's trousers and starched button-up turn to shreds. Beau barely teases the knife down Daniel's flexing abs, and, "Fuck!" he bellows again, his wrists bound and clanking his chains.

"Is that what you want, *human*?" I say the word like a slur. "You want our fuck?"

"Go to hell!"

He gets into character, as do I, roaring with laughter, "Why go to hell when we can fuck you in your world instead?"

Beau and Colton stand like my hungry soldiers, devouring Daniel with their stare. Remnants of his clothes hang from the bench. All that remains are Daniel's black boxer briefs, hardly restraining his cock, thick and hungry for our use.

I glance around.

Scarlett's skirt and blouse are in tatters, too, her high heels in the air. Luca's ripped her bra down. He's sucking her nipples while Ford strokes his cock, preparing himself.

Nick is teasing Zar. Eily and Silas are sharing Stacey's breasts. Mateo and Charlie are lavishing Luke's tip. And Blair? She's feasting on my writhing wife.

Yes, this is going to be a supernatural night.

Redix

CHAPTER EIGHTEEN

REDIX

Damn, I love Halloween so much, it's scary.

I stride across the tent to the table draped in silver. Blair brought the case of sheaths and dildos over while we were corralling humans.

She's lined them up.

It's quite a collection.

Some look like tentacles, others like bulls. Some are ridged and bulbous, and others look truly alien, with odd ridges and asymmetric girth.

While, of course, kink is the game tonight, that's not what's pounding my heart. The ultimate decision is what I want to give to Daniel. What kind of pleasure?

As guilty as he's felt about the future of our show, I feel guilty about the stress he's been under.

I had no idea.

He's so polite and powerful on set. He's so focused on caring for others that I want to take care of him.

I choked back tears when he won the Emmy. I love him so much it's like I won, too. I don't need one for myself. We shared the victory.

We share everything.

But we're still new at this, learning how three very alpha men love each other. How we need to ask for help, too. Because fuck knows, our alpha women sure tell us all the damn time to just talk about it.

Though it seems for some, like me, with testicles and testosterone, talking is an acquired skill.

But right now?

I don't want Daniel's words.

I want his moans.

A large, scaled dildo with a soft, pointed tip and hard middle knot in cosmic blue and pumpkin orange sure looks like it'll help. It has a round, flat base. It can serve as a six-inch plug, and of course, it grabs Eily's attention.

She's at Stacey's bench, on the other side of Daniel's, her eyes growing wide at what's in my hand.

"My god," she marvels. "Is that landing inside Daniel?"

I stroke her hair. "Oh, we'll make him beg for it."

A groan of consent escapes Daniel's lips when he sees it. Blair propped his head on a small pillow. All of our humans have one so they can witness their coupling.

More so they can relish it.

But I want Beau and Colton to relish this, too. "Get him ready to take me," I command.

Beau's eyes spark greedily, his ripped body smeared in blue paint contrasting with Colton's purple body, his brown eyes gleaming with hunger. Somehow. *No.* I definitely know they've done this before.

Because fuck me, it's erotic what they do to Daniel.

They rip his briefs open, his grunts filling the room until all that remains is his thick BOSS waistband.

Pouring generous ribbons of lube over their fingers, they tease before expertly probing Daniel's exposed ass. It makes him groan, his soaring desire infectious.

It makes Beau and Colton equally aroused and hard. They stand between Daniel's spread legs at the edge of the bench, and I stand a few feet away.

Relishing the spectacle.

"Such a manwhore," Beau teases, sliding his finger alongside Colton's, easing two inside Daniel. "He likes it in his ass." Beau's other hand reaches for Colton's raging hard-on.

"Yes," Daniel groans. "Fuck yes, I do."

"Fuck this is hot," Colton growls, seeking Beau's lips.

They kiss, their tongues rolling together. Colton fists Beau's cock, rubbing their shafts together, too. They're moaning, kissing, and frotting, and it's so damn beautiful as Colton reaches for Daniel's surging length.

He starts stroking Daniel while Beau probes him, and I can hear Daniel's grunts of pleasure. He must have the most sensual sight of two men getting off on playing with him, toying with his ass and cock.

It makes me leak.

I let them have their way with him while I untie my loincloth, letting it fall to the rug. Breaking my role, I taunt, "I'm glad you're enjoying my man because your future wife sure enjoys my wife, too."

Colton glances to his left, catching our women. I glance, too.

Blair has Cade twisting, moaning, and bucking over her three fingers and tongue.

"Fuck yes," Colton mutters, pumping Daniel harder, his

other hand tightening his grip over his cock, rubbing against Beau's.

Beau lets Colton guide their pleasure while they watch Beau's two fingers claim Daniel.

"Fuck!" Daniel howls. "Fuck me. I mean … breed me. Now!"

"Is he ready for us?" I ask them.

With lust hooding his eyes, Beau turns his stare to me, his forehead pressed to Colton's. "Yes." His voice is labored with lust, with restraint. "Breed him while we milk him for you."

"Why don't I start him?" I douse the knawty dildo until it's dripping with lube, "and you finish him? I have others to breed, too."

It's more like I'm asking if this is a boundary for them. I respect it if it is. We all have them.

"Yes," Colton rumbles. "Start him, and we'll finish him." He looks at Beau. "Together."

Together.

I share the feeling.

I want this with Daniel, too. I want him to know and trust that he can let us care for him as much as he takes care of us.

Yes, his wife Charlie can snipe someone from a thousand meters, but it's Daniel's instinct. It's in his nature to fight and protect, too.

But now, Beau withdraws. So does Colton as they step around, standing on either side of Daniel, watching as I ask him, "Do you trust me?"

I break character; so does he.

"Yes," he urges, lying bound and on his back. "Always."

Slowly, I ease the blue foreign tip inside as Daniel stares at me, his lips parting, his eyes widening, his cock jumping.

"Milk him," I urge Beau. "Make this good for him."

Colton licks his lips, and Beau nods. As I push further inside, against that tight ring, pressing against it, Beau fists Daniel's thick base while Colton wraps his lips around his swollen tip, sucking it.

"Oh fuck!" Daniel rattles his ankle chains. "Oh, fuck yes!"

"Are you going to take it?" I ease more inside. "Are you going to let us take care of you, too?"

Luca had his turn with Daniel, but this is *mine*.

I didn't know Daniel was suffering at the time. I didn't know he was trying to protect me from the truth. I didn't know he was willing to sacrifice just so I could win, too.

So now I can teach him a lesson—a loving, lustful one from The Six.

We take care of each other.

Always and until the end.

"Yes!" Daniel howls, his eyes locked on mine. "Fuck yes, give it to me. Make me take it."

He loves this, he needs this, he needs us to take care of him sometimes, and we will—we always will.

Colton moans with Daniel in his mouth as Beau watches him fervently.

Beau's not jealous. His pupils dilate. His cock drips. He licks his lips. He's raging hard watching his man enjoy this, watching Colton's bearded lips plunge up and down Daniel's thick shaft, his tongue lashing his tip when he reaches it.

It's shaking Daniel's thighs. He's sweating. He's taking it inch by inch. But when I reach the wide, bulbous knot, I don't know if he can take it.

Beau sees me pause. "Let me," he says. "I know how to

do it. Colt likes it when I use one on him; one just like it. And so does Blair."

Colton lifts from Daniel's cock. "Fuck yeah," he huffs, his spit webbed to Daniel's tip. *Damn, he's hot.* "Fuck yeah, he'll love it. Just go slow."

This is trust.

This is love.

I let go, and Beau takes my place between Daniel's thighs. Walking around, I snake my hand into Daniel's coal waves. Leaning down, I kiss him, and I don't stop.

He writhes, his back bowing, his breath huffing and gasping into our kiss, but his tongue stays with mine. He lets me kiss him and care for him until he's taken it all. Until Beau presses the alien object all the way inside him.

"Fuck, Redix," Daniel growls as his body shakes, still accepting the luscious intrusion. His cock is swollen and dripping for it. "Fuck. Fuck, I ... I lo—"

"I love you, too." I kiss him again, my lips brushing over his. "I got you. We all do. Now, just let us. Let us take care of you, too." I press my forehead to his. "Okay? That's how we do this. That's how we grow old together. Promise me."

"I..." His aqua eyes mesmerize me. "I promise," he sighs. "I love you. I love all of us. Just ... *fuck.*" He writhes, jerking at his restraints. "Just fuck, don't stop."

I turn to Beau and Colton, giving them a nod.

They'll have fun with him. They'll take care of him. They need this, too.

Everyone deserves at least one fantasy fulfilled. If not, why the fuck are we here?

With one more kiss for Daniel, I leave and aim for the table of alien toys, noting with a smirk how others have already taken a few more.

So, I grab a particularly monstrous one before scanning our scene.

And damn, I love Halloween so much, it's scary.

A neon pink scaly monster length glows in Luca's fist. He's twisting it inside Scarlett, making her growl. He's making her fight her orgasm while he smacks her clit.

On the table beside them, it looks like Zar is taking an alarming red bull sheath from Nick. But Luca's telling Zar he can't come, either.

"We're going to fucking breed you human whores all night," Luca sneers. "Until you're dripping with our milk. Say it!" He smacks Scarlett's clit again before he spanks Zar's cock. "Say you love it."

"Yes, my owner," Zar groans, his cock bobbing back even harder.

"Yes, Luca." A scream of ecstasy threatens Scarlett's voice.

Dang. Who knew Luca was an amateur alien actor?

Then again, if sex is involved, he deserves an Oscar.

I want to give a standing ovation to my friend.

Looking to my right, Ford is dedicating quite the performance to his wife, Stacey. My brows raise, shocked by the massive purple curving Kraken cock sheath he's serving her with. But she's loving it. Eily's licking Stacey's clit, making sure of it.

Of course, Silas is behind Eily, strumming her clit while he gives her the real thing.

My stare turns to admire the deep grunts coming from Luke. He's taking a glowing, green strap-on from Charlie before Mateo takes his turn with his husband, giving it to him bare. Luke grunts, relishing it because they're demanding he stroke off while they take quick turns with him.

Dragging my hand down my face, *dayum,* I'm drowning in the erotic scene. Am I in shock? In loving awe? Aroused more than ever?

Hell, check all of the above.

"Redix the Raider," a honey voice calls, and I focus on its source.

Blair hooks her finger, summoning me to where I was headed all along.

My wife.

Cade's purple dress drapes in shreds, her black lace bra yanked down, hefting her gorgeous breasts for my stare. Her matching panties have been cut at the wet crotch, but they still circle, vulgarly tempting around her waist.

"Your next sacrifice is wet and ready for you." Blair licks her glistening lips. "I made sure of it."

And I can tell.

My woman's pussy is so swollen, pink, and slick, dripping with another woman's spit.

Goddamn, Cade's the most beautiful sight in the world.

Yes, I have other partners, and yes, I love them.

But Cade is where I belong. She's my beginning.

She was my first kiss, the only woman I'll *ever* kiss. I want to die with Cade on my lips. I've already come so close.

She was my first touch. I'll never forget the first time I felt her tender heat. We were seventeen. She had never had an orgasm. Frustrated, she had tried on her own but couldn't do it. So, I took my time with her. Together, we learned how to do it, and when she came for the first time on my fingers, her violet eyes were so beautiful, staring into mine ... I groaned, coming in my jeans at the sight of her.

I've been hers ever since.

She was my first taste. I couldn't get enough of her

moans and the way I could make her scream. Making her come on my tongue became an obsession.

Then, she was my first fuck.

But she's even more.

Our first time, I felt why they called it "making love" because I didn't come so damn fast and hard because it felt so good inside her. I mean, it did, but I climaxed in an immediate explosion with my gasping lips pressed to Cade's ... because I was so in love, my heart burst for her, and my body just followed.

I swear, I'm still right there with her.

She still owns my heart.

Honestly, when I'm with our other partners, it feels like I'm sharing a piece of me. I get off on the pleasure of our bodies. I cherish our intimacy and trust because I know what it's like to have that stolen from you.

But when I'm with Cade, she takes me—all of me—gone.

I disappear inside her, my edges blurring, my heart pounding, matching her rhythm, my body melding with hers.

Sometimes, there's that one person, that one love, who makes you wonder if you're actually two people ... because you feel like one.

"Redix." She writhes for me. Blair didn't bind her wrists, so Cade's tugging at her dark rouge nipples. "Redix, please. *Please...*"

My teeth grab my bottom lip, feeling that feral thrum in my veins at the sight of her heels in the air, her ankles chained to poles, her legs splayed for my access.

No, I'm not into pain.

But I am into pleasure worth dying for.

"Damn, Cade," I admire her opening for me.

Blair has her sexed up. But when Cade sees the sheath in my hand, her lips part. Like Daniel, she can't believe she's going to do this.

But she will.

She wants to.

"Ahem." Blair breaks my daze. Tickling Cade's clit with her fingertip, she brings me back to my role. "She's ready for your breeding, sir."

"No," Cade says with a hooded smile. "No, I don't want Redix the Raider's giant cock. It'll hurt."

She's playing. We have a safe word, and I haven't heard it in years.

Blair hands me the lube. I don't miss her licking her lips as I gloss my cock, using it to coat my swollen curve.

"You're worried I'll hurt you, human?" I tease Cade, "With my giant alien cock?"

Sliding on the blue ribbed sheath, I grunt, shocked at the tight texture inside it. My tip pushes to the open end of the sheath. It adds so much girth to my length I begin to doubt she can take it, but damn, it feels good.

"Fuck," I mutter, grabbing a breath with my eyes on Cade. "Are you worried my cock will hurt? Or that it'll feel so damn good for us you'll only want more?"

"Please," Cade sighs. "Please, be gentle. If you're going to fuck me with your big cock, then make it feel good."

I smirk, dousing this thing in lube. "Oh, we'll make it feel damn good."

"We?"

"Yes," I answer Cade before nodding at Blair. "Keep her ready for me. Lick that pretty little clit of hers. Spread her lips open and let me watch your tongue flick it while I fuck her."

Cade moans as Blair grins, leaning over Cade to obey.

Blair's black hair is pulled into a ponytail, so I can watch it all. I can watch her tongue laving over my wife's pearled pink nub while I slowly push in.

Cade's silent. Only gasps and moans escape her straining throat. Blair's tongue strums her clit while Cade's violet eyes anchor to mine while I penetrate, stretch, and taunt her.

"Oh, you love this, don't you? Look at your pretty pink pussy, stretching to take all of my cock. You want it all, don't you?"

"Uhh," she cries out, her legs shaking, another maddening blue inch disappearing inside her. "Uhh, Redix, it's so much. Oh my god," she groans.

"Beg." I cup her ass, spreading her cheeks more. "Beg if you want more. And play with your tits. Pinch your nipples if you're my sweet little human slut wanting me to fuck you with my giant cock."

"Oh fuck, Redix, please!"

Cade obeys. Mercilessly, she tugs, pinching and tweaking her nipples as I watch her slick, straining entrance take another inch.

And I feel my pleasure threatening, too.

This is so fucking right and raw. So beautiful and brave.

We've never done this role-play, and it won't be the last time. It's intoxicating. It's a drug. The room falls away, and all I can feel is the strangle of this tight device, the tip of my cock sensitive and thrilled by Cade's warm, slick, swollen walls, straining to take me.

My stare travels from Blair's tongue, rolling and circling over my wife's clit, getting it so damn hard, to my stunning wife trusting me, wanting me, taking me.

So damn much of me.

I need to breathe.

Slowly, I withdraw, and she's dripping, her milky arousal drizzling to the floor. "Fuck, Cade." So I drive back inside where I left her gaping, and her thighs shake violently.

I won't hurt her with every inch, but what I'm giving her makes her body twist for more.

Her breath ragged, her lungs heaving, her sex swelling, she grabs Blair's hair. "Don't stop. Don't stop. Oh god, lick me. Lick me while he fucks me. Oh fuck, I'm gonna come."

I thrust inside, giving Cade what she's begging for, and she comes with a back-bowing groan that lasts forever. The muscles in her legs twitch. The lips of her pussy pulse. Her whole body shudders.

But she needs more.

Cade is my instrument, and I know how to make her sing over and over and over.

Gently, I caress Blair's hair. "She's mine now. I've claimed her. Go find your men. Make them please you, too." I know she will.

"Redix," Cade cries for me. She scratches the bench's black leather. "Don't stop. Keep going. Please. Please."

We get lost with me inside her, lost to how familiar and foreign this is. Lost when I make her come again, her voice gravel from screaming, her sex convulsing for more.

I barely hear the others around me coming, grunting and moaning, luring me with the dirtiest talk.

Because I'm fucking losing it. Cade is all I see, all I feel: me inside her, taking her, claiming her. I grab her hips, brutally thrusting. I bury myself, giving her all I have because she takes it.

She takes all of me.

"Oh god, Redix. I'm *coming*..." she cries, almost afraid of the pleasure as I feel her do it, sweating in my grasp, shaking in my hands, and wetting my thighs with her pleasure.

I let go, throwing my chin up. I hold still, ready for the familiar, most mind-erasing, breath-taking release inside her, but...

A black and gold mask suddenly greets me in the blindness.

Its sinful face snarls back at me, grabbing my mind, possessing my body. It makes me ruthlessly pump my cock again; one thought driving me—*Cade is fucking mine.*

"Mine, mine, mine," I growl, and it's not my voice, but it's my pleasure. "Mine." It's me inside her, but I'm not the one fucking her, cruelly driving in her so hard. "Mine." It's my orgasm ripping through me and causing hers. I can feel her shudder, wetting my thighs and doing it again.

"Yes! Mine!" I roar before my throat is suddenly strangled in the grasp of something. Some erotic surrender seizes my muscles, exploding my breath. My cock pulses, spilling inside her. I come so fucking hard for Cade.

But it's not my voice in my mind shouting for her.

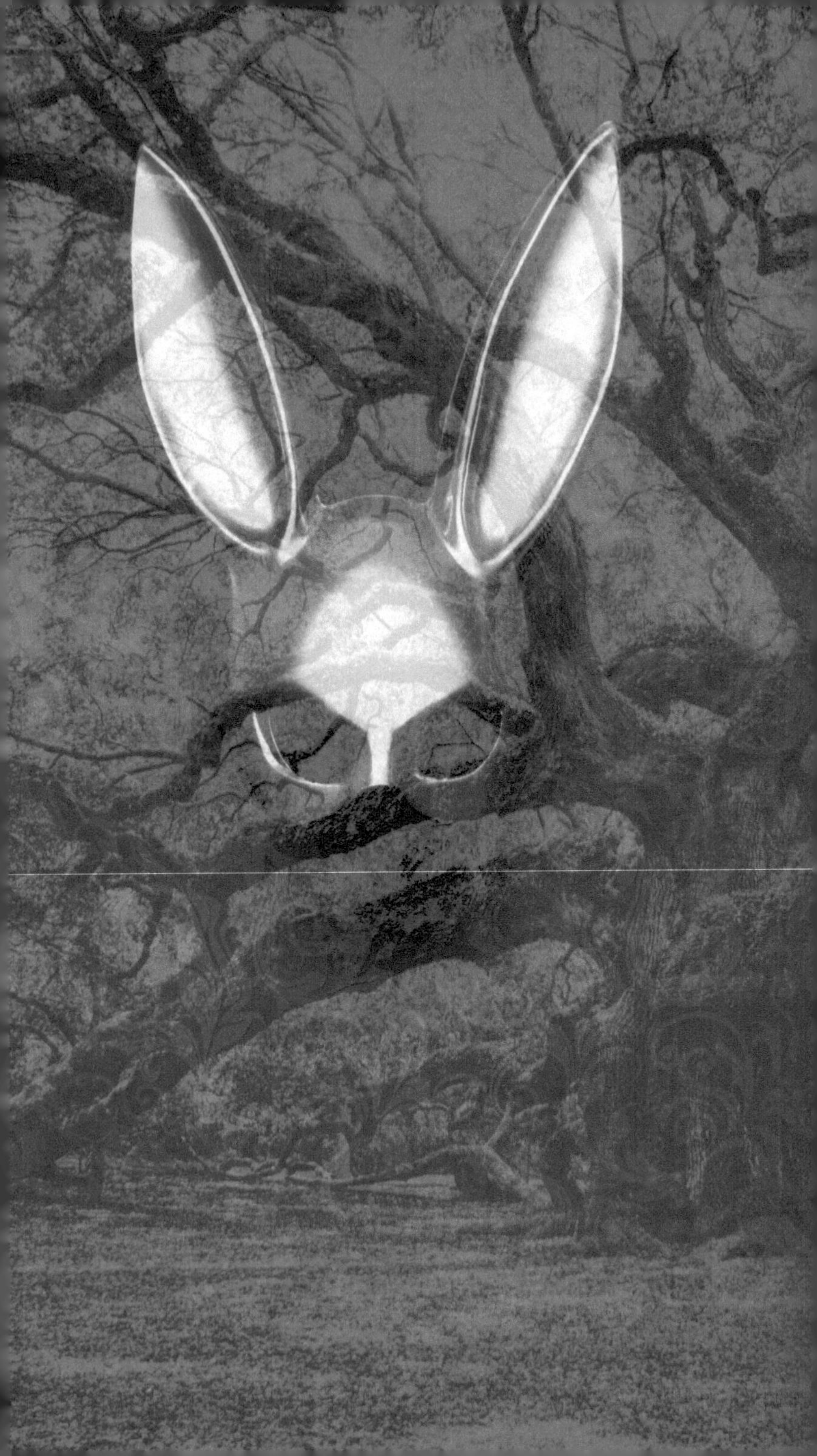

Charlie

"**What do you *usually* do with dildos?**"

"B abe, check."

Shampoo suds stream down my face. The pelting warm water feels so good.

"Babe? Check, please."

Wiping bubbles off my face, I sneak an eyelid open, glancing down, answering Daniel, "You got it all. No more paint in your ass crack."

"I don't know how so much got on me."

"Really? Because there's none left on Redix, Beau, and Colt."

Daniel cocks a guilty grin. "Ah, then it was worth it."

Combing his fingers through his wet strands, his shower is done. The water between us runs clear. Though I'll never want to clean the dirty memory of tonight from my mind.

Tenderly, his grinning lips kiss mine. But I'm curious. "So, is this a new kink? Alien sex?"

"No." He steps out of the shower and onto the bathmat, grabbing a towel. "But it could be a new project. A new series." He pauses, rubbing his chest. "A million says Redix agrees. We'll talk to Blair tomorrow."

"Aliens mating with humans? On Netflix?" I reach for the conditioner. "I'd watch. So would millions. There's enough fighting. We need more romance, more sex on streaming shows. And as long as you and Redix or some other actors are making it hot and not creepy, it could be like *Sex Life* meets *Stranger Things*."

"Well, tonight was sure strange and sexy. And I'm knackered." He leans in for one more peck. Happily, I give it. "See you in bed. I'll warm your spot for you."

He snaps the shower curtain closed. In a few moments, the door to our dressing room in the honeywagon slams.

And I'm alone.

These moments I enjoy. It's not that I don't love my husband. Our partners. Or just the company in general. But a few minutes under the lavender-scented steam is heavenly.

Eily put those aroma tablets in every dressing room shower, and if this fancy wagon weren't on wheels, with a quiet generator humming, it really could be a spa.

Earlier, I let the other aliens go first, taking turns cleaning up. Daniel and I were the last to go. The others are already in the tent.

So, I take my time. I'm still sore and *not* complaining after my sexorcism.

Closing my eyes, I lean back, inhaling steam, letting myself relax and—

Thud.

The door slams again.

"Daniel?"

Silence.

"Did you forget something?" Casually, I ask, but I'm not the kind of woman who gets fooled twice.

I sense it. *I'm not alone.*

The lights flicker.

Do I hear huffing breath?

Wait.

Do haints huff?

Please tell me they do.

Okay, fine. Yes, I want to be haunted. I hope it's my haint. I hope it's my dead uncle, so far removed from my bloodline and dead for centuries, and still, he makes it look good.

Damn, I hope I inherited those genes. I'll save so much money on Botox.

Turning toward the shower curtain, waiting for it to rip open, I have no weapons. No rifle. No 9mm. It's just me and my pruney fingers, and that's enough.

It's a fight.

Or a fuck.

I vote: fuck.

My heart rate knows the drill. My senses heighten. My dripping skin turns to goose flesh. I'm listening. Focusing. Tensing.

Waiting for...

Rip. The shower curtain yanks aside and—

"Shit!" I huff. "Shit. You scared the shit out of me, you little shit."

"Well, shit!" Silas laughs. "I was gonna wash your back and shit."

I roll my eyes.

He smirks. "Well, at least, turn around and let me admire it."

"You were two seconds away from a blinding eye gouge."

"As long as you ain't gouging my dick, I can spare other parts."

I stand naked, my nipples thrilled to see him. His gaze drops, taking a moment to enjoy the sight. His hair hangs damp. His fresh T-shirt and clean shorts smell like laundry detergent. Silas just showered and changed.

And now, he wants me.

For what?

"You were hoping I was your horny haint, weren't you?"

I scoff, "No, I wasn't."

"Yeah, you were."

"Shut up."

"You want me to go get a mask and come back? I can flick the light switch again. Or kill the generator and make it damn creepy for us. I can't speak French, but I know enough to fuck with it."

"Since when do you know French?"

He leans against the wall by the shower, folding an ankle over the other. "From Daniel. I acquired his appreciation for French porn. He's right. It's the best. High-quality productions. Fancy sets. Sexy wardrobe. Good lighting. Great natural tits and dicks. And—"

"Hand me a towel." Silas can wax on about porn for hours. "And tell me what shit you're stirring."

"Can't a man just chat with his best friend turned fourth best fuck buddy?"

"Fourth?" I pat down with the towel he gives me. "Since when is there a pecking order?"

"Pecking? No. None of us have a chicken fetish." He

pauses. "*Yet*, but give it time. But for fucking? You know Eily's first for me. Always. Then I gotta say Redix and your husband take the silver and bronze."

"Because they take your ass."

He laughs. "We take yours, too."

"And you sure moan about it, coming hard like it's a golden privilege."

I brush past him, smiling.

Grabbing my comb off the vanity, I love this—me and Silas. We give each other hell because we've loved each other through it.

Lazily, he smiles, watching my nightly routine. Hair. Teeth. Moisturizer. Finally, I crack. I'm curious.

"Alright, you little shit. What do you want? If it's not my ass, it's something."

"What kinda moisturizer are you using? Cuz you don't look a day over thirty."

"Silas."

"And your tits are timeless."

"*Silasss.*"

"And your ass is immortal."

"Silas!"

"Fine." He sighs, "I need your help."

I ask the mirror, seeing him in the reflection. "What's wrong?"

"Eily."

I whip around. "Is she hurt? Did y'all fight? Is she mad about tonight? I mean, it must be kinda hard watching us fuck others when she's not. When she's only with you."

He cocks a brow. "Ouch, my ego."

"I don't mean it bad, it's just—"

"She's not mad. We're fine. We're great. We love fucking

while others do, too. All she wants is for everyone to have fun, but…"

His gaze falls.

And so does my heart.

I can't bear to see Silas hurt.

When we were younger, and he started to get awkward, teen boy zits, he was so shy about it. So insecure.

So, I took a red Sharpie and made myself chin dots, too, so he and his zits wouldn't be alone.

I knew then, and a hundred other times, he wanted to kiss me. But timing is everything. So is fate.

He needed to find Eily first.

He'll always need Eily first.

Just like I need Daniel.

I reach for his arm. "It's okay. Whatever it is. Tell me, and I'll help."

"First, put some clothes on." A grin lifts his pillow lips. "I worship my wife. But you got a damn pretty pussy."

I punch his biceps.

"Ouch!" He rubs it, laughing.

"Tell me what's going on," I demand, tugging on my jean shorts before slipping a faded USMC sweatshirt over my head.

"Tomorrow is my trick night," he answers. "And I need help. Eily's still ovulating, and I don't know what to do."

I twist my hair into a wet bun, never breaking our eye contact. "Well, then cancel the trick and just be with her and make it romantic. We'll understand."

"But that's not what she wants. She's worked too hard on this week. It'll bum her out if I cancel a night."

"Even if she's ovulating? It'll be her last night this month, right?"

I know Eily's cycle.

So does Cade.

We're so close; we synced up last year.

At first, it was annoying—three Aunt Flos coming to visit at the same time.

We try not to make it a blood bath.

And it's not like our men haven't proudly earned their red wings. It's not like they mind. Hell, Daniel's the one who remembers to put tampons in my purse, not me.

But it does limit things because sometimes it ain't a cakewalk. So, the husbands make it sweet. If we're together and on the rag, they have a ritual. It involves a dozen red roses for each of us. Three gift baskets with Teuscher Swiss chocolates and French wine. And a night of foot rubs, with heating pads on call.

But lately, it's also the time when Eily gets quiet.

Which isn't like her.

It's sweet how Silas knows when to silently hold her tight or when to make her laugh.

But this is one miracle, even with his billions, he can't divine.

"Yeah," he mutters. "The window is closing this month. And with each month—it's been eleven—it gets harder on her."

Softly, I offer, "And you. I know it's hard on you, too. You love her. You want this with her. You're so sweet to her, but I know you're worried, too."

"I am." He tosses his chin up, confessing to me and the ceiling. "This week has been fun for her to plan. You should see how happy it made her, and it's a dream having y'all here. But once it's over and reality returns, it's gonna be rough. I know it. If, in a couple of weeks, she's not pregnant and there's nothing else for her to focus on. Like, to have hope about? Fuck, it's gonna break her heart."

Barely, I touch his chest. I know him so well.

If Eily hurts, his heart breaks, too.

"If you want," I offer, "I'll make sure we're here—all of us. We can cancel work, get the grandparents to watch the kids again, take her somewhere, or do something special."

"I don't know. I feel like I'm all out of tricks." He huffs, hearing his pun, "And treats. I don't know what else to do. I just don't want to fail her."

"You're not failing her. You love her more than anything. I never thought the boy I used to beat in spitting contests would become a prince so in love with his tiny, rebel princess."

A smile lifts his lips. "And I never thought the gorgeous girl who ate crickets for fun would be a Marine so in love with an English gentleman."

Gently, I bang my head against his chest. Memories of our cherished childhood make me smile while he pecks my hair.

There's no word to describe me and Silas.

Well, there's one.

Love.

"So, what do we do?" I ask. "How do we make tomorrow night perfect for Eily? How can we make her ovulating dreams come true?"

He takes my hand. "Come with me."

"Are you *sure* I'm supposed to be in here?"

"What?" Silas asks, flipping on a wall switch. Golden uplights glow from the corners of the room. "It's just our sex room."

"Yeah," I glance around. "It's you and Eily's sex room. I've never been in here. None of us have."

It felt weird sneaking into Silas and Eily's home. Silently, we waved at the staff staying here, and they waved back, raising an eyebrow, watching me disappear upstairs with Silas without his wife joining us.

Then again.

Who cares?

I'd never hurt Eily. I'm beyond loyal to her. I love her, too.

And this room is so her. So elegantly decorated. It's sexy, sumptuous, and chic at the same time.

The walls are painted in dark indigo, the luxe sheen of the rich paint making them almost shine, while the ceiling glows. It's painted gold. Pearl and gold fixtures with warm lamps make it cozy. Champagne velvet chairs and a settee are tucked around the room. Black leather sex furniture—a chaise, a bench, a bed, and a swing—blend into the room like they belong.

You belong.

It's all so inviting.

On my left, a wall of mirrors beckons, its glass looking antiqued. Sliding one aside, Silas reveals neatly arranged gold shelves with rows of acrylic containers and even calligraphy-labeled black leather bins.

It's like The Container Store and Etsy had an orgy with Delta's. It's signature Eily Van de May style.

But what really impresses me are the glass shelves Silas reveals, sliding aside another mirrored wall. Automatic uplights click on, glowing behind the shelves, revealing a shrine.

"Oh my god," I sigh. "I love her so much."

"Right?"

Silas admires the same sight.

Eily built a shrine to her sex toy collection.

And I mean, *collection.*

She has them carefully resting on acrylic stands. Vibrators, plugs, dildos and more in every size and color. Every material, from plastic to latex to glass to metal to wood.

On the top row are toys I've never seen. Not at Delta's. Not online.

"Those are historic ones." Silas catches my wonder. "She collects historic sex toys. We don't use them, of course. And some she donates to the Museum of Sex in New York, but these are her private collection."

I linger my fingertips over a ceramic dildo. Its old, original black glaze cracked in spots.

"My god," I mutter. "Has Stacey seen these? She'd appreciate them, too."

He nods. "Eily's going to curate a show with her at Delta's one day. That's one of her many art projects: a show celebrating historic sex toys, proving how so many cultures never shamed it. They celebrated sex, and so should we."

"So, are you saying we should use one of these on Eily?" I admire a worn wooden dildo made of oak. "For your trick night? Is that what you're thinking?"

Our partners are likely asleep in our tent, assuming Silas and I are missing because we're messing around. That we're still satisfying the sexual tension we denied between us for so long, and they definitely love us so much they want us to.

We know exactly what they're thinking.

And how they'd never suspect what we're really up to.

"Nah," he answers. "I don't think we should use one of her antique toys. Some are too valuable, or I don't trust them. What if I break one off in her?"

I snort, pointing to the modern quartz one with gold inlay. If not for its prominent penis head, I'd guess it was a rare sculpture you'd buy in an art gallery; it looks that fancy.

"But that one won't break," I say. "It's too big and thick." Silas smirks. "Damn, you've already used it on her, haven't you?"

"It was her very happy birthday trip to Paris."

"Okay, then." I point to others. "What about these from Delta's?"

I recognize the new purchases. I bought a few, too. Some of these dildos work great in my strap-on.

Daniel does love a good pegging at the end of a long week.

"We've used them," he says. "Almost all of them, and that's why I need help. I want to do something special for her. Something different."

I grab the unicorn dildo, admiring its twirling length while I ask, "What have you planned so far? Anything?"

"Yeah." He plops down on the sex chaise. "I got some ideas and bought some stuff at Delta's. Vale, Blair's twin. You know her, right?" I nod. "She shipped me some stuff, but..."

His face falls again, his shoulders sagging.

"But what?"

"But what if I get it wrong? What if I do something Eily hates and I miss our last chance this month?"

My throat gets tight, my heart clenching.

I forgot this pressure, while some may always take it for granted.

My first pregnancy, our twins, was a surprise. I wasn't supposed to fuck Daniel Pierce in the first place. Let alone fall in love with him. We married a month before our twins were born.

And our son? Our third?

We planned him. I didn't mind the months it took me to get pregnant. I assumed, naively, I guess, that it would just happen eventually.

But when you've been trying for months, even years, with no luck. Or when, like Stacey, you've lost a couple. It's humbling. It's heartbreaking.

Time feels like torture. Fate feels unkind.

I won't dismiss the pressure on Silas. The helplessness he must feel, too.

"Just tell me what you have in mind, and I'll be honest."

He wrings his hands. "You won't bullshit me?"

"Do I ever?"

"You laugh."

"That's when you're being such a man. Not a sweet husband like this."

"If I tell you, you can't give me shit."

I raise my hand. "Scouts honor."

"You were never a Girl Scout."

"Because I wouldn't promise to wear a smile all the goddamn time."

"I'm serious, Charlie Girl. I got an idea, and it's kinda weird, but..." The sexy lines on his face etch deeper. "It feels right. It feels like it's my last hope."

"Okay," I nod, "just don't do something crazy. I mean ... Eily is a free spirit with a healthy sex drive, and she loves you, but even she has a limit. Like, no super freaky stuff just to get her pregnant and—"

"But how am I supposed to know what's too freaky when it comes to us?" Damn, he sounds stressed about this.

"I mean, in three days, we've fucked like vampires, priests and nuns, and now aliens. Where's the line?"

I smile. "Donkey dicks."

I make him laugh. *He knows our nickname for him.*

"No donkey dicks," he says. "I swear. But I got an idea. More like ... I got an omen."

"A *what*?"

That word: omen.

It raises my pulse, my eyebrows, and that trusted premonition I get when something is coming. Like electricity across a wire, I can always feel it. It's been a blessing and a curse my whole life.

I can often sense when something is going to happen—something ... cosmic, world-changing, life-altering.

I can sense it, but I can't stop it.

"An omen," he says. "It keeps telling me to do this thing with Eily. This *ritual.* I can see it in my dreams, and when I'm awake, it comes in flashes. It's like someone is talking to me, telling me to do it."

"Is his name Redix, and does it involve Lemonheads?"

Now, it's his turn to roll his eyes. "I'm serious, but if you're gonna give me shit, then—"

"I'm kidding. I'm kidding. It's just when you talk about omens it scares me. I believe in them."

"Since when are you scared of shit?" He gestures to the scar on my cheek. "You're the bravest person I know."

"Brave is what you do even when you're scared. I feel fear. I just won't kneel to it. I make fear *my* bitch."

He nods. "Alright then. If I tell you, and if I show you, you can't laugh or get scared or give me shit. Just tell me if you think it'll work. If you think Eily will like it."

I'm about to do the scouts honor thing again, but yeah, I didn't take that oath, so I salute instead. "Promise."

"Alright. Pick out seventeen of Eily's best dildos."

"Umm, *what?*"

"You heard me."

He stands before fetching a basket from the corner. Bottles of lube and batteries rumble in the bottom of it.

He answers my questioning stare, "This is our traveler basket for when we borrow from the shrine and fuck in other places. Like ... *every* fucking where."

I start selecting dildos and setting them in his basket. It's like we're in the produce section, picking the juiciest pricks for an orgy salad.

"Dare I ask what we're going to do with these?"

"What do you *usually* do with dildos?"

"Well, my son, Duke, found one of ours and started using it as a sword in the backyard. He proudly showed it to our neighbor. There was *that* mortifying day. And then there was the day when Caroline found my fingertip vibrator and wore it to preschool, saying she was a princess getting married and it was her wedding ring."

Laughter shakes his chest. "Damn, don't y'all lock up your sex toys?"

"Don't judge." I elbow him. "You'll see one day. I promise. Your kids will be finding your sex toys, too."

He mutters, "God, I hope so."

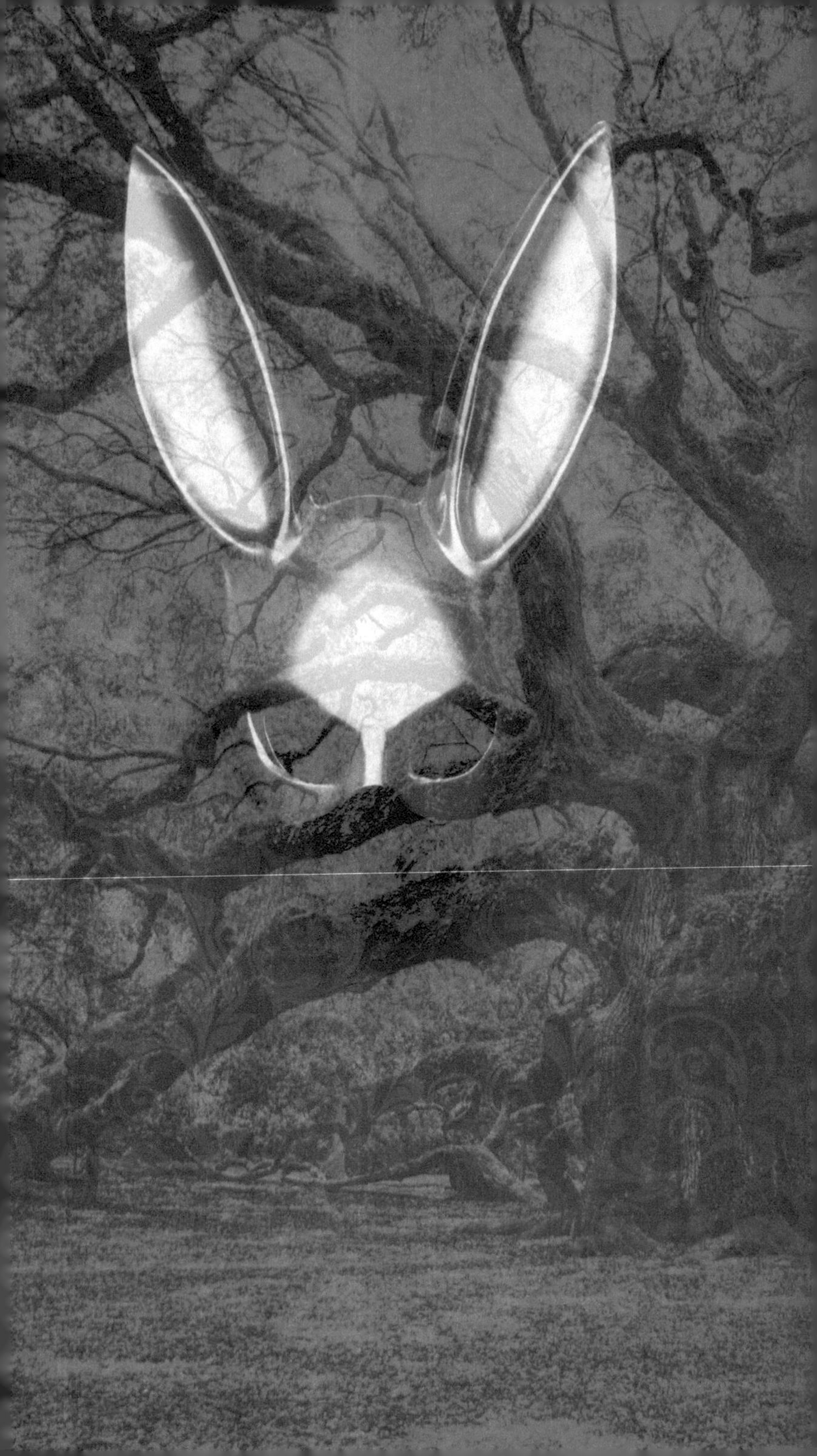

Silas

"I'LL COME BACK AS A GOLDEN BENNY BITCH AND HAUNT YOU
LIKE A HOT HAINT."

Only Charlie will get this. Only she'll understand. Yeah, she'll definitely give me shit for it.

But still.

She believes in me. She always has. Sometimes, she was the only one.

Silently, I lead her down the sandy path between my home and the glamping village. It's a long walk lit by the full moon.

I glance up at it.

I've always heard the moon's voice. She has power and pull. Live by the water, and you respect her.

But now, another voice calls. It resonates with her in an evocative chant. It sounds deep, thrumming in my veins and drawing me near.

On the edge of the camp, between our home and the

tents we've erected, soars the ancient live oak.

Yes, there are others on this island—these magnificent trees, famous for their size and history. There's one so large in Florida, it can be seen from space.

But this is the oldest, the largest one here, and no photo can capture its power.

The base of the tree is so wide that the eleven men here would have to link our arms to circle it. Its thick branches reach so high they tower toward the sky, then swoop back down, grabbing the ground, before rising again.

Charlie stares up at the tree, admiring the moonlight dancing through its autumn leaves, drifting on the breeze to the ground.

She whispers, "What are we doing here?"

"Something found me here."

"Quit talking cryptic and creepy."

"I'm not. Something told me to come here." I point. "To dig here."

She flicks her stare to where my finger aims. "There better not be a skull buried there."

"Not a skull." I kneel, my fingers raking through the rich, decaying soil. "I found something else."

She kneels beside me. "You found a *dildo*?"

I chuckle. "What the fuck? Why would I find a dildo buried at the bottom of an ancient live oak tree?"

"Well, I don't know." She shrugs. "You made me load a basket with them. You made me trek across the island with them. And you said my ancestor did sex rituals here."

"No, *you* said that. You said you saw them ... sorta."

"I did."

"And I believe you. I *know* they did rituals here because I found this..."

Dusting away the dirt, the moonlight catches its golden sheen.

Charlie marvels, "Oh my god. Is it gold bullion? Buried by pirates? I mean. It's almost not fair. You already have billions. You don't need more fucking gold or mon—"

"It's not money or gold. It's this."

I lift the relic, holding it up for her to admire. It takes her a moment to recognize its form.

"Is that a gold rabbit? With a man's dick?"

"It's a rabbit dick."

"Rabbits don't have dicks like that."

"How do you know?"

"Are we really debating this?"

"No." I hand it to her. "Whatever it is, it's a sign. I found it buried here months ago and looked it up. Pagans used rabbits in fertility rituals."

"I know," she says. "Lots of our holidays and rituals are actually pagan ones, like Halloween. The pagans called it 'Samhain,' the night when the veil between the living and the dead is so thin that the dead can visit the living and—"

"Jeez, is this Religion 101?"

"Fuck off. I paid attention in college."

"Well, then, tell me what this means. Why did I find this the day Eily and I started to try to get pregnant?"

"*Noooo.*" Her eyes get as wide as saucers. "The fuck you say?"

"Yeah, the fuck I *did*. It was my first morning with Eily with no birth control, with her ovulating. Twice, we made love, and then I came out here. I started to clear the land for the tents, but something told me to come to this tree. To this spot. To dig. And I found this rabbit."

"What does Eily think?"

"I didn't tell her."

She backslaps my arm. "Don't lie to your wife."

"I'm not lying to her. I just didn't tell her. I mean. What if it's a bad omen? It would freak her out."

With a deep sigh, Charlie studies the figurine, spinning it in the moonlight. "This thing is old."

"It had to be from Lois Ravenel. After the wars, his family lost this island, and it fell into ruins. It's been abandoned since."

"A Ravenel Fuck Rabbit." She shakes her head, so proud. "Finally, the proof. Hot sex *is* in my DNA."

"No, it was in the dirt. And now I think it's telling me to do something. Like, if I want to get Eily pregnant, we need to do a ritual."

"Oh, my pagan gods," she sighs. "Eily would love it."

"So, you don't think it'll weird her out? Or make her think it's bad luck?"

"I think if you want a blessing, you have to offer up a prayer."

"What about a sacrifice?"

She whips her stare at me. "Touch Eily and die."

I lower my brows. "Cut back on the dark romances."

"But you just said *sacrifice*. Like, someone has to bleed or die."

"No one's bleeding or dying. Jeez, gimme credit."

"Then what are you sacrificing?"

"Just trust me. Just tell me if you'll help me."

Tenderly. Aggravatingly. Lovingly. Annoyingly. Charlie rolls her eyes at me.

"I'll always help you, you little shit. Till the day I die, and then I'll come back as a golden bunny bitch and haunt you like a hot haint, making sure you love your wife right."

I flick dirt at her. "See? That's not such a sacrifice."

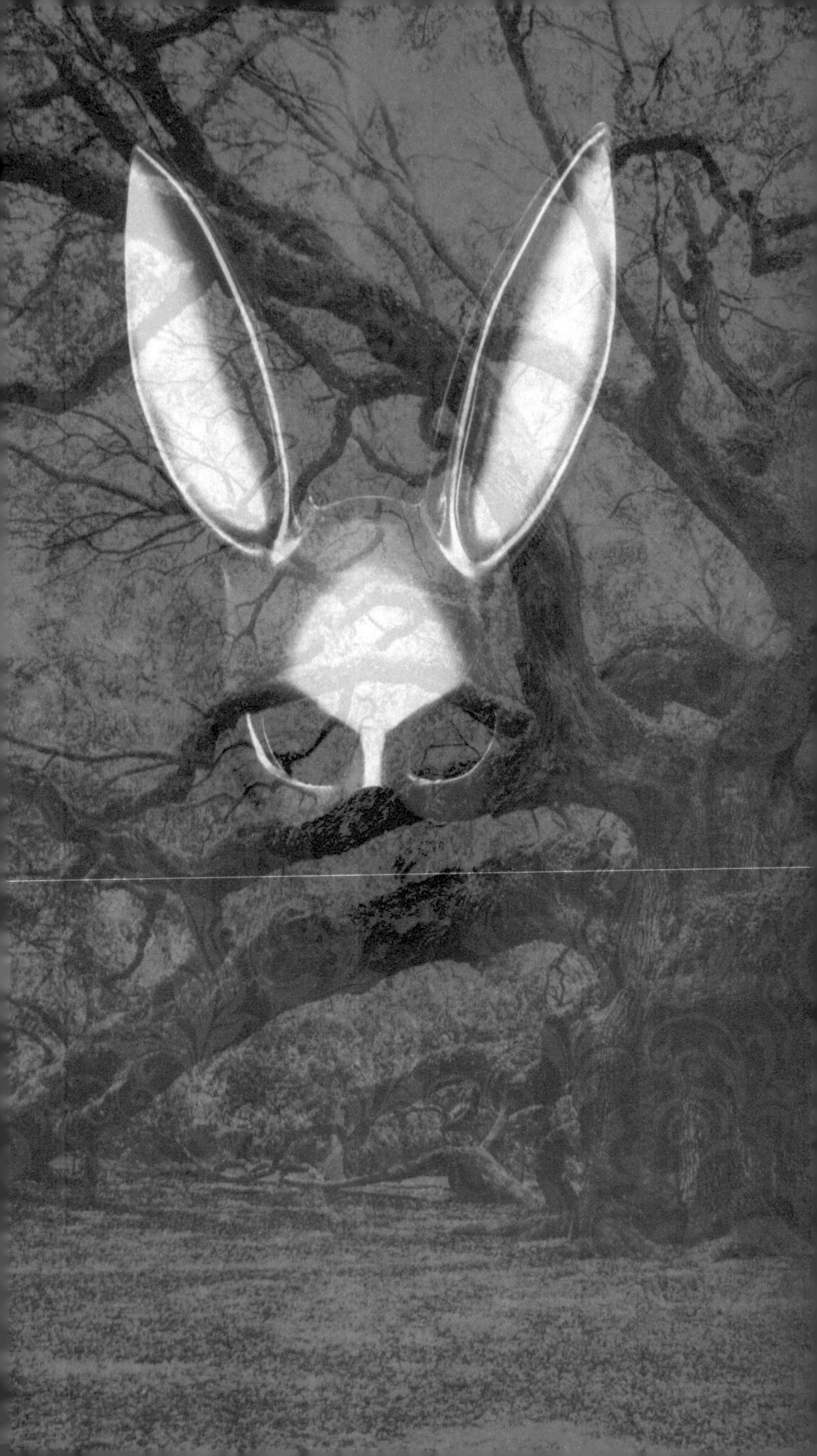

Cade

CHAPTER TWENTY-ONE

CADE

"You won't mind if I finish my misdemeanor. I really need some butt plugs."

I smell bacon and guilt.

Silas and Charlie keep exchanging glances. And not in a we-just-fucked-around way.

They're up to something.

We found them asleep this morning on the cushions in the Treat Tent. They said they didn't want to wake us last night.

Eily smiled, wrapping her arms around Silas's neck, asking him with delight in her eyes, "What did y'all do?"

"We went gigging," he answered her.

Eily believed it, and so did Daniel. We all know how Silas and Charlie love flounder gigging. You have to do it at night.

But I noted Charlie's flip-flops. She's too smart to fish in those. Same with Silas.

And I'm a mom to little ones. A flea fart could wake me. So, I know they never came into the tent overnight to grab their deck shoes.

Stalking the breakfast buffet, I grab a pumpkin latte, a pumpkin muffin, a pumpkin waffle … you know? 'Tis the season. Go gourds or go home.

Finally, when she's alone, I pounce.

"I smell cunty tricks."

Charlie smirks, choosing a green Frankenstein smoothie. "If you'd start using soap when you shower, you wouldn't have such a pungent pussy."

"Don't flip my witch switch." I elbow her. "You're up to something."

"Holster your strap-on. I'm closed for breakfast."

"Eily didn't notice your flip-flops, but I did. The hell you and Silas went gigging last night."

She knows I'm just giving her hell.

Not Charlie. Not one of us would ever hurt the other. But sneak around and try to pull off a surprise?

Pile on a life sentence for that guilt.

Proving my point, she doesn't answer me.

"I have ways of making you talk."

Looking me dead in the eye, she sucks her green smoothie through an orange paper straw. "Uh-huh. And I have ways of making you come."

"I won't put out until you tell me."

Laughing, she answers, "That's why I have four other partners."

"I'll get Redix to go on a fuck-strike, too."

"Hmmm," she jokes. "Guess I'll be calling Stacey and her husbands more often. Or making more trips to Atlanta to visit Blair, Beau, and Colton."

"Oh, come on." I sag, almost dropping my waffle. "I

need two more cups of coffee to put up with this shit. Just tell me."

"Tell you what?"

"Tell me what you and Silas are planning."

Slowly, a warm smile crinkles her scar. In a whisper, she answers, "A fertility ritual."

Lightning fast, I figure it out. "For Eily? For tonight?"

"Yeah," she answers. "But one of us needs to go to Delta's today. And it can't be Stacey. It'll be too obvious if she leaves."

I glance around the Treat Tent. All are gathered around tables, laughing and drinking coffee.

It's our last day. No one wants to leave, not even Colton. Rumor has it he finagled his way out of practice today.

"I'll go. I can say I need to check on the girls. That granddad ran out of diapers or something."

"That's lame," Charlie answers. "Your dad is the best babysitter ever. Eily will see right through it."

"A yeast infection! I can say I need some cream."

"This ain't amateur hour. You know we stocked our fuck pharmacy."

"Fine then," I sigh. "Come up with something better. But it should be me. Other than you and Silas, I know the tides and the water. I can get to the mainland fastest."

Charlie twists her lips, her stare scanning our group. Logic fires across her sapphire eyes. Maybe a little smoke wisps from her ears, too.

"Cummings," she says, whipping her stare back at me. "We say you're going to confront him at Delta's. It's Thursday. He should be there, according to Stacey, and you've been such a cop about him. Why not? Eily would believe it."

"Eily would be pissed. I can't rain on her spooky parade."

"Then say you won't confront him. Just tell her you want to meet him. To make sure he's legit and to encourage him to terrify the men tonight."

I nod. "If that pans out, Eily would love it. And you're not wrong. I want to meet this man."

An hour later, I'm whipping the rope free of the cleat while Eily stands on the dock, begging me, "Just don't pull a Cade."

"A *Cade*?"

"Yeah," she says while Silas unties the bow of his boat, ready to send me on this secret mission. "Just don't kill Cummings if you think he's bad. I mean ... he *is* bad but in a sweet way."

"In all my years, I've never met a *sweet* criminal."

This ruse of Charlie's is actually working because I'm not lying.

Yeah, I'm going to Delta's to pick up supplies for a surprise ritual tonight.

But hell yes, I'm going to Delta's to confront a mobster, too.

The only thing I'm afraid of? The traffic I may fight on the bridge.

"Cade, I'm serious." Eily's fists are on her hips, her pumpkin sunglasses making it hard for me to take her seriously. *She's too cute.* "Do NOT piss off Cummings. I kinda like him."

"You like him because of his fake name." Silas tosses the fenders overboard, prepping the boat to launch. "*Cummings.* That's fucking classic."

"No, I like him because he's good at scaring the shit out of y'all."

"Then where has he been the last two nights?" I ask.

"That's his tactic," she answers. "He keeps you guessing."

"Well, I'm not guessing. I'm getting answers." I grip the key, turning over the engine. "And I'll be back in a few hours. Text me if y'all need me to pick up anything."

Quickly, Silas slices me a look.

He's already schemed with Stacey about what she has in stock at her store. He's already texted Vale, the store manager, who's prepared a box for me to pick up.

Will I happen to stumble up to the third floor and, whoops, pick the lock on a secret black door?

Does a queef make a sound?

Two hours later, I'm standing in Delta's front parlor. Five large, flat black boxes are stacked by my feet.

"Thanks for this," I tell Vale.

"You're welcome."

Of course, her smile is identical to Blair's. Except I notice a new piercing—a diamond Monroe above her left lip. She didn't have it the last time I shopped here.

"You really saved us. It's going to be a hot, haunting Halloween eve." I gotta ask. I can't be a bitch. Not to another woman. "Do you want to join us? And witness your spell?"

Barely, Vale laughs.

No, she's forcing it, tossing her thumb over her shoulder.

A man, an older, hot man with glasses, sits at her desk. He tries hiding his glance, but I catch it.

He's clocking me.

"I gotta pass," Vale says. "I'm in the middle of an audit. Our accountant has me chained to my desk."

The man in glasses coughs.

"All night?"

"Yeah," she twirls her long black braid, "all day, all night—I'm his prisoner."

"Ahem." He clears his throat again.

"I mean, we gotta stay," Vale says. "The IRS will kill me if we don't resolve this taxing issue."

I search her gray eyes. Vale's trying to tell me something. She's not in danger. Not imminently, I can tell.

But something is going on.

Something with the accountant.

"Well, I'm good at math," I offer. "I did some forensic accounting for the Sheriff's Department back in the day."

"We're fine." A gruff voice erupts from the elegant man, and I confront his stare.

He leans back in his chair, lifting his chin, a smile ghosting his bearded lips. "The IRS won't touch her," he assures, "*not* while I'm around."

Plot, meet the thickening.

This guy?

He's clearly more than an accountant. Or at least, he's the hottest fucking one I've ever seen. Sexy, mussed, light brown hair. A shadow of a dark beard. Brown, bedroom eyes under a stern brow. And pillow lips your cat wants to pounce on.

I'd evade my taxes for his internal audit.

Instead, I shrug. "Suit yourself."

Stacey said her historic Charleston row house is haunted. Probably. But rife with testosterone, mobsters, and taxing issues?

I'm on to something.

"Can I shop?" I thumb toward the stairs. "I want to pick out something special for Eily."

Vale winks. "Please, be our guest."

"Ms. Monroe," Mr. Taxing My Clit snarls at Vale, "the

upper floors are closed this afternoon until we finish inventory of your assets."

"Not for Cade," Vale chirps, sounding thrilled to defy him. "The Six are loyal customers. Stacey trusts them."

Vale flits her hand toward the stairs. "Me cunty casa, es su casa."

A bilingual invitation? That's all I need.

With a cheerful wave, I grab a black leather shopping basket and stroll past Mount Beefcake, aka Jace, one of Delta's two bodyguards.

Every time I see him ... I swear I've seen him before.

Leisurely, I climb the wooden stairs. Since the upper floors are apparently closed this afternoon, I'm free to snoop.

On the second floor, I aim for the ivory lacquered drawers in the showroom, quickly selecting two white gowns for Silas to choose from. Surely, he'll love one for Eily.

Folding them in the basket on my arm, I strain my ears. Downstairs, it sounds like Vale is giving the accountant some lip.

Good.

Sorry, but I can just tell...

That man is hotter than the Devil's boxers, but his ass is so tight he'd skin a fart.

Quietly, I leave the showroom and sneak up to the third floor. At the top of the landing, on the right, is the infamous "classroom," as we jest. It's where Stacey and her husbands, or guests, can give or receive "educational" demonstrations of the various sex furniture and toys that Delta's sells.

Gotta say: best oral exam ever.

But not all are allowed. Not all are permitted up here.

Evidenced by the camera monitoring the doorway.

Stacey doesn't allow cameras in the room, but she does ensure safety. Jace, downstairs, can see who enters. So, I make sure he catches me doing so.

I set my basket down and take a moment to admire one of the leather sex chaises in the room. I've been wanting to get one. And if our kids or guests ask what it is, it's mommy's "yoga chair."

You know … for downward doggy style and all.

Waiting a few minutes, I listen again and hear the din of voices downstairs, so I slide against the wall, right under the camera above my head. At this angle, it can't see me.

At the opposite end of the third-floor landing, a black door calls me like *The Bachelorette*.

Magnolia Cade Bryant, pick me. Pick me. Pick me.

Sliding out the decorative spider bobby pin holding back my bangs, I pry it open with my teeth. Squatting down, I wedge the metal into the brass keyhole.

Do I know how to break into shit? Guilty.

Am I a former cop? Guilty.

Do I give a shit? Not guilty.

Because guilty skills can do good sometimes.

Yeah, I taste the hypocrisy.

According to Stacey, Michael Cummings and his crew are guilty criminals who do good work, so how am I any different?

Meh. I shrug. That's why the Fifth Amendment is so much fun.

I'm protected from self-incrimination and being forced to—

"Can I help you?"

Fuck me, Jesus and Joseph. You, too, Mary.

Please tell me Vale Monroe grew a set of balls in five minutes and suddenly sounds like a dangerous man.

"Uh, yeah." *Don't look. Don't look. You're fifty shades of guilty.* "I was hoping to find some more butt plugs in here. Our glow-in-the-dark ones don't work. Then again, butt cheeks get in the way, so what do you ex—"

"So, you need to pick a lock to satisfy your sphincter's needs?"

Sphincter?

Someone plays with Wordle. Or asses. Or both.

"Well, if you knew my husband's fetishes, I'm hoping there's a candy store behind this door, too."

Yes, I'm still squatting. Yes, I'm still facing a keyhole with my guilty spider bobby pin in it. Yes, I can do this all day.

Unless I have to pee.

"I'm well aware Mr. Redix Dean is a very lucky man to have a wife like you so devoted that she commits felonies for him."

Did you hear his asshole tone?

Yeah, me too.

This fucker ain't talking about this damn door.

He knows.

And I'm pissed.

Slowly, I rise, turning to face him. Stifling my surprise, it's not the mysterious Michael Cummings I expected.

No…

I'm glaring at the Anal Accountant.

Black-horned glasses that define a sexy nerd. Starched white button-down that could stand on its own. A gold and navy silk tie knotted so tight it'd survive a hurricane. Tailored navy pants with a razor-sharp front crease over his muscular quads, his cuffs breaking perfectly over spit-shined brown leather oxfords. Damn, I can see my reflection in them.

This man not only counts money, he has it.

And yet, something's off about him.

But here we go…

"Breaking and entering isn't a felony."

It's his intensity that's odd. Is it scary? Or sexy? Dang it, it's Halloween. My horny cat can't tell the difference.

"I wasn't speaking of breaking and entering," he says, casually lacing his hands framing his crotch.

Is he protecting his bulge? Or showing it off? Tough call, but it adds up to be a big one.

"Well, then. You won't mind if I finish my misdemeanor. I really need some butt plugs."

"Sergeant Bryant, did you not complete your anal phase of psychosexual development?"

I scoff, "I wasn't aware they taught Freud's bullshit in Business School."

"And yet," his lush lips tighten, "I'm well-schooled on how they teach law enforcement how to *break* the law."

Yep, there's another veiled threat. And yep, he's standing so close I can taste his cologne: chocolate musk, sweet money, and one big creamy man muscle.

"So, this is your room?"

Checkmate.

"No," he answers calmly. "But I know the gentleman who rents it."

"Who?"

"Someone like you who appreciates privacy." He's so fucking hot, he's cold. "Secrecy. Loyalty. *Protection.*"

Yeah, I could interrogate. Or I could banter. Both are my favorite pastimes.

But I have an orgy waiting.

"Look, we can whip out our verbal dicks and compare the length of our lexicons for hours. But I have a question that *will* be answered, and friends waiting for a Whorey Halloween. And yes, I'm willing to commit felonies for the ones I love. Wanna be next?" His brows tick up. "That's what I thought. So cut the shit and tell me where Michael Cummings is."

Is that a smile or a smirk?

"I don't know that name."

"Oh, so you're one of those?"

His stare burns.

"One of those who thinks because I have breasts, I can't smell bullshit?"

He tsks, "Again. *Shit.* You really have anorectal fixation."

"I really have an asshole-tell-me-before-I-break-your-dick fixation. *Where* is Michael Cummings?"

"Umm?" A deep voice cautions. "Do we have a problem, folks?"

Jace, the bodyguard, looms behind Mr. Assmunch.

"No," I smile at Jace genuinely. "We don't have a problem. Mr. Anocrat here was just about to tell me where I can find Mr. Michael Cummings, the man who rents this room."

Taxy Tush cocks a grin while Jace answers for him, "Perhaps I can relay a message to our tenant for you, and Mr. Allen can return downstairs where he's needed."

"Mr. *Allen*?" I laugh in his face. "Oh, so you're like Mr. *Asshole* Allen? And you claim I have anality?"

It's his turn.

He opens his mouth to say something ... but stops.

Then, I swear it happens in slow motion.

Arrogantly, he removes his geeky glasses, and Clark Kent has nothing on him. Before my eyes, he transforms like Superman, but this time...

He's a supervillain.

That's when I catch the knavish rake of his eyes and the

dark ink hiding under his starched collar. His nipples harden, betraying how they're pierced, too.

Leaning forward, his lush lips curl, his sneer sounding so sexy while his warm mouth steams over my ear. "If we're talking fetishes, it's Mr. Hybristophilia Allen to you, Cade. But, *shhh*, it's my very big secret."

When he pulls away, his smile is pure porn and power.

And, goddammit, I need Google in my brain.

What the hell does hybristophilia *mean?*

While he returns to his innocent disguise, sliding on his geeky glasses, I address Jace.

But really? I'm ordering Mr. Allen.

"Tell Michael Cummings he has one hour to return Eily Van de May's call."

Jace stammers, "May I tell ... er... Mister ... *Cummings* what the matter is about?"

Why does Jace stall over that last name? And not as Eily does, like she's tickled by it?

"Yes," I answer, brushing past Mr. Allen's broad shoulder. "Tell Cummings it's about his next breath if he wants one."

I take a Sunday stroll back into the sexy classroom to retrieve my basket. On my way down the stairs, Mr. Allen follows me like an ominous shadow.

Do I want to turn around and put him in a chokehold until he confesses? I'd climax to it.

Do I want to disrespect Stacey and her business? No, I trust her too much.

Still, there's more to this criminal cock, Mr. Allen, than meets the eye, and I'm an addict for the truth. I'll get my fix soon enough.

In the front parlor, Vale greets me with a hug. It's like I

just gave her a pony. "It's on the house!" she says of my gowns for Eily.

"Please," I insist. "Put it on our tab. And next time I'm in Charleston, I owe you lunch. No audit. No excuses."

"Well, at least let Jace carry all the boxes for you."

"No. I got it."

Because like hell if I'll let Mr. Allen think I'm dainty and dumb.

I lift the teetering pile of boxes with the grace of a hippo, then turn, giving Mr. Allen my model smile. Fortunately, I remember how to fake that like a pro.

"Good afternoon, Mr. Allen." I wink. "I *will* be seeing your ass again. You can count on that."

Take that, Mr. Fuck-You-Philia.

But while I wait with my gift boxes on the sidewalk by the cobblestone street outside Delta's for my car back to the marina, I slightly stomp, cursing myself.

"Fuck! You did it! You totally pulled a Cade. You verbally twisted that man's balls. That man who clearly works with Micahel Cummings."

Eily's going to kill me.

Maybe Stacey will, too.

In the minutes it takes for my car to arrive, I whip out my phone and look up "hybristophilia."

The screen warns, "Hybristophilia: Sexual interest and attraction to criminals, particularly violent ones."

Twisting my stare back to Delta's tall front windows, I search for shadows through the white sheers that block the view inside.

But like he's reading my mind, the curtain pulls back, and Mr. Allen toasts me with a come-hither smile and his cup of tea.

The sexy, sinful, son-of-a-bi...

Wait, I like bitches.
I can be one.
Specifically, to men like Mr. Allen.

By the time I'm back, Silas is pacing the dock. While we tie up the boat, I get an earful.

"Damn, Cade, I'm sweating like a sinner in church. You were supposed to be back an hour ago."

"I know. I'm sorry." I have to lie. I won't ruin tonight for them. "The traffic on the bridge was horrible."

"Do you have the gown?"

"Yeah. I got you two to choose from." He jumps into the boat while I snap off the lid to the storage bin containing the boxes from Delta's. Lifting the lid off a black garment box, I show Silas my selections.

He examines the white silk chemise, then the white lace babydoll.

"They're pretty," he sighs, exasperated. "But they look like what she wore on our wedding night."

"You said 'something virginal,' and nowadays, the only time a woman wants to be a virgin again is on her wedding night."

"But she'll be cold."

"No, she won't." I lift the lid to another, even thicker garment box and show Silas my surprise. "It's a white, faux fur cape with a hood."

"It's perfect!" he marvels. "But how the hell did you get this at Delta's? It looks like something from a fairytale."

"Vale said they have lots of Furries."

"Lots of what?"

"People with a fur fetish. Or anything fuzzy or whatever. Don't ask," I huff. "I've had my fill of fetishes today."

He looks at me like I've lost my mind, and god, I want to tell him about Mr. Allen and Mr. Cummings. I want to tell him that Eily's "sweet criminal" is on my shitlist.

Shit.

Shit.

No. No. No. I do NOT have an anorectal fixation.

I have a protect-my-family fixation.

"Okay," I snap the lid back on the bin. "What's next?"

"I'll take this to Charlie. She's been setting up all day while Blair, Scarlett, and Stacey have kept Eily distracted."

"Distracted with what?"

"They're in the Treat Tent, with everyone carving pumpkins to take home to all the kids tomorrow. And with Eily and her Dremel tools, that means pumpkin Picassos ... and Paw Patrol ones."

"Aww. Is she really?" It hits me hard. "The girls are gonna love it!"

Why am I suddenly getting choked up?

Oh, I know.

Because Eily's so sweet like that. She often does crafts with our kids. I don't even mind when her indigo art turns their little hands blue.

It clenches my heart. I want this so much for Eily and Silas. Our hearts are tethered to the same dream.

Years from now, I can see our front porches in a row, loaded with pumpkins carved by a dozen kids.

Okay. Maybe not a dozen because I'm done at two.

Half a dozen.

Two for me and Redix. Three for Charlie and Daniel. And please, *I pray to whatever bewitching ritual we do tonight* for at least one child for Silas and Eily.

"So, how can I help?"

Silas rushes, "Can you go to the house and get a lantern? Something for her to carry so she can see."

"Uh, they make these things called flashlights."

He rolls his eyes.

Poor fella.

Usually, Silas is immune to stress.

But I have a feeling he'll be a dad soon because that's one big ball of bouncing, blissful stress, and he's getting his first taste.

"Not tonight," he says. "It's an old ritual, so no electricity, nothing modern. It's all lanterns, pumpkins with candles ... you get the idea."

"Oh, my god. That's going to be so beautiful. She's going to love it. All the jack-o-lanterns and flickering candles and her in a long, white cape and—"

"Can we do this Pinterest board later?"

"How do you know about Pinterest?"

"Jeez, Cade." Silas laughs. "Quit investigating. No cops tonight." I raise my eyebrow. "Fine. My wife is an artist. If we have a kid, their middle name will be Pinterest. Satisfied?"

I twitch my nose. "Yep."

"Okay. So, get a lantern for her. And ... and ... boots! She'll need her boots. Get her Doc Martens."

"Doc Martens and bridal lace babydoll? If that doesn't conjure your cock, a coven, and a conception, I don't know what will."

He sighs, a heavy exhale falling from his chest.

Pecking my forehead, he mutters, "How can I tell her I want a baby with her, but *she's* really my dream come true? No matter what happens."

I hug his waist, muttering against his pecs. "You say

exactly that. A million times if you have to."

He kisses my hair. "What if it doesn't work?"

"What if you have twins?"

He jerks back, shocked.

"Look, you can play the what if game, or you get on with life. You decide."

Hope finds his face again.

"Alright. Enough wallowing." I pick up the big bin and shove it into his hands. "Now, go be the baby-making, love liquid sharing, seed-spreading, beefy, breeding, sex shaman you've practiced to be your whole damn life. You know how to do it. And might I say," I blow a kiss, "damn well, so just do it.

"Just love her tonight."

CHAPTER TWENTY-TWO

EILY

> **"I'M CRAVING POTATO CHIPS AND DICK."**

I gotta give it to them. They kept me distracted. All day, I was a pumpkin carving machine.

But now?

Something's up.

The sun started to set, and everyone made silly excuses to leave the tent. All that remains are me, three dozen carved pumpkins, and Blair, setting candles inside them.

"You want to tell me what they're up to, or should I just wait here for the surprise?"

"Hmm?"

She won't look at me. It screams guilt.

I sit on a picnic table, my legs swinging. I just packed my Dremel away, and now I'm bored—and convinced.

"I know Silas is up to something. Just tell me so I won't ruin it."

"Uh," Blair laughs. "*That* ruins it."

"Just please tell me it's kinky, and I'll be happy. I'm ovulating, and I can tell. I'm craving potato chips and dick."

She chuckles. "Is that what it feels like? I wouldn't know. I've been on the pill since I was seventeen."

"Oh, bet your favorite vibrator, you can feel it. Once I stopped using the patch, poor Silas. I had to cut my fingernails because I started shredding his back every time we fucked. Now I know why they make all those maneater songs about women. If I'm not craving his cock, I want to run five miles, cry, scarf down Pringles, or organize my spice rack."

Blair falls on a furry bean bag chair, laughing harder. "Poor Beau and Colton. That'll be me in a few months."

"Oh!" I perk up. "Are you gonna try, too?"

"Yeah. Right before our wedding, I think I'll stop the pill. It's a long story, but Colton really has baby fever. So does Beau."

"And you?"

She pushes her glasses back up her nose. I love Blair's look: sexy librarian. I love her curves, too.

Not that I don't like my little Tinkerbell body.

I mean ... if you got it, haunt it. That's your spell.

"Yeah," she answers. "Stacey told me today you're never really ready for anything. That's the beauty of life. It's predictably surprising."

"She's half right. I mean. I'm surprised by *my* life. I fantasized about Silas in high school but never dreamed he'd be my husband." I twist my lips. "I lie. I did *dream* it. I just didn't expect it. Same goes with this. I dream about being a mom. But I can promise you ... I am SO damn ready for tonight."

I hop off the table. "Come on, just give me a little hint. After all we've done this week, what's left? A graveyard gangbang? A fright night of masked fucks? The forbidden Addams family?"

Blair shivers. "Eww. No. My sister worships Wednesday Addams, and that's a hard pass."

"Then what are they doing to me? Everyone who hasn't hosted a trick or been a treat came up with sad excuses. I mean, really? Zar, Nick, *and* Luke are suddenly too tired? Please. Those guys have constant heat in the meat. So, what does that leave Silas to do? It's his trick night, which means *I'm* the trick again."

Blair purses her lips.

She won't crack.

And I won't make her the guilty party who does.

So, I plop beside her and rest my head on her shoulder. "Hopefully, we can get knocked up together. Cade and Charlie are done. Stacey and Scarlett are taking a break. It'd be nice to have a pregnancy pal."

"I heard your ankles swell."

"I heard my tits will finally swell."

"I heard you get hemorrhoids."

"I heard you get hornier."

Her body shakes with laughter beside mine. "Oh my god, that's a combo from hell. I *am* going to need an expectant vag to vent to."

"Alright, where's our sassy Whoraween?" Suddenly, Cade charges into the tent. "You're coming, *literally*, with us."

She's followed by our Cunty Coven: Charlie, Stacey, Scarlett, and Blair's already rising with them.

"Well, it's about damn time." I stand, too. "My pussy was getting parched with impatience."

"Here." Charlie shoves a full water tumbler in my hand. "Drink, pee, and then shower. You know the drill."

I salute. "Yes, Sergeant Squirt."

Playfully, she smacks my ass while they lead me out of the tent. I start sucking down electrolytes because, one: this ain't my first orgy; two: UTIs are a special hell; and, three: I want to be in top shape for this.

I'm conjuring Simone Biles. I'm going for a gold medal vault with a round-off, back handspring into two flips in a pike position, landing with a perfect mount on Silas's donkey dick.

Just please don't let me break it again.

While they drink wine and giggle in the dressing room, I shower. They make me do it with the curtain open so they can watch.

Yeah, it starts to heat my oven.

With the way Scarlett looks at me, she's getting heated, too.

Then Stacey gives me a blow. With a hair dryer. Not the other fun kind.

"Honey," she coos, "this brings back my beauty queen days. How should we fix all this gorgeous long hair?"

"Down to her waist," Cade insists. "It makes Silas feral."

"Are you sure?" I ask. "Sometimes, if it's down and I'm lying on my hair while we're fucking and I sneeze or something, I can get whiplash."

Blair about falls over on the vanity countertop, laughing. "Whiplash from a wienering? It's too good. Why don't you cut it?"

"Yeah," Cade suggests. "I love having short hair. Redix thinks it's sexy."

"Because," I share, fascinated by Stacey doing something fancy with a round brush, giving my ends some curl, "I've been growing it out since high school. Since the day Silas saved me from those boys."

Stacey flicks off the dryer.

All jaws drop.

All eyes fall on me.

Charlie asks gently, "Eily, are you serious? All these years? That's why your hair is so long?"

"Yeah. It's my tribute to Silas."

"Does he know?" Cade asks.

"Of course. That's why he loves it so much. Did you notice his leather necklace and the glass bead on it? Look closely. It's a lock of my hair trapped in the glass. I made it for him."

"Stop it." Scarlett stomps, throwing her chin up and blinking back tears. "That is too damn sweet. Y'all are like a fairytale, and my ovary just burst. Luca's gonna shoot right through my diaphragm tonight and get me pregnant again."

I'm feeling the fairytale, too.

Dare, I pray it actually comes true tonight.

"Can one of you witches just tell me what's happening?"

Cade leans down, kissing my cheek. "Quit asking, my little witchy poo. It's a surprise."

"Well, I'm getting fucked by Silas. I know that."

Every pair of eyes darts away, admiring the boring white walls of the dressing room.

"What?" I blurt. "Are there more? Are all the guys gonna—"

"No!" Charlie hollers, half-laughing. "No way. No sexorcism for you. You're all Silas's tonight."

"Phew." I slump in my chair. My heart was racing there for a second. "I mean, I loved it when we did it before. Remember when I had to put my foot down with Silas on our first New Year's cruise? When I had to insist on my double dose with Daniel?" Charlie nods, smiling. "Yeah. Fun times. But now, I only want Silas."

"Well, you're gonna get him," Cade assures. "And then some."

They laugh with sweet delight, and I love them. Our cunty coven is a potion that would cure any heartbreak.

Even if it doesn't happen tonight, I just know. I just trust.

I'll be okay.

If you have love, you can make it through anything.

In a giddy whirl, my hair is done. Then Blair does my makeup, all fairy-to-be-fucked style: my lips petal pink, my lashes touching my brows.

Cade hands me long, white cashmere socks and my Docs to lace on. I'm naked in them before Scarlett makes me stand, slowly slipping a sheer, white lace babydoll over my frame.

It's innocent, I'm not, and that makes it sexy. My nipples are already excited, but Scarlett surprises me, leaning down to lick them through the lace, and I softly gasp.

Dear God. Goddess. Halloween deities of dicks and dark holes. Whoever. Please. I'm so damn ready for my fucking surprise.

"Now, now," Stacey purrs at Scarlett. "You're not supposed to eat our treat yet."

"Yes, you can," I sigh. "My beaver buffet is wide open."

Blair giggles while Scarlett insists, kneeling before me. "Well then. Just a little taste."

It silences the room, energy shifting from play to passion.

The other women lean against the vanity, watching. They're dressed in the black silk pajama tops and bottoms I gifted to all guests, each monogrammed for them. But now I notice some tops are unbuttoned, glimpses of cleavage tempting me.

So, I stand in the middle of the room, letting this happen to me.

This whole night can happen to me.

I trust.

I love.

I hope.

With a tender, teasing lick, Scarlett laves her warm tongue over my clit, and I gasp, wanting to fist her flaming hair, but I don't. I keep surrendering as she does it again. And again. And again, while I stare at Blair, who's opened her shirt. She's proudly pinching her nipples and chewing her lip, watching us.

When Scarlett flutters her tongue over my sensitive nub, I moan, staggering back.

"Okay," Charlie rises, but Scarlett doesn't. "She's almost ready."

From a black box, Charlie lifts a long white fur cape. I almost can't focus on the breathtaking garment while my pussy is getting licked to delight.

Standing behind me, cloaking me in luxe faux fur, Charlie fastens the gold buttons, securing the soft, warm cape over my body before she reaches inside it, pinching my erect nipples, twisting and tugging while Scarlett sucks my clit.

"Oh god, y'all," I sigh. "Is this what we're doing? Please? All five of you will have me first?"

Cade coos, "Patience."

Gently, Scarlett retreats. So does Charlie. They grin, their cheeks flushed while they take sips of wine.

But I stammer. I'm so aroused. "So ... so ... what now?"

Cade answers, "So, now we take you to where you started."

"Where I *started*?"

"Where you and Silas started. As a married couple."

I cock my head. "Our dock? Where we tossed my shoe in the water on our wedding day?"

"Yes, our Cinderella," Charlie replies, her smile sparkling. "Tonight is your next ritual." She pauses. "Your *fertility* ritual."

What?

Is this for real?

After all my lonely journaling, spicy romance novels, "educational" porn, and believing books about manifesting my destiny, it actually *worked*?

"I'm gonna be ritually fucked?"

Wait.

That didn't sound right.

"I mean," I babble. "In a good way? In a hot and kinky and sweet and spiritual way?"

"You know, a week ago," Blair chuckles, "I wouldn't have believed that emotion potion was possible. But after this week with the seventeen of us? Yeah. That's exactly what we are. Spiritually salacious. Sinfully sweet. Se—"

"So fucking late," Charlie interrupts, glancing at her watch. "Sorry to end the soliloquy, but we have very horny men and a ritual waiting."

I rub my naked thighs together. "But I'm not wearing panties."

Cade laughs, "Since when do you wear panties? You hate them."

"Tonight," I beam. "I want to. I want it to feel different. To feel special."

"Here, my sweet." Stacey hands me the white lace fluttery pair matching my babydoll slip. "Put these on. They'll be like honey to horny bees."

"Hang on." Blair turns to her makeup carrier, opening the jewelry drawer. "I have something, too." She lifts a pair of dainty nipple clamps, pearls dangling from their ends. "Do you like these?"

I bite my lip, nodding.

So she does the honors.

Lifting my away cape, then sliding my thin lace aside, she leans down, sucking my nipple, still wet from Scarlett's mouth, gently biting it too until it pebbles between her teeth.

"Yes," I moan.

With a grin, she lifts away, carefully securing the gold clamp over my nipple, slowly adjusting the tension on it until I groan. Until it's the perfect, pleasuring pinch.

"Good?" she asks.

I nod, relishing how she prepares my other nipple, too.

By the time she's done, my nipples sing with sensation, the pearls on the clamps dangling with exquisite weight, making my pussy slick with thirst.

"She looks so hot, so ready to share," Scarlett practically growls at the sight of me. "We gotta start because I'm dying."

"Same," Stacey adds.

I readjust my slip and cape before Cade takes my hand, leading me out of the honeywagon. My women, my coven for tonight, follows us, and I have to will my feet to work, thankful for my trusted Docs because my thighs are already weak with desire.

On our path through the camp, I glance around. Shocked. Delighted. Overwhelmed to see what they've done.

Real ivory taper candles drip. Their wax pouring down tall iron stakes in the ground. Their ancient glow illuminating our path. The jack-o-lanterns we carved today decorate the platforms of every darkened tent.

It's the only light I see, taking my breath away.

"Did Silas do all this?"

"All the men did this for *you*."

Cade squeezes my hand. Our feet crunch over leaves fallen on sand and pine needles, following the long, winding path to the water.

I glance back at my friends and beg, "Will someone take a picture of the camp? It's so pretty; I gotta put it on Pinterest."

Stacey chuckles while Blair promises, "We got ya covered. Don't worry."

"Where are the men?" I ask.

"You have to find them," Scarlett teases.

"What?"

"Shhh." Cade tugs my hand through the dense forest, lanterns left along the twisting trail lighting the way. "No more talking. The ritual starts soon."

Normally, that's an impossible task. Me, not talking. Me, not blurting.

I can't control my mouth, and most of the time, why should I? I was silenced for too many years.

But tonight ... yes ... this feels special.

Sacred.

The cool night air thrills the small peeks of my flesh not kept warm by this mythical white fur cape. The smell of pines, autumn leaves, and the salty air of the island wafts my senses. Our footsteps softly clomp in our procession down the long, wooden dock.

We don't need lanterns out here.

The light of the full moon shimmers like diamonds over inky water. It's the most ethereal yet eerie sight.

Then I notice an unlit lantern beside a white velvet cushion on the center of the dock, a sleek black box with a gold ribbon sitting beside it.

Cade leads me to the cushion. Charlie guides me, telling me to kneel on it, facing the water. Gently, she reaches between my naked thighs, easing them apart like I'm opening to the water before me.

"Close your eyes," Cade soothes, and I obey, drawing in a stuttering breath.

Though my pulse races, I'm relaxed. Though I'm not sure, I know. Though I'm a little scared, I trust.

I hear them murmur. I hear them shuffle. I hear the golden ribbon over the black box whisper free. They're lifting something from the box, its gift tissue rustling.

Water sloshes against the floating dock, the current making it gently bob. In the distance, a barred owl calls, followed by a gentle splash in the water. It could be a fish, a dolphin, or a gator.

I'm not worried.

Me and Mother Nature got this.

I'm wet with anticipation.

"Eily Van de May?"

Cade's sultry rasp coaxes my name.

With eyes closed, I answer, "Yes?"

"Tonight, you will complete an opening ritual with all of us. You will see love, feel love, and receive love. May it open you to even more life to come."

She pauses, pulling away as I murmur, "I love Halloween."

"Now ... open your eyes and turn around."

CHAPTER TWENTY-THREE

EILY

I WISH I DIDN'T BELIEVE IN HAINTS.

Fluttering my eyes open, I look over my shoulder and gasp.

I know I'm supposed to be silent, but...

Oh, my gold-naked bunny God.

I mean ... *Goddesses.*

The women are all nude. They're all wearing gold bunny masks covering half of their beautiful faces. They're kissing. They're fondling. They're fingering.

While Blair moans, devouring Charlie's neck, her two fingers sliding inside Charlie's slick pussy, Charlie does the same to Blair while she looks at me.

"Tonight," Charlie orders warmly, "you watch. You witness love as it opens you for more. You will wait for yours to arrive, and you will trust. No matter what ... he will come for you. Do you believe?"

"Yes," I sigh.

Blair starts sucking Charlie's nipple, her fingers unrelenting between her legs. She's making Charlie's thighs shake while she tells me, "But you cannot come. Not until he's inside you. No matter the pleasure tempting you, you must wait for him, and ... and ... uhhh..."

Charlie moans as Blair suddenly squats, hungry for her, and she lets her. She opens her stance so Blair can pleasure her, so she can grab her hair while she writhes her pussy over Blair's eager tongue. Then I glance at Stacey, who's kneeling beside Scarlett. They're taking turns feasting on Cade, too.

"What ... what ... what do I do?"

"Watch. Feel. Open," Cade stammers, so I obey.

I turn around, still on my knees, and admire Blair's luscious ass while she quickly makes Charlie come on her tongue. All while Stacey moans into Cade's pussy, her fingers pounding, making Cade come with a shuddering gasp before Scarlett takes over, boldly lying Stacey on her back, nude on the dock.

We watch them twist into a sapphic sixty-nine, and I'm soaked.

My legs are trembling.

Their wanton moans echo over the water ... then I hear a thick branch snap on the shore.

We're being watched.

Charlie hears it, too, and smirks.

She helps Blair to her feet, turning Blair's naked body toward the island a hundred feet away. It's close enough, and the moon is bright enough for anyone to see as Charlie kneels before Blair now, slinging her leg over her shoulder. Blair throws her head back, her moan needy and loud, her hips rocking over Charlie's face.

Beside them, Scarlett and Stacey devote their mouths

between each other's open legs, their lusty cries filling the night air.

To the men watching on the shore, it must be the most erotic sight, their gold bunny masks adding to the fetish, to the ritual.

Cade approaches me, her naked body incandescent in the moonlight.

Lifting a lighter from the black box, she ignites the small lantern beside me.

"This is for you." She hands me a small gold parchment scroll tied with a black bow. "When you hear the drum calling, read it, then take your lantern and find us."

"*Find* you?"

"Yes." She squats beside me, her kiss lush and gentle. I kiss her back as I hear women gasping and moaning. *They're coming.* "But remember. You must watch. You must wait. You must open and receive. And you must trust. You can't come until he's inside you."

I grin. "You're so bossy."

"Shhh." She smiles, pressing her fingertip to my lips. "This is supposed to be serious."

"But I'm horny as fuck."

"Oh, my sexy bitch in heat, we're just getting started with you."

She rises while the others catch their breath. Then, one by one, they approach me, my lantern illuminating their curves as each kisses me, letting me taste the feminine arousal on their tongues, leaving me hungry for more.

Without a word, they walk away, their beautiful backsides swaying in the moonlight.

More branches break as our audience retreats. They don't want to be caught by the bunny queens while I kneel, watching them disappear into the forest.

Finally, I only see darkness, and the faint silhouette of the pines and palms before me, the shallow waves lapping the sandy shore under the moonlight.

I only hear water.

I only taste desire.

I only feel hope.

I only sense time taking forever.

I realize this is part of the ritual. It's part of life. All the plans we make. All the hopes we have. All the dreams we share.

Fate still reigns supreme.

All you can do is worship it.

Finally, after I start shivering, though wrapped in a cape, I hear a drum—a slow, thumping, primal beat.

Then it stops.

With trembling hands, I open the parchment, and it reads...

WHO HAS MARRIED MANY WOMEN BUT NEVER MARRIED?

"Oh, *come on*," I say to no one, annoyed. "I gotta use my brain?"

This isn't a ritual, this is a damn riddle.

I'm about to get mad when I only want to get laid, and then it pops into my head. My partners know my rebel mind too well.

A priest!

Of course. The ones who made rules about marriage and sex but have no clue about it, but I do. I know the answer: Colton and Mateo.

They played the priests this week, but which one? And do I go to one of their tents?

Fuck it.

I'll figure it out along the way.

Rising to my feet, my knees ache from kneeling while I brush off my cape before lifting my hood. Cloaked in fur, I grab my lantern by its warm wooden handle and aim for camp.

Yep, it's dark and creepy.

Yep, I feel way too vulnerable under my flowing cape, wearing only skimpy lingerie and wandering alone at night through the wild woods.

And yep, it's kinda fucking crazy.

But hey, it's exactly what I want.

Because this is my home. This is my sentimental spot with Silas, our dock. These are our trails, which we walk almost every day, holding hands. And this is our island where I feel safe.

But when my booted feet meet the sandy path, a sudden, chilling gust whips across the shore. A horror petrifies my bones, a panic pouring through my veins as it comes back to me...

My villain?

The haint?

Peering into the darkness, the familiar forest before me suddenly swallows all light. Someone extinguished the lanterns, and mine pales to the blackness drowning the world around me.

Who blew the lanterns out? Our women wouldn't. And who was that on the shore watching us? I thought it was our men.

But what if it was—

Snap!

A branch breaks in the distance.

I whip my eyes in its direction and see only the dark

curtain of an evil nothing, an eerie presence staring right back at me.

"Hello?"

After a panicked minute, the barred owl calls again, and I freak out.

They only call at night to warn an invader. Silas taught me that.

"Mr. Cummings?" I don't snort at his name this time. "If that's you, I'd love to know so I don't piss myself right now."

Silence replies before palms rustle with an ominous squall, screaming through the tree canopy. Dead leaves startle by. The air plummets, dry and chilling, making the hairs on my arms stand, my flesh rising, too.

Oh, no.

Something's coming.

A storm.

A villain.

A haint.

Staring down the haunting void before me, I have a choice. Give up on my fantasy and go back to the dock and scream for help. Eventually, they'll hear me. Or step bravely into terrifying, spine-chilling, blind uncertainty and complete this ritual.

I squeeze my eyes closed and see the only thing, the only one I want ... Silas.

He's waiting for me.

"Fuck this," I mutter and start marching faster, my cape sweeping the sand and dead leaves behind me.

Never has this trail felt so long. Never have I been afraid on our island. Never have I been absolutely sure...

Someone is following me.

Their breath chills my neck.

"Fuck you, demon."

I surprise him, spinning around, aiming my lantern into the howling silence, and I'm greeted by mocking shadows. The canopy above me kills the moonlight, my eyes playing wicked tricks on me.

I see nothing.

Yeah, but…

I feel someone.

"Okay, motherfucker!" I shout. "Come out now, or let me get on with my ritual. Because you're really killing my lady boner."

Silence.

Then…

Wind howls through the leaves. A sudden chill slithers like snakes up my naked legs. A sensation screams up my spine as something whispers over my ear.

"Run!"

I whip around and sprint as fast as I can, terror and threats chasing me. My heart hammers so hard; it's all I hear. My hand clutches my lantern, my knuckles white, though I can't see them. I see nothing except my booted feet stumbling through sand, leaves, and fear.

I wish Silas were here.

I wish I didn't believe in haints.

I wish I could revoke my invitation to a hot-ass criminal to scare us because it's working.

I *am* fucking scared. I'm afraid. I'm alone. And I hate these feelings; they rush back, haunting memories long buried.

So I keep running.

Another branch snaps behind me, and I gasp, glancing over my shoulder at an invisible threat. I keep waiting for it to grab my throat and steal my voice, dragging me down into the darkness. Instead, it shoves me, making me trip over branches, gripping my lantern tight.

But I keep going. I won't stop. I have to trust I'll reach Silas, I'll reach the clearing, and finally...

There it is.

Our tent village.

But this again?

Who the fuck blew out the pretty Pinterest pumpkins and candles? I can barely see a thing.

I'm writing a strongly worded one-star review on this. This isn't sexy glamping anymore.

This is scary.

This is creepy.

Because damn, our island looks haunted as hell in the pitch-black solitude.

I'm about to scream, "Stop it! I'm too cute to spook!"

Then, suddenly, a lone candle flickers. Someone lights one of the pumpkins I carved, etched with a glowing floral design.

It's Blair's tent—her tent with Beau and Colton ... the priest.

I made it.

Squaring my shoulders, I turn, lifting my chin and flipping off the dark terror behind me.

If it's Mr. Cummings.

If it's a haint.

"Eat my cunt," I sneer at the night. "You'll see! I'd rather be fucked by them than scared by you."

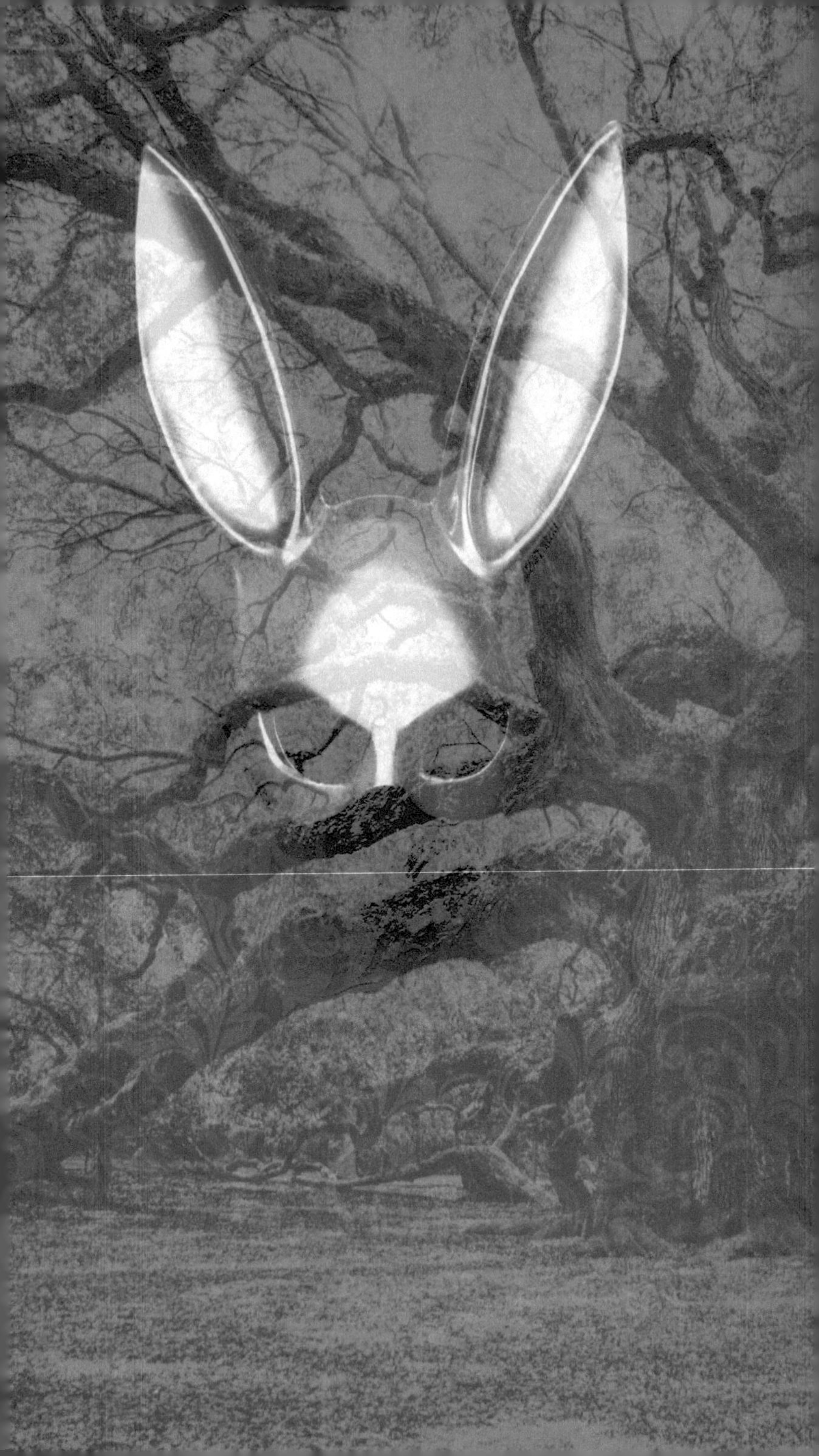

Eily

CHAPTER TWENTY-FOUR

EILY

By the time I storm across the clearing, through the safety of the camp, my fear turns into fiery determination.

I don't care how creepy it gets, I will have my fucking ritual.

I approach Blair's tent, and that's exactly what I hear.

Fucking.

Really hot fucking.

It changes my racing pulse from panic to passion. The terror in my body turns to thirst. My haunting becomes a hunger.

I rush up the platform, then pause...

Am I supposed to enter? To watch? To join?

"Eily." It's Blair's gasping voice. She must've heard me, and I guess one of them saw me on the edge of camp. "Come in."

I peel back the flap of their tent and almost moan at the sight.

Beau, Colton, and Blair are nude, glowing in the lantern light, and wearing gold rabbit masks.

Blair kneels on their bed, her cheek pressed to the white blanket, her eyes on me with her ass in the air, her pussy open for Beau and Colton's glistening hard cocks.

They've already been inside her, and now they stare coaxingly at me.

"What..." I stammer. "What do I do?"

"Sit," Blair sighs, barely nodding to the simple wooden chair by the foot of their bed. "And spread your legs. Let us watch how we make you wet. How you open while you watch us."

By the sound of Beau and Colton's rough, ready breath, they're holding back. Their muscles look tense. They stroke their cocks, waiting for me to obey, to participate in the ritual.

So, I do.

I sit on the antique French chair. In honor of the history of Indigo Island, I put one in each tent.

My furry cape forms a warm blanket beneath my bare legs as I spread them, my eyes locked on their naked bodies. My babydoll is so short and see-through; it conceals nothing. But when I tug my white lace panties aside so they can watch my arousal, my opening, Beau's eyelids drop even heavier with desire.

"Fuck," he mutters.

"Damn." Colton's nostrils flare.

They stare at me with lust.

"Keep going," Blair urges them. "Keep going and show her our love so she can open for more."

Without even grabbing her hips, Beau fists his base and

thrusts his jutting cock back inside her. Pumping into her waiting pussy, he makes Blair moan, spanking her ass as he growls, "Spread 'em."

So, she reaches behind her, pulling her cheeks even farther apart so he can admire his claim.

Then he pulls out, spanking her clit with his hard dick. "That's it, kitten. Show us that wet pussy." He makes her cry out as Colton takes his place.

While he thrusts slower than Beau, Beau kisses him, fondling Colton's balls and making him grunt. Then they switch again, and this time, Beau stays shallow. He teases Blair's entrance, making her arch, begging for more.

"Yes," she cries. "Keep going back and forth. I love it. I love feeling both of you share me."

This is too hot, too beautiful, and dirty.

While Colton takes his next turn with Blair, Beau reaches for something on the bed. When he lifts it, I want to clap, but I don't.

I'm too aroused.

I feel it slicking my sex.

"Thank you for this," Beau says of the pumpkin glow-in-the-dark butt plug in his hand. "Now watch how much our dirty girl loves it in her ass, too."

With a filthy thrill in his blue eyes, Beau spits, wetting the spot he'll relish, and Blair groans.

"Our little kitten likes it dirty." Beau eases the toy inside her while Colton claims her pussy. Blair mewls at the pleasure they give her until the plug is seated in position, then Beau smacks her ass again. "Tell her. Tell her how our dirty girl likes it."

"I like your cock in my ass," Blair gasps.

Then Colton grabs her hair, his thrusts getting brutal. "Where else? Where else do you beg for our cocks?"

"My pussy," she cries. "I want your cocks in my pussy. Taking turns with it. Please. Show her. Show her how you fuck me so hard."

They do. They let me watch their union, and I know this is one of the many intimate ways they express their love because it starts to burn through them. I can tell. I can feel it, too.

They're not only showing me, they're sharing it *with* me; their lust bleeding into love.

Beau grabs Blair's hips, his thrusts getting deeper, seeking and making her pant. *She's going to come.* Colton kisses Beau while Beau is buried inside her, and once Colton tugs on her plug, Blair locks her eyes on me and screams, her orgasm shaking her thighs.

Instantly, Beau comes with her. He throws his chin up, his pecs and throat straining as he spills inside Blair. And even though he's still huffing and dripping cum, he pulls out, and Colton takes his place inside her. He pounds Blair so hard she grabs the mattress and keeps coming, and with Beau's kiss, Colton comes, too, grunting and thrusting until he's done.

My lips part, both pairs. Like them, I'm huffing for breath. Desire burns inside me. I almost can't take the heat. I need to touch myself. I need to come. My sex aches, empty and waiting.

But I obey.

I want this ritual to work.

Blair keeps her eyes on me while I curiously watch Beau slip a small, beaded bracelet off her wrist. Then, he and Colton stalk my way, their cocks still hard, glossed, and dripping with their seed as their eyes devour my exposed pussy.

Oh my god, they look so primal, so carnal, and beautiful.

It matches how I feel.

Leaning down, Beau kisses my cheek before whispering, "Did we make you wet and open?"

"Yes," I sigh against his beard.

Colton leans down, too, their manly musk intoxicating me. With a gentle kiss on my cheek, he asks, "Did you feel our love?"

"Yes." I'm pressed between their heat, feeling safe, exposed, and *so* ready.

"This is from us." Beau gently lifts my left wrist, slipping the bracelet on. It's simple. It looks handmade out of a thin leather strap and three ruby beads. "This is our wish for you and Silas."

What? I blink back tears. "Did you make this?"

"Yes," Beau answers. "We made it for you today while you were carving pumpkins."

I'm so touched, I can't speak.

It's like their sex, their love is blessing ours.

"Now," Colton cups my cheek, "you have to find who's next."

"Please," I murmur. "No more riddles. I'm too horny to think."

Colton chuckles, gently taking my hand. He helps me stand before he thoughtfully adjusts my cape and hood, telling me, "No more riddles. Just find the other priest."

"We love you," Blair calls out, and I turn back. She's smiling my way, lying on their bed, and watching my exit.

"I love you all, too."

I'm glowing and flushed with desire, but the same haunting chill I felt in the forest suddenly threatens when I step back into the pitch-black night.

It's here. It's waiting for me. It didn't leave. It's hunting, but I'm too heated to care.

Oh my god, if this is what I'm supposed to do all night —watch each couple, each group, share their love and sex —I'm going to burst into flames, consume Silas, or both.

A pumpkin, one I carved with roses, is lit on Stacey, Mateo, Ford, and Luke's platform.

And indeed...

This is the ritual.

I enter their tent to find the profile of their bodies, joined in the most erotic chain of lust. They wear nothing but their golden masks, turning my way as they silently watch me enter.

Taking my seat, I know what to do.

I sit on the French wooden chair by the edge of their bed. Spreading my legs, I pull my soaked lace panties aside, feeling the wet rush of arousal, watching Ford and Luke lick their lips at the sight of me.

Then, they resume what they desire, and I stifle my moan.

It's so salacious, it's sacred.

Stacey rides Mateo's mouthwatering length, her hips held tight in his grasp. Luke kneels behind her, his hands laced with Mateo's. He's fully claiming her ass while Ford stands behind him at the edge of the bed, his body draped over Luke's while he greedily thrusts inside him.

All four of their bodies are connected, their hearts, too. You can hear it in their devoted moans.

This is their ultimate coupling; you can tell by the stirring kisses they exchange. By the nightly turns they must take, switching bodies but the alignment the same.

With parted red lips in a shameless smile, Stacey looks my way in her bunny mask and lets me watch her get a merciless double penetration.

Luke stares at me, too, with hunger in his eyes while I

witness his ultimate pleasure, a cock in his ass while he drives into a wet pussy. He's sweating and moaning for it. Mateo proudly groans at their weight and power as Ford grunts, commanding their pace.

At first, it's slow; they edge their desire, showing me. But then lust takes over. Ford starts driving harder into Luke, grabbing his shoulders. It makes Luke grip Stacey's hips harder, taking and giving, so Stacey braces herself over Mateo. He's licking her nipples swaying in his face.

The look in Stacey's eyes is pure ecstasy.

"Show her," Ford orders. "Show Eily how we open her, how we make her come, how we fill our woman with our cum until she drips with it, and how we love to clean her, too."

"God, yes," I moan, my sex pulsing, milky desire seeping from my core; I can't help it.

Stacey sees me. She witnesses my thirst, and it makes her buck, coming and shaking with her men driving into her. They climax, one after the other, their carnal grunts and locked muscles so arousing.

They kiss mouths. They kiss Stacey's sex, licking and cherishing what they shared. They murmur their love before their bodies move.

Stacey turns my way in her bunny mask, lying on her side, her body flushed, her smile bliss. She takes off her bracelet and hands it to Mateo, and then again, the men stalk my way, all three of them. Again, they're still hard and dripping.

They kneel to kiss my cheeks, and I'm suffocating in their masculine pheromones, the smell of their sex, their insemination.

It's raiding my senses.

I'm lightheaded as Mateo carefully slips the bracelet over my left wrist. Similar to the one I just received, its band is thin and leather, but theirs has six pink beads.

"We love you all so much," Luke says, his smile so warm, his hand on my naked thigh hot. "Thank you for letting us share this with you. This is our wish for you and Silas. Our blessing."

At first, I'm confused by their bracelet. They're a marriage of four. It should be four beads, but then I remember their cute little daughter, who looks just like Mateo, and their baby boy, who looks like Luke.

That makes them six so far.

"Thank you so much," I sigh, overwhelmed.

Stacey gently shares, "I almost gave up, too, but stay strong. Look at the life I found when I kept believing in love."

I smile at her. I'm blinking back tears, holding back a storm of emotions. Love, lust, and life collide through my veins. Witnessing their sex, watching their love, it makes everything feel so natural, so heightened. I stand to leave but don't know where I'm going, and I'm dizzy with desire.

Ford sees it daze my eyes, and his gruff, sexy face turns tender. "I got ya," he says, scooping me up.

Draped over his arms, he carries me to Luca, Scarlett, Nick, and Zar's tent. There, we find another carnal coupling, another sight that overwhelms with lust.

Ford gently sets me on the chair by the foot of their bed but stops to admire their love, too.

I thought we'd find them indulging their kinks in Luca's tent. They do it so well, and I've relished watching it before.

But not tonight.

It tightens my throat.

It melts my heart.

Because they're showing me their more tender side, the more intimate moments they must share behind closed doors. And they're wearing their masks for me, too.

Luca is coupled with Scarlett, passionately kissing her while slowly driving deep inside her in a missionary position. She's wrapped around him, holding him, and moaning for more.

Nick and Zar are coupled right beside them. Nick is taking Zar in the same position, their kiss unwavering with moans.

Quietly, Ford leaves, and I follow the ritual. It feels right.

I expose myself; I open myself to their love, too. I let Luca see when he glances my way, and his groan is ravenous when he stares at my pussy, weeping with want.

It's beyond erotic what Luca is letting me watch. He's not a Dom tonight. His beautiful bronze body sweats. His shredded muscles strain. His deep breath labors, a slave to his desire. Tonight, he's serving the love he feels for Scarlett, for Zar and Nick, too. They share it. They show it.

I stay quiet, feeling it stir so deep inside me, too, that it finds my bones. They're turning liquid, passive, and pliant as they've never been before.

I have so much fight in me, but not now.

Not tonight.

I surrender.

I chew my lip, watching Scarlett's hunger mount as Luca takes her. He thrusts several times inside her, then pulls out, climbing up her body before he roughly whispers, "Taste us. Taste where I belong."

Scarlett sucks his cock, glossed with her arousal, moans

erupting from their throats as Luca fists her strands. He fucks her mouth until her back arches, and then he climbs down, thrusting into her waiting pussy. It makes her cry out, scratching his back, driving Luca's hips harder.

It matches Nick's intensity, pounding inside Zar's ass, and Zar loves it. He's feverishly stroking his swollen cock to it, his throat straining with grunts. The way his abs flex, his forearm straining, his cock dripping as he begs Nick, "Yes, baby. Fuck my ass. Fuck me harder," it's breathtaking.

"Look," Nick coaxes. "Look at what me fucking you does to her."

Zar turns to see me exposed, swollen, and wet, and he comes, shooting over his chest. Nick quickly follows, his massive pecs quaking, the sound of his grunting orgasm setting Scarlett off.

With a scream, her nails draw blood from Luca's flesh. She comes hard, biting his shoulder, but he's not done.

Resting her legs over his shoulders, Luca gives her all his power. He starts grinding in ruthless circles, his glutes flexing like rocks. He's hitting that tender spot deep inside Scarlett, making her thrash and come again; I know.

Silas does the same to me, and I'm in so much sweet pain waiting for him, needing him.

I watch Luca finish. He's so beautiful when he comes, grunting, his lips parting, letting his muscles relax as he spills inside Scarlett. All his dark Dom falls away, and he looks like a bronze god in heaven. It's so tender how he kisses Scarlett, whispering his love while he's still inside her.

Then, he slides the bracelet off her wrist, and he and Nick repeat the ritual. They come to me after coupling with their mates, kneeling to kiss my cheeks.

"Sometimes," Nick whispers sweetly over my ear, "we get more than we ever dreamed of. That's what Zar and I wish for you, my dear."

I kiss Nick's cheek before, tenderly, Luca lifts my wrist.

Smiling, he sees the two bracelets on it. Reverently, he kisses my pulse point before sliding their bracelet on, too.

It has six Grecian blue beads. Four for them and two for their children so far.

"I cannot express how we adore you." Luca cups my cheek, tears threatening his crystal eyes, making them burn in mine. "How we love you and Silas, all six of you. So please take our blessing, and keep your hope alive, my little Aphrodite."

"Never give up," Scarlett gently assures me from her bed, blowing a kiss as Zar blows one, too.

Well, fuck.

Half of me wants to cry; half of me needs to come as I sigh, "Thank you. We love y'all, too."

I feel so softened by love, I can't move. I let Luca lift and carry me out of the tent.

I expect him to take me to our tent. It must be next. But shock hits me along with the chilling night air.

Luca doesn't take me to our tent. Naked and in a gold rabbit mask, he silently carries me into the middle of the clearing, like I'm being offered to the eerie night.

He's being so sweet and caring as he gently sets me down. But then he asks, his accent gravel with desire, "Are you open for him?"

I nod at his towering form.

"Show me," he demands, so I step my feet apart.

Deliciously, Luca reaches inside my panties, his thumb teasing my swollen clit. Skillfully, his thick middle finger circles my entrance, never penetrating but finding me waiting and wet.

I stifle my moan, my body trembling as he groans, "Hmm, so tight and tender." He's still rimming my aching entrance with his finger, his thumb barely strumming my nub.

The man is a god at making you come. I'm fighting it, and he's teasing me; I know with Silas's permission, and it makes this even hotter.

"Are you ready for him?"

"Yes, master."

I love saying it, and Luca smirks, loving the sound.

He gazes down at my form so tiny before his. His stare finds my breasts peeking out from behind my cape, my nipples pinched by clamps and covered in lace.

It swells his cock, hungry again, and my breath thins, marveling at his surging size.

Knowingly, he glides my lingerie aside, exposing my breast to the cool air. He tugs on the pearls, rattling the clamp over my nipple while his fingers coax me to come.

I moan, my thighs shaking while he probes, "Will you wait for him?"

"Yes, master," I sigh.

His thumb strums harder over my clit, his tug pulling my nipple taut. The tension in my body is so tempted to release. "Are you sure? Your pussy feels so wet and ready to come."

This is a test. I know. My instinct makes my hips writhe over Luca's coaxing hand. My body is in pain to let go, but my heart resists.

"Yes," I stammer. "I'm waiting for him. I need *him*. Please. Where's Silas?"

Tenderly, Luca slowly withdraws his touch, kissing my forehead.

"Go to him," he orders.

"But where is he?"

I look around. I can barely see the lanterns inside the tents where I've been and the pumpkins on the platforms, but that's it. All else is dark and terrifying.

"Trust," Luca starts to walk away, "and he'll come."

"But *I* need to come!"

Luca even laughs like a Dom.

"So," I call to his nude backside, "is this like Trick or Treat? Do I go back to each tent?"

"This is Halloween," he answers, not looking back. "You go where you're most afraid."

And damn, Luca Mercier has the hottest naked ass, and yes, I'm poised to orgasm all alone in the middle of a field. Arousal coats my thighs. My nipples tingle with need. My clit is sobbing. Literally, I'm weeping down there.

I feel possessed by lust, just like Charlie was. But holy haunting hell, I don't want to be scared again.

In the distance, Luca disappears inside his tent, and I don't know how they planned it, but all the tents go dark.

It's silent.

It's like they vanish, and I'm alone again. It's just me, the moon, and my hope.

I twist my lips, fighting back tears. It's not from sadness. It's because it's all I feel now. The wish from Blair, Beau, and Colton. The strength from Stacey, Ford, Mateo, and Luke. The hope from Scarlett, Luca, Nick, and Zar.

I know this is a rite of passage, a way to give me gifts so I'm prepared, so I won't give up.

But it's cold.

And dark.

The night feels super kinky and creepy, and suddenly...

I don't feel alone.

"Silas?" I whimper, afraid to let anyone hear me.

But something does.

An icy gale gusts through the camp, fluttering the tents and extinguishing the jack-o-lanterns.

Silvery moss, dripping from oak branches, hisses free, slithering on the breeze, snaking my way into a coil around my boots. An eerie current rises from the ground, climbing over my boots, winding up my naked legs, its seeping fingers seeking my heated wet core, a clawing haunt wanting inside my sex.

I can't move as a silent scream strangles my throat. Terror starts to steal my breath, then...

Thrum. Thrum. Thrum.

A drum beats again. Silas's djembe: I'd know its resonance anywhere. Sometimes we sit on the porch, and he plays while I paint.

His call makes the spirit retreat, sliding down my body and bleeding back into the ground as a flickering light lifts my stare to the dark distance.

The live oak.

The ancient tree on the edge of camp.

Someone ... no, Silas ... lit a fire on the other side of it, making the tree's towering silhouette glow in the fiery light.

I'm called to it.

I love this tree.

I know it's special.

Don't tell Silas, but I offer fruit to the tree every month. And the week before we started trying to get pregnant, I buried wooden eggs I carved and dyed with indigo ink as an offering to her.

That's by day when the world feels right, when the tree is welcoming.

But tonight?

It looms on the edge of something dark and haunting. It feels like a man with snaking branches twining around me, its shadow dragging me into its darkness.

Still, I go.

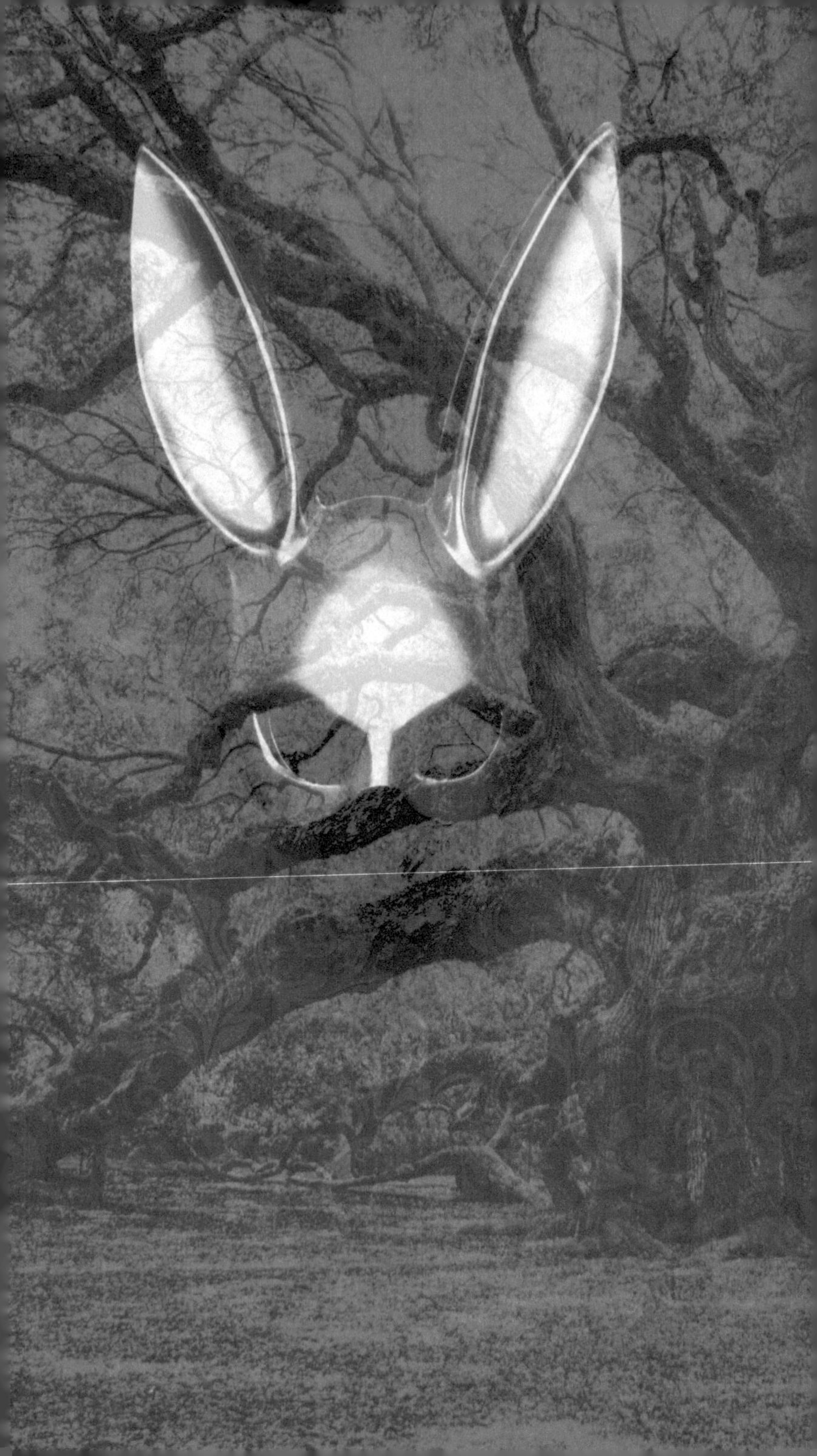

Eily

CHAPTER TWENTY-FIVE

EILY

I know it's Silas calling me.

And I know we're not alone.

So I race, crunching over the tree's fallen leaves, until my gaze falls on where I buried my indigo eggs almost a year ago. Fresh acorns have fallen over it, and I bite my lip.

Acorns mean fertility.

At least, that's what some used to believe.

Tonight, I'll believe anything, though I'm a wreck of terror and desire. Who knew the body could feel both at the same time?

Peeking around the tree trunk, maybe I'll see dead people like I joked with Charlie. Maybe it'll be my hot villain, roasting marshmallows … or his enemies.

Or maybe it'll be…

Cade and Redix!

Charlie and Daniel!

I screech to a halt because they're standing by the edge of a bed. *Our bed*. The one from my bedroom with Silas. I'd know it anywhere. Its headboard and frame are wrapped in handwoven seagrass braids.

But, oh my decorating gods, they moved it outside? Under the tree?

Ringing our bed, it's not a campfire. No, it's the flickering ivory candles on iron stakes. Silas even draped our bed in white faux fur like my cape, with violet pansies fluttering over it.

"I... I..." My hand covers my mouth. The one that won't work.

Call a doctor. I can't even blurt my surprise.

It's magical.

It's beautiful.

It's so seductive.

"Come here, fun size." Redix aims my way.

Damn, he and Daniel are nude, making those rabbit masks look lecherous and hot. I mean, everyone did, but these are my men, too, and I'm a feral female. They look like my next meal.

Redix scoops me up, tossing me over his shoulder, and I giggle, relieved to be with them. Playfully, he flops me on the bed, and I bounce with laughter.

My partners sit, surrounding me as Charlie eases, "Before we start, we have a bracelet for you, too."

"Y'all didn't have—"

"Hush."

A naked Cade lifts something sparkling in the candlelight, and all I can wonder aloud is, "Where were you hiding that? In your cooch?"

Redix laughs. "Yeah, and I went mining for the diamonds."

"And I went diving for the pearls," Daniel adds.

That's what Cade carefully clasps around my wrist: a platinum bracelet with six diamonds and the rest pearls.

"Oh my god, it's so beautiful," I marvel. "Thank you!"

If the symbolism is the same...

"It's six diamonds for us," I note, feeling teary until I keep counting, "and ten, eleven, twelve ... *thirteen pearls*? Holy tree of life, who's popping out all these kids? Y'all have five, and we want one. Maybe more than one, but *eight*? I'd lose my uterus or my mind."

"Definitely both." Cade laughs.

"No pressure," Charlie assures. "Thirteen is a lucky number. Maybe it'll be our grandkids one day."

"Can we not talk geriatrics?" I beg. "I'm trying to stay horny, and you have no idea the night I've already had."

"Well, I'm fucking until I die at ninety-two," Redix swears. "I'm going out inside Cade's pussy with Lemon-heads in my mouth."

I shake my head, laughing, because Redix is dead, dying serious.

"Okay, y'all, hush," Charlie gently chides. "We have a ritual to continue."

"So help me, Halloween," I sigh, "if you give me any more riddles, live hot sex shows, or freaky rites of passage, I'm done. I'll rub one out right here and call it a night."

"The horny hell you say." Redix tugs my ankle while Daniel takes my wrist.

I know what they're doing. Under our bed's mattress, hide the straps Silas and I use for our Tie-Me-Up Tuesday tradition.

But this feels new and erotic—my body in restraints, bound to my bed under a spell-binding tree. The night is chilly and spooky, but the furry blanket is warm, and my partners are hot.

Daniel binds my wrists, then unclasps my cape, revealing my babydoll. His fingertips caress my cleavage, giving me goosebumps. "Are you warm enough?"

I nod because there's a solar flare in my panties.

Redix restrains my booted ankles, my legs wide open, and then, like infrared, he spots my drenched heat.

"Damn." He leans down, burying his face in my lace and making me gasp. With a deep inhale, he moans. "Y'all, she's hurting for it. She's so sexed up after watching the others; her panties are a sponge of lady cum."

"Oh yeah?" Daniel spots my pearled nipples. "Let's see if we can make her cream the bed, too."

Shocking me, he rips my slip, not a lot. Just enough to reveal my breasts, my lungs heaving.

"Okay," Cade rasps, sounding aroused. "Let's get her ready for him."

"Ready?" I beg. "I left READY miles ago. I took a cruise across a creepy ocean, then a caravan on humping camels through the land of live porn, to a sprint across a barren field of terror, and now I've crossed the border into This-Bitch-Better-Get-Her-*Cuntry*-Fucked-By-Her-Husband, or this is war."

Cade chuckles, but Daniel leans down. "Shhh." He licks my nipple. "We have to fuck you first."

"What?" I start tugging at my restraints. "No. I don't want your cocks. I mean ... I *want* your cocks ... but I love Silas, and right now, he's all—"

"Trust us," Charlie soothes. "We know who you belong to."

Reaching under the bed, she searches for something.

When she lifts the basket from our sex room, it dawns on me.

It's like the heavens open, clouds part, and the dildo gods sing...

Wait?

Or are they dildo goddesses?

Nope, in my world, it's both. We all praise sex toys.

"You know, in ancient times," Charlie picks up my gold inlay quartz favorite, "they used these in rituals to please women, preparing them for sex."

She licks it while Daniel says, "They used them on men, too."

"You know Silas wanted each of us to use one on you," Charlie says. "All fifteen of us."

"Please," I peep. "He knows me so well."

"But we told him it may be too much," Cade warns.

"No, it's not."

"I told you she's hurting for it," Redix says. "She feels possessed by the devil to fuck like we have all week."

Cade doubts, "Possessed? Or *horny*?"

He laughs. "Exactly. Is there a difference?"

"Here, here," Daniel says. "When I'm randy, I feel possessed. So, if not fifteen, let's give her a few at least."

I'm about to debate the definition of "a few" because tonight ... sorry ... it equals *fifteen*.

But when Daniel pulls aside my drenched lace, and Charlie slides the cool, smooth quartz inside me as Daniel leans down, flicking his warm, talented tongue over my lonely clit...

"Oh god!" I scream to the night. "I'm gonna come."

"But you can't." Charlie pulls it out, and Daniel stops.

"That's why we *said* ... Fifteen. Was. Too. Much," Cade

lectures in tempo, tapping her cheek with my treasured, flopping, red tentacle dildo.

You know, if she weren't a hot, nude bunny, looking like a fetish fantasy, she'd be a know-it-all school marm. Lucky for her, I love playing a naughty schoolgirl. And I love her.

But tonight?

"Wait. This is my ritual, right?"

They nod.

"And you've made all the rules so far. Even that, I can't be fucked by fifteen people with fifteen dildos."

Okay, that *is* sounding excessive.

"We'd thought you'd like the ritual," Charlie worries.

"I do like it. I love it. It's just that if this is my ritual, can I have something *my* way?"

They exchange glances before Redix gently rubs my thigh. "You're right." Of course, he'd understand. "What's your wish, fun size?"

"Other than I wish you'd stop calling me 'fun size'?"

He grins, guilty. "Our dirty little princess?"

"Better." I grin back. "And on that note, your dirty little princess wants to watch her partners together." Eyes dart. "I know Silas is somewhere waiting for me. He's probably watching, but it doesn't feel right. I've watched everyone else while waiting for him and I want to watch you, too. It makes me feel loved." I pause. "And very horny."

"Mates," Daniel rubs his palms together, "it is her night. Let's not keep a lass waiting."

"Okay, eager beaver," Cade asks. "What do you want?"

"Untie me first."

"But he wants you tied."

"You can tie me back," I assure Charlie. "But since I'm not getting fifteen of my phallic friends from my favorite friends, I'll play with one while y'all play as I tell you to."

"Damn," Redix mutters. "It twitches my cock when you act like Luca."

They untie my ankles and wrists while I consider my options.

More ... I'm considering them.

I'm taking in the sight of the ones who show me love.

Redix always texts me articles and posts about art shows. We try to go to as many as we can.

Daniel shares my love of cereal. On his global travels, he finds new ones for us to try.

Charlie loves dying indigo fabrics with me. She's making more throw pillows to piss off Daniel.

Cade and I have been working on sketches for a tattoo all six of us would be willing to get. That's not been an easy task.

And somewhere tonight, Silas is waiting on me. But I know tomorrow night, once everyone leaves, we'll spend the night on our shore, helping any new baby sea turtles that hatch.

I could call it a night and just demand Silas join us now.

But I've come this far...

"Hey." Redix cups my cheek. "Where'd you go there for a second?"

I smile. "My memories with y'all. It's a happy place."

His other hand lingers up my thigh. "How else can we make you happy?" His fingers brush my panties. "And horny?"

It comes to me in a flash, something I've never seen between us. Yeah, it's possible, and I wonder why it hasn't happened yet.

"Is there a reason I've never seen Daniel top you?" I ask Redix, and all four fall quiet.

Daniel searches Redix's eyes, asking the same question. Charlie and Cade do, too.

"I guess because Daniel's always wanted to be our bottom," Redix answers thoughtfully. "Honestly, the top does all the work, and I like taking care of him. So does Silas."

"But you bottom for Silas sometimes."

"Yeah." Redix isn't mad. He's sitting beside me, pondering the issue when maybe there isn't one. "Silas was my true first, and he's been the only one."

"So, is that it? You'll only bottom for Silas?"

"No. He's asked me the same thing. He said he'd like it. He wants to watch Daniel top me, too."

I lower my voice. "Is he watching us right now?"

Redix smirks.

Yes, Silas is watching us.

So is an elusive mafia lawyer. And a haunting, horny haint.

We should've popped popcorn.

"Is it what you want?" I reach for Redix's hand. We share a similar past. "I mean, I'd understand if—"

"Maybe I should have the balls to ask him myself," Daniel's voice lulls, hesitant and husky. "I've always wanted to."

Redix turns to him, softly shocked. "So, why didn't you?"

"I didn't want to pressure you. I mean, with your scars, I'd never—"

"You wouldn't be pressuring me. I love you."

"Then you want me to fu—"

"Yeah, I want you to. I just didn't know *you* wanted to."

"Of course I do."

"Can I just point out," Charlie eases, "that this is why we tell you guys to talk more?"

Redix shrugs. "We talk all the time."

"You talk about scripts," Cade says. "You talk about football. Soccer. Whatever. You talk about calf raises and leg day when you clearly need to talk about feelings and other body parts, too."

"If we're all gonna live together," I add, "we need to be *always* talking."

Daniel cuts a look at Redix, both flaring their nostrils, trying not to laugh.

"What?" I ask. "What did I say?"

Daniel snorts. He can't hold it back, but he sure tries.

"What? What's so funny?"

Cade rolls her eyes. "I think they'd rather get root canals than be surrounded by us three, *always talking*."

Redix bursts, laughing. "Hell, a root canal would be the only thing keeping y'all from yapping all damn day."

"Shut up." I slap his leg. "You love it, and you know it. And besides, by me making you two talk, Daniel finally gets to fuck your ass."

"Why, yes, our dirty little princess. Thanks to you, he does."

Redix looks at Daniel.

Silence fills the air as their stares get heavy … and hungry.

"Fuck me," Daniel mutters, clenching his jaw. "Goddamn, I can't believe we're finally doing this." He slowly strokes his cock, telling Redix, "I've wanted you for so long."

His cock juts, needing Redix, needing someone, so Charlie reaches, making him moan as she strokes it for him.

"How do you like it?" I ask Redix. His length surges hard for it, too.

"I want to ride him." Redix stares at Daniel but answers me, "I want him to watch how much I love it, how much I love *him*."

"What do you want us to do?" Cade asks.

"We have to complete the ritual," Charlie reminds us, pumping Daniel's shaft. "The men have to plant their seed inside us."

I giggle, "We're not aliens tonight."

"No," she answers, "but it's good luck. It's what we want to do for you, like the others did. It's like a blessing."

"Do we have condoms?" Daniel gruffs, watching Charlie's handiwork. "And wipes?"

"Yeah." Cade rummages through the basket, plucking a condom from the bottom. "It looks like the Van de Mays have been going from butt to beaver."

I raise my hand. "Nothing says Happy Friday like a double hole punch."

Charlie stops stroking Daniel. "But can you last long enough?"

He scoffs, "Bloody right, I can last. I've had a lot of practice of late. I can last all night."

"Not all night," I warn. "I've been waiting forever for Silas, so no dick-dallying. Let's do this."

Redix grins as he stands, waiting for Daniel's next move.

Daniel proudly rises beside him, grabbing his neck, fully taking Redix in a kiss that makes their cocks swell, rubbing together.

But it's how they moan over their tongues. It's passionate. It's loving. It's complete. It conjures the deep connection that binds us.

And … it makes Charlie hand me the gold quartz dildo while she takes a realistic one for herself, and Cade plays with the tentacle in her hand because this is so hot, too.

My women lie beside me, propped on pillows against the headboard. Somewhere, I can sense Silas watching us, loving us. Loving it as we play with our pussies, watching Daniel prep Redix.

He bends him over the bed, his hands braced on the mattress, as Daniel kneels behind him. Caressing his buttocks, Daniel gently kisses Redix's scars. It makes Cade gasp back tender tears at the sounds of trust and desire graveling through Redix's moans.

But when Daniel starts tonguing him and moaning into his cheeks, his fingers teasing him, too, Redix groans even louder, the swollen tip of his cock dripping on the bed.

Their arousal makes us moan, enraptured by the sight. There's so much pent-up desire between them. It looks like Daniel's tongue and fingers are driving Redix insane.

"Goddamn, Daniel." Redix groans. "Damn, I want you. God, fuck me now."

With his hand still on Redix, gliding over his flesh, Daniel lies across the foot of the bed. It's like he doesn't want to break their connection. It's like the one I've seen for years between Redix and Silas. Their bond is beautiful. But now, I don't know whether to come or cry at these men sharing it, too.

Daniel grabs the condom on the fur blanket, then Redix helps him roll it on before taking the lube and glossing his shaft.

Greedily, Redix straddles Daniel, reaching behind to guide him in, but, "Come here," Daniel pulls him down. He fists his long hair and kisses Redix, huffing over their lips, "Go slow. Take your time. I want it to feel so good for you."

"If it's you or Silas," Redix nips his lip, "it'll always feel so damn good."

Then, he rises, reaching behind him, his eyes locked on Daniel's as Redix slowly wedges him inside.

The strain across his shredded, shaking quads reveals the stretch Redix takes from Daniel. The penetration. The pressure. The burn before the pleasure. We've all felt it as Redix hungrily sinks down on him, making Daniel bow his back with a sudden groan, "Oh fuck yes, take my cock."

He starts riding Daniel. It makes his dick screaming hard for him. "Yeah," Redix mirrors Daniel's lust. "Fuck yeah, I'm taking your cock."

Daniel won't stop groaning and grabbing Redix's flexing pecs. So Redix grabs his, too, hanging on to Daniel's trapped stare, his lips parted in awe. It beckons Redix. He leans forward, taking Daniel's kiss, riding him as their groans of lust echo through the woods, rousing any creature with a heartbeat because mine is pounding.

I've always wanted this. I've always wanted every union between the six of us, and now we have it.

I know Silas is watching. This is the night he divined, and he's loving this.

Months ago, Silas told me this was his wish. He wanted Redix to trust Daniel fully. He needed Daniel to love Redix as much as he does.

For all of us to love each other—it's all Silas has ever wanted.

And now it's like he's the Marquis, the new ruler of this island. This is Silas's love ritual, whether watching like a spirit or here with us.

You can feel his spell in the air as Daniel starts stroking Redix, making him shake.

"Fuck, you're dripping," Daniel marvels, his thumb

smearing beads of cum over Redix's tip. "Damn, your cock is so fucking hard, loving mine fucking your arse."

"Harder," Redix orders him. "Do it harder." So Daniel lets go and hammers his hips, pounding inside him, making Redix's length bounce. He howls, his cock leaking, "Oh, fuck. Cade! Cade!"

She crawls across the bed, straddling Daniel, too. Bracing herself against Daniel's chest, she opens for Redix, sliding back on his curving length as he guides it inside her.

"Oh fuck!" Redix roars, grabbing her hips. "Oh fuck, he's gonna make me come so fucking hard inside you."

Daniel groans. He's fighting it. It's not easy with Cade's luscious breasts tempting above him, so he reaches for one, pinching her nipple. It makes Charlie, beside me, moan, but Cade moans louder.

Ruthlessly, she grinds back on Redix, circling her hips. She's seeking her end and his. He reaches around for her clit, rattling it, and she gasps, shuddering with an orgasm.

"Do it, too," Daniel growls, thrusting inside Redix. "Come inside her. Come with my cock fucking your tight arse."

With proud grunts, Redix obeys. He comes hard, with every muscle tensed, his stare trapped on the forest. It's like he's staring at Silas while Daniel makes him come inside Cade.

Redix grabs her neck, pulling her lips to his, kissing her as every muscle on his frame quivers, softening with release.

"Fuck, babe," Daniel begs. "Fuck, I need Charlie."

Cade and Redix roll off him while Charlie responds.

Daniel snaps off the condom, taking the wipe Charlie hands him. Quickly, he preps for her while Redix moves to lie beside me, pulling Cade into his arms and keeping me warm.

I assumed Charlie would ride Daniel and finish him off, but she gets on all fours, facing us, and it rouses him.

Daniel climbs to stand at the edge of the bed. Grabbing her shoulders, he sinks inside her while she moans with her eyes on us, watching her get fucked. Brutally and ruthlessly, Daniel does it.

He does it how Charlie loves it because she's strong … but he's stronger. He makes her cry out with each smacking thrust of his powerful hips.

"So. Fucking. Wet," he growls. Leaning over, he grabs her throat, taunting her ear, "Such a naughty girl. You got wet watching your husband fuck another man's arse, didn't you?"

"Yes," she pants.

"Do you love it when I fuck your naughty arse, too?"

"Yes, sir," she huffs, her breasts jolting at his force. "Yes, please. Fuck me."

Like a devilish rabbit, Daniel sneers, pushing his fingers over Charlie's lips. She obeys, sucking them before he plunges them in her ass, making her moan while his other hand squeezes her throat tighter, her eyes framed by a gold bunny mask, rolling back in lust.

"That's it, naughty girl," he taunts. "Fucking take it in the arse and pussy. Fucking squirt on me. Squirt this sweet, wet cunt all over my cock. Come on. Do it. Do it, Charlie." He hammers harder, flesh slapping against flesh. "Show them who this pussy belongs to. Say it!"

"Daniel," she cries before a scream grabs her throat. Violently, she shakes, her watery cum streaming down her thighs and wetting his.

"Aaaa, fuck, babe." He bites her back, just enough to

make her gasp while he grunts, spilling inside her, his breath labored and loving her.

"*Fuck*," Redix sighs. "Fuck, Eily, if you aren't ready for your man by now, I don't know what will do it."

"Yes," I sigh. "Yes, I'm ready for him."

I'm almost in tears, and I don't know why.

Maybe it's because I can't take anymore. I'm brimming, my edges overflowing from their love, but I feel so empty, needing mine, too.

I need Silas.

"Please," I beg. "Please get him here. *Now*."

Quietly, almost reverently, they prepare me.

Daniel and Redix bind me again.

Gently, Daniel kisses my cheek. "You look so beautiful for him," he praises. Redix does the same. Then, he thoughtfully stacks the bracelets on my wrist as he whispers, "Eily Van de May, we love you, our princess."

Cade kisses me, arranging my cape and covering me so I stay warm once their bodies leave. But I catch the tears brimming in her eyes as she smiles. She can barely mutter, "It's gonna work out. I promise," and I believe her.

Charlie approaches with a black silk blindfold. Tenderly, she secures it with a warm kiss on my lips, vowing, "He's coming for you," as I fall into darkness.

And suddenly...

With our past week.

With all that's happened to the others.

With the journey I've had tonight, sailing through a sea of emotions, swells of lust, love, and terror.

I'm not sure...

Who is coming for me?

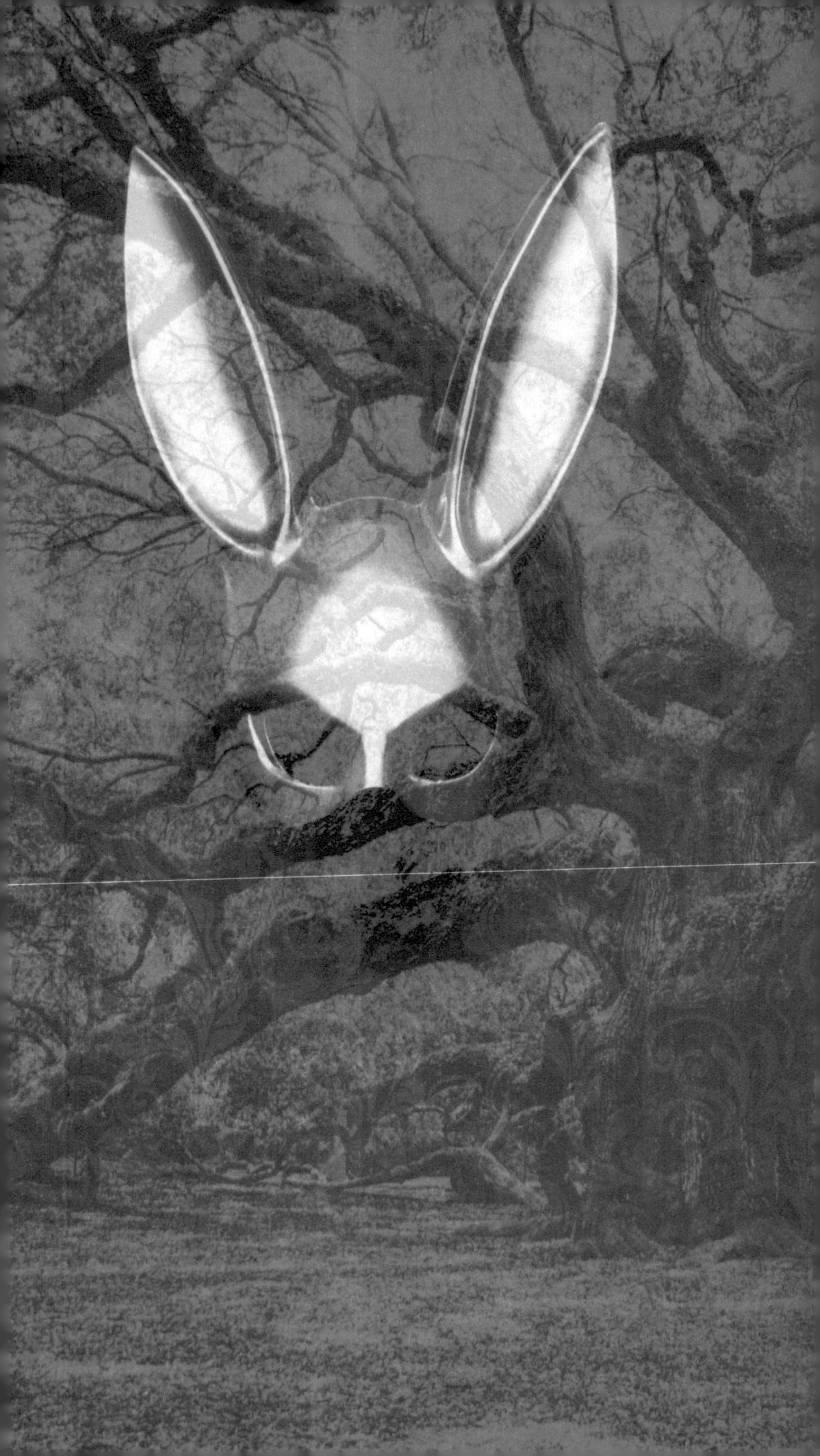

Silas

"You're still my ghostest with the mostest."

I watch our partners kiss Eily, then quietly leave.

Redix reaches for Cade's hand, holding it while his other hand cups Daniel's shoulder. So Daniel rubs Redix's back, his other hand never letting go of Charlie's while she lifts a lantern, lighting their path back to our tent.

Yeah, I fucking adore them.

But I'm still standing here, hiding behind a grove of windmill palms, treasuring my wife.

Damn, Eily's breathtaking like that. Her black Docs and white lace babydoll. Her pretty cape and sexy blindfold. Her beautiful body, ripe and waiting for me.

"Silas?" she whispers to the night.

But I need one more moment to watch.

To catch my breath.

To be thankful.

Because I'm so damn in love with her.

I don't want a life without her.

When I was growing up, my grandma had a nest of seven pet rabbits. She had the dwarf kind and kept them in a pen that took up an entire bedroom.

As a kid when I visited her, I was in heaven.

They were all cute, but my favorites were a little gray male named Smoke and a little brown female she let me name Turtle.

I learned then that rabbits, of course, have multiple mates, but they form deep bonds in their nest. Smoke and Turtle would share food. They'd groom and cuddle each other. So, when Smoke died ... Turtle grieved. She barely moved for a week.

I guess I learned something about love from those rabbits. How you can be with others, but there's only one you live for.

And damn, I sure saw how they made lots of babies, too.

But me?

I only want my mate. I only want my dreams with her, the dreams we share with the others in our nest. And if that includes a baby for us ... well, I sure love trying to make one with her.

This night has been sweet torture waiting for Eily.

I guess that was *my* ritual.

Hoping.

Watching.

Waiting.

Hell, that's all a man can do once his part is done. Right?

Standing in the shadows, I watched our partners greet her and give her our bracelet. Then, I chuckled, hearing Eily put her lopsided foot down and insist on her part of the ritual.

Of course, she wanted what I wanted, too.

I've been waiting a long time for Redix to trust Daniel fully. Then again, it seems Daniel had to learn to fully trust Redix, too.

Because trust ain't just about telling the truth and keeping promises. It's also about sharing your pain. And for some men, that shit doesn't come easily. Not that we don't feel it; we're just raised not to talk about it.

Don't judge.

Three rutting bulls gotta learn how to navigate our horns. Me and Daniel figured that shit out years ago. I know his points, and he knows mine. But me and Redix? We never locked horns. We saw each other's pain at first glance.

So, yeah, I got hard watching Daniel finally top Redix. Well, Redix sorta topped him, and that's so like him. Even after finally letting Daniel in, Redix is still so alpha.

But when I saw Daniel kissing Redix's scars, my throat got tight. I blinked back tears.

I knew the six of us were finally complete.

Fuck, I'm getting my man-period.

Lately, I get it when Eily ovulates. I'm all horny and emotional, and I'm not complaining. It makes me feel even closer to her.

"Silas?" she whispers again. "Is that you?"

She must hear me.

Or maybe she can smell me. I'm standing upwind from her. It's a gusty night, and I always wear my Creed cologne.

"Ahh," she sighs, squirming on our bed. She's restrained how I wanted her, but she's lifting her hips for me. "Silas," she's sighing for me. "Please."

Good girl.

She knows I'm out here, watching her, and I grin. *She's trying to seduce me, and it always works.* My dick is getting hard for the ... shit, I've lost count of how many times tonight.

"Ahh," she moans again, her back arching. "Ahh, yes. Please, Silas, I'm so wet for you."

Damn, if I had antlers like a buck, I'd rub them on a tree, snort, then scrape my massive rack on the ground before chasing her down and mounting her. I'd stand by her side for days, mating with her while I fought other males, keeping them away until I was sure she was mine.

This is how I want Eily. Writhing. Wet. Waiting. Ready.

For me.

I've made her wait long enou—

"Yes," she gasps. "Yes, that feels so good."

That?

I look down.

Nope, I'm standing here. Twenty feet away. Looking like a naked dumbass wearing an erection, boots, and a mask in the forest for a crazy mating ritual.

So, what in the fuck is *that?*

I lift my weathered Timberland boot to storm her way, then—

Snap!

On my left, deep in the woods ... who knows what the fuck that was, but I ain't waiting. I charge Eily, my boots crunching over leaves, cracking branches, and whipping past palms.

"Silas?" Eily stammers. "Wait. Where are you? What—"

"Eily." I reach our bed. I reach for her bare leg, and she jumps. "Baby girl, it's me."

Her head jerks side to side, blindly searching. "But who—"

"Who were you talking to?"

"You!"

Eh, no, she wasn't.

But I know her voice. She's starting to freak out, and that'll fuck up our plans.

Gently, I straddle her and tug down her blindfold.

"Aaaaaah!" She screams. "Fuck you, horny demon!"

Shit! *My mask.* I rip it off. "It's me."

She stares. Eyes wide. Lungs huffing.

"Eily, it's me."

"Silas?" She swallows, "But where... Where did you get that mask?"

"This?" I hold up the black and gold demonic disguise. "On Etsy. They sell carnival masks and—"

"Carnival?" She huffs, "No, Silas, you looked like the horned devil. I thought it was you. The one who was just—"

"It *is* me." I cup her flushed cheek.

"But who?" She glances around. "Who was just..."

Her voice falls away.

Oh shit, she's scared.

"Shhh." I lean forward, gently kissing her shaking lips. "It's okay. I'm here. It's just us now."

"But, I don't understand," she sighs. "I just felt—"

I kiss her again. I keep my lips softly pressed to hers, tasting our shared breath, until her tongue slowly meets mine, letting me gently soothe her. Letting me remind her *—It's okay. I'm here, and you're mine.* And I don't stop with my kiss until she's kissing me back.

Until her whimpers become soft mewls into my mouth.

Until her body rises to meet mine.

Until she's tugging at her restraints and begging over my lips, "Silas, please. I've waited all night. Please, I need you and—"

"And I need you too, Eily." I kiss her tender neck, biting

and licking, feeling the resonance of her moans against my lips. "Always."

I smell her vanilla-scented strands. Lacing my fingers through her long, silky chestnut hair, tortured visions of how I lost her years ago and tender memories of how I found her again grab my heart.

They make me sigh, my lips kissing her clavicle, my nose reveling in the sandalwood perfume she wears.

But with my next breath … I smell … *her*.

I suddenly inhale her sweet, intoxicating feminine musk. It calls from between her legs, her sex open and crying for me.

"Fuck, Eily." It's my instinct, primal and with a chemical rush. It's powerful and savage, and I follow it.

I steam down her flesh, trailing my tongue past where her gown has been torn, past her tempting, little jeweled nipples. I'll play with them later.

I need to taste her.

Kissing her belly, my lips make her quiver. She sucks in an aching breath. "God, Silas. Please."

But when my nose tickles over her little white panties, I inhale, and a feral groan crawls up my throat. I'm not a man; I'm an animal. I rip one delicate side of her lace, making her gasp, before I tear the other.

Rising on my knees, I lift her panties to my nose, watching Eily as I inhale her, letting her scent mark me forever. Then I suck on them, thirsty for the soaked cotton spot saturated with her arousal, her tangy sugar filling my mouth.

She watches me, her stare in awe. It roams between my rabid worship of her cum-soaked panties to how fucking raging hard her scent makes my dick.

"Fuck, baby girl," I growl down at her. "You're in *heat*."

"Yes," she writhes. "So, stop making me wait, Silas. Hurry."

She's so cute when she's mad.

She's so goddamn sexy when she's fierce.

Now, she's both, and she's all mine.

Leaning down, I can't help it. I'm not in control; my appetite is. I'm hungry, trailing my tongue up the inside of her thighs. Closing my eyes, I'm a husband, relishing his wife's taste, but when I open them to her pretty little pussy, I'm a beast.

Her bare ivory lips are so swollen and glistening. The sexy brunette triangle she keeps groomed, curls damp with desire. With my fingers, I part her rosy petals, and her clit is a pink pearl, shimmering with want. Her opening is milky and weeping for me.

I take one lick through her ripe sex, and she yanks at her restraints, screaming, "Silas! God! You're gonna make me come, but they told me to wait."

I lift, gazing over her tiny terrain, teasing her, "Wait for what, baby girl?"

"Your dick," she huffs. "I need to come on your dick."

I grin. "I can't make you come on my tongue first?"

"No," her legs squirm, "it's the ritual. I can't come until you're inside me."

"Well then." I crawl between her legs. "Let me make you do it a hundred times."

What drives me more? The sweet love I feel for Eily, my wife forever, or the savage urge I have to fuck her like an animal right now?

I want to feel her tight little pussy come on my cock while her sweet lips gasp into my mouth. I want her body shaking in my grasp while she drips down my shaft. I want her nipples hard and demanding my suck. I want every part of what we've been waiting for.

But I'm tall, and she's tiny. So, I reach over and rip her wrist restraints off. Then I stand at the edge of the bed and free her ankles.

Yanking her to me, she squeals as I tower over her, holding her legs open.

Fuck, look at those big green eyes. My ring on her finger. That sweet, virginal lace slip. Those pert, tempting tits. Her hungry, wet cunt.

"Make it drip for me, Eily."

She obeys, squeezing until a little drop leaks from her opening, and I lick my lips, my dick dripping at the sight of her.

"Do it again. Show me you're in heat for me."

With a moan, she does it, making her milky arousal trickle from her sex, and I lose it. "Who owns your pussy, Eily? Who loved it first and made it his?"

"Silas," she gasps as I press her legs back, splaying her open. I can smell her intoxicating scent as I stare at its source. As I crouch down for one more taste of it, lapping my tongue into her little creamy pool, making her hips jump. "Oh god," she pants. "Silas. *Please.*"

So I rise, gripping my swollen dick. I press down, rubbing my wide tip over her hard clit until she's shaking. Then I drag it down to her wet entrance but halt, barely pressing inside her.

Her mouth parts, her breath panting as I aim my lips for hers, swearing, "All night, Eily, and all my life—You. Are. Mine."

I kiss her, my tongue slowly penetrating her mouth as I squeeze my heavy cock into her tight heat. *Fuck, I'm trying to go slow, but it's overwhelming.* How much I need her. How much I love her. How much I want to fuck her, and I do.

I gently thrust, but her swollen walls grab me. They pull me deep inside her, making me pump harder. "Fuck, Eily." I huff over our lips. "Fuck baby, I love you."

"Silas," she cries, in love or lust, I don't know. Tears leak from her eyes as she grabs my shoulders, scratching, hanging on to me as she bucks, convulsing and coming so fast and hard I can't believe it.

It's like she's in pain with pleasure and moaning for so much more.

"Damn, baby." So I pull out.

Quickly grabbing her legs, I press them back again and take another soothing lick over her pulsing pussy, making her scream and grab the bed before I do it again and again and again until she's panting for more.

I hold her tiny leg so she's open to me. "So beautiful." I tease my tip through her lips. "So open. Damn. You're swelling even more for me." I circle my crown over her entrance. "Do you want more?"

"Yes," she can barely talk, and it's so fucking breath-taking watching my thick cock slide inside her. Sometimes, I'm amazed I fit, but tonight, she's never been this wet and open. She won't stop shaking and panting.

I thrust, going faster, holding her leg, my other thumb strumming her clit, and I don't stop until I make her come again, jolting on the bed. She groans as her pussy contracts so hard it's pushing me out, but I fight to stay in until she's done.

Then, I pull out and press her legs farther back, licking her little hole until she's pliant and passive for more.

"Fuck, Eily." I lean over her, making her taste her cum, laving it over her tongue. "You're so sweet and dirty tonight. You're fucking me and fighting me at the same time."

"I'm not fighting you." She reaches down and grabs my glistening shaft, guiding it to her entrance while she demands, "So, don't stop fucking me, Silas."

Her eyes narrow, heavy with lust. She props up on her elbows while I hold her leg, and we watch my cock claim her. I reach down, tugging the pearls on her nipple while I pump faster and harder, and she screams, her shaking legs trying to close to me while she comes again.

Fuck, my baby girl is a little animal tonight.

I want to laugh, but I'm so goddamn in love and insane with lust my instinct prevails.

I keep fucking her, making her come, and each time she bucks, jerking away, I yank her back to me. To the edge of the bed, where I pin her legs back and suck her clit, making her groan before I rise and guide my cock inside, slowly splitting her open again.

I've never seen Eily's beautiful green eyes so hooded with lust. I've never watched her little body come so hard, so many times. I've never felt her pussy so swollen and slick before she contracts around me, grabbing and fighting for more.

I'm going to lose my goddamn mind, and I do. I can't fight this urge anymore.

"Eily, baby. Come here."

I sit on the edge of the bed, and like a doll, I lift her, her cape sweeping behind while I make her straddle my lap. Then, I wrap her legs around my waist.

I stare at her beautiful face, overwhelmed in this posi-tion. I suck her clamped, pebbled nipples. I caress her soft back. I fist my hard dick, my raw tip rubbing, seeking her dripping entrance until I feel it. Until she sinks down on my shaft, wrapping me in her wet heat, and I groan with her nipple in my mouth.

"God, Silas," she moans, scratching my back while she glides her tight little hungry cunt up and down my shaft. *My baby knows how to take me.* From my tip to my base, she owns me.

"Eily." I need to feel her come on my cock once more before I lose it all inside her. I grab her hip. I grab her hair. "Ride me. Ride me hard." I press my forehead to hers. "That's it. Grind on me. Just like that." We gaze down, watching us. "Look at you, taking all of me inside that pretty little pussy. Yes, rub your clit on my cock until you come." Her body obeys. "Fuck baby, yes, I can feel you."

I can feel everything.

My swollen ache for her. A tight heat coiled in my spine. The sweet tension pulled taut to snap. An insane hunger. An intense need.

A tender hope.

I can't get enough of her, so I claim her kiss. I make her ride my cock, our breath rising. She's too small to fight me. She has to take me. I make her open. I make her love it until she's about to come; I love her gasping breath. I love *her*.

I have to watch as her eyes shake as she falls apart for me. "Silas," as she sings for my soul, releasing something inside me. Something only she has.

"Eily," I can barely speak. I stare into her green eyes. I bruise her hip. I hang on to her hair. I can't breathe, forcing her to take everything I have. It belongs to her. *Only her.*

Even the tears I fight.

Even the kisses I give her while we catch our breath.

Even the way I hold her tight, lying our bodies down, pulling her cape around us to keep her warm.

Even the way I stay inside her while I brush the hair off

her face so I can see her. So I can fall even more in love with her.

She stares back at me, searching my eyes before she whispers, "What if we don't get pregnant?"

"Even if we don't get pregnant, I need you to know you're my dream come true. I've only ever wanted *you*, Eily. I swear I marry you every morning we eat cereal. Every day we go for a walk. Every afternoon while I fish and watch you paint. Every night, when you burn our dinner." She smiles, tears welling in her eyes. "You're my family, Eily, no matter who else joins us."

"Can we foster?" She won't stop searching my eyes. "Or adopt?"

"Of course." Her cheeks are so flushed, I have to touch them. "We can adopt as many as you want and watch; I'll probably get you pregnant too, and then we'll have a mess of kids until you're so happy, you're fussing at them all the time."

She tickles her fingertip down my nose. "I only wanna fuss at you."

"Hmm, good." I roll on top of her. "Because right now, I only wanna fuck you, too."

She giggles until my kiss grabs her laughter. Then she lets me slowly take her one more time. And deep in my heart, I don't need to know what will happen next.

I just need her.

An hour later, I'm tugging at the fur blanket on our bed. The night is getting colder, and the candles are burning out.

"What are you doing?"

"I'm getting our bed ready." I brush the flower petals off the pillows. "Woman, you wore me out."

"Huh-uh." She shakes her head. "I'm not sleeping out here."

"But it's romantic and shit. Besides, getting our bed out here took me an hour."

Her head, with her mussed pretty hair, won't stop shaking. "No way we're sleeping under this tree. It's official; our island is haunted."

"Pfft." I set the basket of dildos on the ground. "I could've told you that. We got a horny haint on this island and, according to you, a sexy mobster, too."

"But," she kneels on our bed, staring at the canopy over us, "doesn't that scare you? Because I felt him. Someone was touching me before you did. And don't tell me I'm crazy because I'm not. A woman knows when her pussy's being worshiped."

"Well, it wasn't Michael Cummings doing it because I watched you the whole time. Once everyone left, it was just you and Casper, the cunt hungry ghost."

She chews her lip. She's trying to decide whether to freak out or be thrilled; I know my woman.

So, I tell her about the gold rabbit I found, and she insists I show it to her. Then she melts my heart, showing me the indigo eggs she buried on the other side of the tree. Together, we decide to bury the gold rabbit with her eggs.

We kneel, our hands patting the rich soil firmly. But silently, I say a little thank you, too.

To Lois Ravenel. To this tree. To our island. To our partners and friends.

I believe in haints *and* prayers.

"I need to say something," Eily insists, brushing her dirty hands across her white cape.

"Baby girl, you need to blurt a *million* things."

"True." She shrugs. "So, let me just say: the mask you wore *tonight*? The black and gold devil one from Etsy?"

"Yeah? I ordered it two weeks ago."

"Well, I just saw it two hours ago while I was blindfolded." She pauses. "I saw it in a vision while something was touching me. And then ... I saw it on *you* when you took off my blindfold."

"Boo, ha, ha!" I wiggle my dirty fingers in her face. "You can't escape me. Even my devilish ghost wants to fuck you."

"Be serious," she huffs. "Doesn't that scare you? Like, we're legit haunted by the ghost of Lois Ravenel."

"Nah." I shrug. "He must've seen me wearing the mask, then possessed you with a vision of it."

"Silas! That's freaky!"

"Yeah, but it's kinda sweet, too. He called me to that tree months ago to find his gold rabbit. I know it. Hell, he probably called you to plant eggs by it, too. And now it's Halloween. It's like Charlie said: this week, his spirit is closer. He can touch us. All week he's been fucking with us while we fuck. I mean, Charlie said he possessed her, too. So did Redix. And Daniel and Cade saw him. We've all felt him. That's what Halloween is all about."

"And that doesn't scare you?"

"No. Spirits are always around us. Our energy never dies; it just changes form."

"Is this a science class?"

"No, it's true. So, it doesn't scare me. It makes me feel better. It's like he's watching over us." I take her hand. "It's like he's helping me get you pregnant."

She chews her petal lip, her stare considering the tree.

"Think of it this way," I tell her. "He's one of our guests, but he only visits during Halloween. The rest of the year, it's our island."

She talks to the tree. "I'm not naming our first kid Lois!" She mutters, "Though it is a pretty name."

"We already know our first child's name, no matter how they're laid in our arms."

She turns to me, a smile ghosting her lips. Yep, here come our tears again. *She believes it, too.*

"Come on." I stand before scooping her up. "Let's go back to the tent with the others before we have another threesome with a hot haint."

Her legs swing over my arm while I carry her across the dark, spooky clearing. An icy gust suddenly lashes my naked backside, dead leaves rustling over our path. I sense something … or someone following us, making the hairs on my neck stand.

But Eily wraps her arms around my neck, too, resting her head on my chest while she sighs, "We may have a hot haint, but you're still my ghostest with the mostest."

And I'll always be so hauntingly in love with her, too.

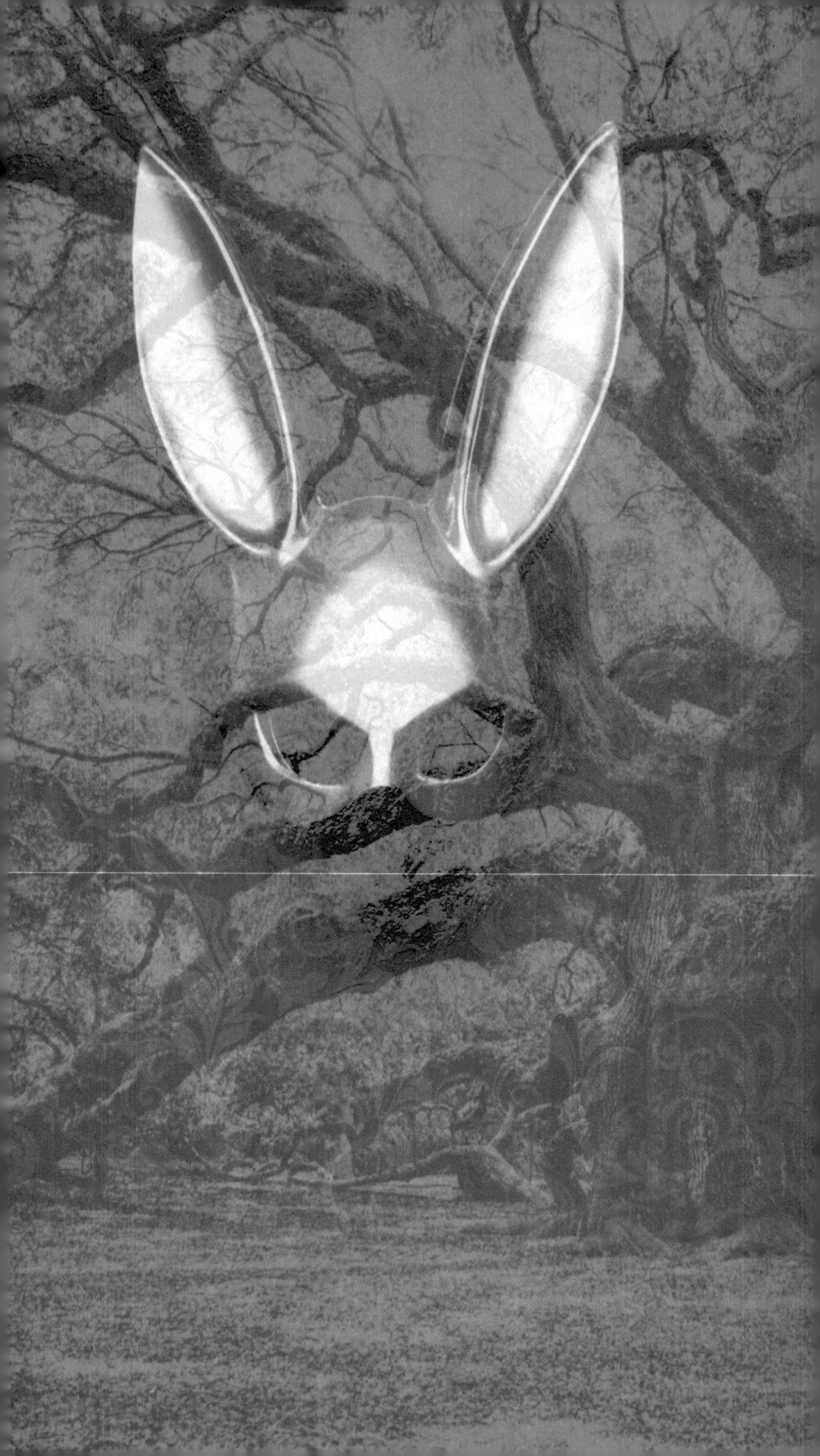

Silas

CHAPTER TWENTY-SEVEN

SILAS

"Whose turn is it?"

"Not mine."

"Daniel's."

"Bollocks. I did it yesterday morning."

Cade groans, "And I did it the day before."

"Jeez," Eily mutters into our pillow. "Next year, I'm buying coffee makers with timers."

"Don't spoil them." I squeeze her tighter, refusing to open my eyes. "Their ass ain't too precious to get up and press a button."

"Mine is," Redix murmurs.

"Same," Charlie yawns.

"Thirty more minutes."

Daniel orders us to sleep more, so I sigh, burrowing my nose in Eily's hair as she wedges into me. Then Charlie twists with Daniel, stealing covers. They make Redix rub against my backside, trying to stay warm, so I burrow against him, too, while Cade's soft yawn sounds cute.

Finally, our cuddling silence fills the air.

Until...

"Let me do the honors."

A bassy voice rumbles, and I jolt upright.

We all do.

Sitting in a chair at the edge of our bed is a large, looming silhouette of a man. There's enough foggy morning light to see his black cropped hair. Raven wool coat. Sable leather gloves. Kohl fitted turtleneck. Onyx tailored pants. Black scuffed boots.

And glacial eyes staring at us.

"Who the fuck?" I lean for my rifle under the bed, but—

"No need for your Remington, Mr. Van de May," he says. "Or Ms. Ravenel's Tanfoglio 9 in her handbag. Or Ms. Bryant's sleeper hold. Or any of you gentlemen rising. By all means, stay warm and cozy where you are."

He leans over in his chair, its wood creaking, while he presses the button on the coffee maker sitting on the table for us.

"Thanks, Mr. Cummings." Eily yawns with a big stretch. "I'll take mine with five sugars."

I snarl, "While I'll take a fucking explanation as to why you're here."

"And how you want to die if you take one step our way," Daniel warns.

"And where you want your unmarked grave." Redix isn't joking.

"My, my," he taunts. "Someone's grouchy in the morning."

Eily chirps, "We just need coffee."

"We just need answers," Cade growls. "*Now*."

I glance at her. She's dead serious and stunningly topless: a dick-stirring combo. One Mr. Cumming's smirk makes it obvious he appreciates.

"I think you have all the intel you require, Sergeant Bryant," he corrects her. "I answered your call. I'm here and taking my next breath. I'm minding my manners, though they seemed to have escaped you when you met my colleague yesterday."

"*Cade*," Eily sighs with an eyeroll in her voice, "what did you do at Delta's?"

"Nothing."

Cade's guilty.

"Nothing?" Cummings raises a dark brow. "Mr. Allen informed me you were trying to break into my meeting room."

"Who the bloody hell keeps a meeting room in a sex shop?"

Daniel's fuming, I'm clenching my jaw, and I know Redix has a fist cocked.

Cummings smirks. "Who the bloody hell wouldn't convene in a sex store? It makes for meaningful meetings."

Eily giggles. "I told y'all he's sexy."

Barely, Cummings grins, nodding at my wife, and ... *oh, hell no*. I rise from our bed, buck naked and fucking pissed. "Answer our questions, or you're not leaving my island alive."

His stare boldly rakes my frame, from my glaring eyes to my bare feet back up to my hard morning wood, pausing to admire it.

Then he slants a look at the others in bed. "I quite admire your lifestyle. Swinging intrigues me."

"We don't swing." Charlie's not amused. "We love each

other. There are deep emotions involved. Strong relation-ships and bonds. Care to test them?"

"No test needed," his response is low.

There's something cold about this man with heat in his eyes—eyes that look like clear, blue ice. They're so intense, his frigid stare burns. It's an unnatural mix and it flares my nostrils.

"Were you here this week?"

Cade starts her interrogation while I watch his gloved hands. If they make one move for his jacket, I'm on him. No matter the cost.

But he rubs them, palm to palm, like he's contemplat-ing. "No."

"Bullshit," Charlie says. "I heard you last night."

"Wasn't me."

"You were on the shore."

"Wasn't me."

I seethe, "I heard you in the woods."

Calmly, he answers, "I first arrived an hour ago, Mr. Van de May. My Cigarette is at your dock."

"A racing boat," Redix scoffs. "Like that doesn't scream, 'Criminal on the run.'"

The muscles in Cumming's jaw flex. It's hard to detect under the shadow of his dark beard, but any man would see it—any man about to beat the shit out of another.

"Y'all, quit being rude." Eily jerks the blanket, making everyone look at her. "He's my guest. I asked him to come, and now he's here and telling the truth." Eily turns, smiling at him. "Mr. Cummings, would you like a cup of coffee?"

"No, thank you, Mrs. Van de May."

"We have warm biscuits and sweet tea in the black tent. Not the one with sex furniture in it. That's where we fuck.

The other tent is where we eat." She pauses. "Eat *food*, I mean. Care to join us for breakfast?"

A smile tickles his lips. "No, thank you, Mrs. Van de May."

Of course, my wife has him bewitched.

The rest of us?

We'd be another blood splatter on his clothes worn to hide it.

"Why did you help her?" I ask. "Why did you agree to do this spook-us-shit for my wife, but then you bailed on her? Where are *your* manners?"

Cade sneers, "Criminals don't have them."

Again, his jaw clenches.

Again, Eily groans, "*Caaade*. Stop."

But Cade can't help it. She'd kill for us, and I love that about her.

"And why would you risk your arrangement with Stacey?" Daniel talks business. "She clearly trusts you if she allows you in her establishment. So why did you bugger off and not help Eily?"

"My apologies." He watches us closely. "I enjoyed helping Mrs. Van de May last year and—"

"The Chucky dolls in the bathroom?" Eily sounds smitten. "Was that you last year?"

He blinks.

"Nope, that was me," Redix confesses.

"The eyeball gummy candies in our cereal?"

"Again," Redix answers Cade, "me."

"The red Kool-Aid in the shower head?" Daniel probes.

Cummings nods.

"The bloody handprints on my new white bedspreads?"

"Red food coloring and latex gloves," Cummings answers Eily. "I'll send replacements."

"The bloody envelopes left with pictures of us all week?" Redix sneers.

"You were captivating subjects."

"The chainsaw we heard one night?"

He unclasps his hands, telling Charlie, "Thought I would clear a few things away for you."

"My missing Shun Kaji knives?"

His stare challenges, but his words assure me, "You'll find them back in their block this morning."

This man is an enigma. An enigma who's been in my house.

Cade clocks it, "So, you get off on scaring people with blood and weapons?"

His eyes sharpen. "Dolls and sweet things aren't my style."

"Yeah, and bullshit ain't mine," I answer. "So why were you here last year, but not this week?"

"Regretfully," he addresses Eily, "business kept me from helping you this year. Again, my apologies, Mrs. Van de May."

"You never answered Silas," Cade persists. "Why did you agree to help Eily in the first place?"

"I've seen her around." A faint smile lifts his lips. "I'm quite fond of her."

"Fond of my wife will get you found dead."

"Oh, Silas." Eily shivers with a grin. "I get so wet when you talk like that." Then she urges, "But y'all, seriously, settle down. He belongs to Ms. Faye's sex club. I saw him there, then we bumped into each other on Meeting Street."

"Where your firm is," I add. "You've closed some deals for us. Like this island. We know who you pretend to be."

"Pretend to be? No." For a moment, he's fire and fury. "I *am*."

He is … *what?*

It's the question in our threatening eyes before his turn to ice, cooly answering, "I was the attorney who represented the seller in the closing on your island, yes. That's what brings me here this morning." He stares down Cade. "Despite Ms. Bryant's felonious invitation, I came to bring you this."

He reaches inside his black coat, and Charlie barks, "You better move that fucking hand so slow, I can count the stitches on your glove."

She shocks me, lifting her 9mm from underneath her pillow with Daniel and aiming it at Cummings.

But Daniel yawns, not surprised. Guess that's how Charlie sleeps well at night nowadays, and I can't blame her.

And Cummings doesn't flinch. No, he expected it from Charlie. We're playing his game now, and it's fun for him.

The wicked fucker smiles.

Leisurely, pulling a small black gift box out of his jacket's inside pocket, he offers it to me, explaining, "I thought you and Mrs. Van de May would appreciate having this. My firm found it doing their due diligence on this island."

Like a kid at Christmas, Eily beats me to it.

She crawls to Mr. Cummings like he's Santa Claus.

Yes, she does it naked and across our group bed, so there's a part of me that ain't scared of this man. We'd fucking kill him, and he's not here to hurt us.

But every cell in my body knows he's capable of hurting others.

Scratch that.

Capable? No. Culpable.

Cummings wears guilt like his thin, platinum nose ring. I just noticed it. And the diamond studs in his ears.

Does he look like your typical genteel Southern lawyer?

Hell to the mafia, no.

Still, he didn't draw a weapon. He offered a gift, so Charlie lowers her gun, resting it on her lap, while Eily pops the box open.

"What is it?" Cade sounds suspicious. "A bloody horse head?"

That makes Cummings laugh. It sounds unwelcome in his gravel voice. "Hurting innocent animals isn't my style either."

"But hurting innocent people is?" Charlie's got the 9 and the upper hand.

"Never," he replies. "What an utter waste of life and time."

"Oh my god."

But Eily's gasp grabs our attention. She's staring into the box like Pandora is staring back at her.

"Eily, what is it?"

I don't like this man's affection for my wife.

Yeah, I'll share her with the ones we love. But I'll gut someone who hurts her. I practice on fish all the time.

"It's him," Eily answers. "It's Lois Ravenel."

She turns to crawl across the bed, showing the gift to Charlie while showing her sexy, naked pussy to Cummings, too.

He cocks his head at it, and I warn, "Erase the sight from your mind, or I'll erase you."

His stare won't leave Eily, who's showing something to Charlie while Cummings casually scoffs, "Relax, Mr. Van de May. I find my feminine amusements elsewhere."

"Yeah, well, I find them with my wife, so avert your eyes." Then I boss, "Eily, get under the sheets with Charlie. And Daniel, cover her up."

Do I sound like a possessive asshole?

With goddamn bells on, I do.

But Eily doesn't care. She shows Charlie whatever is in that box.

"What is it?" I bark.

Casually, Cummings answers, "It's an antique, hand-painted miniature portrait we found of Marquis Lois Armand de Ravenel. The nobleman who immigrated from Orléans, France, and came to Charleston to hide as a pagan among the Protestants."

"It *is* him," Charlie gushes. "It's the man I saw in my—"

"When you were possessed?"

"Yeah," she answers Cade. "Except he's wearing a wig or has super long brown hair in this painting, but it's him. It's my great, great, great, whatever uncle."

"Oui!" Eily sounds thrilled. "It's our haint, and he's hot! I bet he was getting lots of oh la la love in his day."

"So, what is this?" I challenge Cummings, "An apology for letting my wife down?"

"No, it's a deal," he answers. "I'll stay off your island, and you'll stay out of my meeting room."

"Or?"

Cade loves danger.

"Or," he answers, "you'll join us."

"Please," Charlie laughs, "you're on a first-name basis with the bottom of the deck, and we know which end is up."

"She means hell no," I translate.

"You want Silas's money," Redix sneers.

"No, I have money." Cummings gestures to my island. "But I appreciate his resources. They're valuable. As is your fame, Mr. Dean." He nods at Daniel. "Mr. Pierce. You can get meetings with powerful people."

"And do what?" Cade asks. "Extort them? Is that the deal your colleague Mr. Allen offered Vale? And Stacey? Join us, or else?"

He sneers, "Nash would *never* hurt Vale."

"Nash?"

"Yes." The ice in his eyes blazes. "Nash Allen. He'd never hurt Vale; she's his daughter's best friend. And we're protective of Stacey, of all her staff at Delta's. We're ... *close* with them."

I have no idea why a man like him would invite people like us to join him. I guess Stacey's right. Deep down, I have to trust her.

I have to trust Cummings is not who he seems.

"So help you mafia god, if you're coercing Stacey or Vale," Cade swears, "Mr. Nash Allen knows exactly what we'll do to him *and* you. Now, *that's* a felonious invitation."

Cummings coldly seethes while we burn with warning.

"Okay!" So, Eily climbs to her feet, standing on the bed. "That's enough."

Tension, testosterone, and coffee waft through the tent, and so much for my wife's modesty and my possessiveness. She has no shame about her naked body.

Please take a picture. She'd smile for it.

But not now.

She's pissed.

"This is some boo-shit!" Eily stomps her foot on the mattress. "Y'all are NOT ending our Trick and Treat week like an anal fissure."

Redix snorts.

He knows.

"Now," she bosses, "we have a goodbye, silent, naked play party with our guests after breakfast this morning. Then we six,"—she stabs her finger at us—"are sketching some house ideas because we're starting next week on our dream for Indigo Island.

"And you," she whips around to Cummings, "are not hurting our friends. Promise."

Smoothly, Cummings stands. He buttons his coat before turning to the coffee. Pouring some into a mug, he smirks, "I promise, Mrs. Van de May."

Like wolves, we watch him lift a silver spoon and neatly add five scoops of sugar. His black-gloved hand stirs before turning with the steaming mug and carefully handing it to Eily, standing naked on our bed before him.

It's like the lion and the mouse.

But somehow, that lion knew the "I Put the Boo In Booty" mug with a cute, tushy ghost belonged to my mouse, Eily.

"May you six enjoy building your dreams together," he says before turning to leave.

"Wait!" Eily shouts.

He turns around.

"What's your *real* name?"

His lip curls.

"For me? Pretty please?" She swishes, "I'll give you all my Halloween candy."

She makes his eyes laugh as he takes a long look at us, and I know it's not the last time we'll meet.

He studies Eily, swiping his gloved thumb over his bottom lip. It leaves a trail of blood behind before he turns around and walks out, answering over his shoulder.

"Axel."

Sipping her coffee, Eily turns around and finds us staring at her like she just flirted with the devil.

"What?" She smiles, batting her lashes. "I told you we'd get our spooky freak on."

EPILOGUE

EILY

Three weeks later

"I hope we're stocked up on turkey and fixings because we're trapped." Charlie peers out of the front windshield of our luxury motorhome. "I count three dozen fans surrounding us."

"I told y'all we shouldn't stop at a rest area on the interstate," Redix says while chomping candy corn with his feet propped on our dinette table.

In the driver's seat, Cade fumes, "But you said the number one rule on RVs is no number twos in the bathroom. So, where else can we go? The woods?"

Daniel sips a beer, sitting on the sofa. "I'd rather dig a hole and bury it than be buried under these fans with their phones up."

Silas stands at the kitchenette sink, washing dishes.

"Well, while we were in the fancy roadside facilities, dropping kids off at the pool, one of those fuckers spotted your famous faces and then knifed our tires. So now we're stuck. And it's the weekend before Thanksgiving. Everyone's traveling. When I called, they said the wait for roadside assistance is nine hours for an RV."

"You know what RV stands for?" I sit across from Redix, stealing his candy. "Ruined vacation."

Redix laughs while Charlie frets, "But we wanted to do something special this week."

"Oh," I answer, "this is special, alright. We're stuck overnight at a Georgia rest area with fans tailgating around our RV, waiting for a rare sighting of Hollywood's Sexiest Man Alive."

"Sorry, y'all." Silas brags, "I just got that kind of swagger."

"You can have it." Daniel laughs. "See how jolly fun it is?"

"Aw, we can't complain about it," Redix says. "At least we're trapped together."

"Now I know how a goldfish feels at PetSmart." I stare out at people staring in at me. "Are we sure they can't see us in here?"

"Positive," Silas answers. "They're tinted windows."

"Well, they're loving what they've already seen outside," Charlie advises, scrolling through her phone. "Daniel's 'stans' spotted him in his tight, flannel shirt that's giving quote 'yes, daddy' vibes. And, Redix, you have a hole in the ass of your jeans living quote 'rent-free' in the minds of your Instagram stans."

"Welp," Redix winks, "asses are where holes belong."

"Well, if we're gonna belong here for the next nine

hours," I warn, "someone is breaking the number one number-two-rule."

"God, help us," Cade mutters.

We fall quiet, listening to the chatter of fans outside and the football game on the flatscreen inside.

Then, Daniel groans, "Ugh, this is bloody torture. It's a tied game between Carolina and Atlanta, and I can't stand to watch Nick *or* Colton lose."

"They're fine," Charlie assures, kicking her feet up on the dash. "No football game can come between them."

They watch the fourth quarter of the game, sipping beer and cheering for both teams, while I watch Silas's back. Under his thin black henley, I can see the tension in his muscles.

"Hey." I get up and wrap my arms around his waist, kissing his back. "You're quiet. Are you okay?"

"No." He turns around in my grasp, cupping my cheeks. "I'm sorry, but I'm ready, Eily. We've been waiting all weekend, and we're not going anywhere, so can we just take the test now?"

The others drop their voices.

All we hear is the game.

Silas has been so patient, and our partners have been so sweet. They dropped everything to share this weekend with us. We sat by the campfire Friday and Saturday night, making s'mores and house plans. We hiked yesterday by the waterfalls, and today, we're stuck at a rest area three hours from home.

And I'm stuck, not sure if I want to know.

I glance down at the bracelets on my wrist. I haven't taken them off. "But what if it—"

"But what if it all works out," Silas interrupts softly,

lifting my gaze to his. "Have faith, Eily. What if we're stuck in an RV next year with us six *and* our six kids?"

Daniel mutters, "That could well be a ruined vacation."

He makes me smile, while Silas makes me brave. "Okay. Hand me the piss stick. I'm doing it."

Charlie gets up, dashing past me, aiming for the bathroom on the other side of our king-size bedroom. "The test should be accurate," she says. "It's been three weeks."

"Y'all just give her some space." Cade crawls out of the driver's seat. She plops beside Daniel, grabbing a handful of pretzels. "She doesn't need an audience to pee."

"I'd sure appreciate one," Redix jokes. "I want a standing ovation for my aim."

Standing by the bathroom door, Charlie hands me the white stick. I've had a love/hate relationship with these over the past eleven months.

But when I peek inside the swanky little bathroom on wheels, I see a neatly folded white towel where I can set the stick and a bouquet of pink and burgundy dahlia flowers beside it.

"I got those for you." Silas stands behind me.

I turn around, startled and overwhelmed.

"For *you*, Eily." He laces his hand through my hair. "Remember, we already have our family right here, and we have many years to make our dreams come true."

His kiss is warm and tender.

"You're gonna make me snot-cry," I tell him. "And then I won't be able to see, and I'll pee all over my hand."

"I can help."

"I draw the line at peeing on your hand."

He grins, about to say something sweet and dirty, so I gently shove him.

"Wait outside."

I do the test and don't even make a wish or prayer this time. I can't. Visions of gold rabbits and indigo eggs are watercolors in my mind.

I set the test down, wash my hands, and linger my fingertip over the pretty pink flower petals before I shout, "Okay, set the timer for five minutes."

Sliding the bathroom door open, I jump, staring at my audience of five.

"Did y'all hear me pee?"

"Nope," Redix lies.

"We got the timer set for you." Daniel holds his phone in his palm.

Cade pecks my cheek before Charlie gently shoves everyone past our bed and back into the living area. "Alright, y'all. Give them space."

Silas takes my hand and pulls me down onto the bed with him, lying on our sides. He stares into my eyes and plays with my hair.

It's been an adventure these past two nights. The six of us squeezed into this king-size bed, and I loved it. We slept with the windows open, letting the cold air and smell of campfires lull us to sleep after we tangled in the sheets together.

"I've been thinking," Silas says, sounding deadly serious.

"If this is about Michael Cummings, or Axel, or Nash, or whoever again, don't worry," I sigh. "You're making it a thing when it's not. They can't hurt us. They *won't* and—"

He presses his fingertip to my lips. "They're not who I think about. I only think about *us* and how we seriously need to put a wooden bench underneath our oak tree."

God, I love him so much.

"Someone's been watching *Notting Hill* again."

"It's my favorite movie," he says. "I like the goofy room-mate. He reminds me of Redix, except Redix ain't that hot."

I laugh. "And Daniel reminds you of Hugh Grant?"

"If Hugh Grant had a cleft chin and a hundred pounds of muscle on him."

"And Cade and Charlie?"

"They're the loyal, wise girlfriends who'll save our asses."

"And me?"

"And you'll be my Julia Roberts, lying with your head in my lap while we rest on our bench. Only your hair is longer and brown, and the fuck if I'm reading a book while I'm holding your hand. I only want to look at you."

He holds my hand now and has my heart forever. Because he leaves out that one big part at the end of the movie; the one where she has a tiny baby bump as she lies on the wooden bench with him.

I know he does it because Silas means it—I'm his family. He'll love me no matter what.

PING!

Daniel's phone chimes.

"You do it," I whisper to Silas.

He kisses me. "I love you." And he kisses me again.

"I love you, too."

He doesn't stop until I gently nudge him, and he goes. I watch him slowly rise from the bed and disappear into the bathroom while I hold my breath.

And maybe I make a little wish.

And maybe I say a silent prayer.

And maybe I believe dreams come true.

Exactly how they're supposed to.

Amazingly, when they're meant to.

And not when you plan.

Silas appears in the threshold, and I can't read the expression on his sweet face before he fights back tears … and smiles.

"Really?" I blurt with joy, tears springing from my eyes. "The rabbits worked! We did it? We're finally pregnant?"

I rise to my knees on the bed while he rushes my way. Little squeals erupt from Charlie and Cade while I hear the smack of flesh, the high-five between Redix and Daniel.

They crowd into our bedroom doorway, hugging, while Silas crawls over me, making me fall back on the bed.

"Now, my little rabbit," he teases, gently kissing my tear-drenched lips, "I'm gonna want four more with you."

And even though Halloween has passed and the villains and haints are gone … for now … Silas casts a magical spell.

Because over six years, it happens.

This rabbit has five babies.

Four loving partners.

One soulmate.

On an island.

Forever…

Or until we become hot haints, too.

Thank you for reading!
Please share your review. It means so much.

Get a free bonus scene from
HALLOWEEN FOR SIX
featuring
Nash and Axel,
the first beasts in the Belles & Bratva Beasts Series.

To discover what happens in eighteen years for **THE SIX**,
follow my special offer coming soon!
***Hint: It's the second generation,
the grown kids of The Six***.
The Six Collector's Special Edition Hardcovers

To enjoy more of these characters and their stories, see
Also by Kelly Finley

LUCA & SCARLETT

MAKE HIM

BEAU, BLAIR & COLTON

SHAMELESS PLAY

SHAMELESS GAME

Join my newsletter for the next books coming in this spicy world.
I also share sneak peeks, giveaways & more.

KellyFinley.com

ACKNOWLEDGMENTS

My husband and silver fox: Thank you for being my number one fan. I promise to take you to paradise to read my books as long as you keep making our love paradise, too.

My Book Team: Deborah, it's lucky number thirteen! Thank you for sharing this journey with me. Thank you, Lori, for another gorgeous cover design. As always ... big hugs to my BTS team: Bree, Brit, Erica, Kenzie, and more.

My Beta Team: Brittany, Deborah, Heather, Jay, Jessica, Katelyn, Marsha and Rachel. I love y'all! Thanks for your comments and edits. You give me giggles and inspo.

My Spicy Gals & ARC Team: I love our spicy family! I cherish your posts, reviews, and support. Our DMs and chats kick my feet and warm my heart. I truly can't do it without you all.

#Bookstagram, #BookTok, and FB Spicy Book Babes: You make me smile every day. I love hearing from you! You keep me writing. Thanks for your comments and love.

Author Friends & Mentors: You inspire me. You school me. You help me. Thanks for the Zooms, emails, and chats. You keep me strong.

Best for last - You, my readers: Thank you for giving your time to share this story with me. I welcome your messages, posts, and emails. They are the greatest gifts. And I promise to keep giving you more spice.

Xoxo,
Kelly

ABOUT KELLY

Kelly Finley hates writing bios but appreciates that you made it this far. So here you go…

She lives in the Carolinas with her sexy husband and cherished family. A rebel with many causes, she fancies black leather, dirty jokes, big hearts, and smart mouths.

She believes in loud and proud love, so much so that her readers started calling her **"The Queen of Spice,"**… and she wears her crown with pride.

Dedicated to writing books with shameless heat, she's most likely at her keyboard putting the next spicy story on the page for you.

Want to connect with Kelly and her readers? Get her newsletter at KellyFinley.com, join her Spicy Book Babes on Facebook, and share the fun on her socials.

instagram.com/kellyfinleybooks

tiktok.com/@kellyfinleybooks

facebook.com/KellyFinleyBooks

bookbub.com/authors/kelly-finley

goodreads.com/goodreads_kelly_finley

amazon.com/author/kellyfinley

Halloween For Six

Kelly Finley

© 2024 Kelly Finley Publishing, LLC

Visit the author's website at kellyfinley.com

ISBN: 979-8-9890644-6-5 (eBook)

ISBN: 979-8-9890644-7-2 (paperback)

Proofread by Deborah Richmond

Cover design by Lori Jackson

 Formatted with Vellum